STORY AND ART BY
NORIYUKI KONISHI

ORIGINAL CONCEPT AND SUPERVISED BY LEVEL-5 INC.

YO-KAI WATCH™
Volume 9
TOOTHACHE
Perfect Square Edition

Story and Art by Noriyuki Konishi
Original Concept and Supervised by LEVEL-5 Inc.

Translation/Tetsuichiro Miyaki
English Adaptation/Aubrey Sitterson
Lettering/Zack Turner
Design/Izumi Evers
Editor/Joel Enos

YO-KAI WATCH Vol. 9
by Noriyuki KONISHI
© 2013 Noriyuki KONISHI
© LEVEL-5 Inc.
Original Concept and Supervised by LEVEL-5 Inc.
All rights reserved.
Original Japanese edition published by SHOGAKUKAN.
English translation rights in the United States of America,
Canada, the United Kingdom, Ireland, Australia and New Zealand
arranged with SHOGAKUKAN.

Printed in Canada

Published by VIZ Media, LLC
P.O. Box 77010
San Francisco, CA 94107

10 9 8 7 6 5 4 3 2 1
First printing, July 2018

YO-KAI WATCH™

9

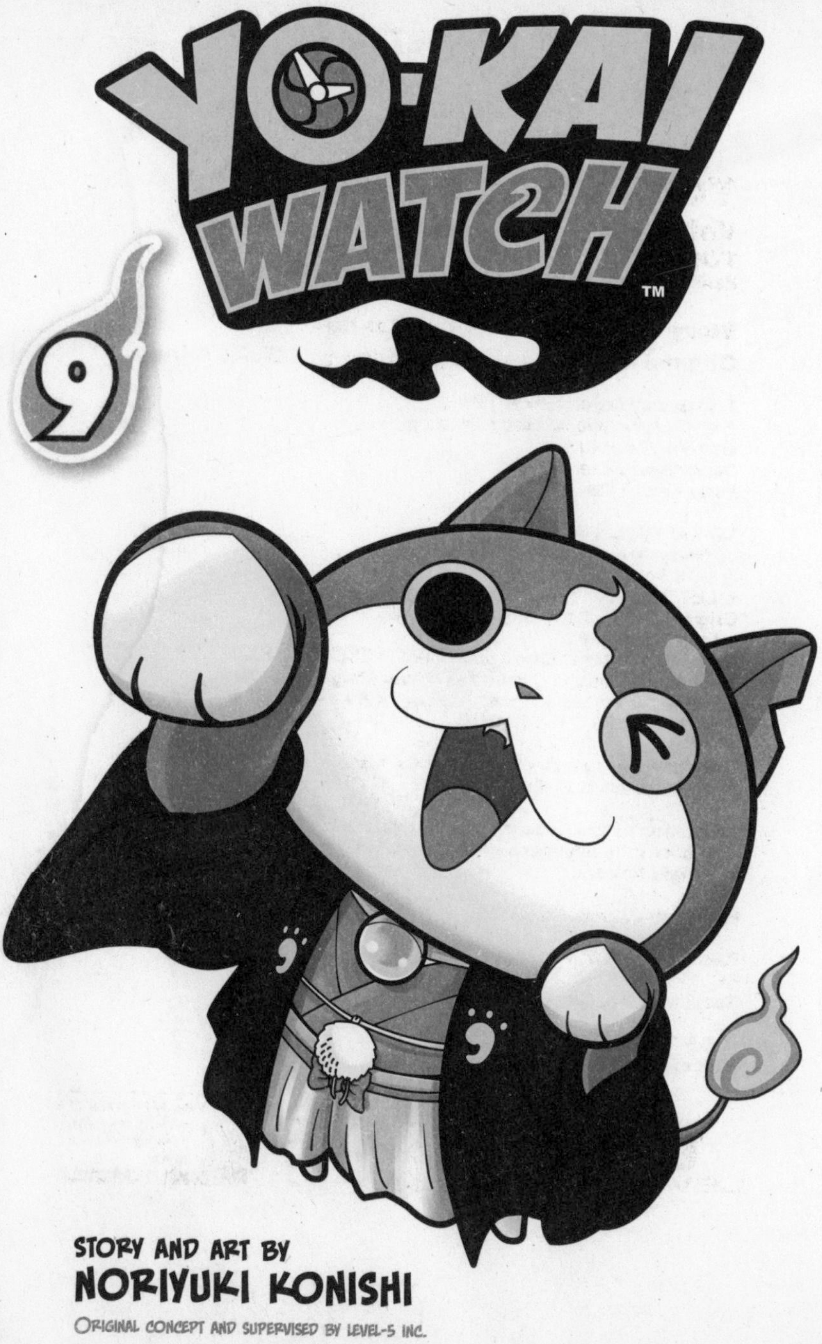

STORY AND ART BY
NORIYUKI KONISHI

ORIGINAL CONCEPT AND SUPERVISED BY LEVEL-5 INC.

CHARACTER INTRODUCTION

NATHAN ADAMS

AN ORDINARY ELEMENTARY SCHOOL STUDENT. WHISPER GAVE HIM THE YO-KAI WATCH, AND THEY HAVE SINCE BECOME FRIENDS.

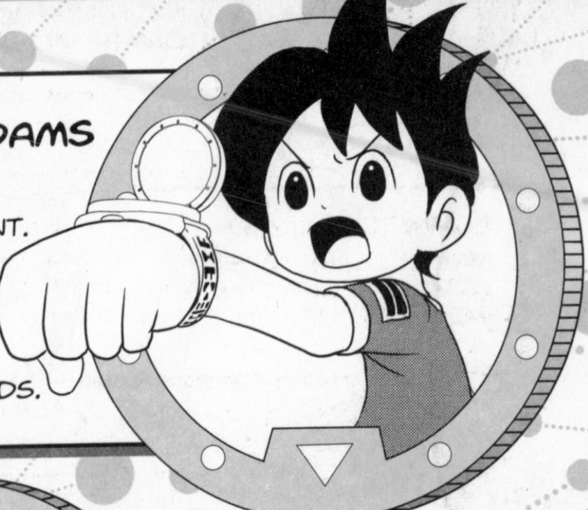

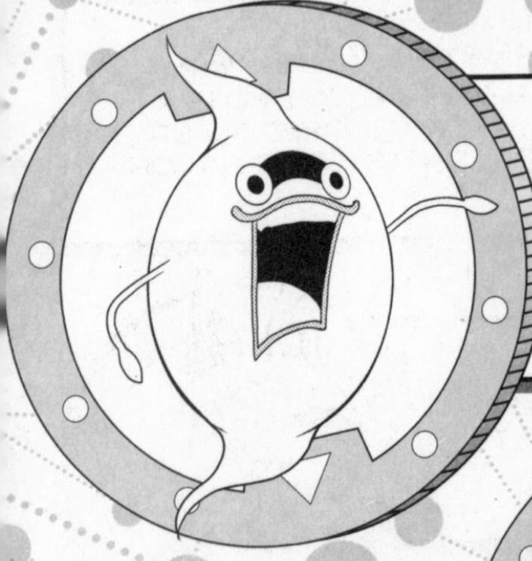

WHISPER

A YO-KAI BUTLER FREED BY NATE, WHISPER HELPS HIM BY USING HIS EXTENSIVE KNOWLEDGE OF OTHER YO-KAI.

JIBANYAN

A CAT WHO BECAME A YO-KAI WHEN HE PASSED AWAY. HE IS FRIENDLY, CAREFREE AND THE FIRST YO-KAI THAT NATE BEFRIENDED.

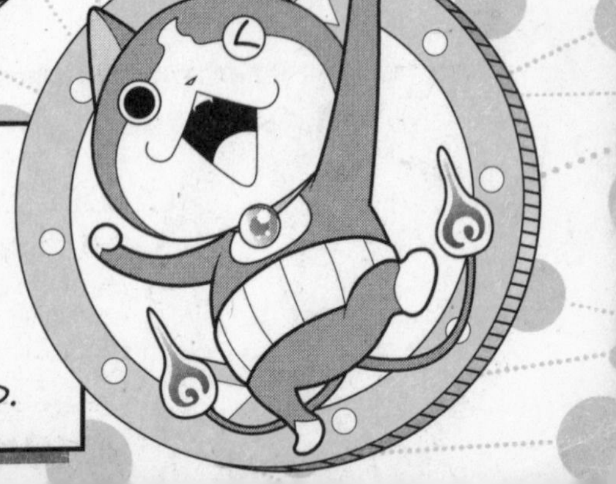

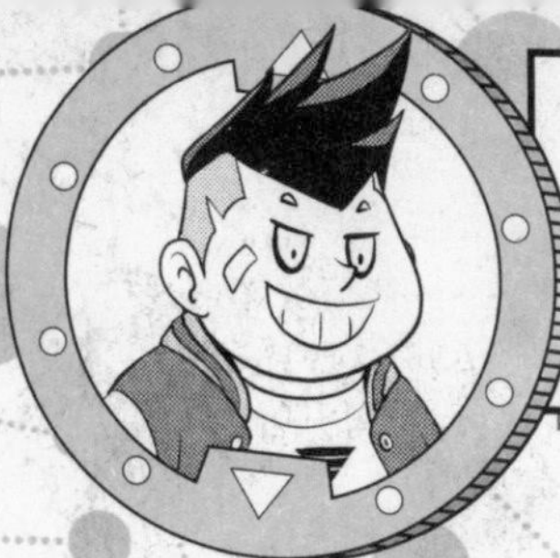

BARNABY BERNSTEIN

NATE'S CLASSMATE.
NICKNAME: BEAR.
CAN BE MISCHIEVOUS.

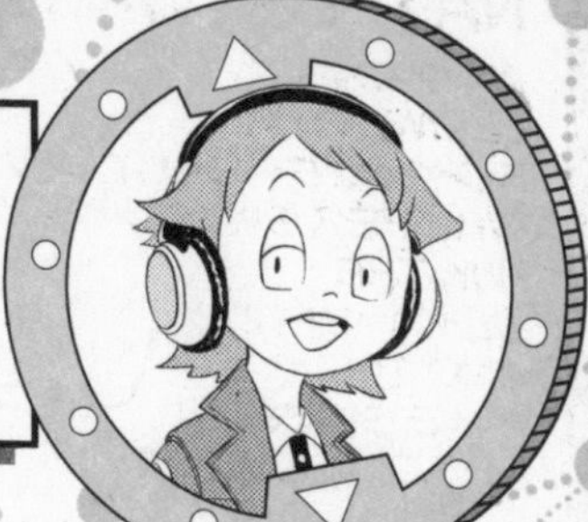

EDWARD ARCHER

NATE'S CLASSMATE.
NICKNAME: EDDIE. HE ALWAYS WEARS HEADPHONES.

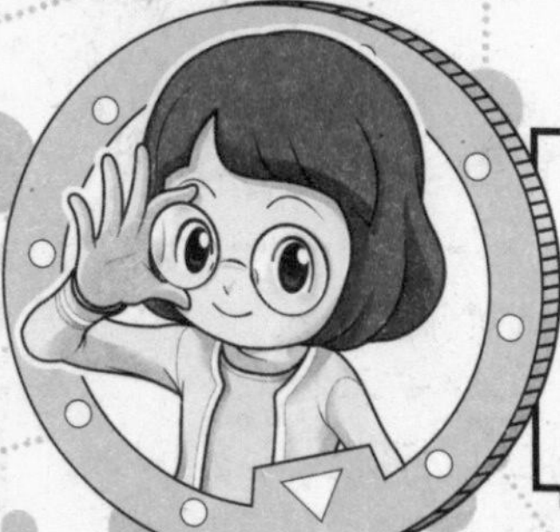

HAILEY ANNE THOMAS

A FIFTH GRADER WHO IS A SELF-PROCLAIMED SUPER-FAN OF ALIENS AND SAILOR CUTIES.

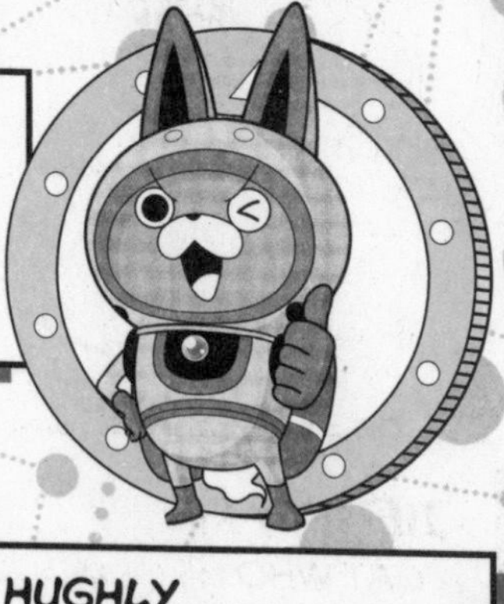

USAPYON

A RABBIT-ESQUE YO-KAI IN A SPACESUIT. HE'S SEARCHING FOR SOMEONE.

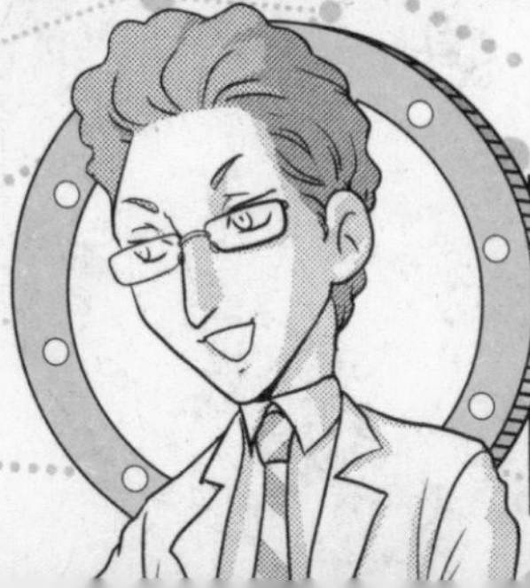

DOCTOR HUGHLY

AN AUTHORITY IN SPACE ENGINEERING. HE TOOK RESPONSIBILITY FOR A ROCKET ACCIDENT AND LEFT HIS RESEARCH INSTITUTE.

TABLE OF CONTENTS

CHAPTER 77: EVERYONE WANTS TO BE NOTICED!!

FEATURING LOW PROFILE YO-KAI DIMMY

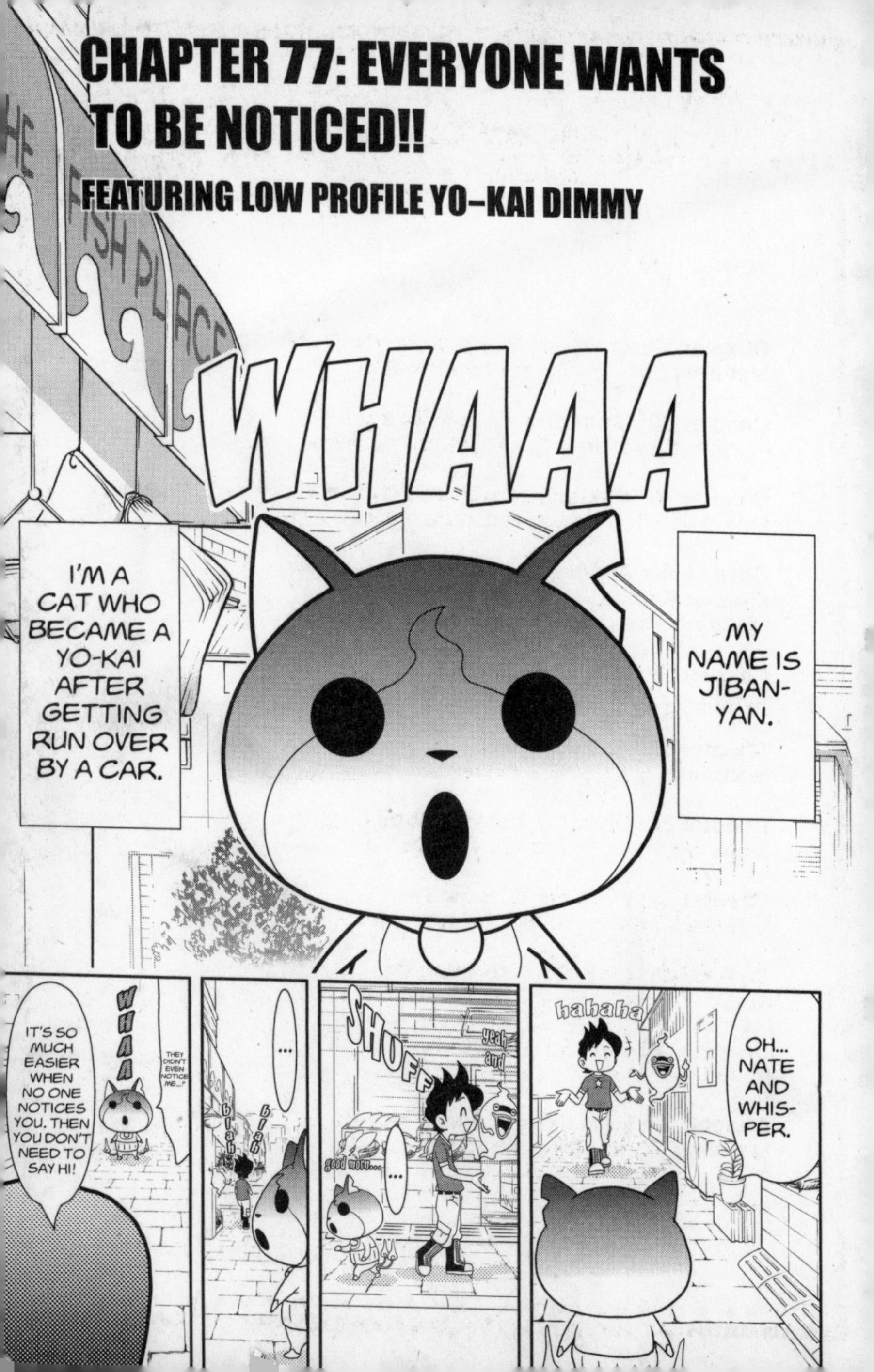

WHAAA
MY NAME IS JIBAN-YAN.
I'M A CAT WHO BECAME A YO-KAI AFTER GETTING RUN OVER BY A CAR.
hahaha
OH... NATE AND WHIS-PER.
SHUFF
yeah and
good morn...
...
...
blah
blah
THEY DIDN'T EVEN NOTICE ME...?
WHAA
IT'S SO MUCH EASIER WHEN NO ONE NOTICES YOU. THEN YOU DON'T NEED TO SAY HI!

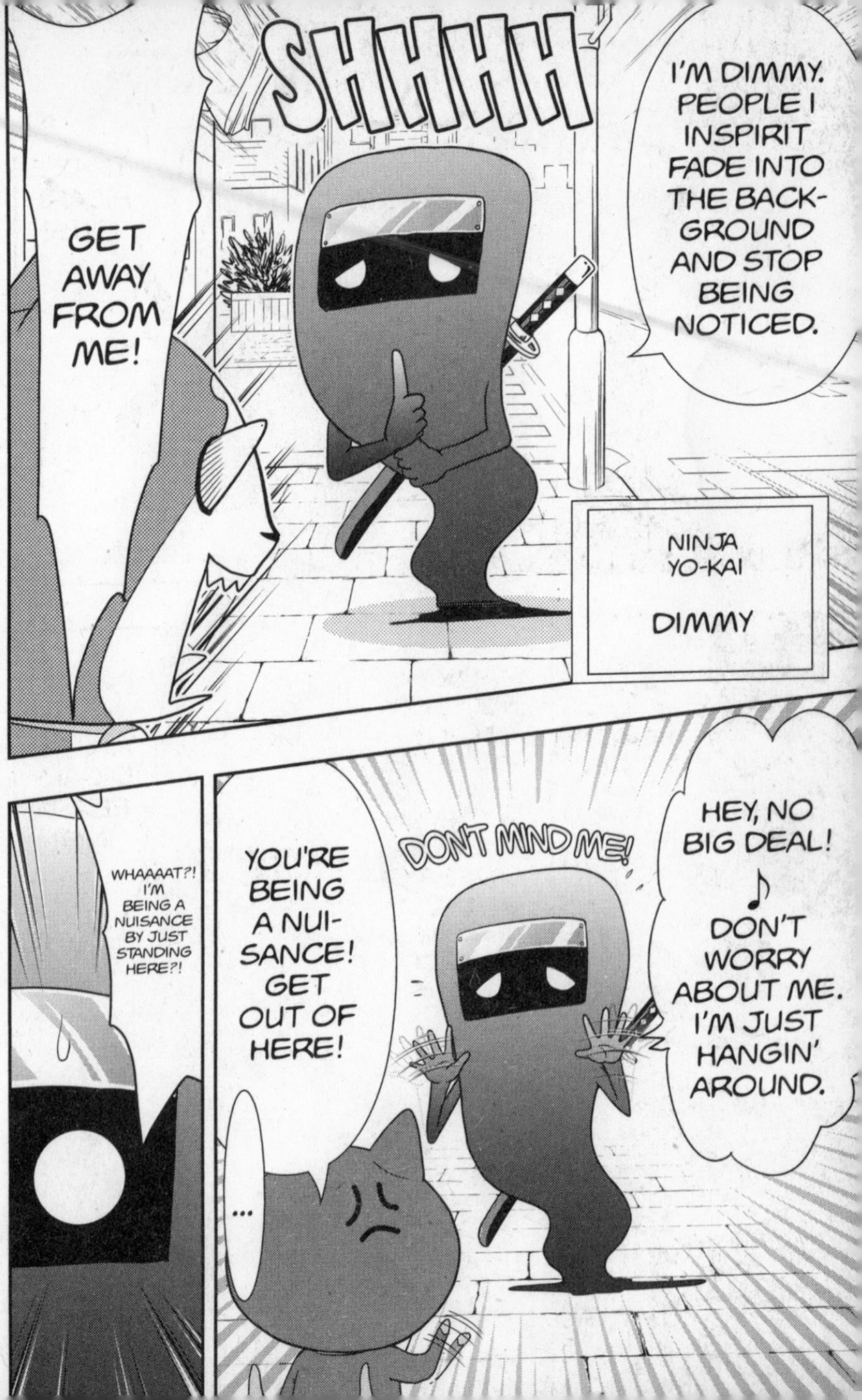
I'M DIMMY. PEOPLE I INSPIRIT FADE INTO THE BACK-GROUND AND STOP BEING NOTICED.
SHHHH
GET AWAY FROM ME!
NINJA YO-KAI
DIMMY
HEY, NO BIG DEAL! ♪ DON'T WORRY ABOUT ME. I'M JUST HANGIN' AROUND.
DON'T MIND ME!
YOU'RE BEING A NUI-SANCE! GET OUT OF HERE!
...
WHAAAAT?! I'M BEING A NUISANCE BY JUST STANDING HERE?!

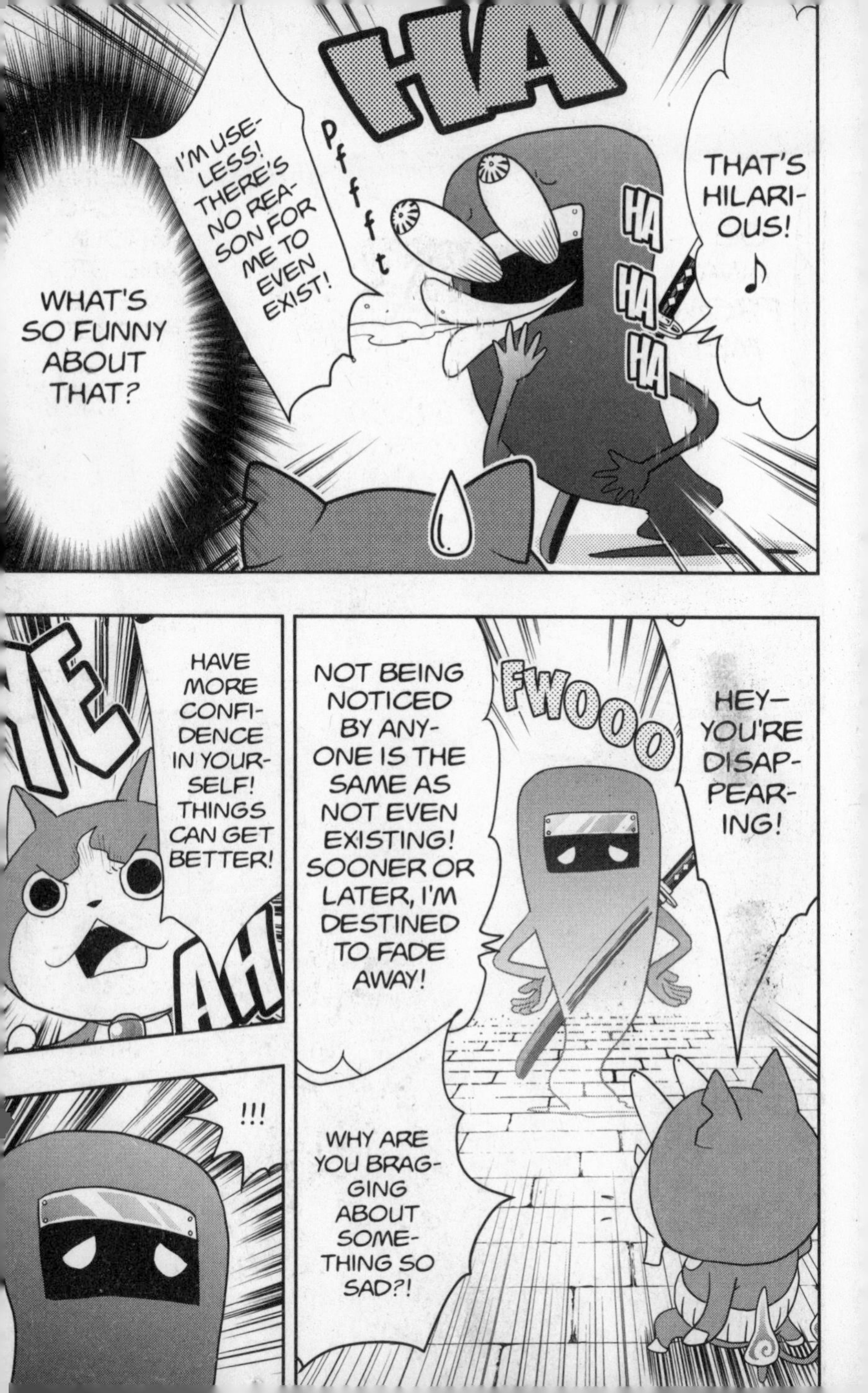
HA
THAT'S HILARIOUS! ♪
HA HA HA
Pfffft
I'M USELESS! THERE'S NO REASON FOR ME TO EVEN EXIST!
WHAT'S SO FUNNY ABOUT THAT?
HEY—YOU'RE DISAPPEARING!
FWOOOO
NOT BEING NOTICED BY ANYONE IS THE SAME AS NOT EVEN EXISTING! SOONER OR LATER, I'M DESTINED TO FADE AWAY!
WHY ARE YOU BRAGGING ABOUT SOMETHING SO SAD?!
VE
HAVE MORE CONFIDENCE IN YOURSELF! THINGS CAN GET BETTER!
AH
!!!

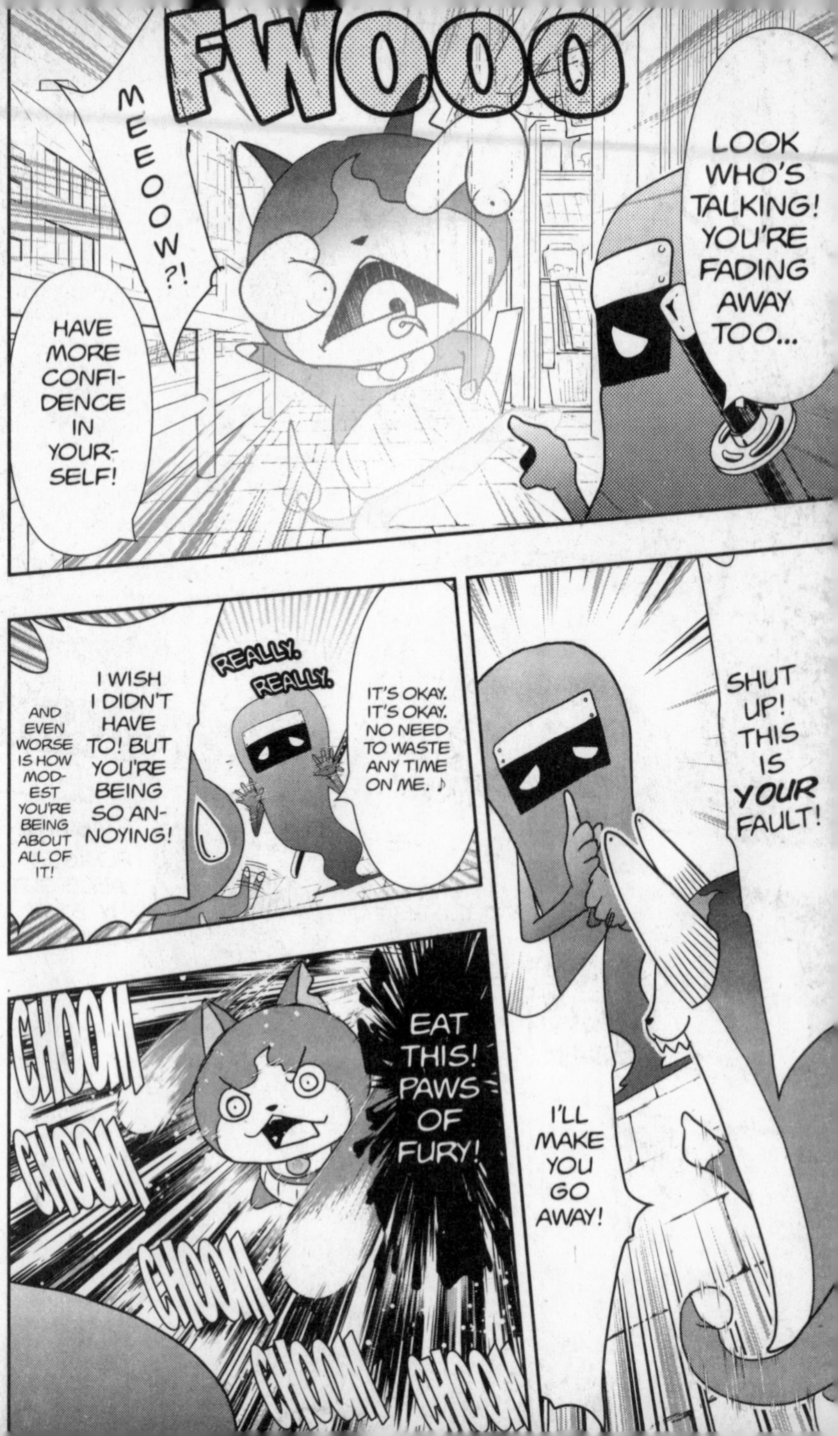
FWOOO
LOOK WHO'S TALKING! YOU'RE FADING AWAY TOO...
MEEEOOOW?!
HAVE MORE CONFIDENCE IN YOURSELF!
SHUT UP! THIS IS YOUR FAULT!
I'LL MAKE YOU GO AWAY!
IT'S OKAY. IT'S OKAY. NO NEED TO WASTE ANY TIME ON ME. ♪
REALLY. REALLY.
I WISH I DIDN'T HAVE TO! BUT YOU'RE BEING SO ANNOYING!
AND EVEN WORSE IS HOW MODEST YOU'RE BEING ABOUT ALL OF IT!
EAT THIS! PAWS OF FURY!
CHOOM CHOOM CHOOM CHOOM CHOOM

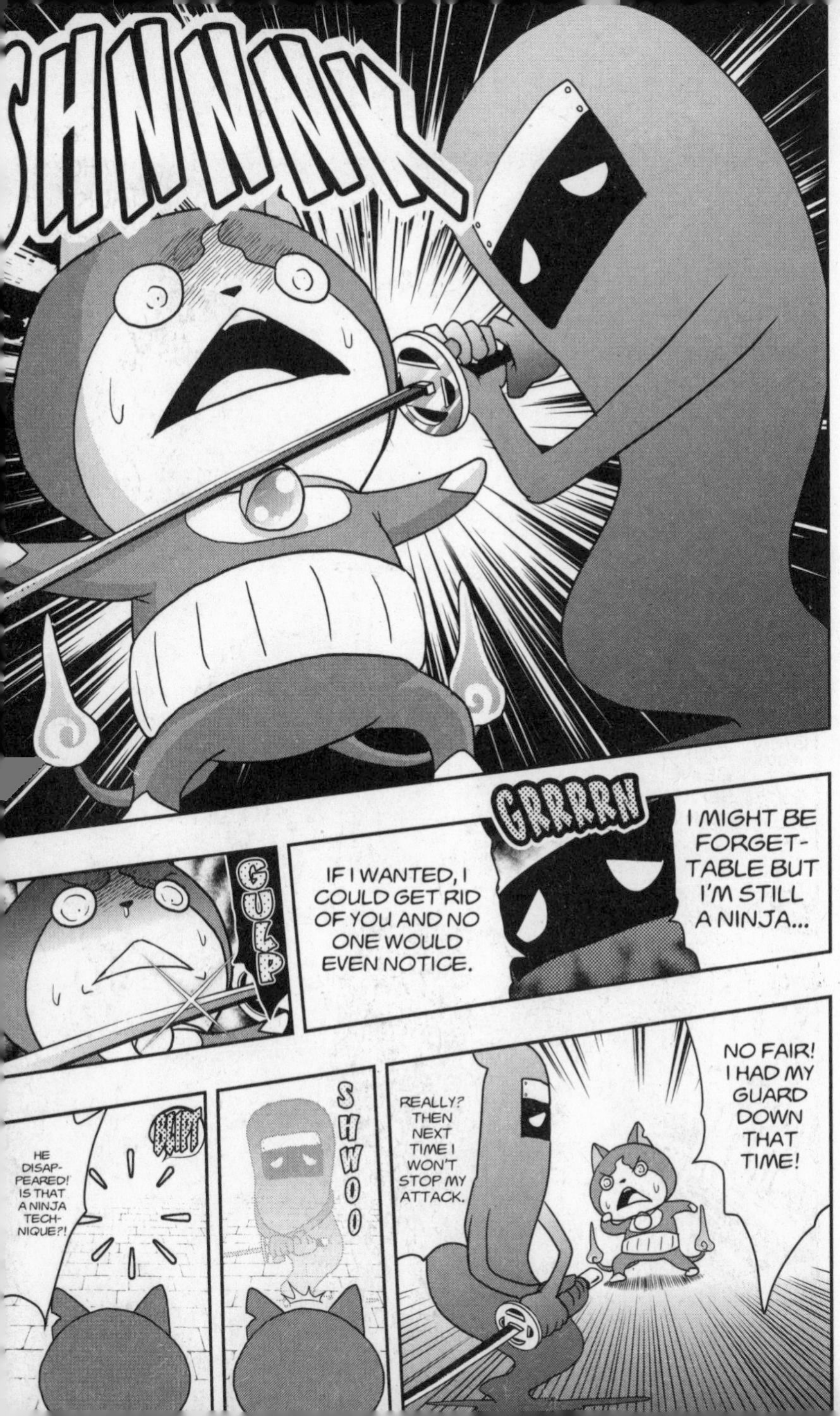
SHNNNNK
GRRRRN
I MIGHT BE FORGETTABLE BUT I'M STILL A NINJA...
IF I WANTED, I COULD GET RID OF YOU AND NO ONE WOULD EVEN NOTICE.
GULP
NO FAIR! I HAD MY GUARD DOWN THAT TIME!
REALLY? THEN NEXT TIME I WON'T STOP MY ATTACK.
SHWOOO
HE DISAPPEARED! IS THAT A NINJA TECHNIQUE?!

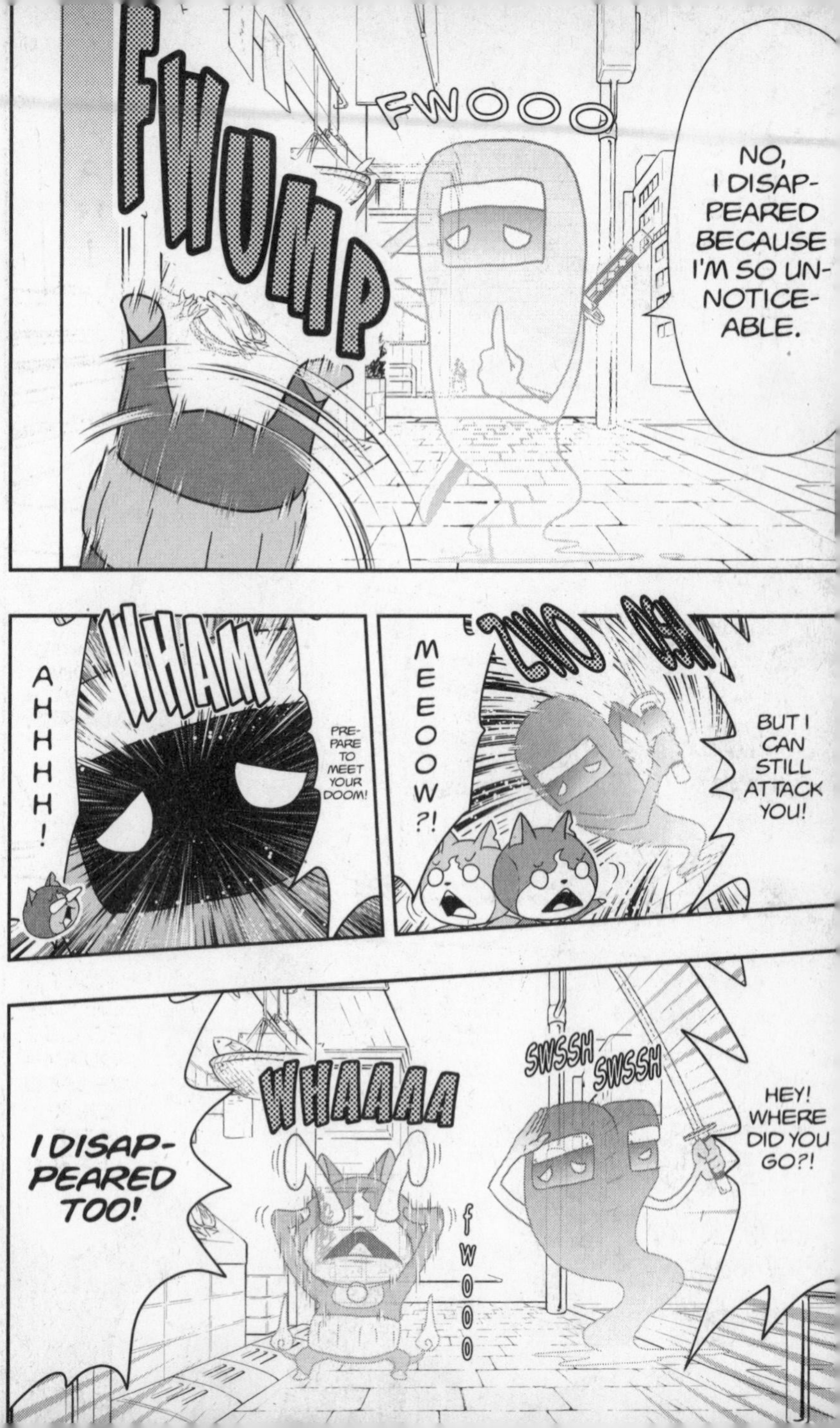
NO, I DISAPPEARED BECAUSE I'M SO UNNOTICEABLE.
FWOOO
FWUMP
BUT I CAN STILL ATTACK YOU!
MEEEOOOW?!
PREPARE TO MEET YOUR DOOM!
WHAM
AHHHH!
HEY! WHERE DID YOU GO?!
SWSSH SWSSH
WHAAAA
fwooo
I DISAPPEARED TOO!

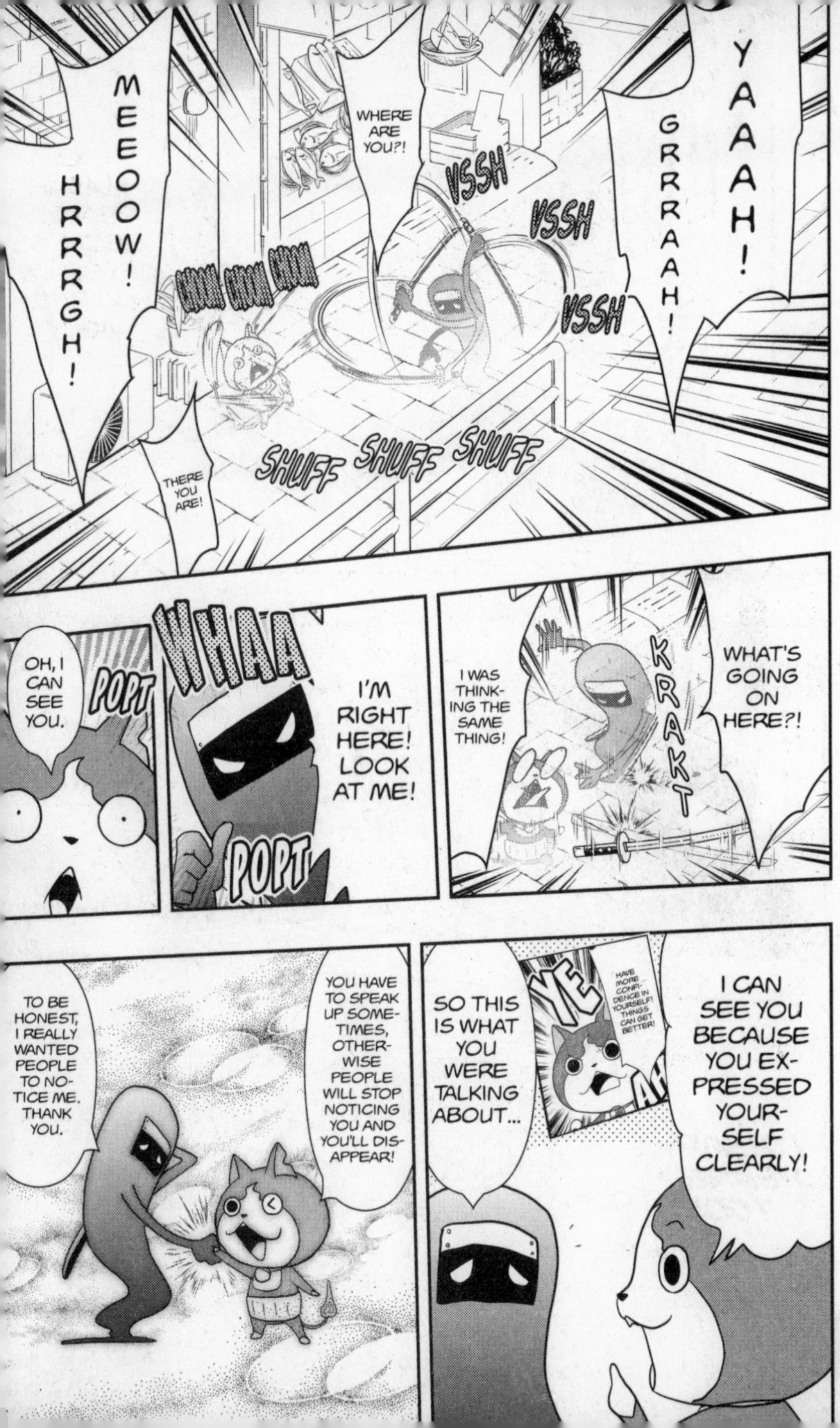
YAAAH!
GRRRAAH!
WHERE ARE YOU?!
VSSH
VSSH
VSSH
MEEOOW!
HRRRGH!
SHUFF
SHUFF
SHUFF
THERE YOU ARE!
WHAT'S GOING ON HERE?!
KRAKT
I WAS THINKING THE SAME THING!
I'M RIGHT HERE! LOOK AT ME!
WHAA
POPT
POPT
OH, I CAN SEE YOU.
I CAN SEE YOU BECAUSE YOU EXPRESSED YOURSELF CLEARLY!
HAVE MORE CONFIDENCE IN YOURSELF! THINGS CAN GET BETTER!
YE
AH
SO THIS IS WHAT YOU WERE TALKING ABOUT...
YOU HAVE TO SPEAK UP SOMETIMES, OTHERWISE PEOPLE WILL STOP NOTICING YOU AND YOU'LL DISAPPEAR!
TO BE HONEST, I REALLY WANTED PEOPLE TO NOTICE ME. THANK YOU.

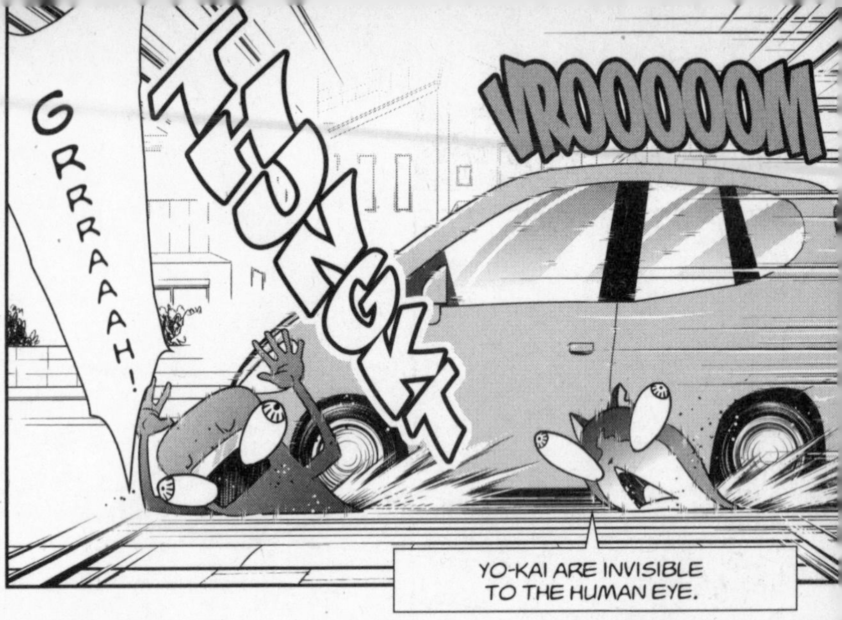
VROOOOOM
GRRRAAAAH!
YO-KAI ARE INVISIBLE TO THE HUMAN EYE.

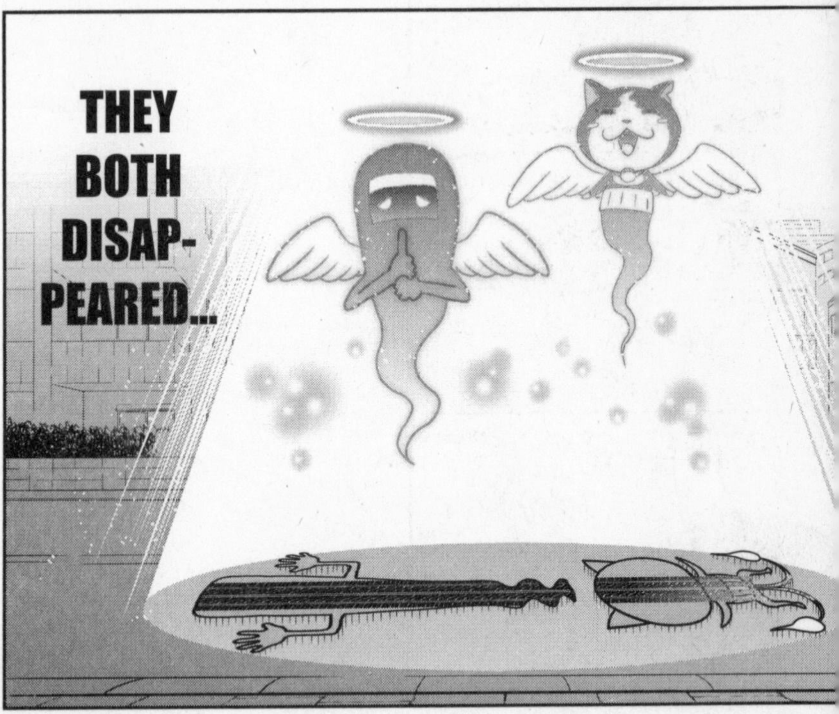
THEY BOTH DISAP-PEARED...

A YO-KAI NAMED DIMMY

ZWOOSH
MEOOOOW! I REFUSE TO DIE!
WE HAVE TO GET BACK TO OUR BODIES!
M-MMEOW!
SHMPT
THAT WAS TOO CLOSE.
I WAS ABOUT TO DIE...
SHUMPT
WAIT...
SHFF SHFF
WHERE'S MY BODY?!
...
UNNOTICEABLE.

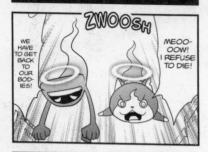

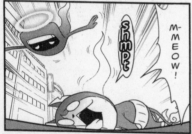

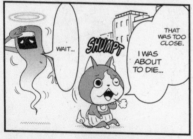

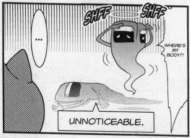

CHAPTER 78: EMOTIONAL ROLLER COASTER?!

FEATURING ATTITUDE-ADJUSTMENT YO-KAI REVERSA

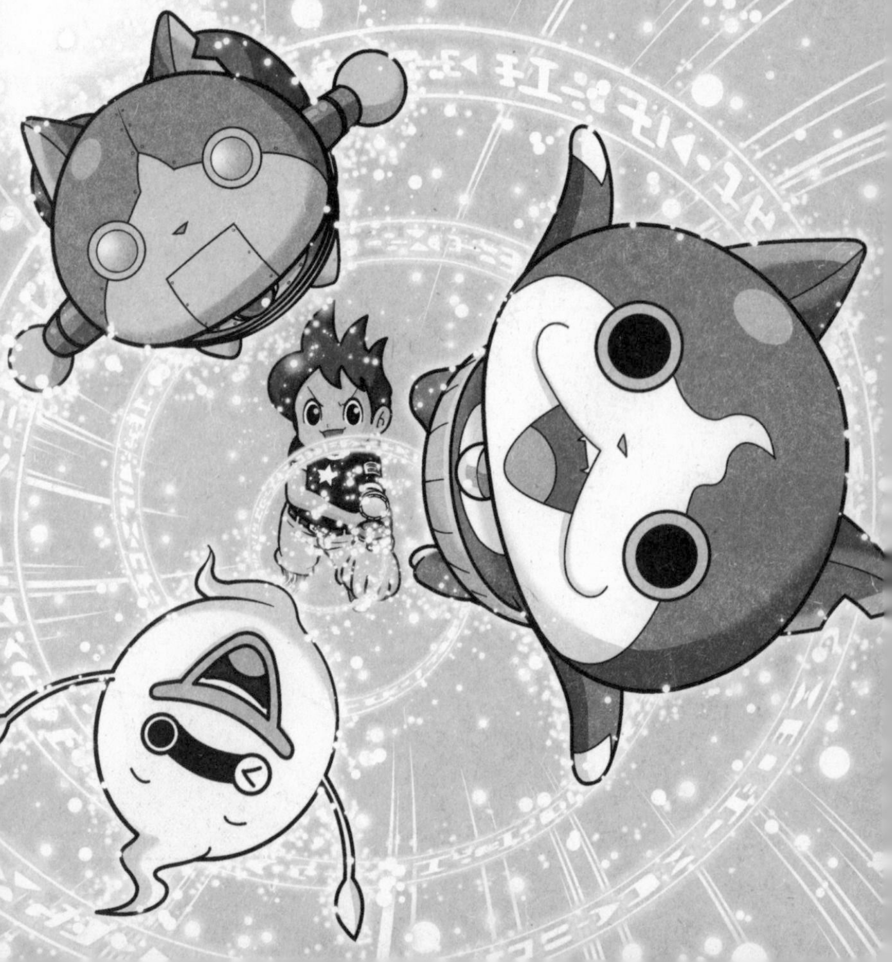

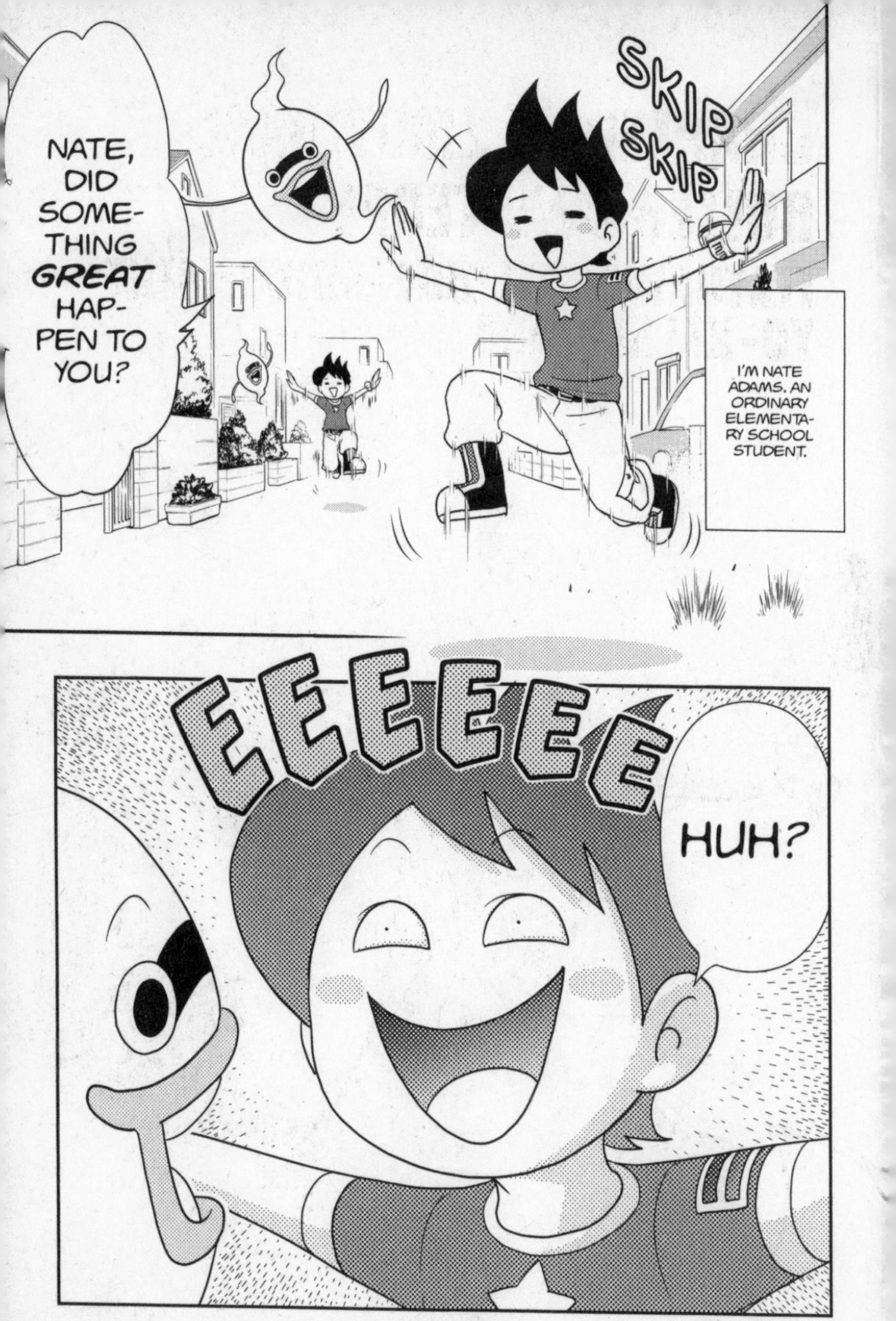
SKIP SKIP
I'M NATE ADAMS. AN ORDINARY ELEMENTARY SCHOOL STUDENT.
NATE, DID SOMETHING GREAT HAPPEN TO YOU?
EEEEEE
HUH?

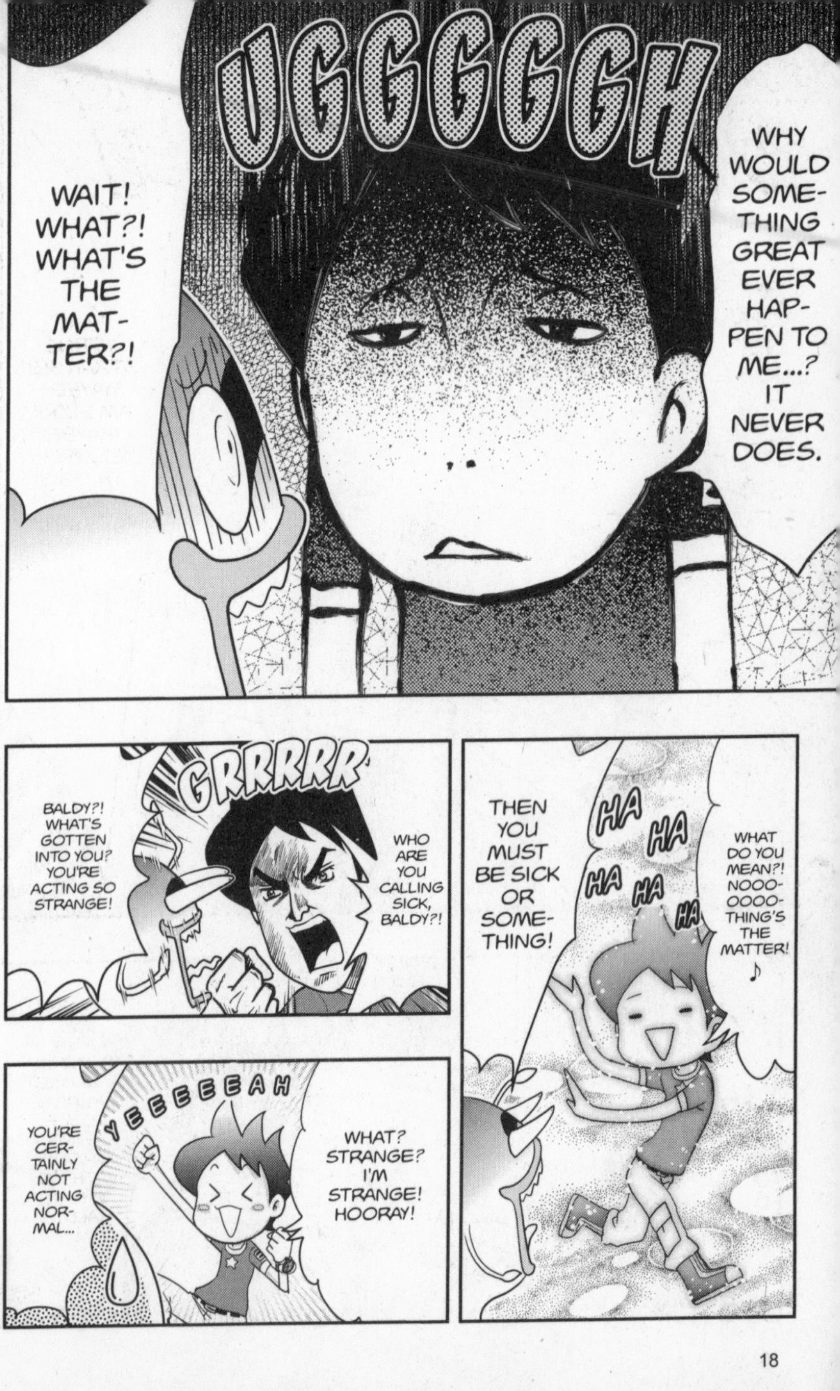
UGGGGGGH
WHY WOULD SOME-THING GREAT EVER HAP-PEN TO ME...? IT NEVER DOES.
WAIT! WHAT?! WHAT'S THE MAT-TER?!
HA HA HA HA HA
WHAT DO YOU MEAN?! NOOO-OOOO-THING'S THE MATTER! ♪
THEN YOU MUST BE SICK OR SOME-THING!
GRRRRR
WHO ARE YOU CALLING SICK, BALDY?!
BALDY?! WHAT'S GOTTEN INTO YOU? YOU'RE ACTING SO STRANGE!
YEEEEEAH
WHAT? STRANGE? I'M STRANGE! HOORAY!
YOU'RE CER-TAINLY NOT ACTING NOR-MAL...

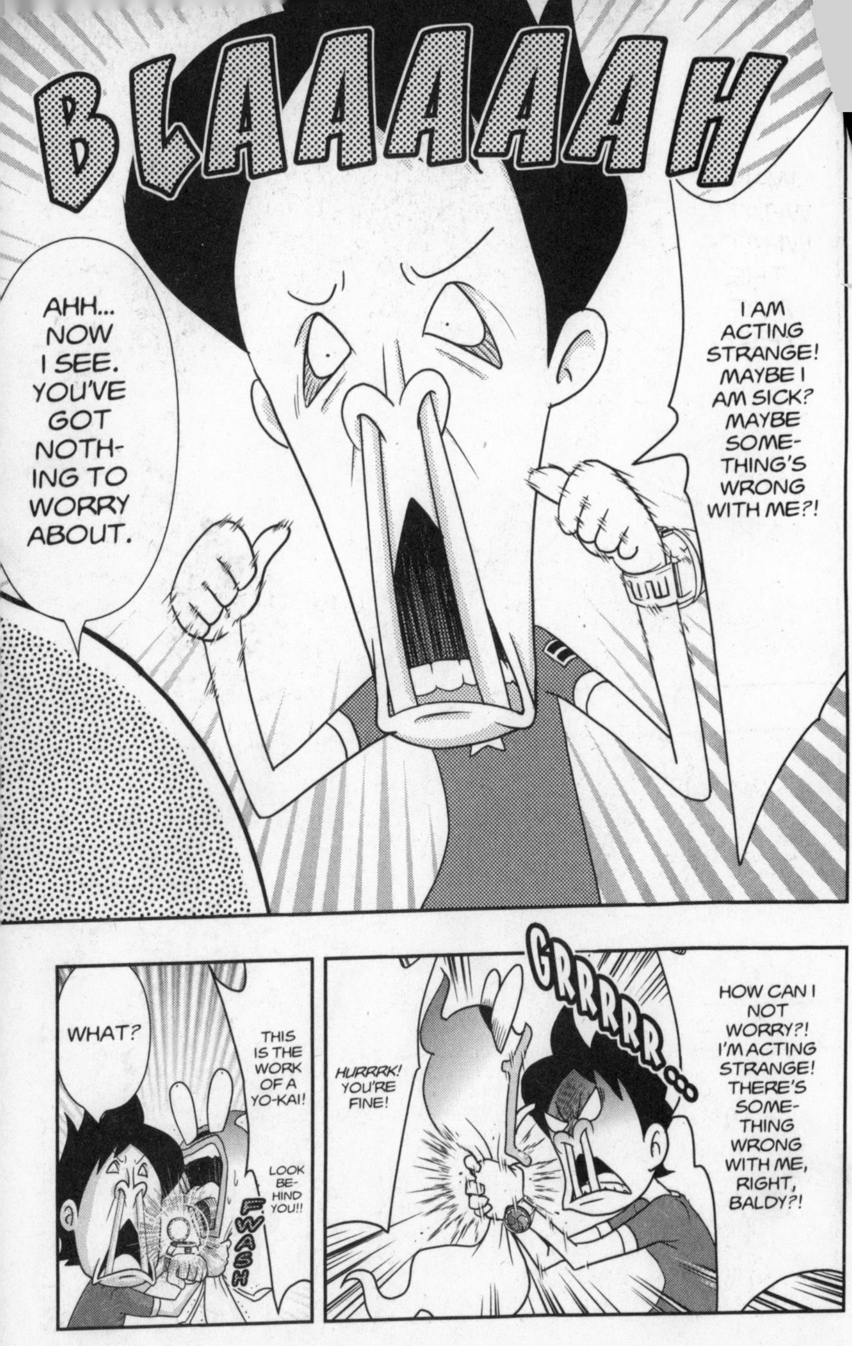
BLAAAAAH
I AM ACTING STRANGE! MAYBE I AM SICK? MAYBE SOME-THING'S WRONG WITH ME?!
AHH... NOW I SEE. YOU'VE GOT NOTH-ING TO WORRY ABOUT.
GRRRRR...
HOW CAN I NOT WORRY?! I'M ACTING STRANGE! THERE'S SOME-THING WRONG WITH ME, RIGHT, BALDY?!
HURRRK! YOU'RE FINE!
THIS IS THE WORK OF A YO-KAI!
WHAT?
LOOK BE-HIND YOU!!
FWASH

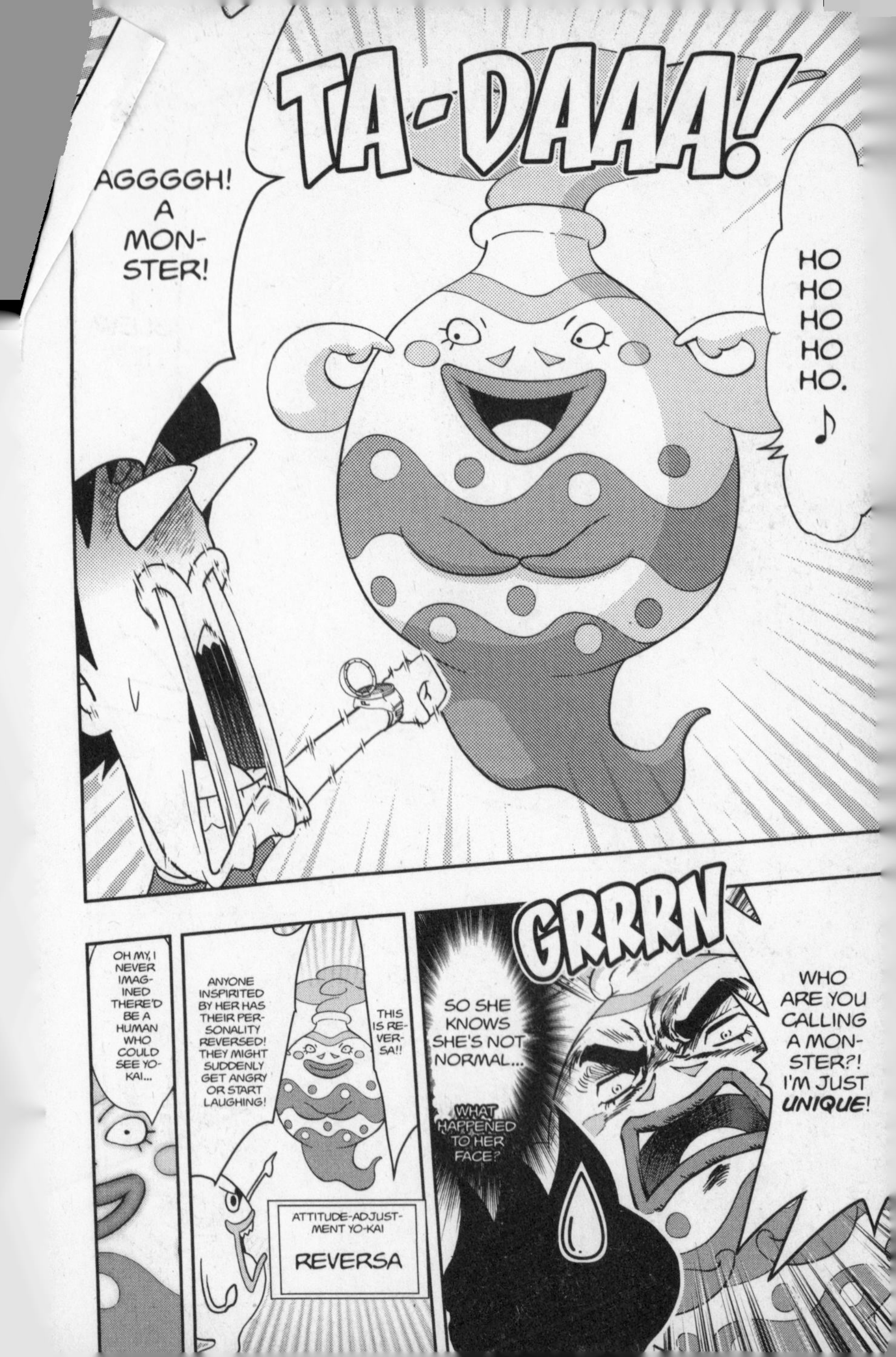
TA-DAAA!
HO HO HO HO HO. ♪
AGGGGH! A MONSTER!
GRRRN
WHO ARE YOU CALLING A MONSTER?! I'M JUST *UNIQUE*!
SO SHE KNOWS SHE'S NOT NORMAL...
WHAT HAPPENED TO HER FACE?
THIS IS REVERSA!!
ANYONE INSPIRITED BY HER HAS THEIR PERSONALITY REVERSED! THEY MIGHT SUDDENLY GET ANGRY OR START LAUGHING!
ATTITUDE-ADJUSTMENT YO-KAI
REVERSA
OH MY, I NEVER IMAGINED THERE'D BE A HUMAN WHO COULD SEE YO-KAI...

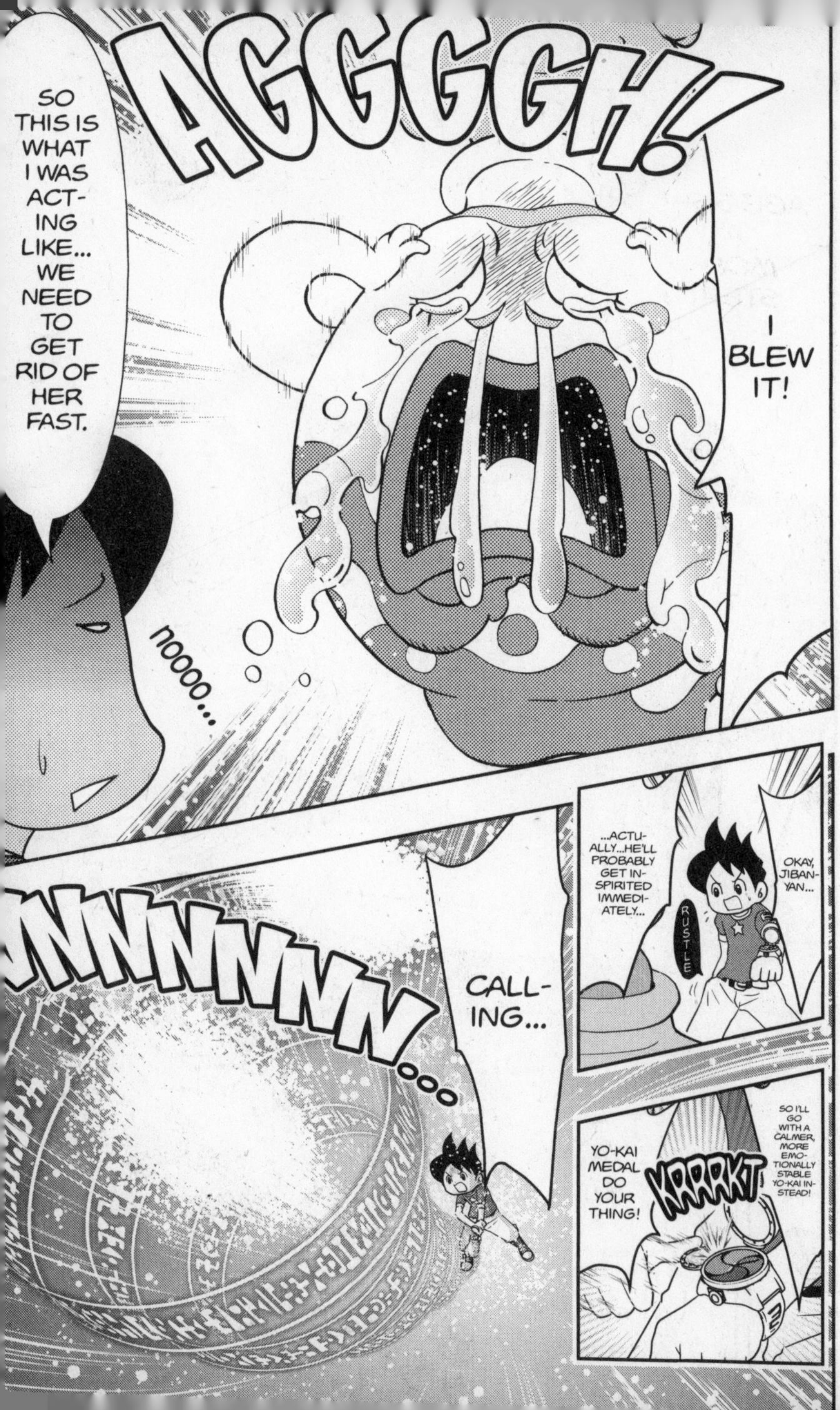
AGGGGH!
I BLEW IT!
SO THIS IS WHAT I WAS ACTING LIKE... WE NEED TO GET RID OF HER FAST.
nooooo...
OKAY, JIBANYAN...
...ACTUALLY...HE'LL PROBABLY GET INSPIRITED IMMEDIATELY...
RUSTLE
SO I'LL GO WITH A CALMER, MORE EMOTIONALLY STABLE YO-KAI INSTEAD!
YO-KAI MEDAL DO YOUR THING!
KRRRKT
CALLING...
NNNNNNNNN...ooo

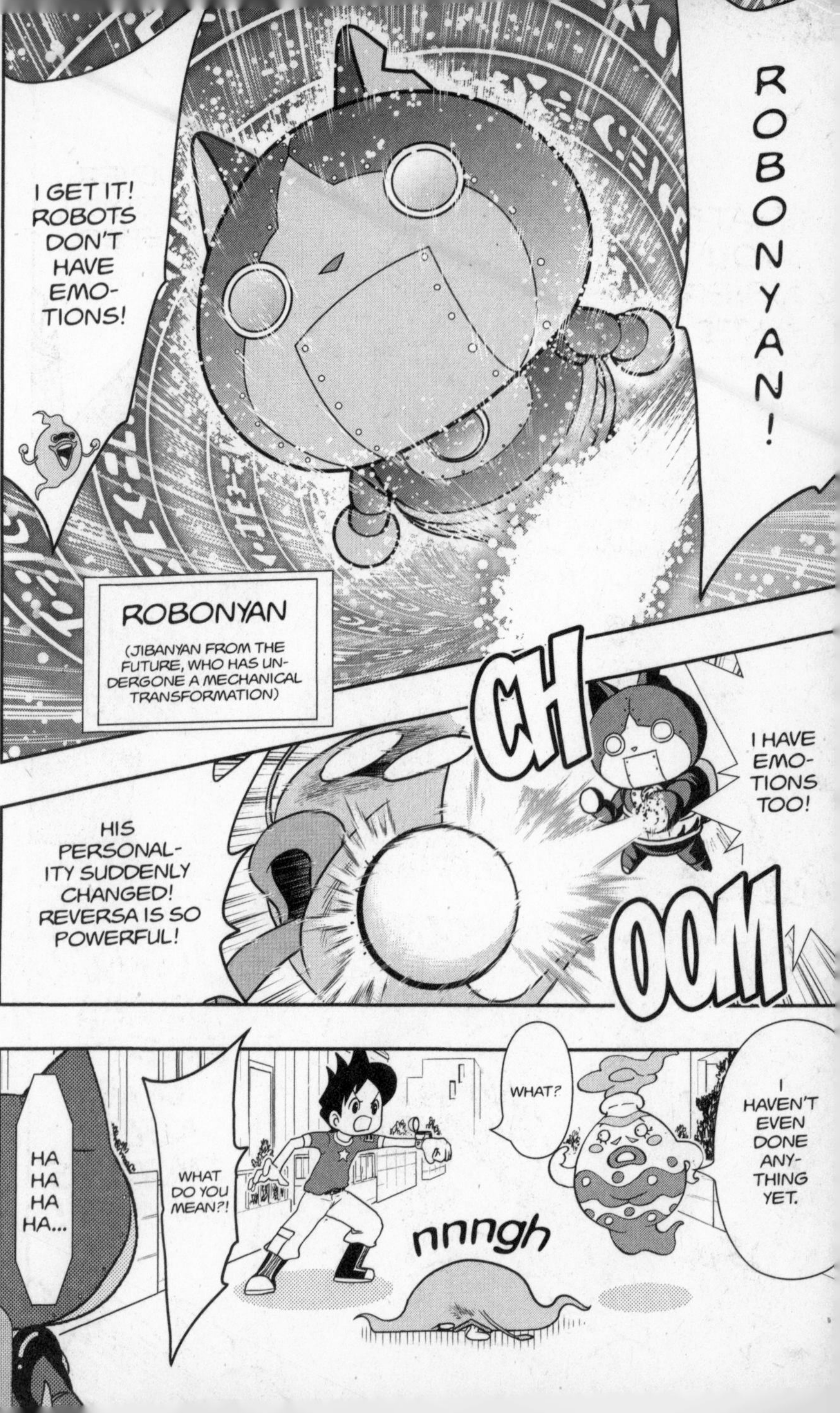
ROBONYAN!
I GET IT! ROBOTS DON'T HAVE EMO-TIONS!
ROBONYAN
(JIBANYAN FROM THE FUTURE, WHO HAS UN-DERGONE A MECHANICAL TRANSFORMATION)
CHOOM
I HAVE EMO-TIONS TOO!
HIS PERSONAL-ITY SUDDENLY CHANGED! REVERSA IS SO POWERFUL!
I HAVEN'T EVEN DONE ANY-THING YET.
WHAT?
nnngh
WHAT DO YOU MEAN?!
HA HA HA HA...

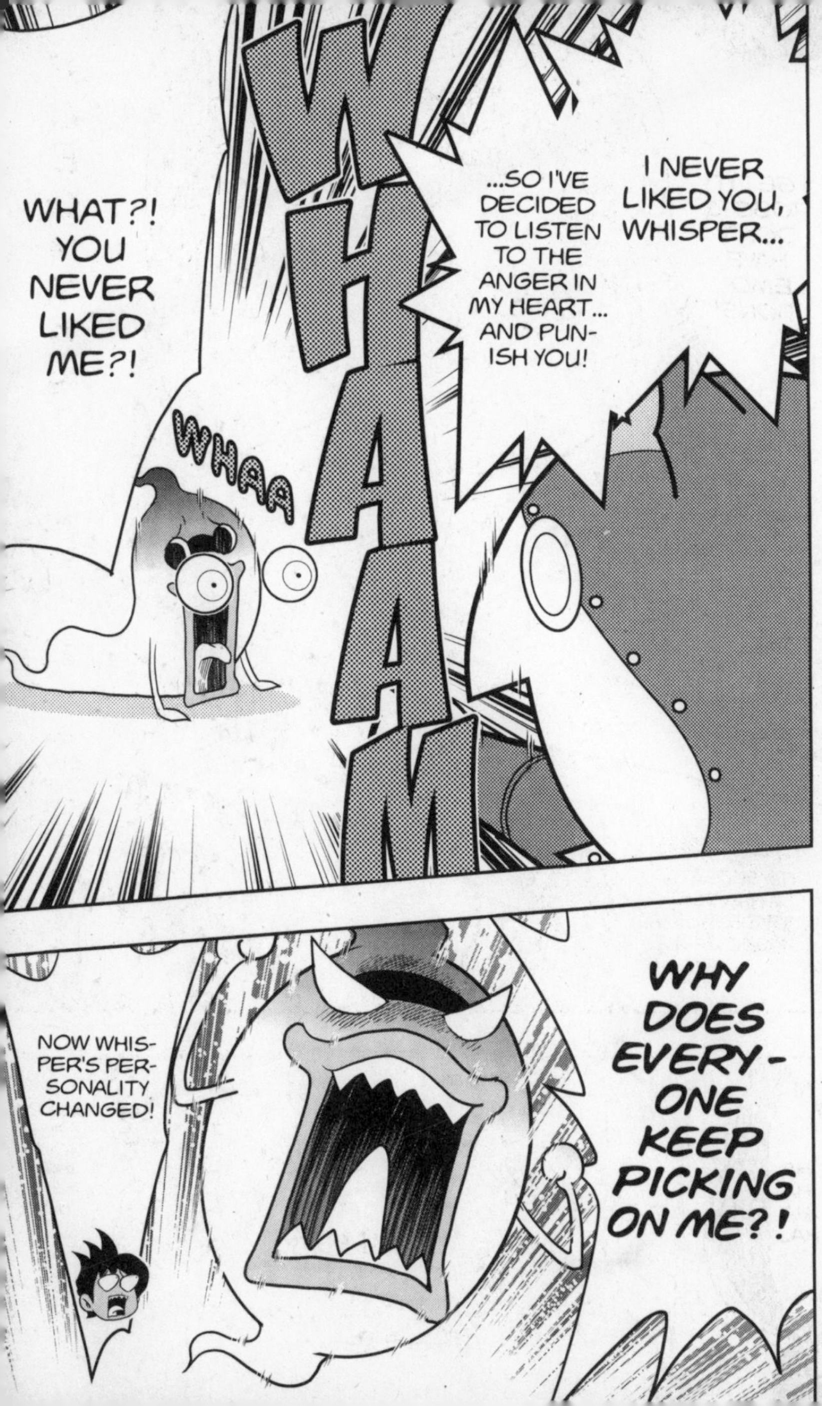
I NEVER LIKED YOU, WHISPER...
...SO I'VE DECIDED TO LISTEN TO THE ANGER IN MY HEART... AND PUN-ISH YOU!
WHAM
WHAA
WHAT?! YOU NEVER LIKED ME?!
WHY DOES EVERY-ONE KEEP PICKING ON ME?!
NOW WHIS-PER'S PER-SONALITY CHANGED!

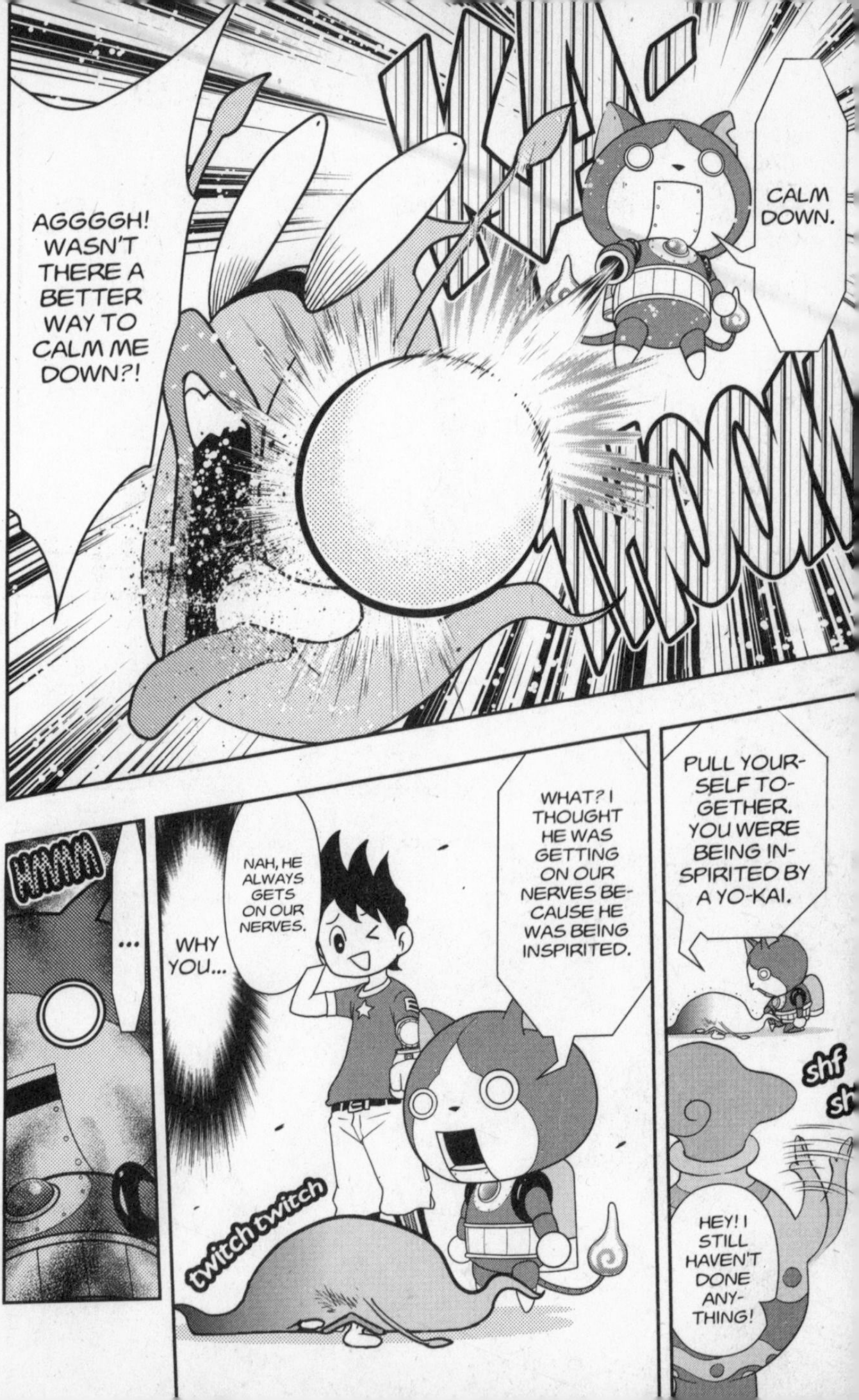
CALM DOWN.
AGGGGH! WASN'T THERE A BETTER WAY TO CALM ME DOWN?!
PULL YOUR-SELF TO-GETHER. YOU WERE BEING IN-SPIRITED BY A YO-KAI.
shf shf
HEY! I STILL HAVEN'T DONE ANY-THING!
WHAT? I THOUGHT HE WAS GETTING ON OUR NERVES BE-CAUSE HE WAS BEING INSPIRITED.
NAH, HE ALWAYS GETS ON OUR NERVES.
WHY YOU...
twitch twitch
HMMM
...

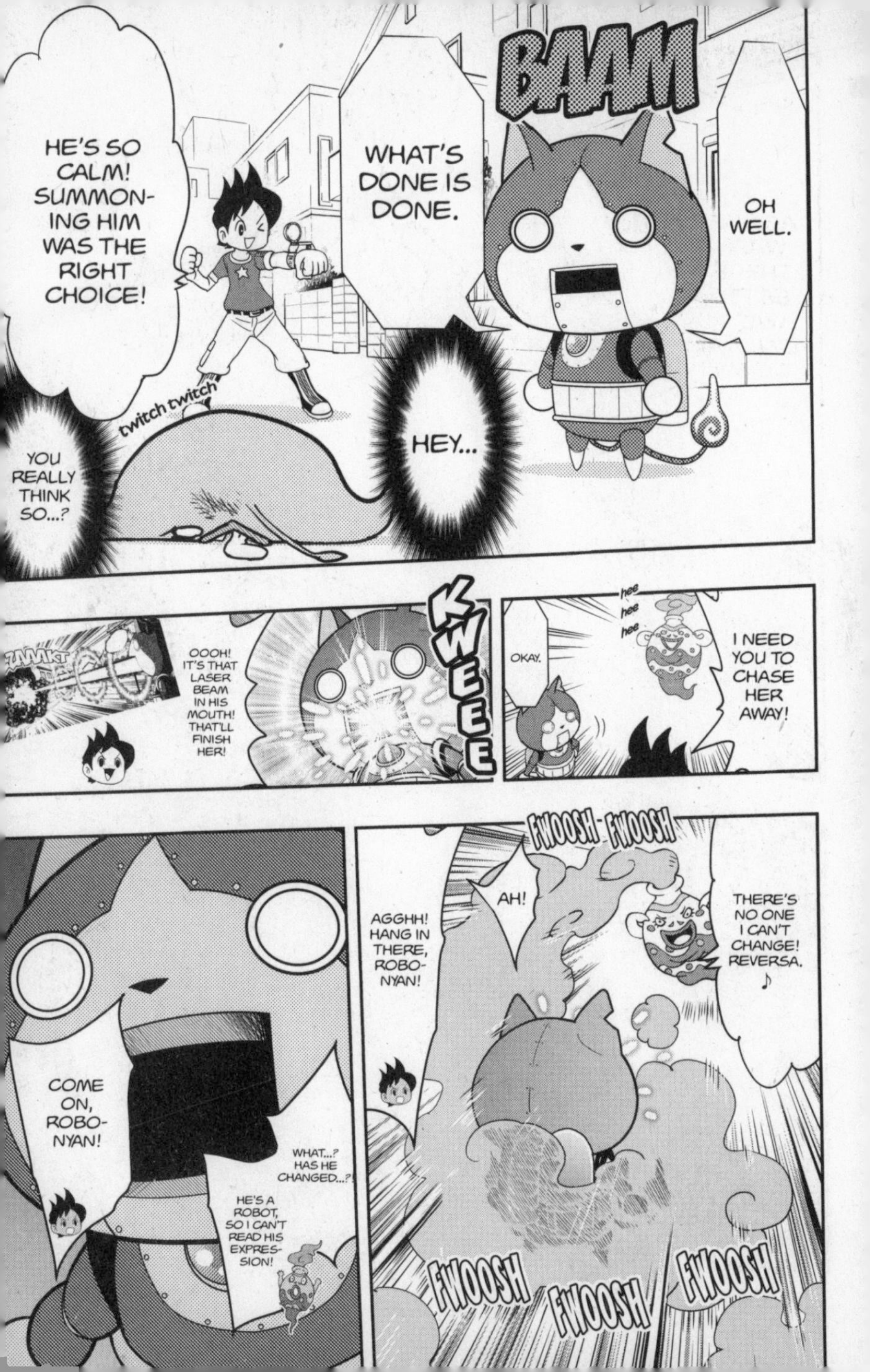
BAAM
OH WELL.
WHAT'S DONE IS DONE.
HE'S SO CALM! SUMMONING HIM WAS THE RIGHT CHOICE!
HEY...
twitch twitch
YOU REALLY THINK SO...?
hee hee hee
I NEED YOU TO CHASE HER AWAY!
OKAY.
KWEEE
OOOH! IT'S THAT LASER BEAM IN HIS MOUTH! THAT'LL FINISH HER!
FWOOSH FWOOSH
THERE'S NO ONE I CAN'T CHANGE! REVERSA. ♪
AH!
AGGHH! HANG IN THERE, ROBONYAN!
FWOOSH FWOOSH FWOOSH
COME ON, ROBONYAN!
WHAT...? HAS HE CHANGED...?!
HE'S A ROBOT, SO I CAN'T READ HIS EXPRESSION!

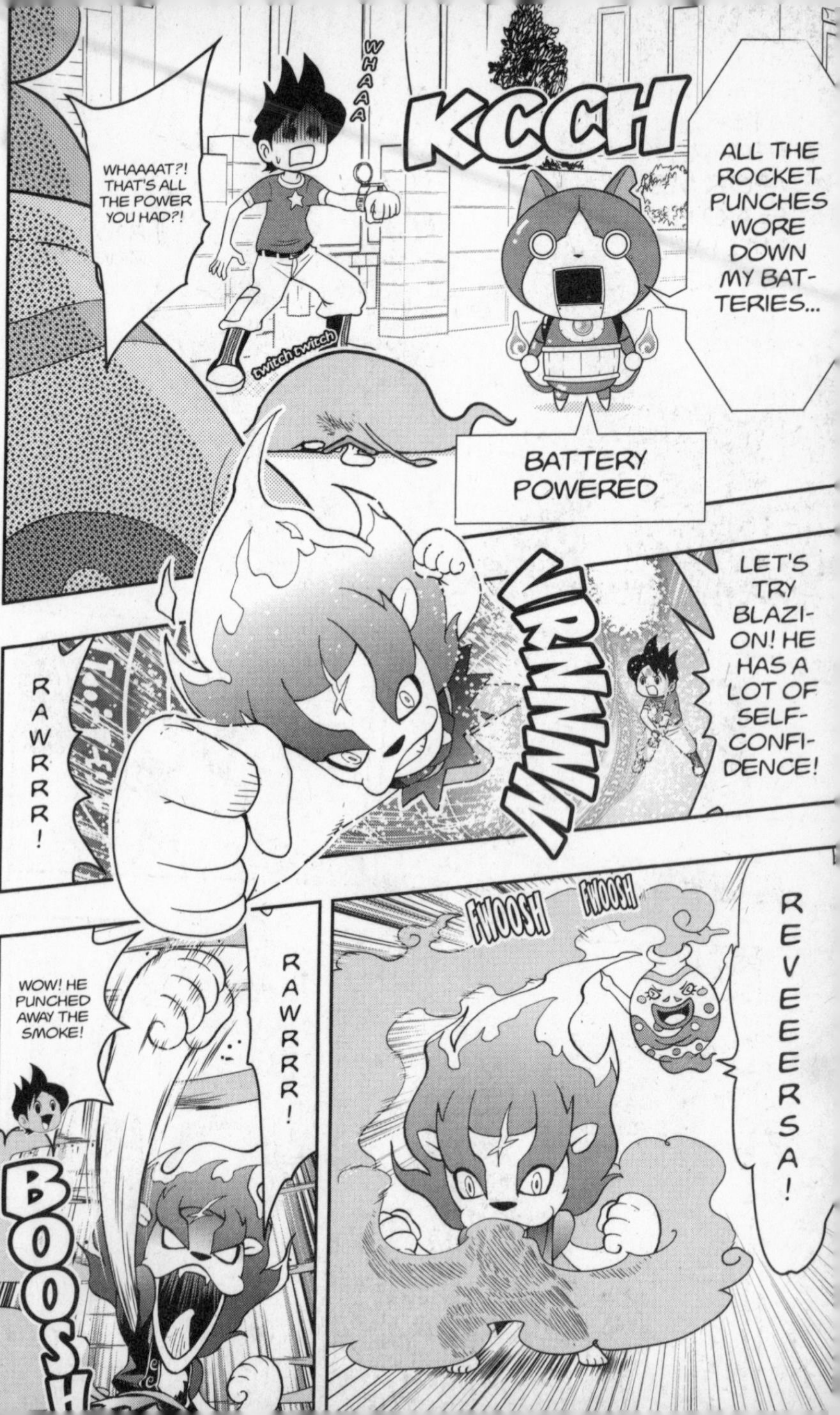
ALL THE ROCKET PUNCHES WORE DOWN MY BATTERIES...
KCCH
WHAAAA
WHAAAAT?! THAT'S ALL THE POWER YOU HAD?!
BATTERY POWERED
twitch twitch
LET'S TRY BLAZION! HE HAS A LOT OF SELF-CONFIDENCE!
VRNNN
RAWRRRR!
REVEEEERSA!
FWOOSH
FWOOSH
RAWRRRR!
WOW! HE PUNCHED AWAY THE SMOKE!
BOOSH

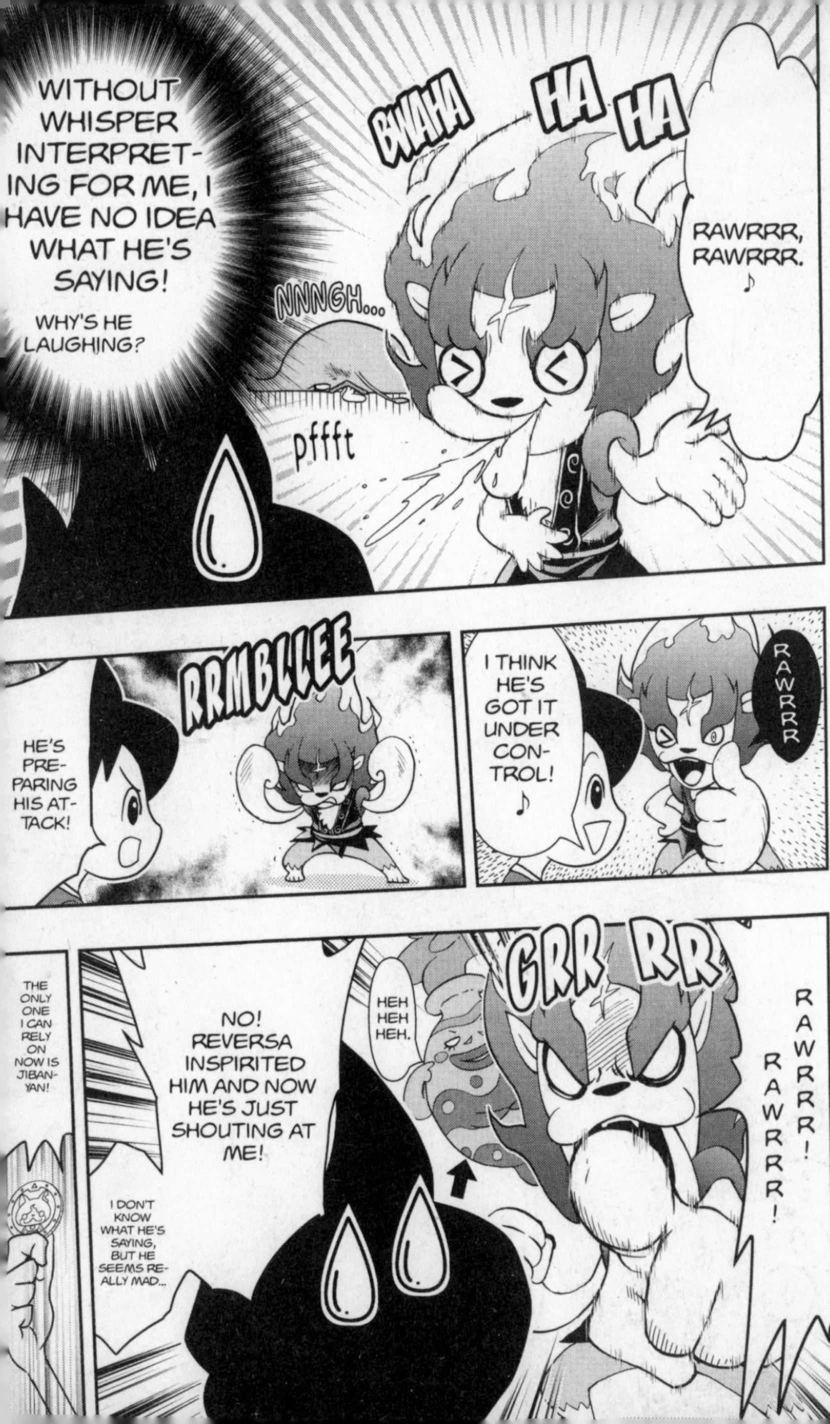
BWAHA HA HA
RAWRRR, RAWRRR. ♪
WITHOUT WHISPER INTERPRETING FOR ME, I HAVE NO IDEA WHAT HE'S SAYING!
WHY'S HE LAUGHING?
NNNGH...
pffft
RAWRRR
I THINK HE'S GOT IT UNDER CONTROL! ♪
RRMBLLEE
HE'S PREPARING HIS ATTACK!
RAWRRR!
RAWRRR!
GRR RR
HEH HEH HEH.
NO! REVERSA INSPIRITED HIM AND NOW HE'S JUST SHOUTING AT ME!
I DON'T KNOW WHAT HE'S SAYING, BUT HE SEEMS REALLY MAD...
THE ONLY ONE I CAN RELY ON NOW IS JIBANYAN!

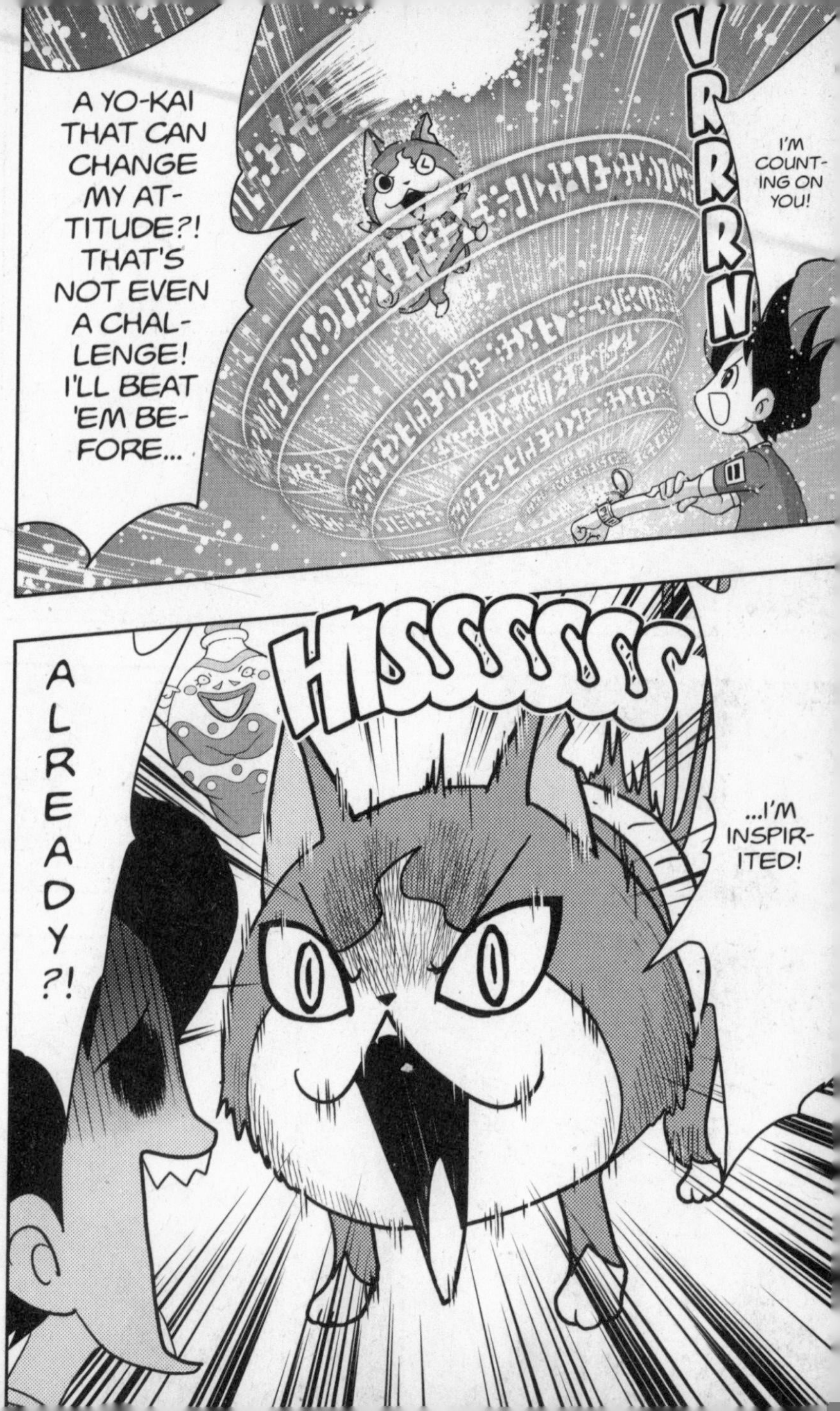
VRRRN
I'M COUNTING ON YOU!
A YO-KAI THAT CAN CHANGE MY ATTITUDE?! THAT'S NOT EVEN A CHALLENGE! I'LL BEAT 'EM BEFORE...
HISSSSSS
...I'M INSPIRITED!
ALREADY?!

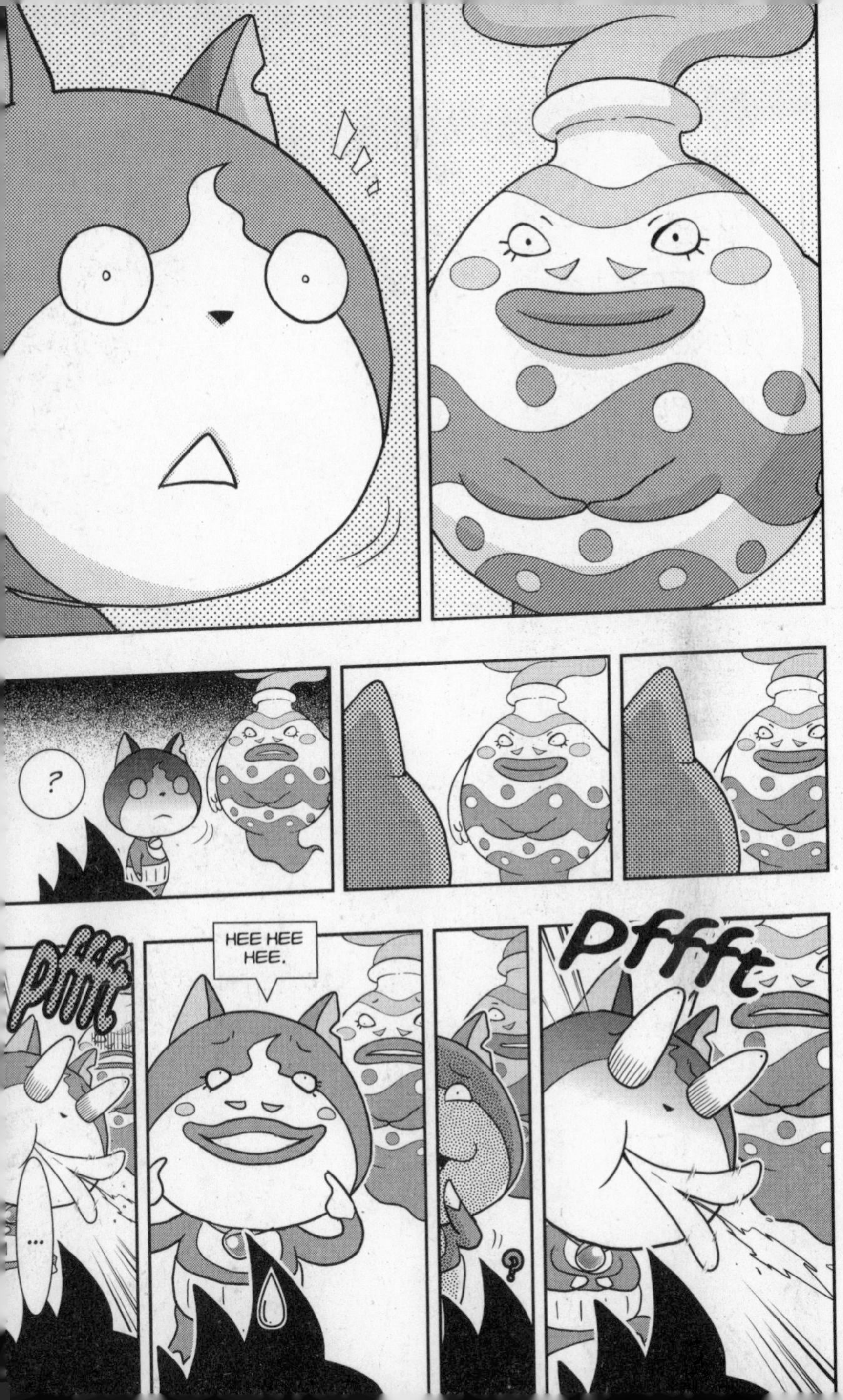
?
Pffft
?
HEE HEE HEE.
Pffft
...

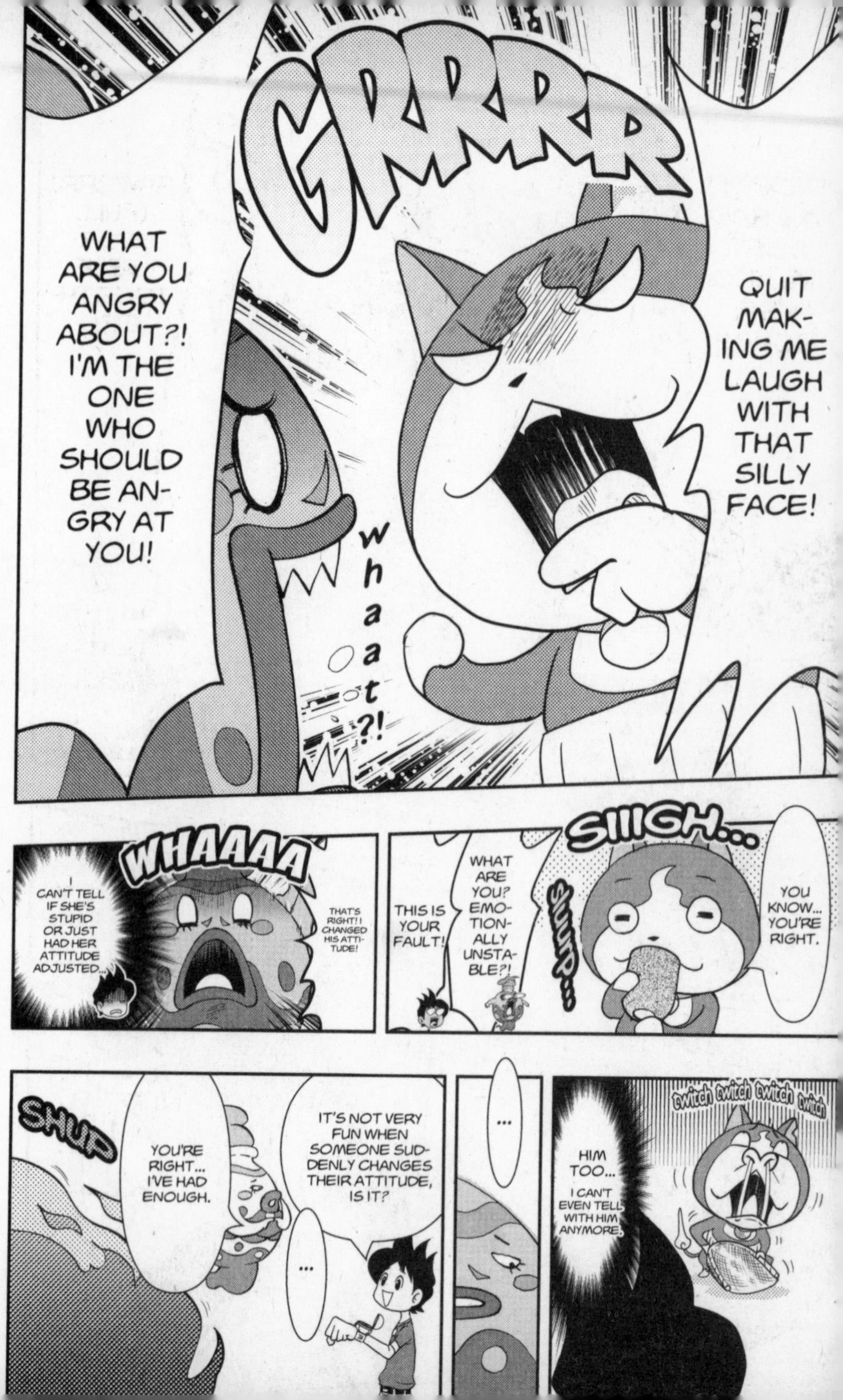
GRRRR
QUIT MAKING ME LAUGH WITH THAT SILLY FACE!
whaaat?!
WHAT ARE YOU ANGRY ABOUT?! I'M THE ONE WHO SHOULD BE ANGRY AT YOU!
SIIIGH...
YOU KNOW... YOU'RE RIGHT.
shurp...
WHAT ARE YOU? EMOTIONALLY UNSTABLE?!
THIS IS YOUR FAULT!
WHAAAAA
THAT'S RIGHT!! I CHANGED HIS ATTITUDE!
I CAN'T TELL IF SHE'S STUPID OR JUST HAD HER ATTITUDE ADJUSTED...
twitch twitch twitch twitch
HIM TOO... I CAN'T EVEN TELL WITH HIM ANYMORE.
...
IT'S NOT VERY FUN WHEN SOMEONE SUDDENLY CHANGES THEIR ATTITUDE, IS IT?
...
YOU'RE RIGHT... I'VE HAD ENOUGH.
SHUP

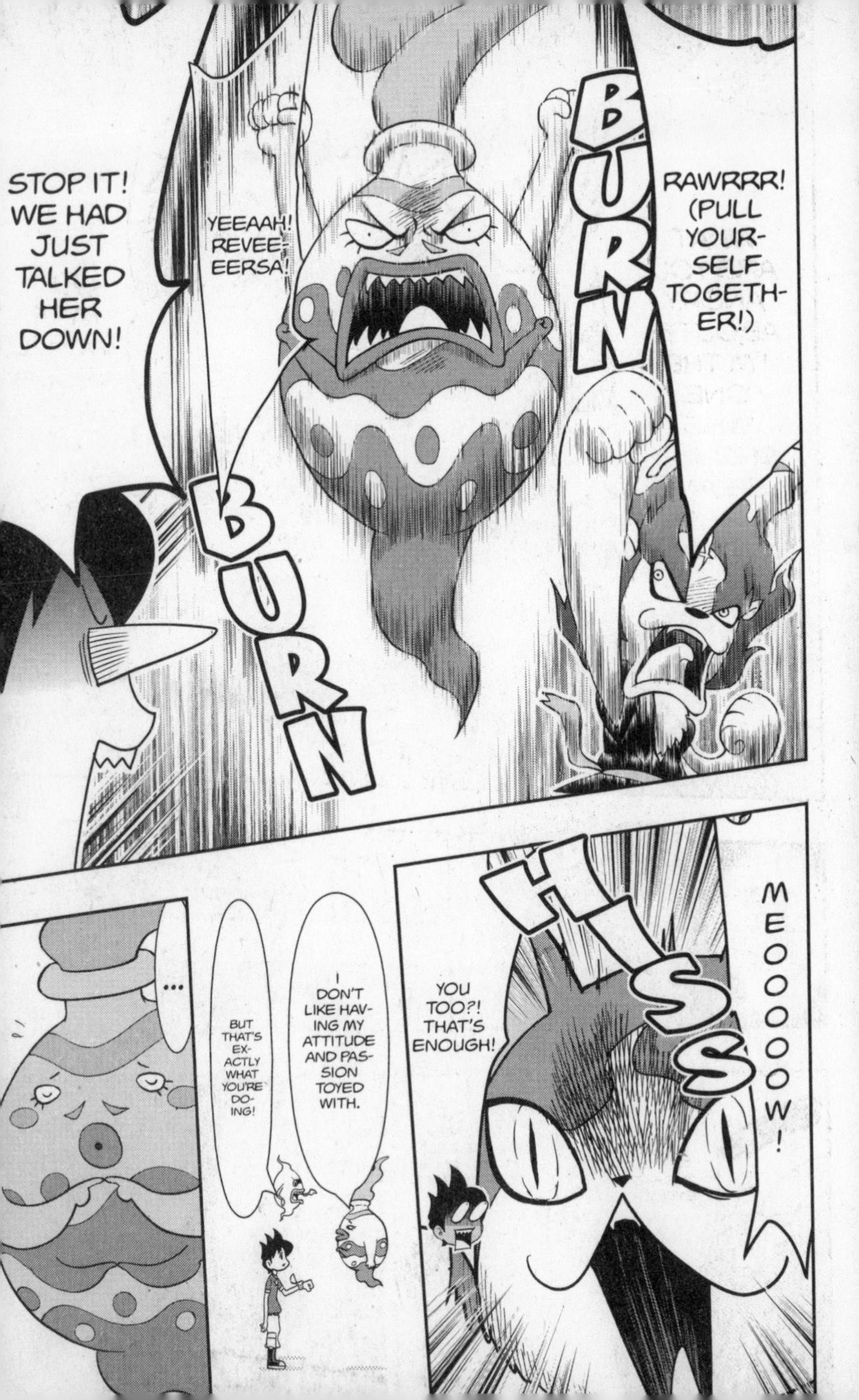
RAWRRR! (PULL YOUR-SELF TOGETH-ER!)
BURN
YEEAAH! REVEE-EERSA!
BURN
STOP IT! WE HAD JUST TALKED HER DOWN!
MEOOOOOOW!
HISS
YOU TOO?! THAT'S ENOUGH!
I DON'T LIKE HAV-ING MY ATTITUDE AND PAS-SION TOYED WITH.
BUT THAT'S EX-ACTLY WHAT YOU'RE DO-ING!
...

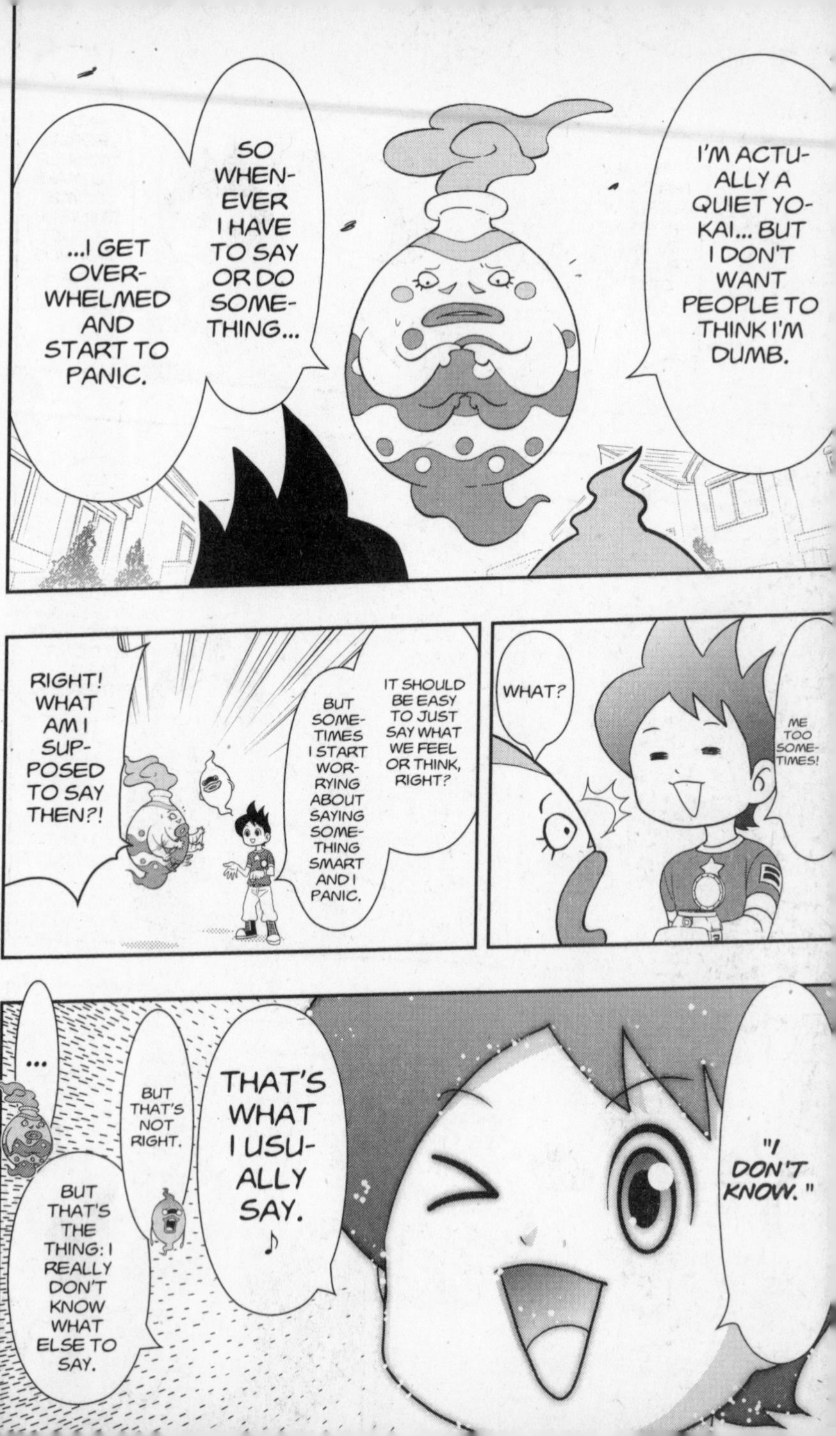
I'M ACTUALLY A QUIET YOKAI... BUT I DON'T WANT PEOPLE TO THINK I'M DUMB.
SO WHENEVER I HAVE TO SAY OR DO SOMETHING...
...I GET OVERWHELMED AND START TO PANIC.
ME TOO SOMETIMES!
WHAT?
IT SHOULD BE EASY TO JUST SAY WHAT WE FEEL OR THINK, RIGHT?
BUT SOMETIMES I START WORRYING ABOUT SAYING SOMETHING SMART AND I PANIC.
RIGHT! WHAT AM I SUPPOSED TO SAY THEN?!
"I DON'T KNOW."
THAT'S WHAT I USUALLY SAY. ♪
BUT THAT'S NOT RIGHT.
...
BUT THAT'S THE THING: I REALLY DON'T KNOW WHAT ELSE TO SAY.

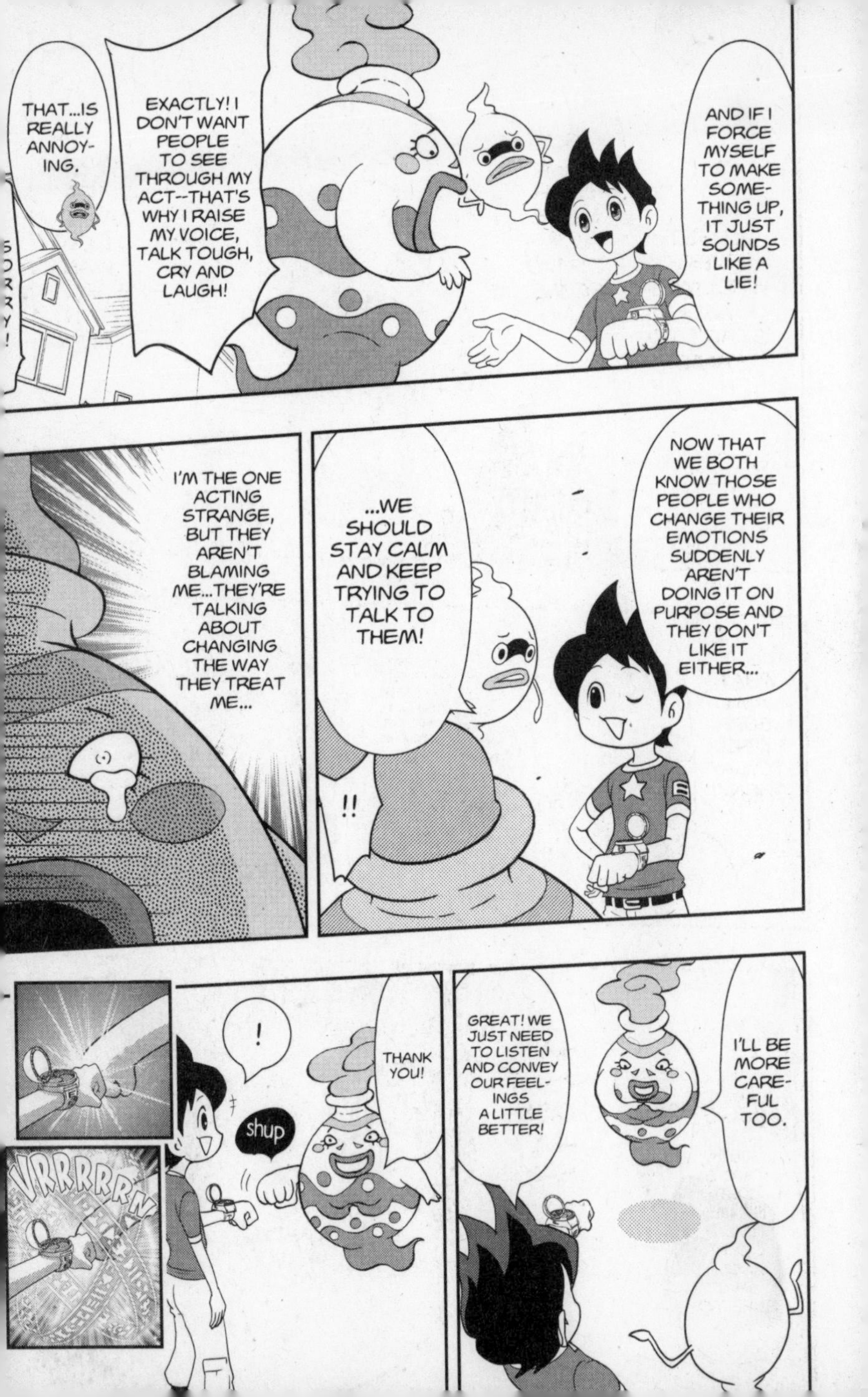
AND IF I FORCE MYSELF TO MAKE SOMETHING UP, IT JUST SOUNDS LIKE A LIE!
EXACTLY! I DON'T WANT PEOPLE TO SEE THROUGH MY ACT--THAT'S WHY I RAISE MY VOICE, TALK TOUGH, CRY AND LAUGH!
THAT...IS REALLY ANNOYING.
SORRY!
NOW THAT WE BOTH KNOW THOSE PEOPLE WHO CHANGE THEIR EMOTIONS SUDDENLY AREN'T DOING IT ON PURPOSE AND THEY DON'T LIKE IT EITHER...
...WE SHOULD STAY CALM AND KEEP TRYING TO TALK TO THEM!
!!
I'M THE ONE ACTING STRANGE, BUT THEY AREN'T BLAMING ME...THEY'RE TALKING ABOUT CHANGING THE WAY THEY TREAT ME...
I'LL BE MORE CAREFUL TOO.
GREAT! WE JUST NEED TO LISTEN AND CONVEY OUR FEELINGS A LITTLE BETTER!
THANK YOU!
!
shup
VRRRRRN

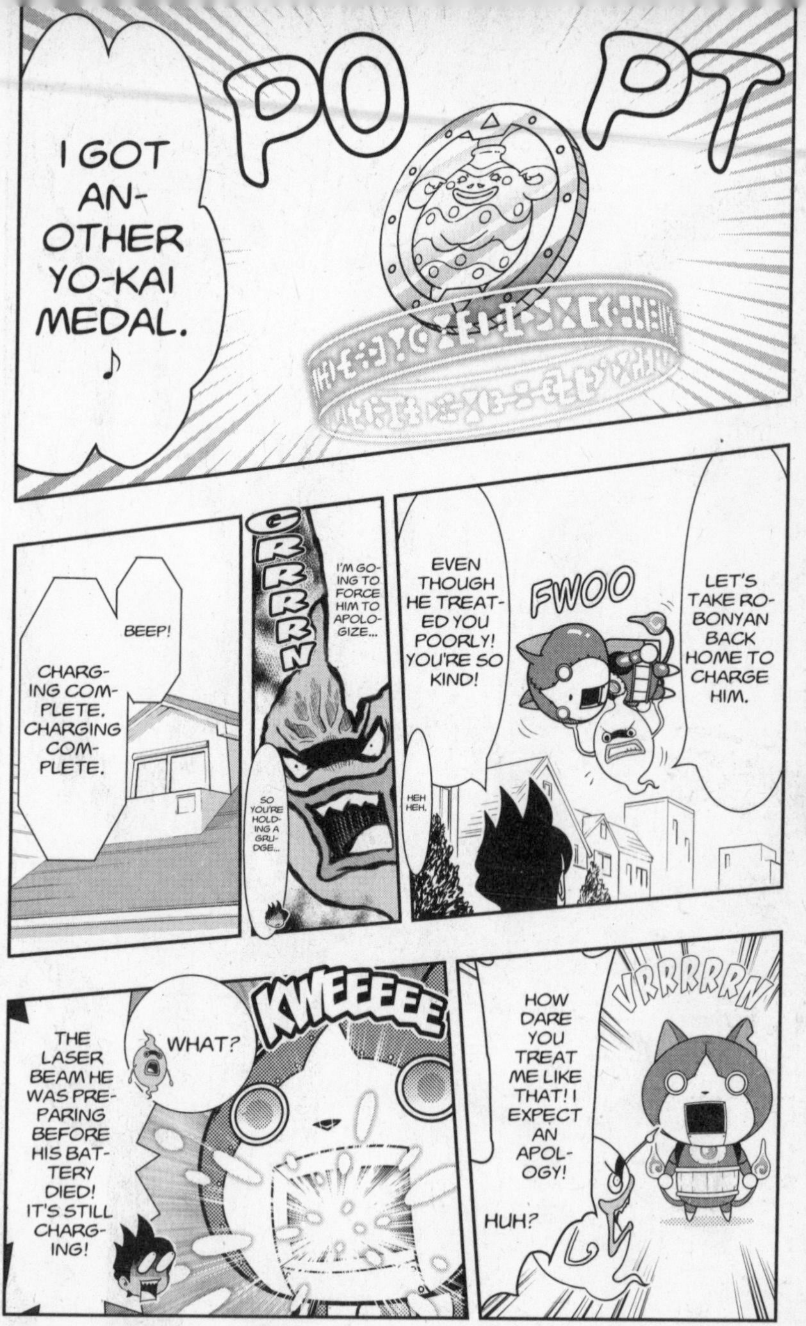
PO PT
I GOT AN-OTHER YO-KAI MEDAL. ♪
LET'S TAKE RO-BONYAN BACK HOME TO CHARGE HIM.
FWOO
EVEN THOUGH HE TREAT-ED YOU POORLY! YOU'RE SO KIND!
HEH HEH.
I'M GO-ING TO FORCE HIM TO APOLO-GIZE...
GRRRRN
SO YOU'RE HOLD-ING A GRU-DGE...
BEEP!
CHARG-ING COM-PLETE. CHARGING COM-PLETE.
VRRRRRN
HOW DARE YOU TREAT ME LIKE THAT! I EXPECT AN APOL-OGY!
HUH?
KWEEEEE
WHAT?
THE LASER BEAM HE WAS PRE-PARING BEFORE HIS BAT-TERY DIED! IT'S STILL CHARG-ING!

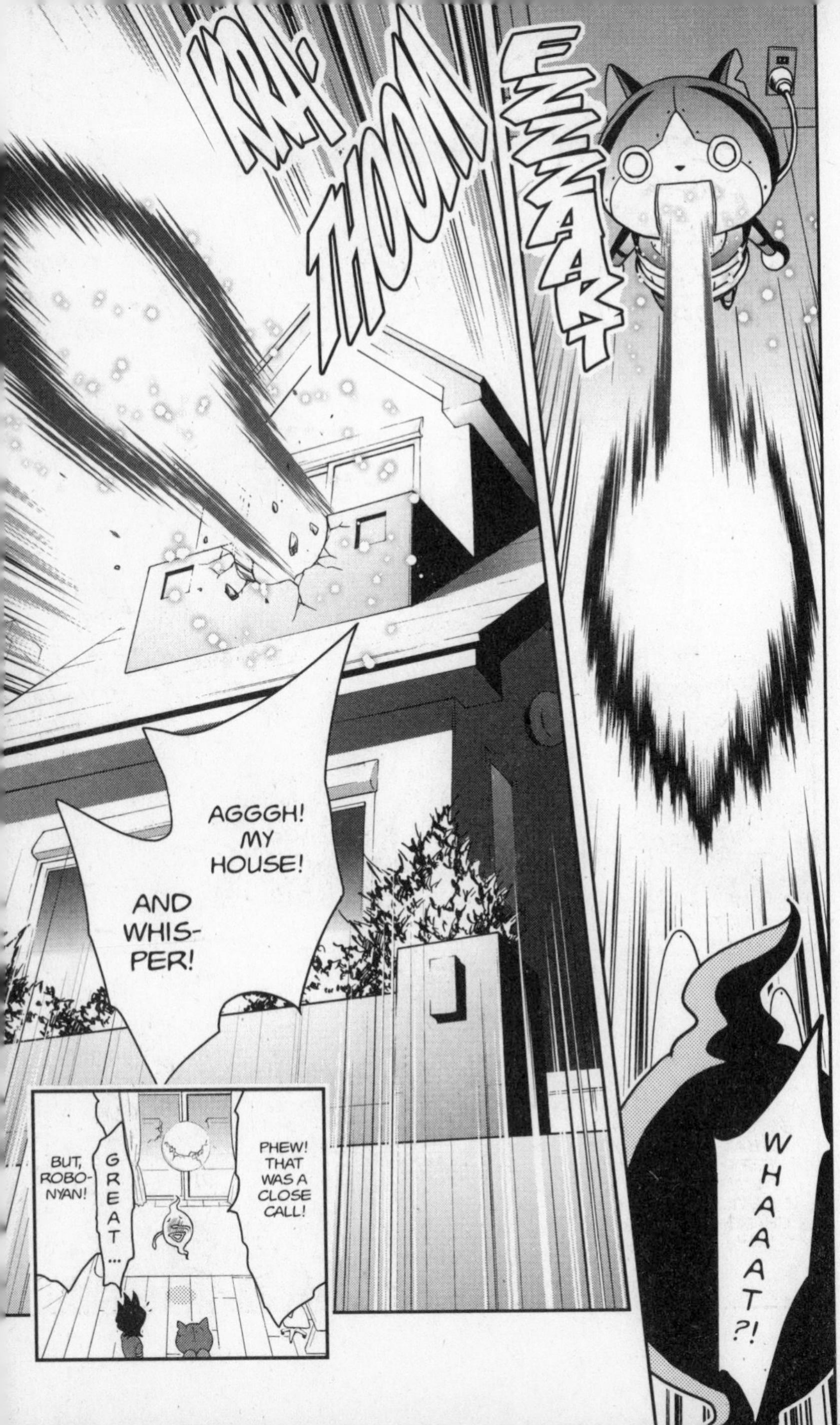
EMMAAK
WHAAAT?!
KRA-THOOM
AGGGH! MY HOUSE!
AND WHISPER!
PHEW! THAT WAS A CLOSE CALL!
GREAT...
BUT, ROBONYAN!

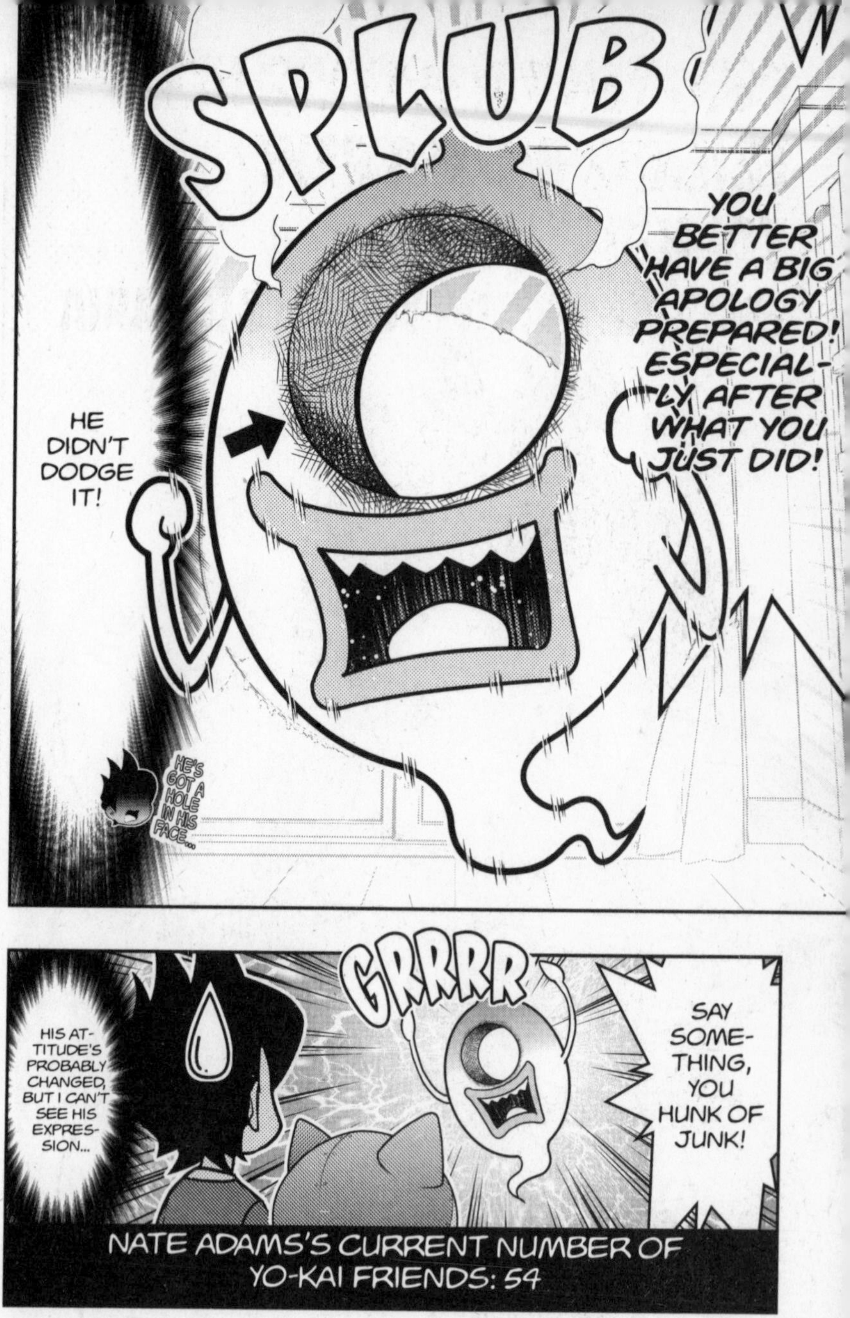
SPLUB
YOU BETTER HAVE A BIG APOLOGY PREPARED! ESPECIALLY AFTER WHAT YOU JUST DID!
HE DIDN'T DODGE IT!
HE'S GOT A HOLE IN HIS FACE...
GRRRR
SAY SOMETHING, YOU HUNK OF JUNK!
HIS ATTITUDE'S PROBABLY CHANGED, BUT I CAN'T SEE HIS EXPRESSION...
NATE ADAMS'S CURRENT NUMBER OF YO-KAI FRIENDS: 54

CHAPTER 79: MAKING NEW FRIENDS WITH A NEW YO-KAI WATCH!!

FEATURING SNOW YO-KAI BLIZZARIA

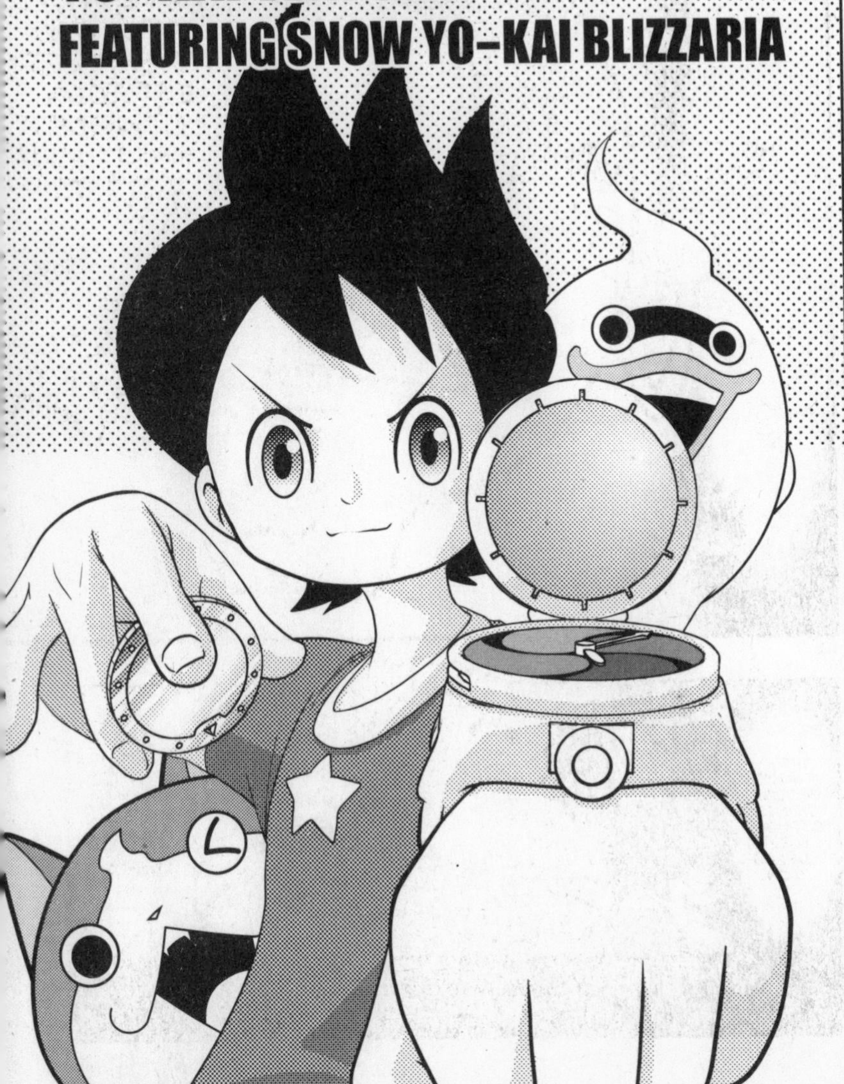

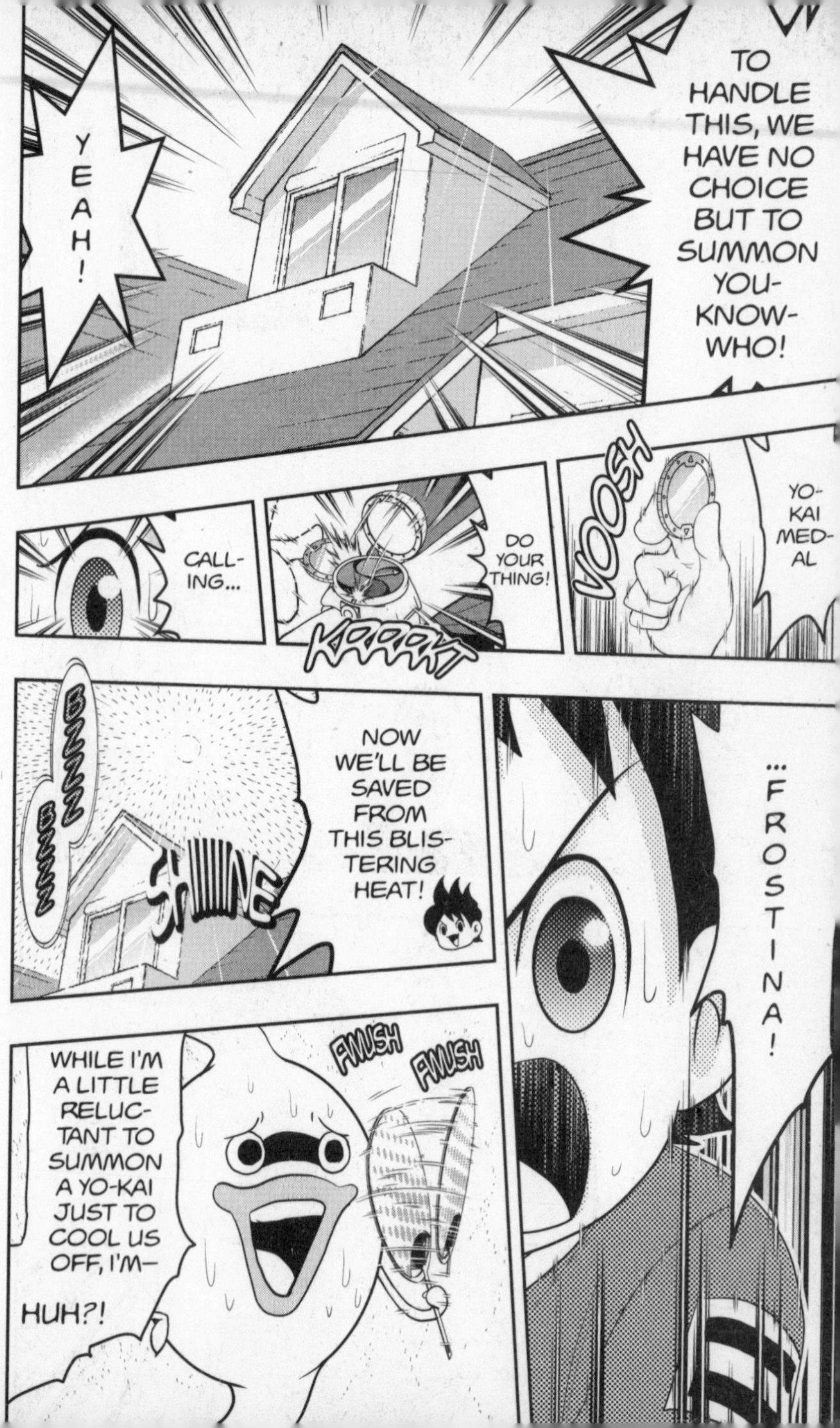
TO HANDLE THIS, WE HAVE NO CHOICE BUT TO SUMMON YOU-KNOW-WHO!
YEAH!
YO-KAI MEDAL
VOOSH
DO YOUR THING!
KRRRKT
CALLING...
...FROSTINA!
NOW WE'LL BE SAVED FROM THIS BLISTERING HEAT!
SHIIINE
BZZZZ
BZZZZ
FWUSH
FWUSH
WHILE I'M A LITTLE RELUCTANT TO SUMMON A YO-KAI JUST TO COOL US OFF, I'M—
HUH?!

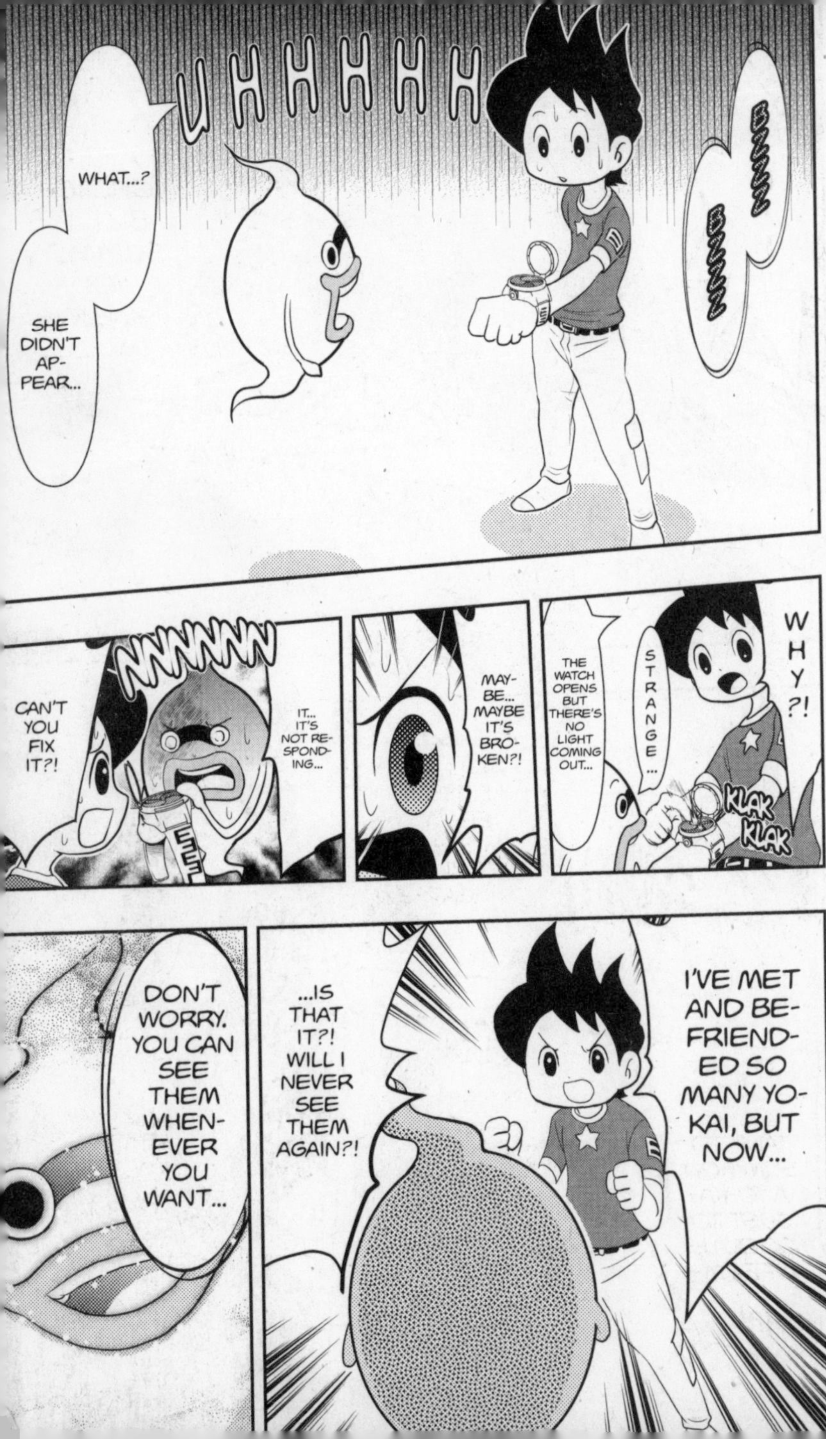
BZZZZZ
BZZZZZ
UHHHHHH
WHAT...?
SHE DIDN'T AP-PEAR...
WHY?!
STRANGE...
KLAK KLAK
THE WATCH OPENS BUT THERE'S NO LIGHT COMING OUT...
MAY-BE... MAYBE IT'S BRO-KEN?!
IT... IT'S NOT RE-SPOND-ING...
NNNNNN
CAN'T YOU FIX IT?!
I'VE MET AND BE-FRIEND-ED SO MANY YO-KAI, BUT NOW...
...IS THAT IT?! WILL I NEVER SEE THEM AGAIN?!
DON'T WORRY. YOU CAN SEE THEM WHEN-EVER YOU WANT...

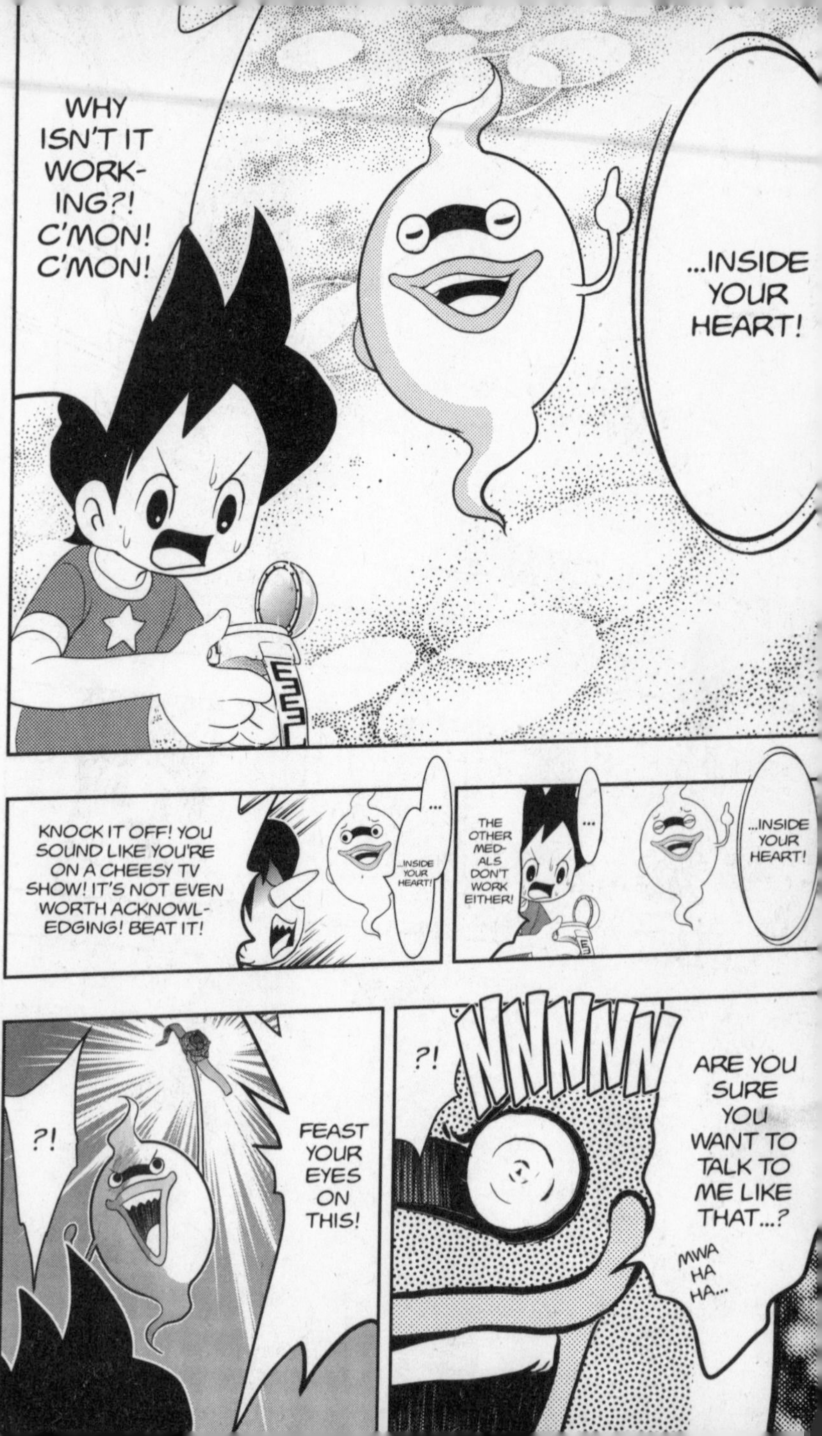
...INSIDE YOUR HEART!
WHY ISN'T IT WORKING?! C'MON! C'MON!
...INSIDE YOUR HEART!
...
THE OTHER MEDALS DON'T WORK EITHER!
...
...INSIDE YOUR HEART!
KNOCK IT OFF! YOU SOUND LIKE YOU'RE ON A CHEESY TV SHOW! IT'S NOT EVEN WORTH ACKNOWLEDGING! BEAT IT!
NNNNNN
?!
ARE YOU SURE YOU WANT TO TALK TO ME LIKE THAT...?
MWA HA HA...
FEAST YOUR EYES ON THIS!
?!

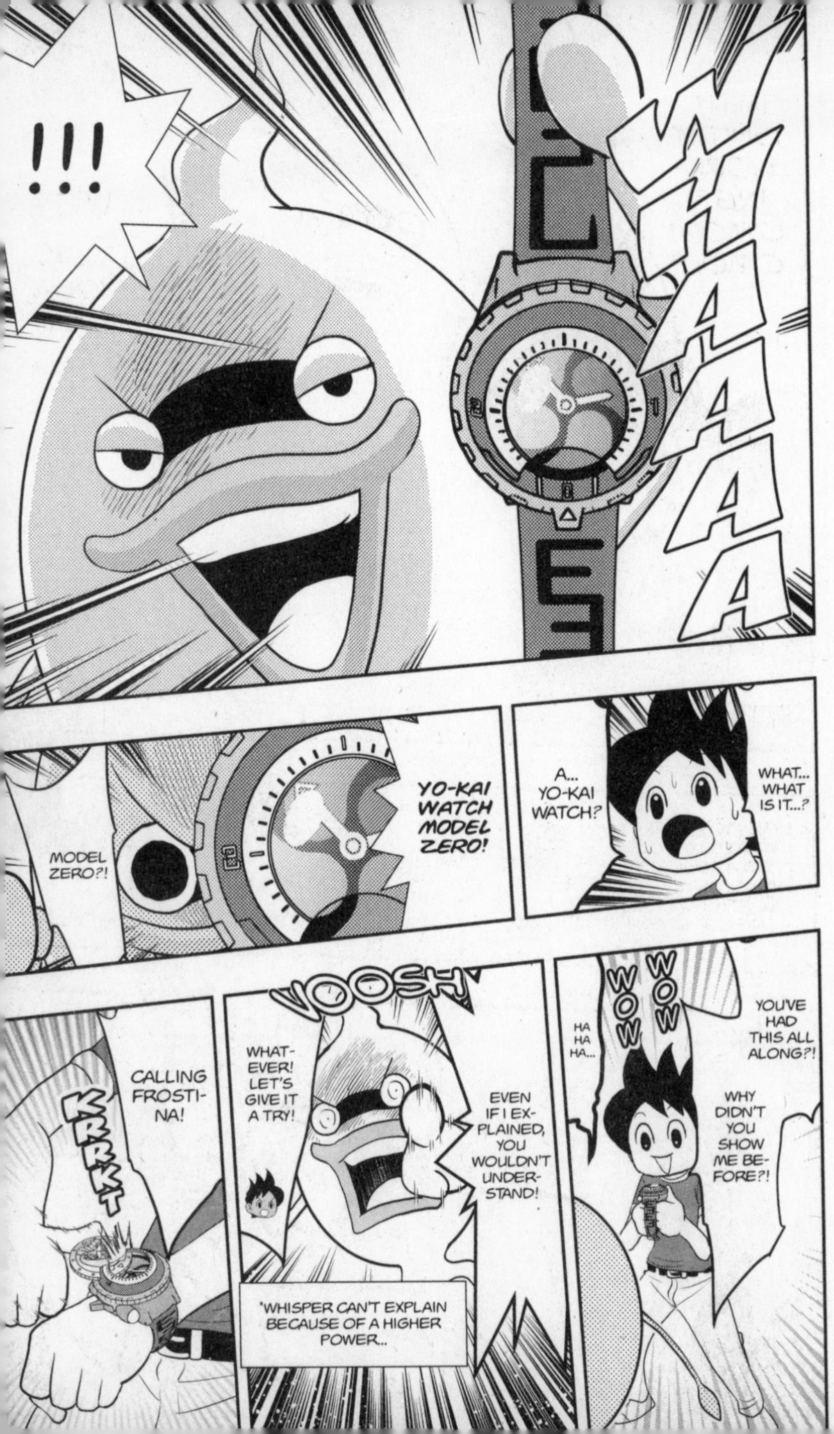
WHAAAA
!!!
WHAT... WHAT IS IT...?
A... YO-KAI WATCH?
YO-KAI WATCH MODEL ZERO!
MODEL ZERO?!
WOW WOW
YOU'VE HAD THIS ALL ALONG?!
HA HA HA...
WHY DIDN'T YOU SHOW ME BE-FORE?!
VOOSH
EVEN IF I EX-PLAINED, YOU WOULDN'T UNDER-STAND!
WHAT-EVER! LET'S GIVE IT A TRY!
*WHISPER CAN'T EXPLAIN BECAUSE OF A HIGHER POWER...
CALLING FROSTI-NA!
KRRKT

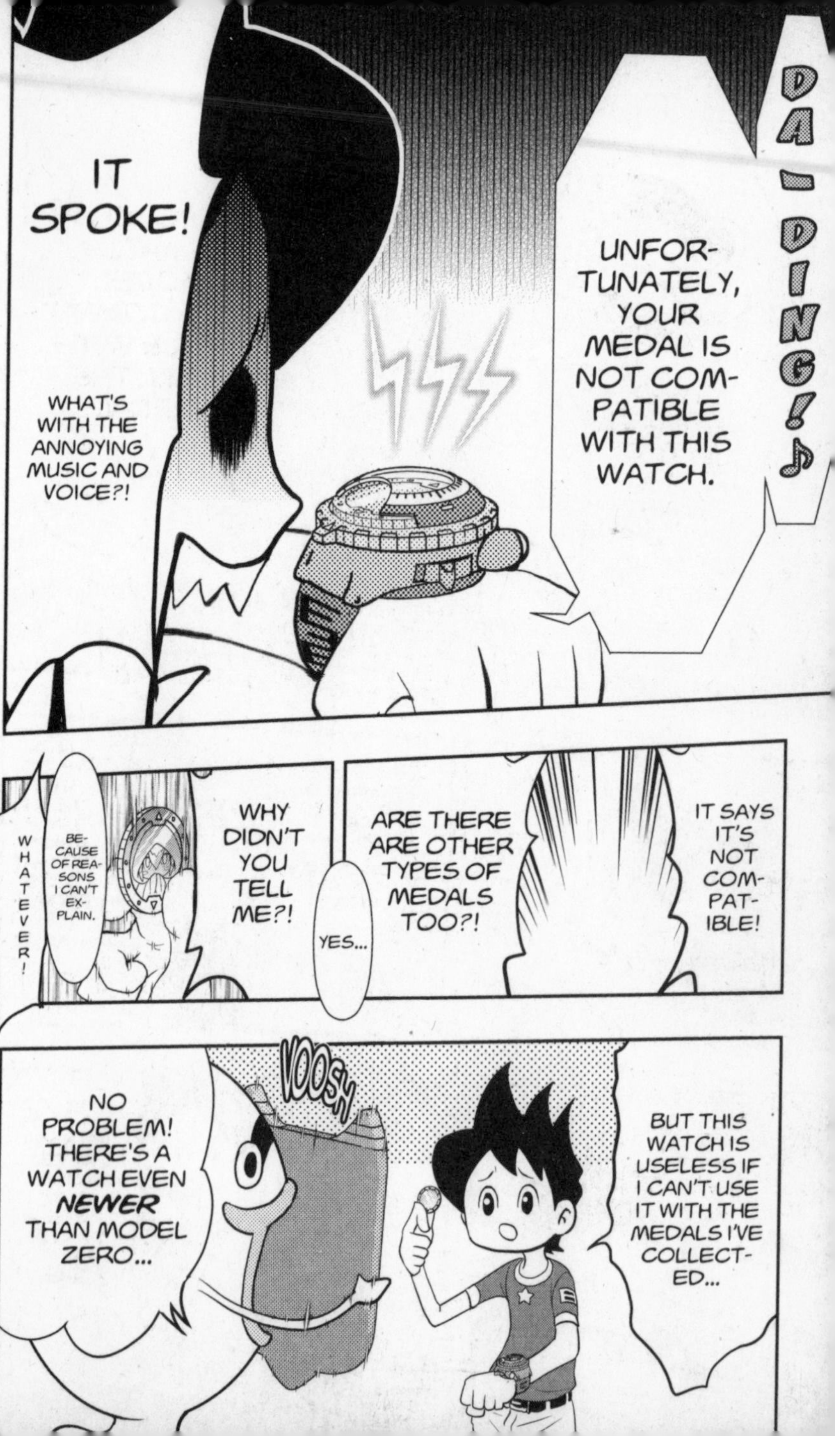
DA-DING!♪
UNFORTUNATELY, YOUR MEDAL IS NOT COMPATIBLE WITH THIS WATCH.
IT SPOKE!
WHAT'S WITH THE ANNOYING MUSIC AND VOICE?!
IT SAYS IT'S NOT COMPATIBLE!
ARE THERE ARE OTHER TYPES OF MEDALS TOO?!
YES...
WHY DIDN'T YOU TELL ME?!
BECAUSE OF REASONS I CAN'T EXPLAIN.
WHATEVER!
BUT THIS WATCH IS USELESS IF I CAN'T USE IT WITH THE MEDALS I'VE COLLECTED...
VOOSH
NO PROBLEM! THERE'S A WATCH EVEN ***NEWER*** THAN MODEL ZERO...

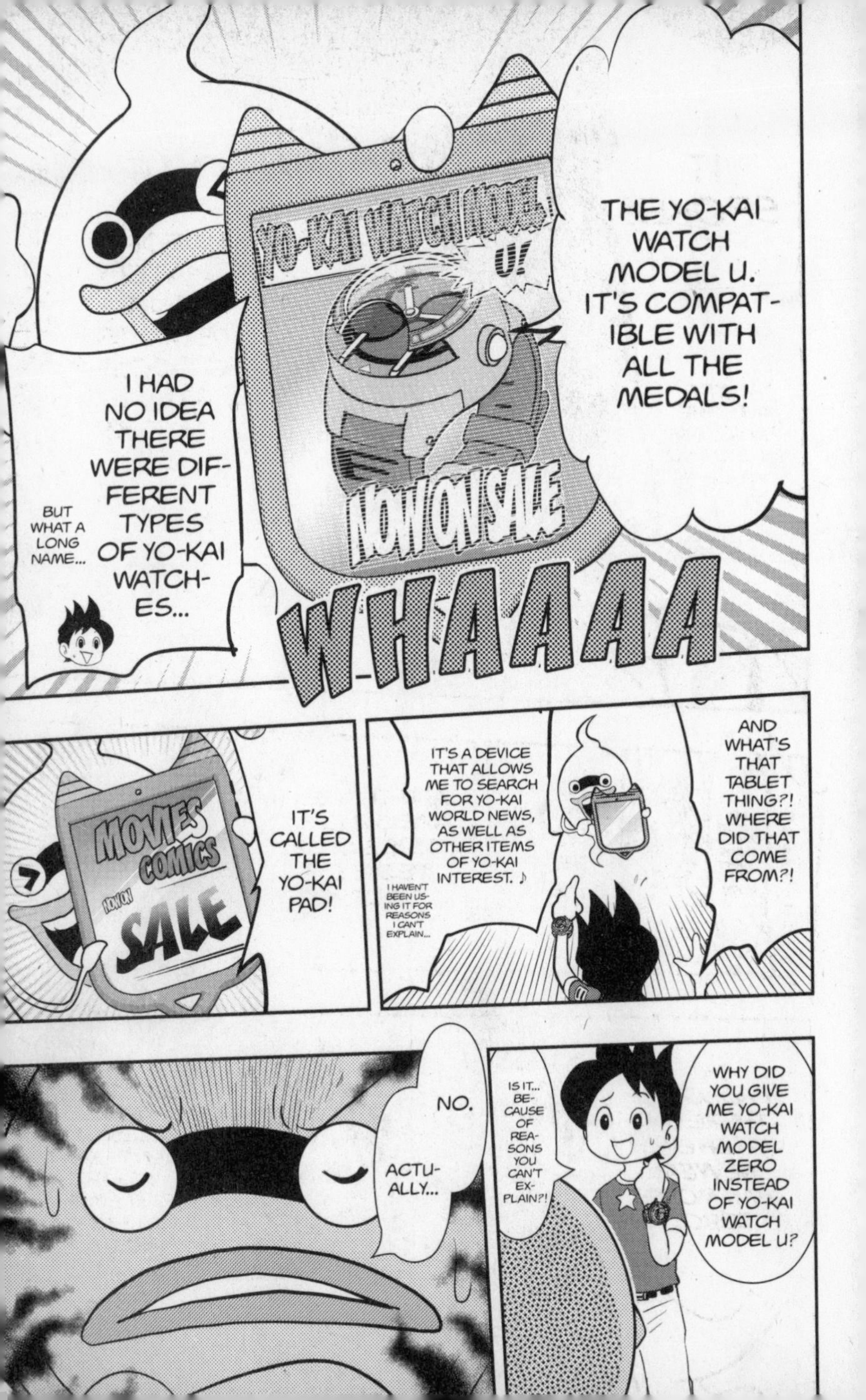
THE YO-KAI WATCH MODEL U. IT'S COMPATIBLE WITH ALL THE MEDALS!
YO-KAI WATCH MODEL U!
NOW ON SALE
WHAAAA
I HAD NO IDEA THERE WERE DIFFERENT TYPES OF YO-KAI WATCHES...
BUT WHAT A LONG NAME...
AND WHAT'S THAT TABLET THING?! WHERE DID THAT COME FROM?!
IT'S A DEVICE THAT ALLOWS ME TO SEARCH FOR YO-KAI WORLD NEWS, AS WELL AS OTHER ITEMS OF YO-KAI INTEREST. ♪
I HAVEN'T BEEN USING IT FOR REASONS I CAN'T EXPLAIN...
IT'S CALLED THE YO-KAI PAD!
MOVIES
COMICS
NOW ON
SALE
WHY DID YOU GIVE ME YO-KAI WATCH MODEL ZERO INSTEAD OF YO-KAI WATCH MODEL U?
IS IT... BECAUSE OF REASONS YOU CAN'T EXPLAIN?!
NO.
ACTUALLY...

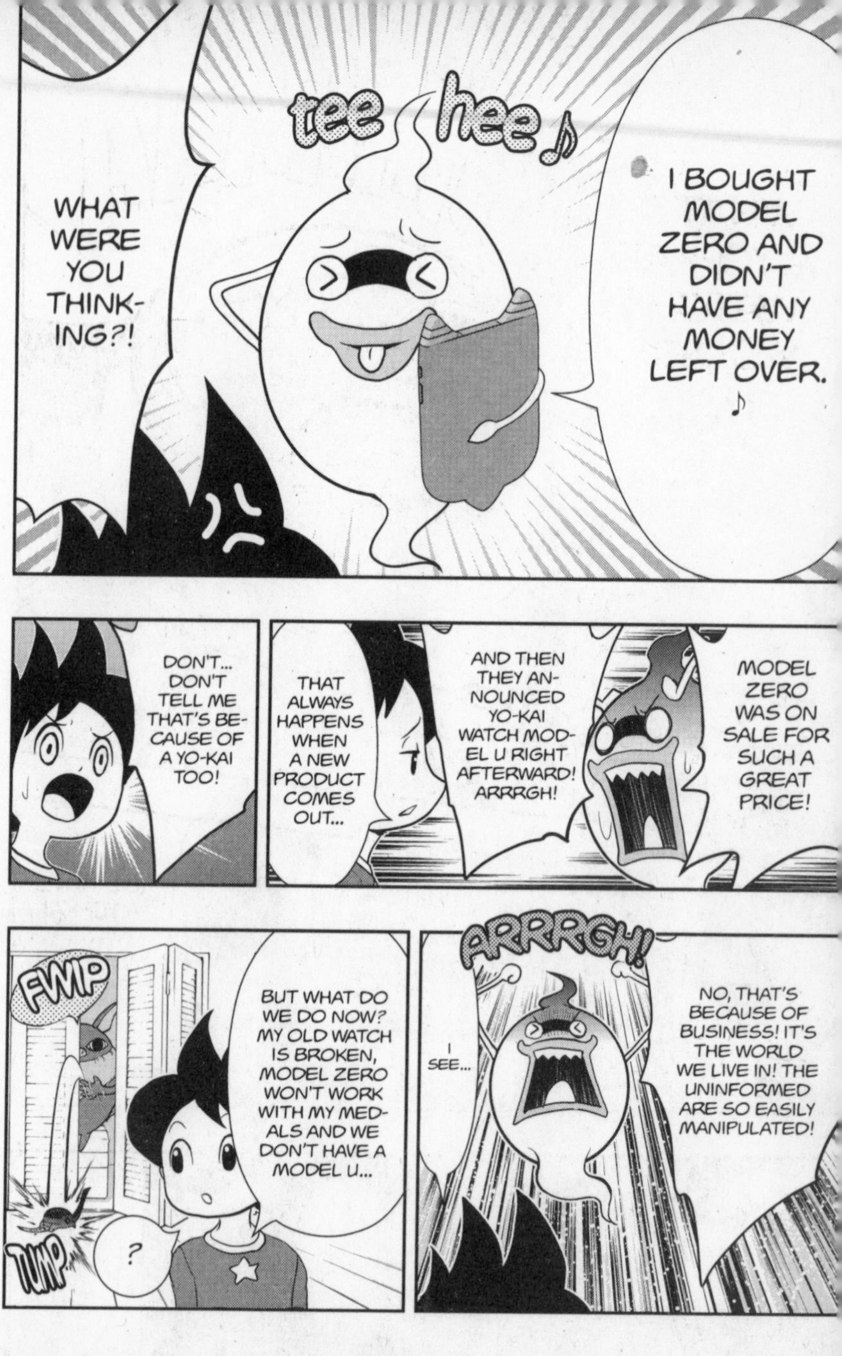
tee hee ♪
I BOUGHT MODEL ZERO AND DIDN'T HAVE ANY MONEY LEFT OVER. ♪
WHAT WERE YOU THINK-ING?!
MODEL ZERO WAS ON SALE FOR SUCH A GREAT PRICE!
AND THEN THEY AN-NOUNCED YO-KAI WATCH MOD-EL U RIGHT AFTERWARD! ARRRGH!
THAT ALWAYS HAPPENS WHEN A NEW PRODUCT COMES OUT...
DON'T... DON'T TELL ME THAT'S BE-CAUSE OF A YO-KAI TOO!
ARRRGH!
NO, THAT'S BECAUSE OF BUSINESS! IT'S THE WORLD WE LIVE IN! THE UNINFORMED ARE SO EASILY MANIPULATED!
I SEE...
BUT WHAT DO WE DO NOW? MY OLD WATCH IS BROKEN, MODEL ZERO WON'T WORK WITH MY MED-ALS AND WE DON'T HAVE A MODEL U...
FWIP
?
TUMP

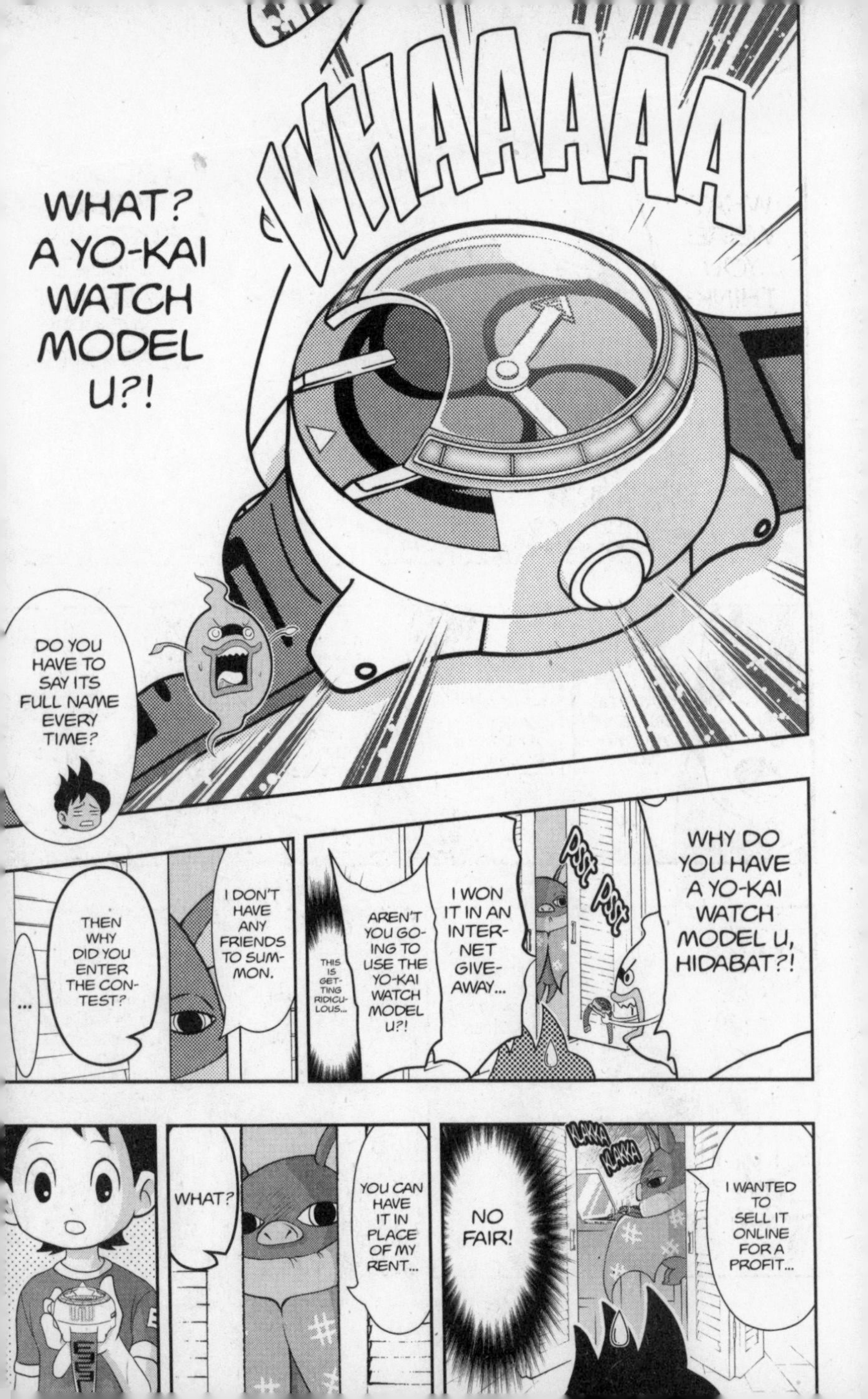
WHAAAAA
WHAT? A YO-KAI WATCH MODEL U?!
DO YOU HAVE TO SAY ITS FULL NAME EVERY TIME?
WHY DO YOU HAVE A YO-KAI WATCH MODEL U, HIDABAT?!
PSST PSST
I WON IT IN AN INTERNET GIVEAWAY...
AREN'T YOU GOING TO USE THE YO-KAI WATCH MODEL U?!
THIS IS GETTING RIDICULOUS...
I DON'T HAVE ANY FRIENDS TO SUMMON.
THEN WHY DID YOU ENTER THE CONTEST?
...
KLAKKA KLAKKA
I WANTED TO SELL IT ONLINE FOR A PROFIT...
NO FAIR!
YOU CAN HAVE IT IN PLACE OF MY RENT...
WHAT?

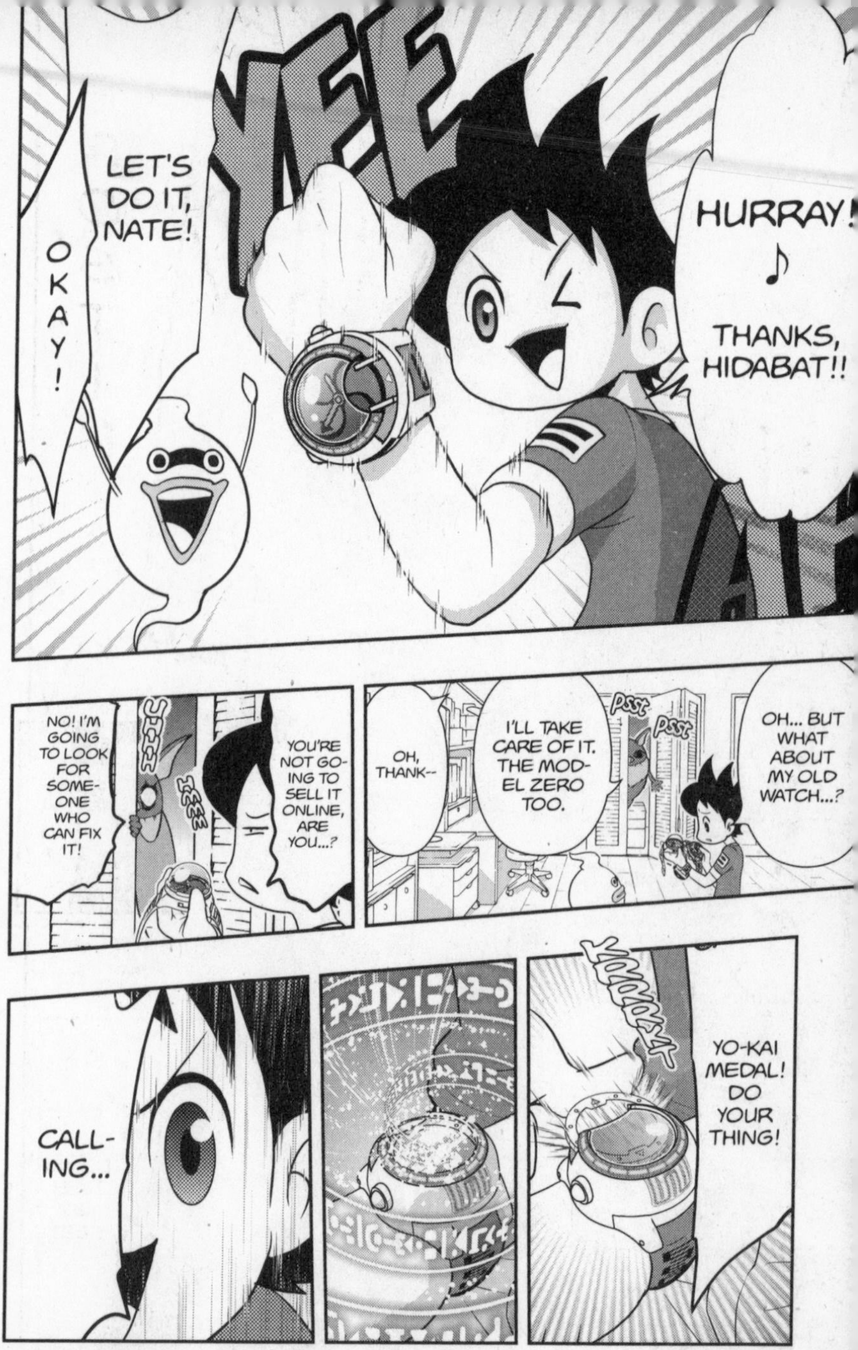
HURRAY! ♪
THANKS, HIDABAT!!
LET'S DO IT, NATE!
OKAY!
OH... BUT WHAT ABOUT MY OLD WATCH...?
PSST
PSST
I'LL TAKE CARE OF IT. THE MOD-EL ZERO TOO.
OH, THANK--
YOU'RE NOT GOING TO SELL IT ONLINE, ARE YOU...?
NO! I'M GOING TO LOOK FOR SOME-ONE WHO CAN FIX IT!
YO-KAI MEDAL! DO YOUR THING!
CALL-ING...

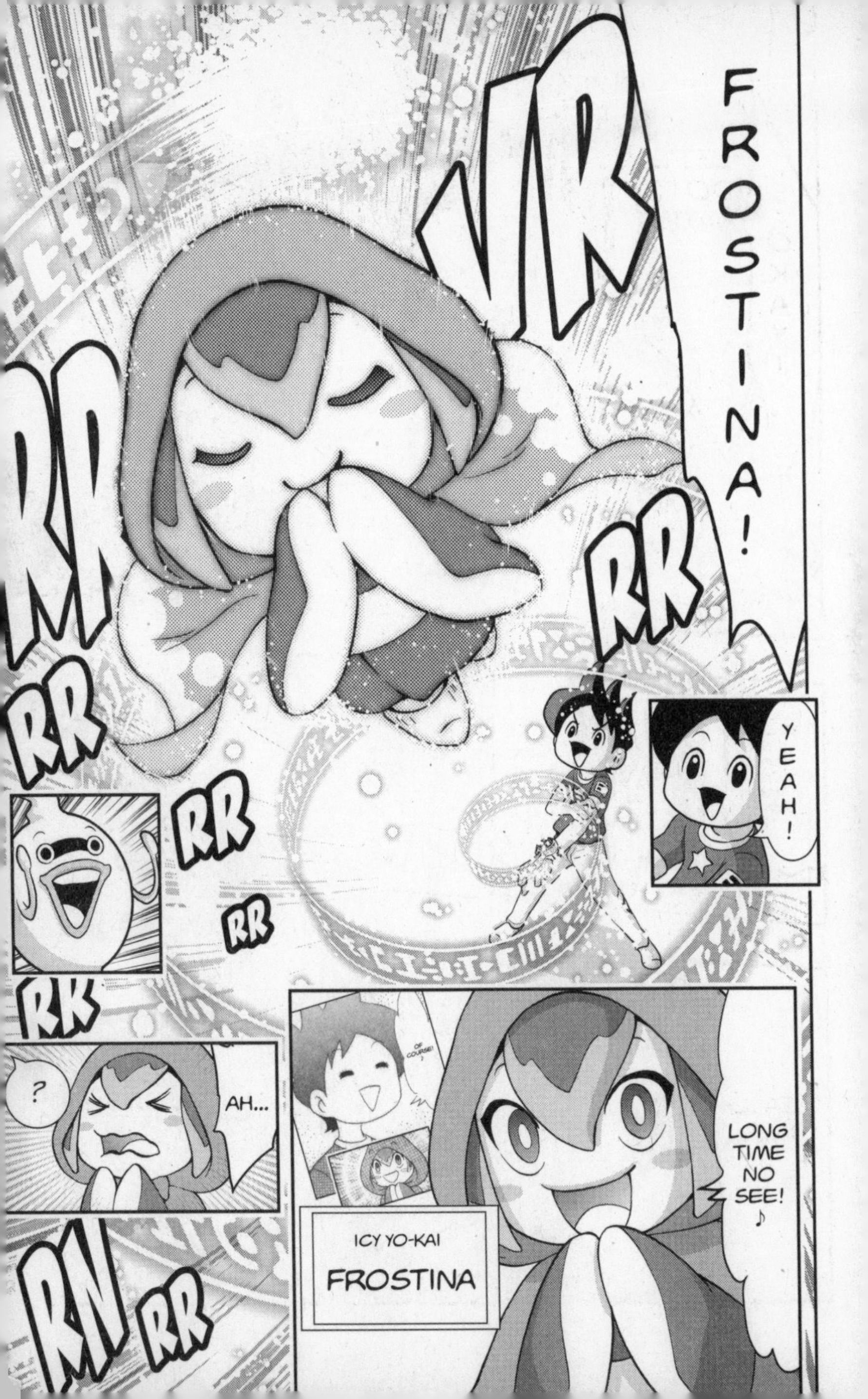
FROSTINA!
VR
RR
RR
YEAH!
RR
RR
RR
RK
LONG TIME NO SEE! ♪
OF COURSE!
ICY YO-KAI
FROSTINA
AH...
?
RN
RR

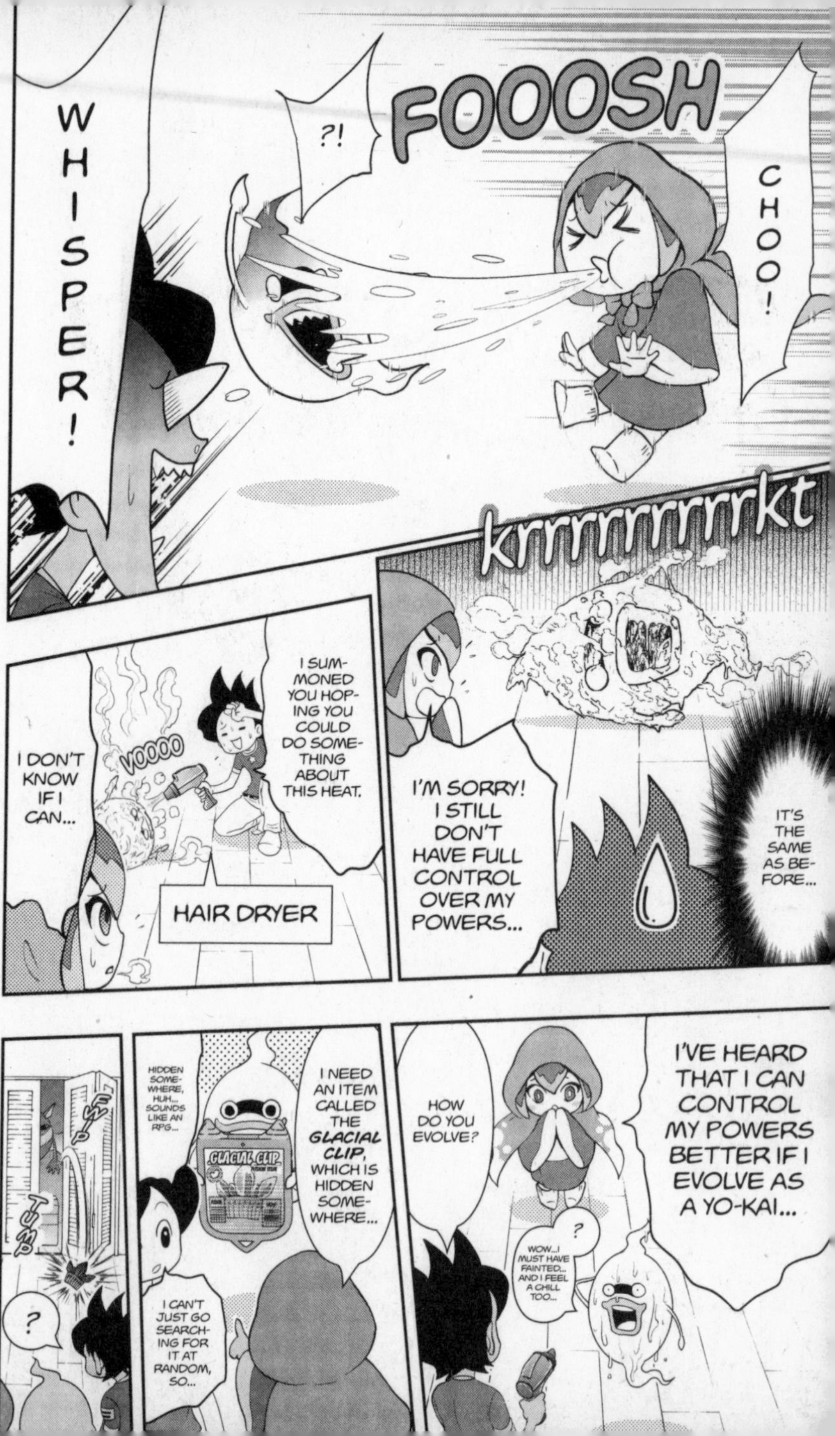

CHOO!
FOOOSH
?!
WHISPER!
krrrrrrrrrkt
IT'S THE SAME AS BEFORE...
I'M SORRY! I STILL DON'T HAVE FULL CONTROL OVER MY POWERS...
I SUMMONED YOU HOPING YOU COULD DO SOMETHING ABOUT THIS HEAT.
VOOOO
I DON'T KNOW IF I CAN...
HAIR DRYER
I'VE HEARD THAT I CAN CONTROL MY POWERS BETTER IF I EVOLVE AS A YO-KAI...
HOW DO YOU EVOLVE?
?
WOW...I MUST HAVE FAINTED... AND I FEEL A CHILL TOO...
I NEED AN ITEM CALLED THE *GLACIAL CLIP*, WHICH IS HIDDEN SOMEWHERE...
HIDDEN SOMEWHERE, HUH... SOUNDS LIKE AN RPG...
GLACIAL CLIP
I CAN'T JUST GO SEARCHING FOR IT AT RANDOM, SO...
FWP
TUMP
?

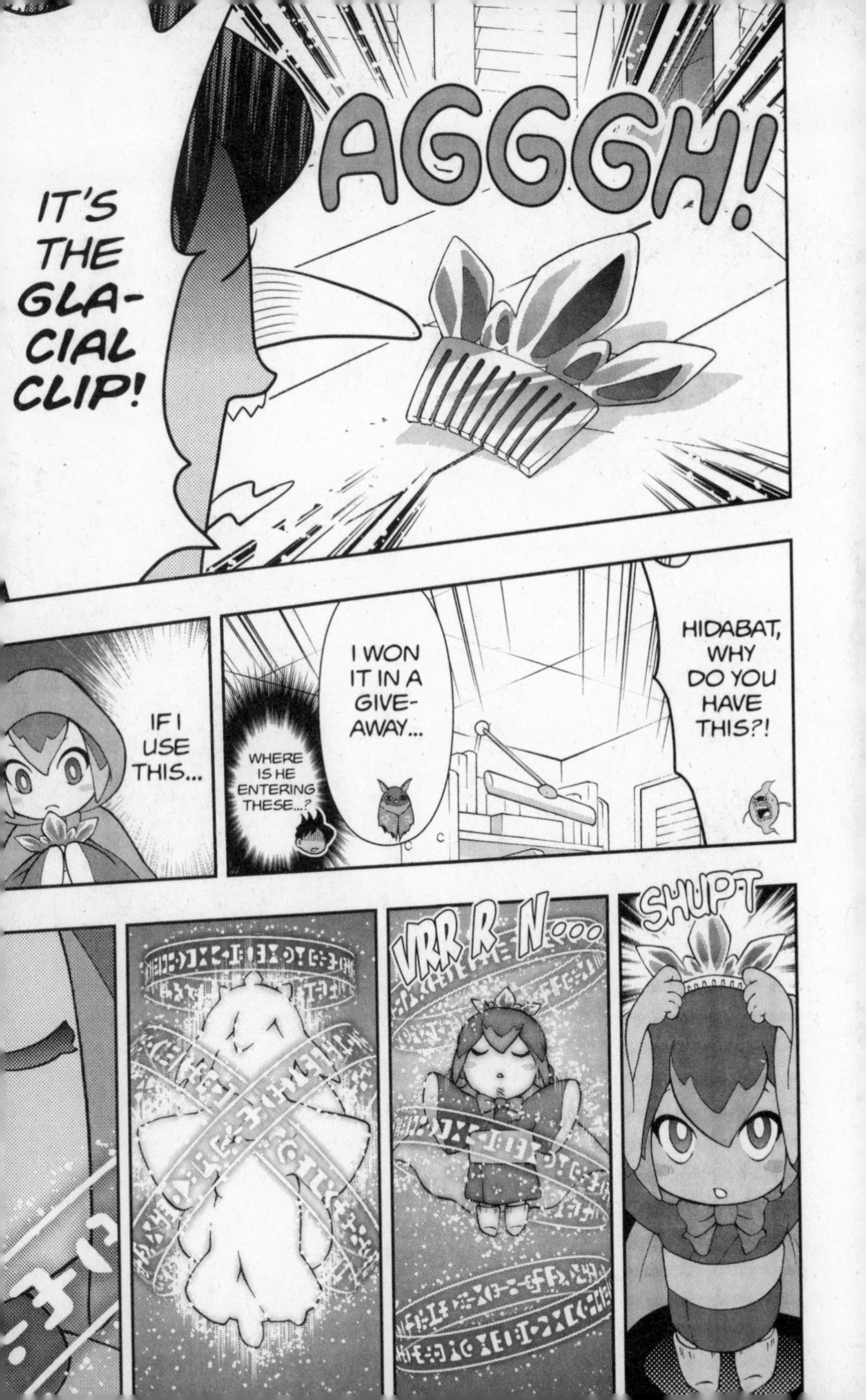
AGGGH!
IT'S THE GLA-CIAL CLIP!
HIDABAT, WHY DO YOU HAVE THIS?!
I WON IT IN A GIVE-AWAY...
WHERE IS HE ENTERING THESE...?
IF I USE THIS...
SHUPT
VRR R N...

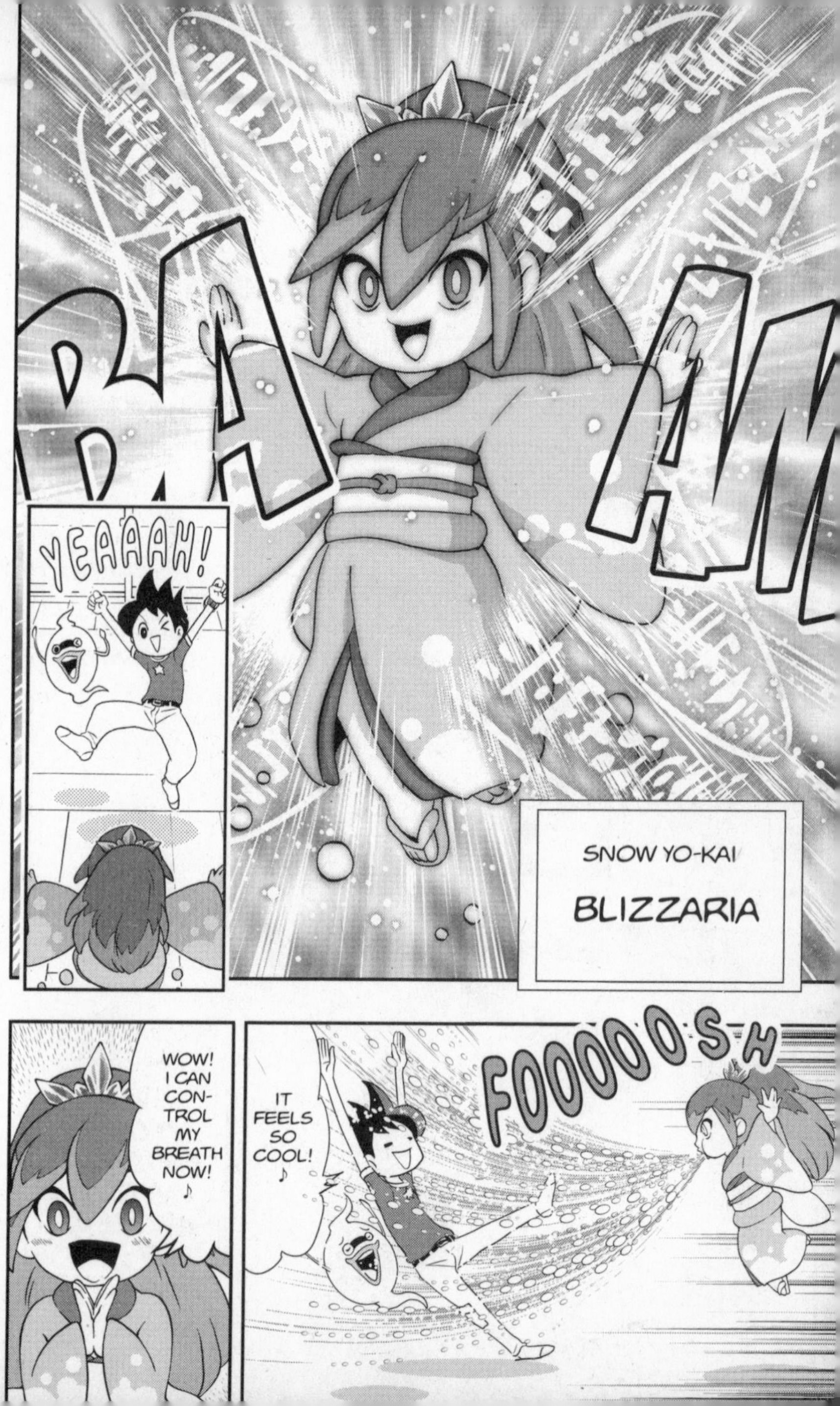
BAAM
SNOW YO-KAI
BLIZZARIA
YEAAAH!
FOOOOOSH
IT FEELS SO COOL! ♪
WOW! I CAN CONTROL MY BREATH NOW! ♪

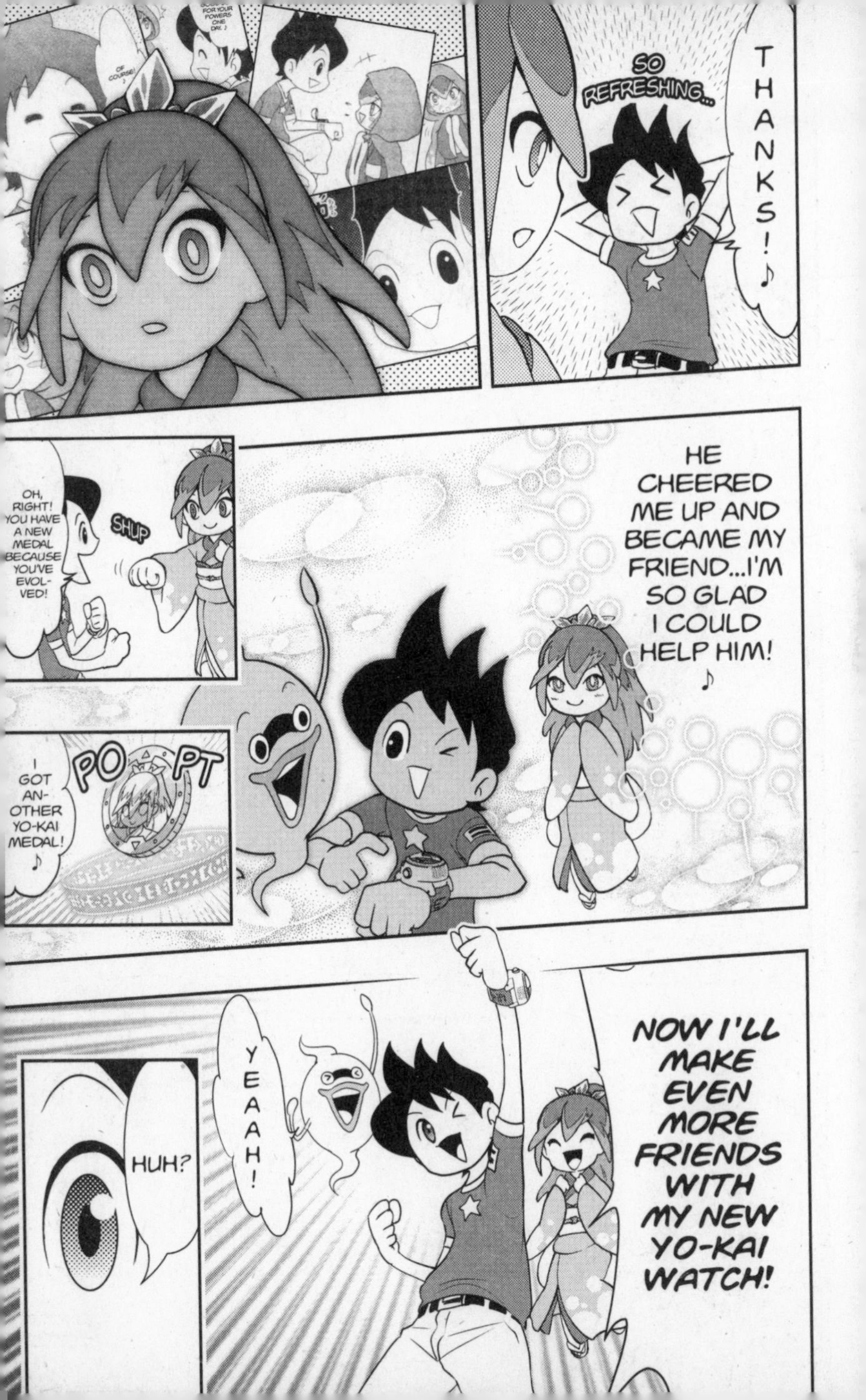
SO REFRESHING...
THANKS! ♪
FOR YOUR POWERS ONE DAY. ♪
OF COURSE! ♪
HE CHEERED ME UP AND BECAME MY FRIEND...I'M SO GLAD I COULD HELP HIM! ♪
OH, RIGHT! YOU HAVE A NEW MEDAL BECAUSE YOU'VE EVOL-VED!
SHUP
I GOT AN-OTHER YO-KAI MEDAL! ♪
POPT
NOW I'LL MAKE EVEN MORE FRIENDS WITH MY NEW YO-KAI WATCH!
YEAAAH!
HUH?

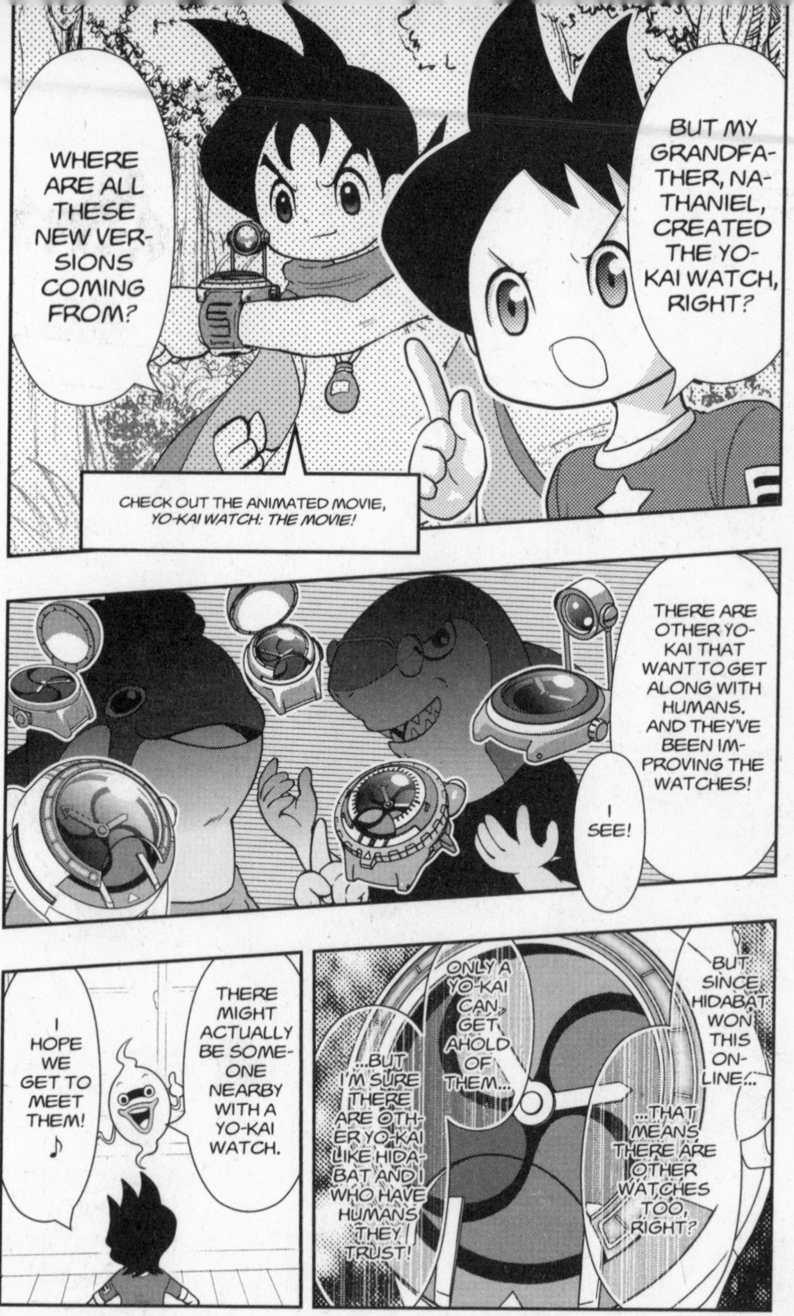
BUT MY GRANDFATHER, NATHANIEL, CREATED THE YO-KAI WATCH, RIGHT?
WHERE ARE ALL THESE NEW VERSIONS COMING FROM?
CHECK OUT THE ANIMATED MOVIE, *YO-KAI WATCH: THE MOVIE!*
THERE ARE OTHER YO-KAI THAT WANT TO GET ALONG WITH HUMANS. AND THEY'VE BEEN IMPROVING THE WATCHES!
I SEE!
BUT SINCE HIDABAT WON THIS ONLINE...
...THAT MEANS THERE ARE OTHER WATCHES TOO, RIGHT?
ONLY A YO-KAI CAN GET AHOLD OF THEM...
...BUT I'M SURE THERE ARE OTHER YO-KAI LIKE HIDABAT AND I WHO HAVE HUMANS THEY TRUST!
THERE MIGHT ACTUALLY BE SOMEONE NEARBY WITH A YO-KAI WATCH.
I HOPE WE GET TO MEET THEM! ♪

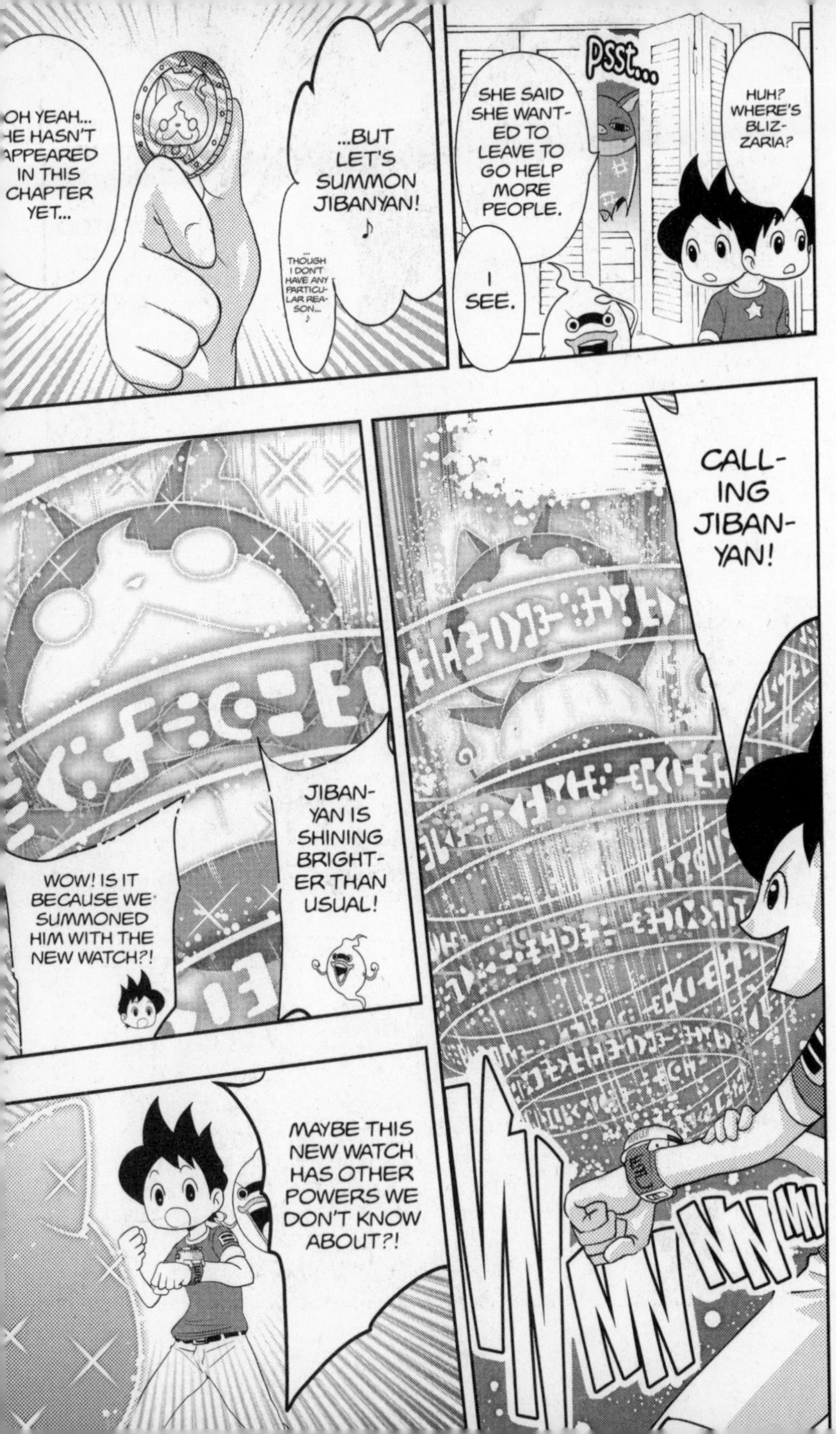
HUH? WHERE'S BLIZ-ZARIA?
PSST...
SHE SAID SHE WANT-ED TO LEAVE TO GO HELP MORE PEOPLE.
I SEE.
OH YEAH... HE HASN'T APPEARED IN THIS CHAPTER YET...
...BUT LET'S SUMMON JIBANYAN! ♪
...THOUGH I DON'T HAVE ANY PARTICU-LAR REA-SON... ♪
CALL-ING JIBAN-YAN!
JIBAN-YAN IS SHINING BRIGHT-ER THAN USUAL!
WOW! IS IT BECAUSE WE SUMMONED HIM WITH THE NEW WATCH?!
MAYBE THIS NEW WATCH HAS OTHER POWERS WE DON'T KNOW ABOUT?!

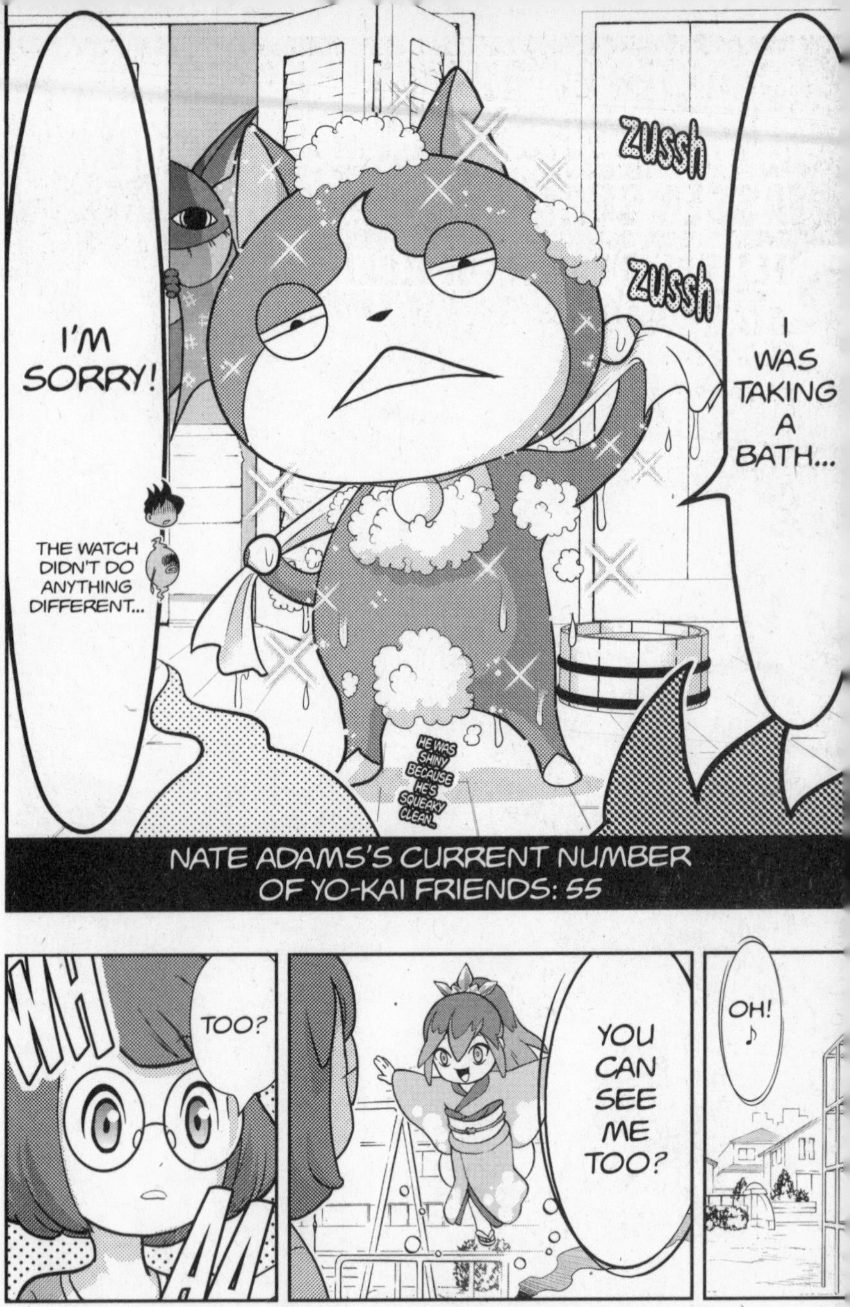
ZUSSH
ZUSSH
I WAS TAKING A BATH...
I'M SORRY!
THE WATCH DIDN'T DO ANYTHING DIFFERENT...
HE WAS SHINY BECAUSE HE'S SQUEAKY CLEAN...
NATE ADAMS'S CURRENT NUMBER OF YO-KAI FRIENDS: 55
OH! ♪
YOU CAN SEE ME TOO?
WHAA
TOO?

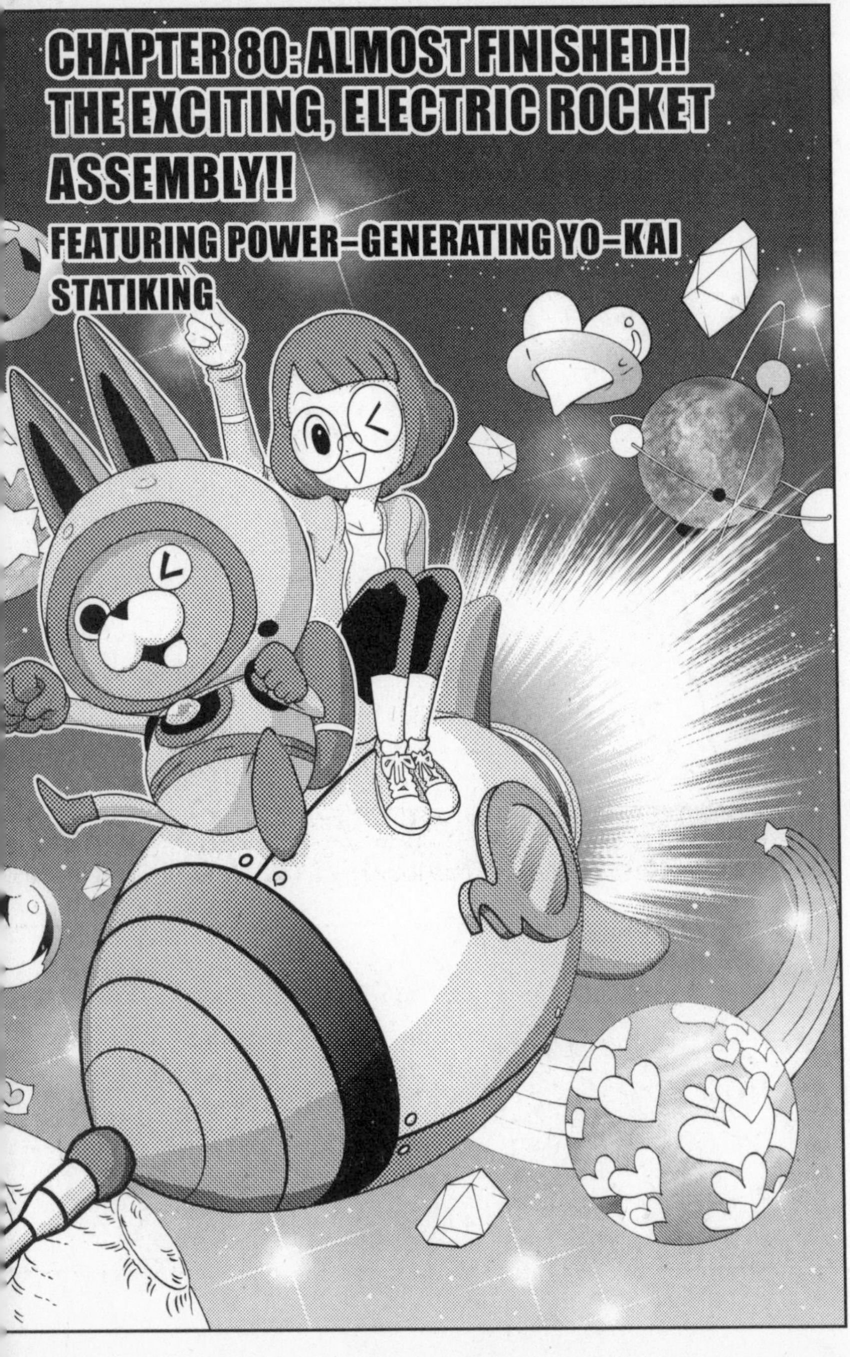
CHAPTER 80: ALMOST FINISHED!! THE EXCITING, ELECTRIC ROCKET ASSEMBLY!!
FEATURING POWER-GENERATING YO-KAI STATIKING

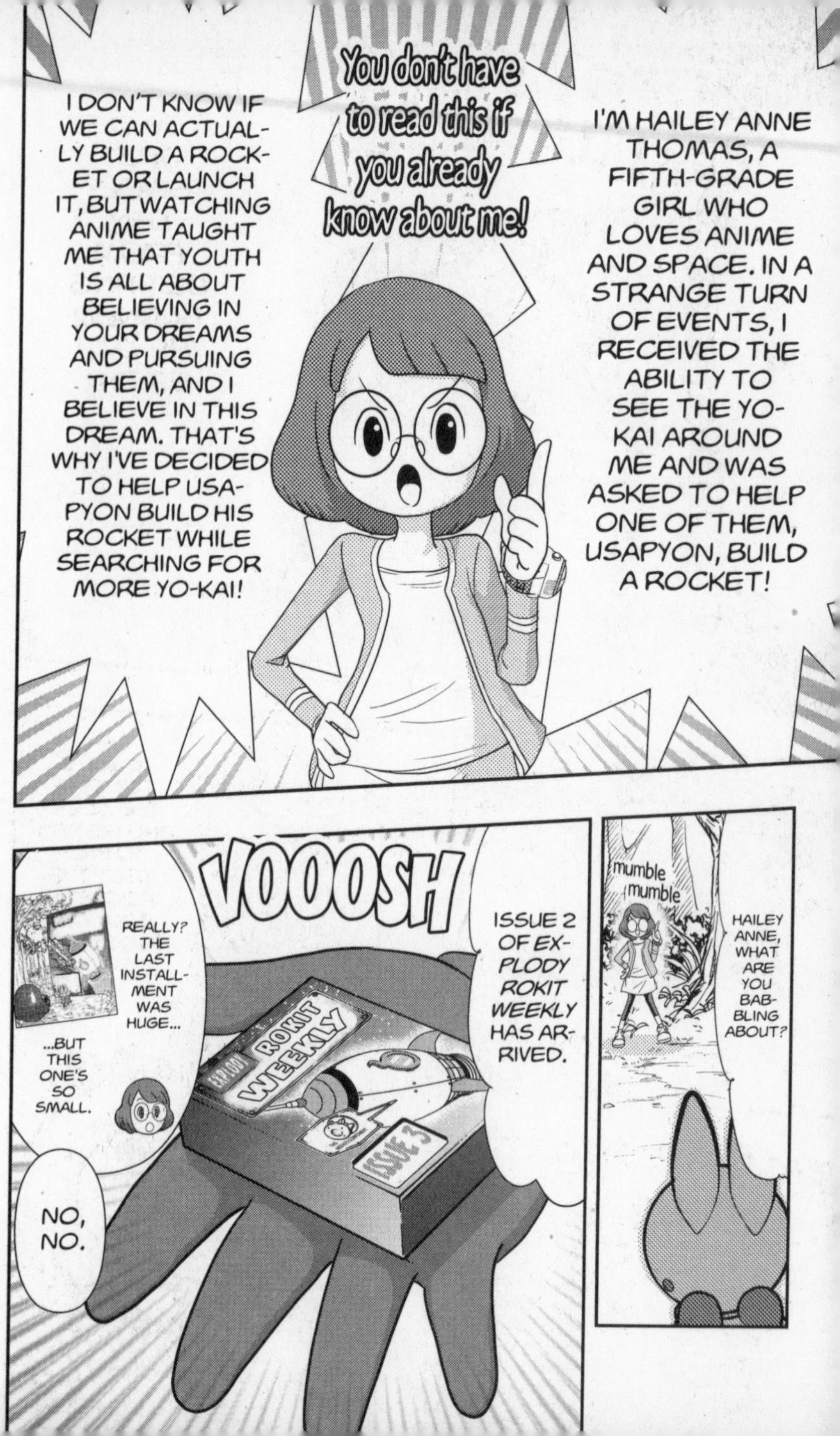
You don't have to read this if you already know about me!
I'M HAILEY ANNE THOMAS, A FIFTH-GRADE GIRL WHO LOVES ANIME AND SPACE. IN A STRANGE TURN OF EVENTS, I RECEIVED THE ABILITY TO SEE THE YO-KAI AROUND ME AND WAS ASKED TO HELP ONE OF THEM, USAPYON, BUILD A ROCKET!
I DON'T KNOW IF WE CAN ACTUALLY BUILD A ROCKET OR LAUNCH IT, BUT WATCHING ANIME TAUGHT ME THAT YOUTH IS ALL ABOUT BELIEVING IN YOUR DREAMS AND PURSUING THEM, AND I BELIEVE IN THIS DREAM. THAT'S WHY I'VE DECIDED TO HELP USAPYON BUILD HIS ROCKET WHILE SEARCHING FOR MORE YO-KAI!
mumble mumble
HAILEY ANNE, WHAT ARE YOU BABBLING ABOUT?
VOOOSH
ISSUE 2 OF EXPLODY ROKIT WEEKLY HAS ARRIVED.
EXPLODY ROKIT WEEKLY
ISSUE 3
REALLY? THE LAST INSTALLMENT WAS HUGE...
...BUT THIS ONE'S SO SMALL.
NO, NO.

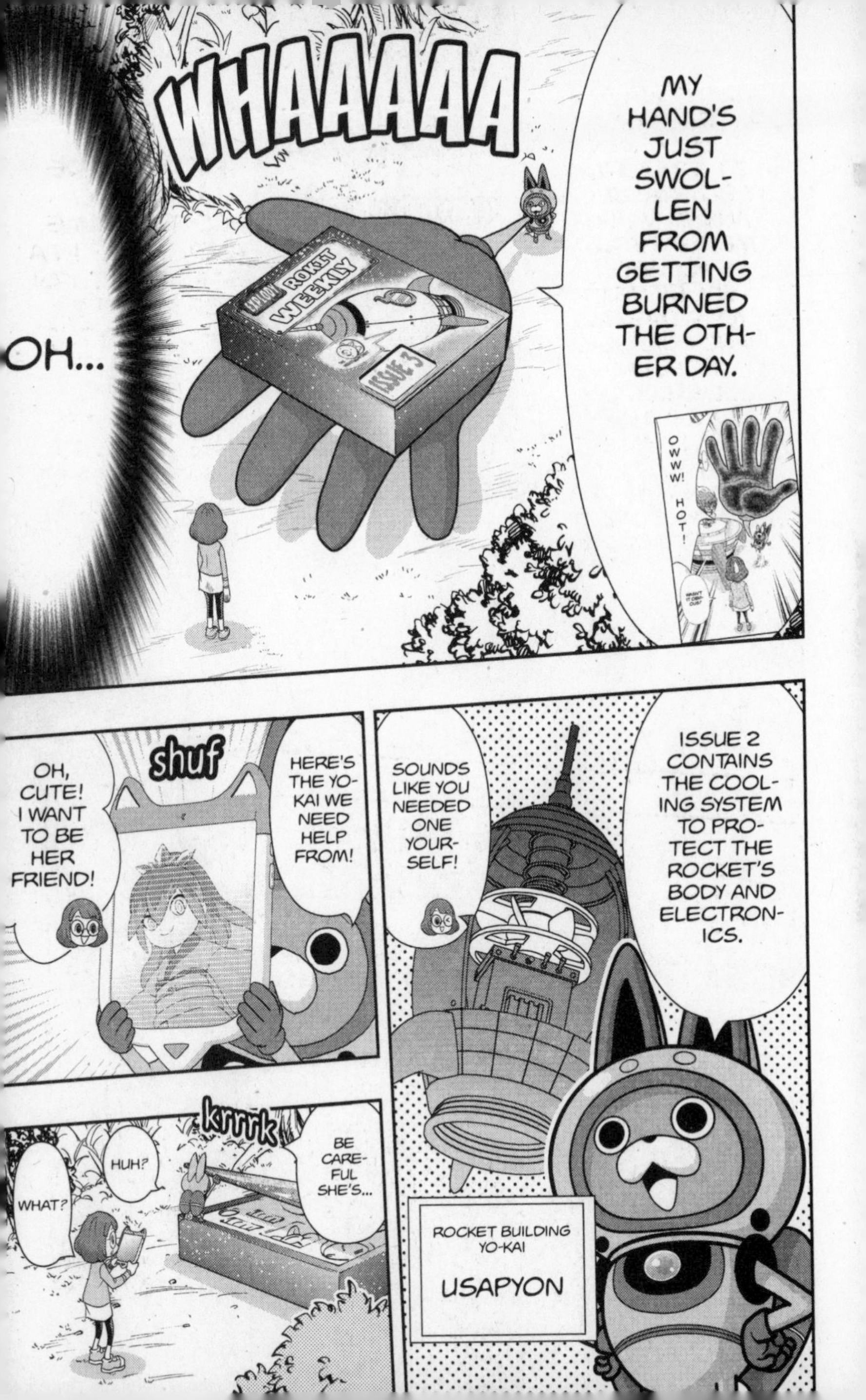
MY HAND'S JUST SWOL-LEN FROM GETTING BURNED THE OTH-ER DAY.
OWWW! HOT!
WHAAAAAA
ROKIT WEEKLY
ISSUE 3
OH...
ISSUE 2 CONTAINS THE COOL-ING SYSTEM TO PRO-TECT THE ROCKET'S BODY AND ELECTRON-ICS.
SOUNDS LIKE YOU NEEDED ONE YOUR-SELF!
ROCKET BUILDING YO-KAI
USAPYON
HERE'S THE YO-KAI WE NEED HELP FROM!
shuf
OH, CUTE! I WANT TO BE HER FRIEND!
krrrk
BE CARE-FUL SHE'S...
HUH?
WHAT?

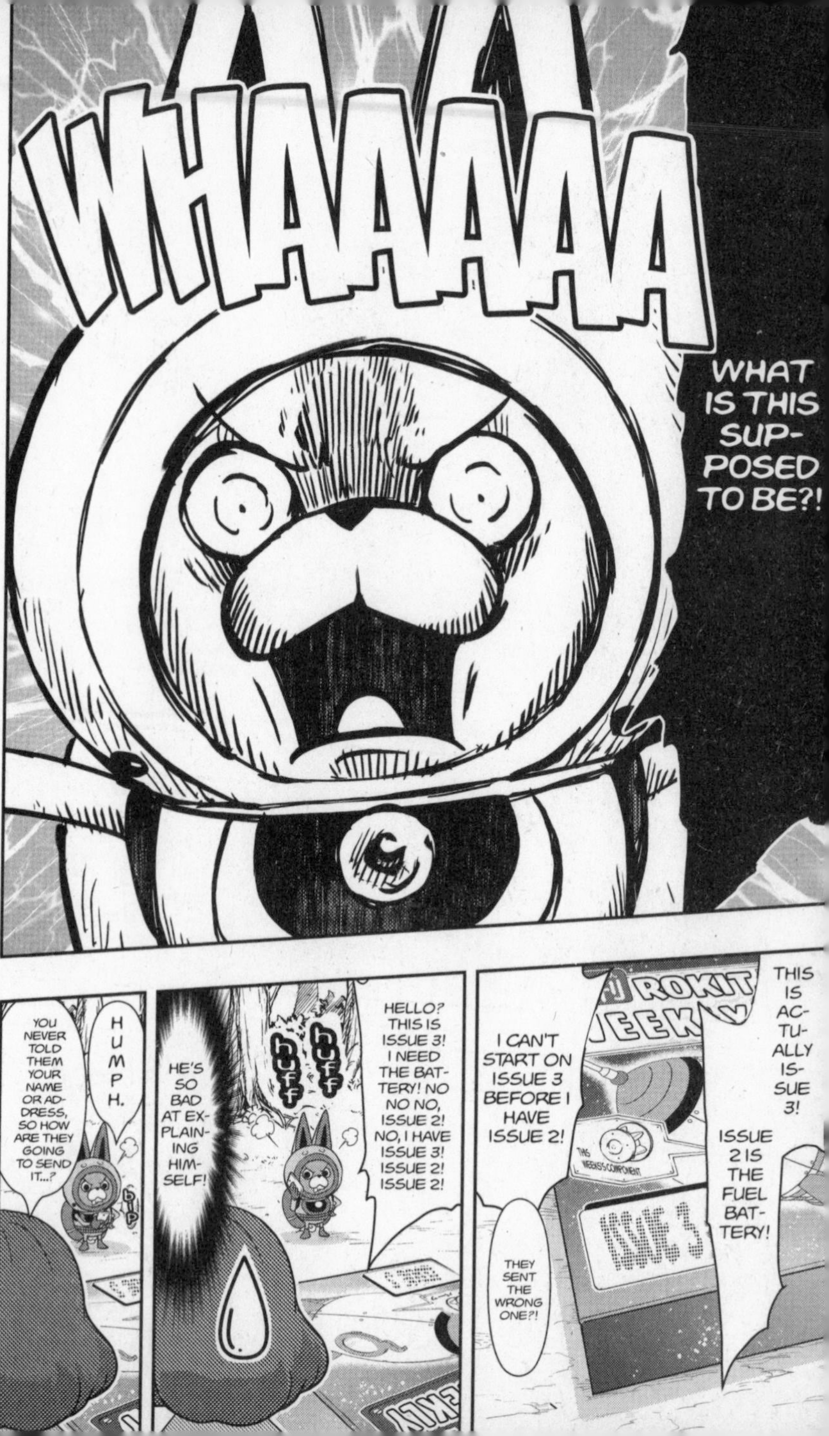
WHAAAAA
WHAT IS THIS SUPPOSED TO BE?!
THIS IS ACTUALLY ISSUE 3!
ISSUE 2 IS THE FUEL BATTERY!
ROKIT WEEK
THIS WEEK'S COMPONENT
ISSUE 3
I CAN'T START ON ISSUE 3 BEFORE I HAVE ISSUE 2!
THEY SENT THE WRONG ONE?!
HELLO? THIS IS ISSUE 3! I NEED THE BATTERY! NO NO NO, ISSUE 2! NO, I HAVE ISSUE 3! ISSUE 2! ISSUE 2!
huff huff
HE'S SO BAD AT EXPLAINING HIMSELF!
HUMPH.
YOU NEVER TOLD THEM YOUR NAME OR ADDRESS, SO HOW ARE THEY GOING TO SEND IT...?
bip

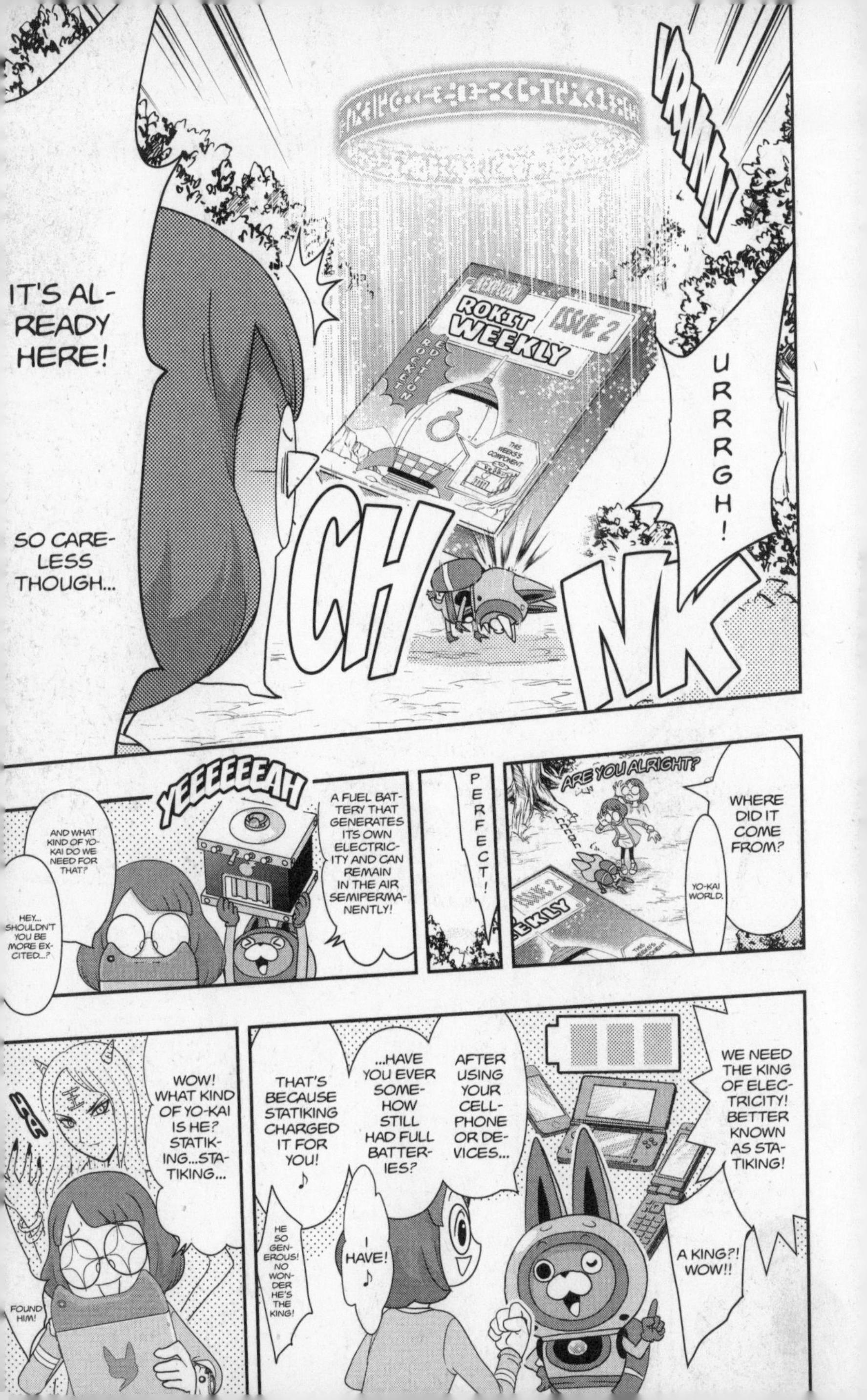
VRAWN
ROKIT WEEKLY
ISSUE 2
ROCKET EDITION
THIS WEEK'S COMPONENT
IT'S ALREADY HERE!
URRRGH!
CH
NK
SO CARELESS THOUGH...
ARE YOU ALRIGHT?
WHERE DID IT COME FROM?
YO-KAI WORLD.
PERFECT!
A FUEL BATTERY THAT GENERATES ITS OWN ELECTRICITY AND CAN REMAIN IN THE AIR SEMIPERMANENTLY!
YEEEEEEAH
AND WHAT KIND OF YO-KAI DO WE NEED FOR THAT?
HEY... SHOULDN'T YOU BE MORE EXCITED...?
WE NEED THE KING OF ELECTRICITY! BETTER KNOWN AS STATIKING!
A KING?! WOW!!
AFTER USING YOUR CELLPHONE OR DEVICES...
...HAVE YOU EVER SOMEHOW STILL HAD FULL BATTERIES?
I HAVE! ♪
THAT'S BECAUSE STATIKING CHARGED IT FOR YOU! ♪
HE SO GENEROUS! NO WONDER HE'S THE KING!
WOW! WHAT KIND OF YO-KAI IS HE? STATIKING...STATIKING...
FOUND HIM!

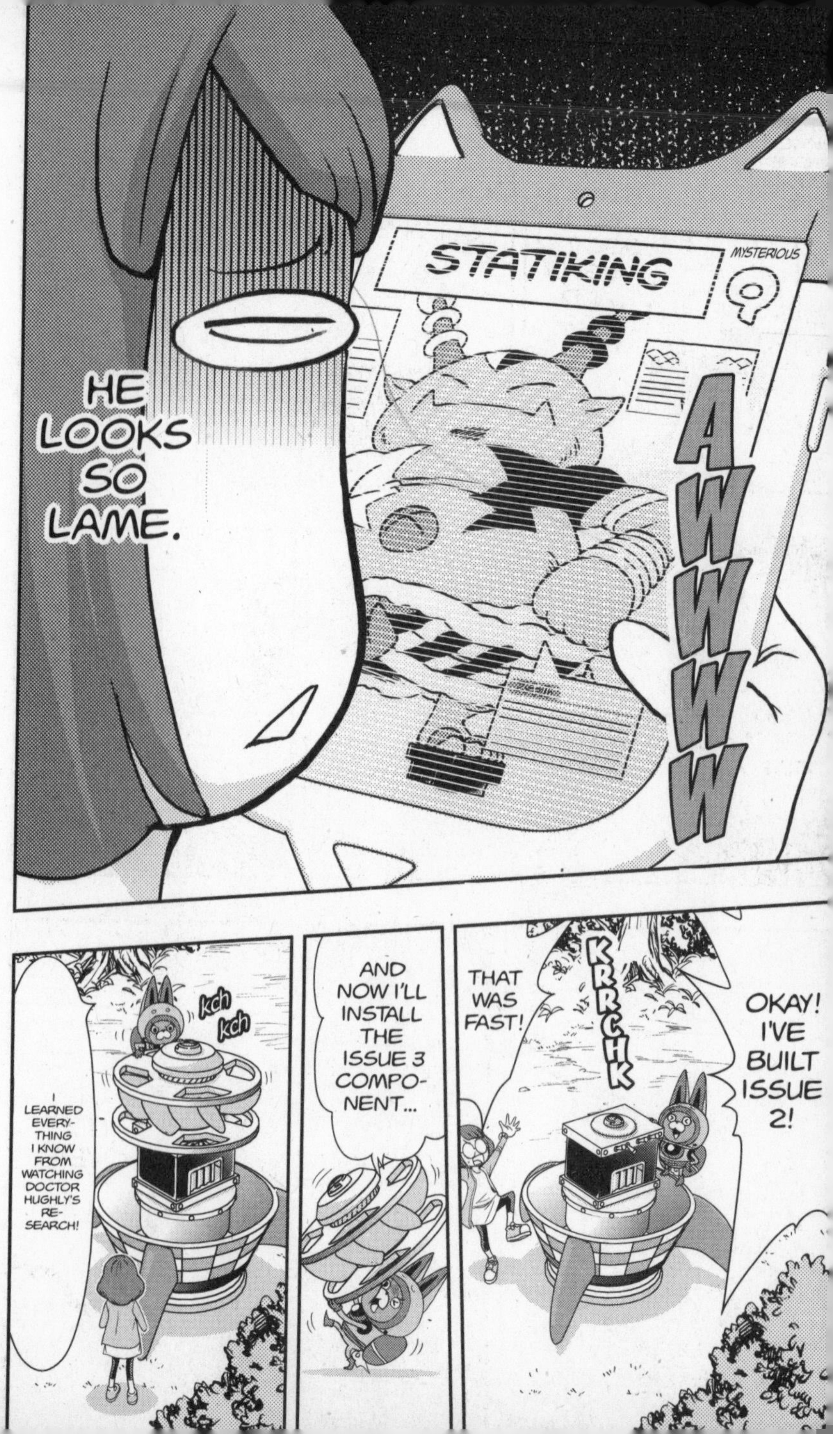
MYSTERIOUS
STATIKING
AWWWWW
HE LOOKS SO LAME.
OKAY! I'VE BUILT ISSUE 2!
KRRCHK
THAT WAS FAST!
AND NOW I'LL INSTALL THE ISSUE 3 COMPONENT...
kch kch
I LEARNED EVERYTHING I KNOW FROM WATCHING DOCTOR HUGHLY'S RESEARCH!

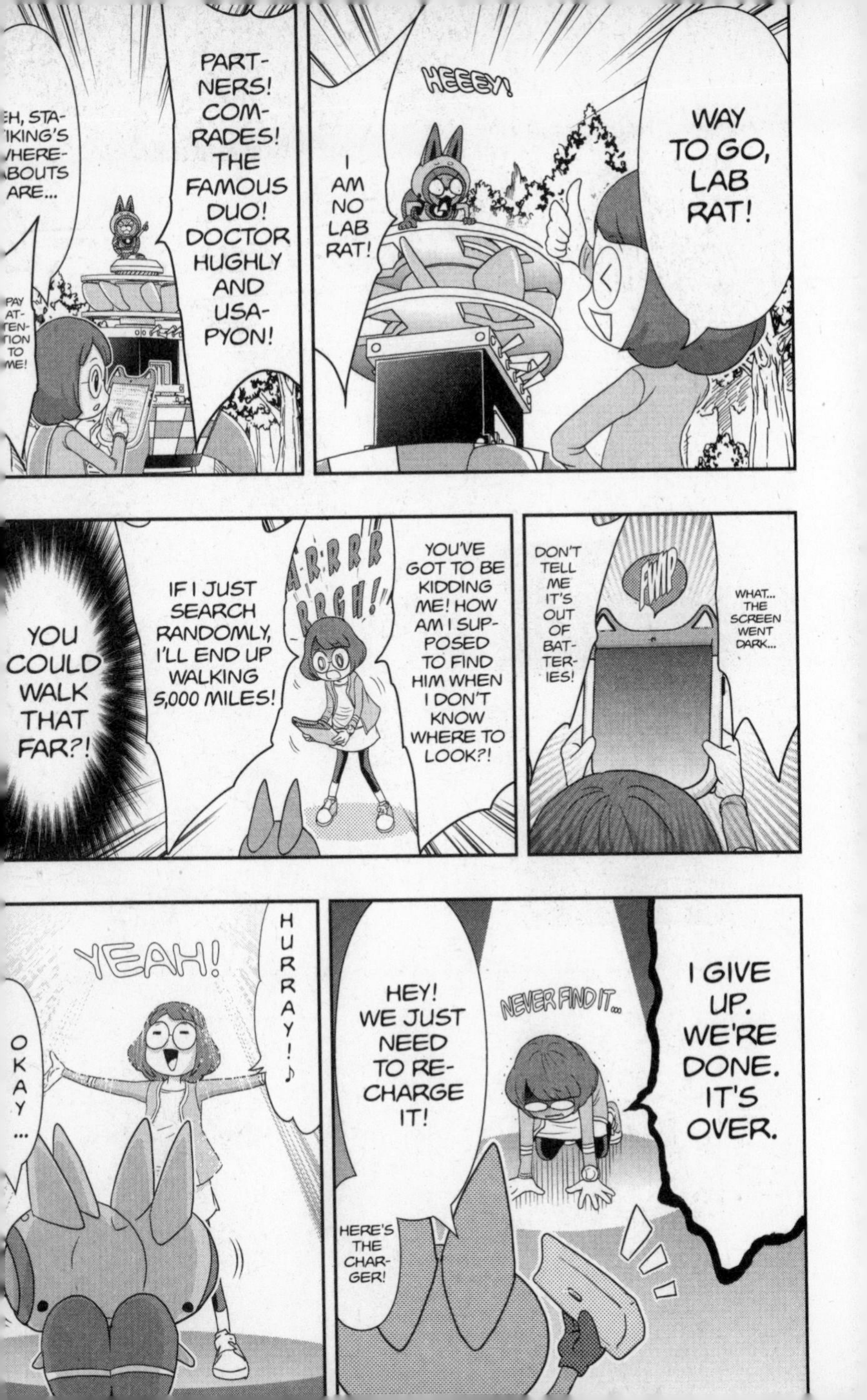
WAY TO GO, LAB RAT!
HEEEY!
I AM NO LAB RAT!
PARTNERS! COMRADES! THE FAMOUS DUO! DOCTOR HUGHLY AND USAPYON!
H, STA- KING'S HERE- BOUTS ARE...
PAY AT- TEN- ION TO ME!
WHAT... THE SCREEN WENT DARK...
FWIP
DON'T TELL ME IT'S OUT OF BATTERIES!
YOU'VE GOT TO BE KIDDING ME! HOW AM I SUPPOSED TO FIND HIM WHEN I DON'T KNOW WHERE TO LOOK?!
ARRRRRGH!
IF I JUST SEARCH RANDOMLY, I'LL END UP WALKING 5,000 MILES!
YOU COULD WALK THAT FAR?!
I GIVE UP. WE'RE DONE. IT'S OVER.
NEVER FIND IT...
HEY! WE JUST NEED TO RECHARGE IT!
HERE'S THE CHARGER!
HURRAY!♪
YEAH!
OKAY...

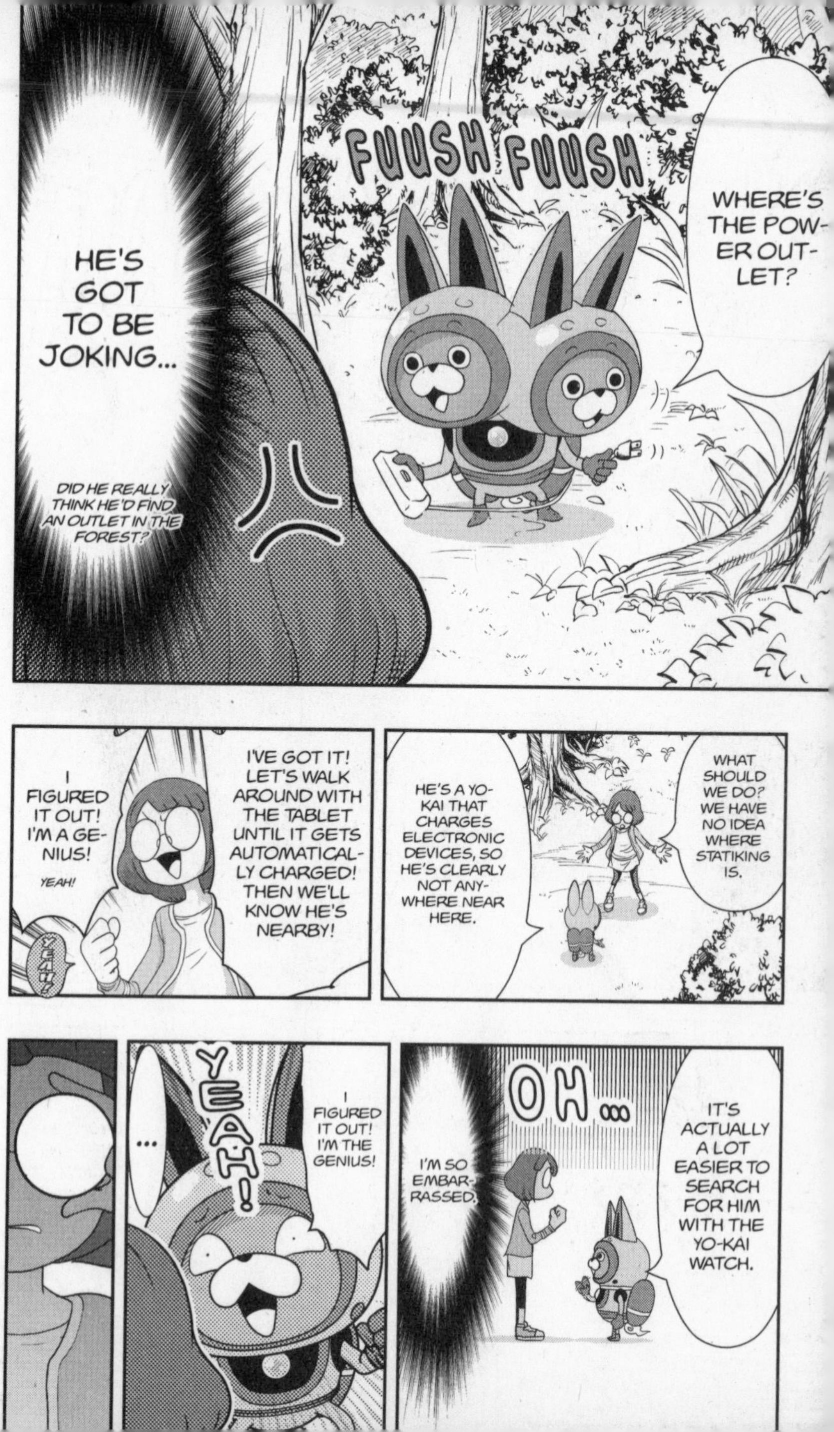
WHERE'S THE POWER OUTLET?
FUUSH FUUSH
HE'S GOT TO BE JOKING...
DID HE REALLY THINK HE'D FIND AN OUTLET IN THE FOREST?
WHAT SHOULD WE DO? WE HAVE NO IDEA WHERE STATIKING IS.
HE'S A YO-KAI THAT CHARGES ELECTRONIC DEVICES, SO HE'S CLEARLY NOT ANYWHERE NEAR HERE.
I'VE GOT IT! LET'S WALK AROUND WITH THE TABLET UNTIL IT GETS AUTOMATICALLY CHARGED! THEN WE'LL KNOW HE'S NEARBY!
I FIGURED IT OUT! I'M A GENIUS!
YEAH!
YEAH!
IT'S ACTUALLY A LOT EASIER TO SEARCH FOR HIM WITH THE YO-KAI WATCH.
OH...
I'M SO EMBARRASSED.
I FIGURED IT OUT! I'M THE GENIUS!
YEAH!
...

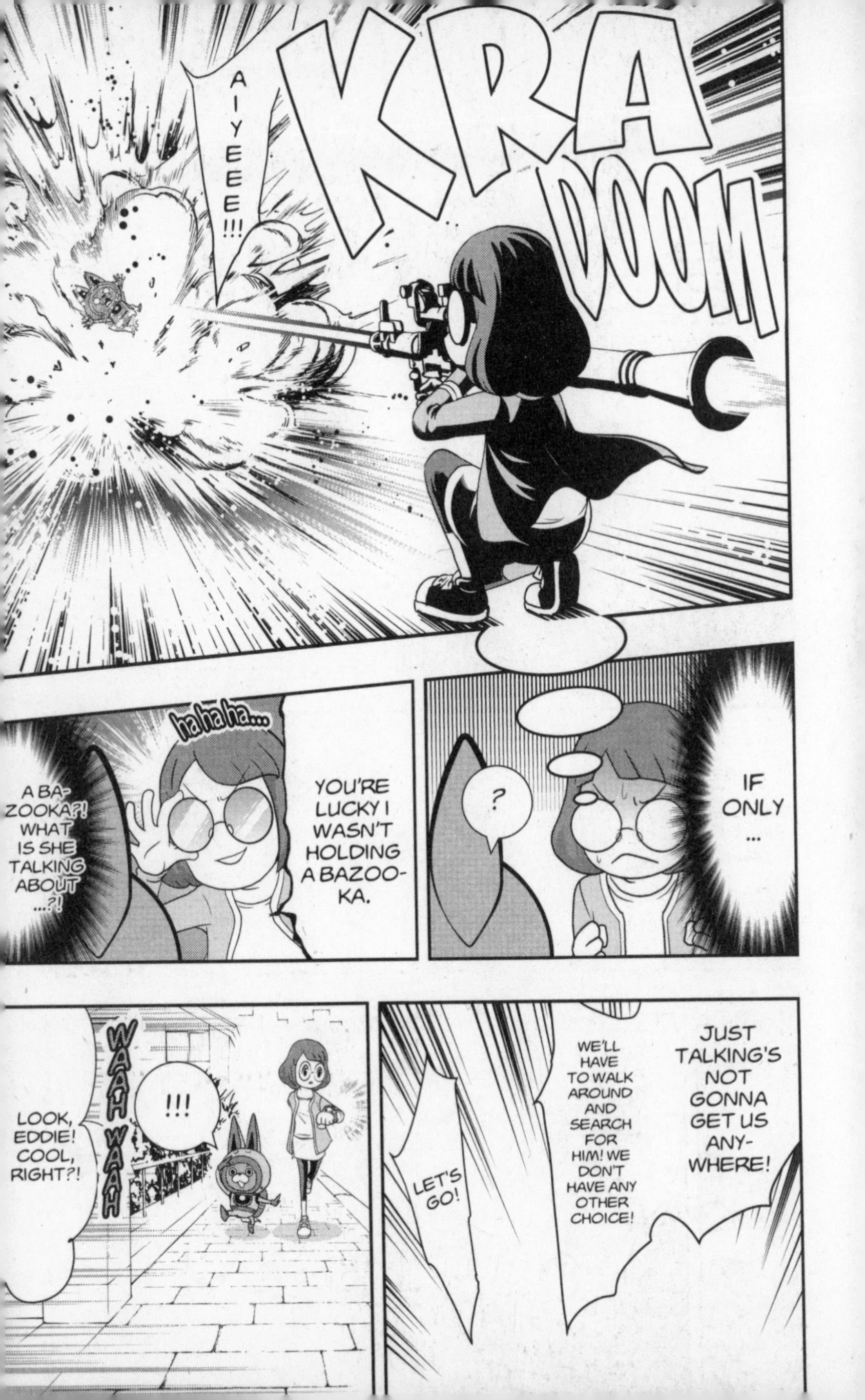
KRA
DOOM
AIYEEE!!!
IF ONLY ...
?
ha ha ha...
YOU'RE LUCKY I WASN'T HOLDING A BAZOO-KA.
A BA-ZOOKA?! WHAT IS SHE TALKING ABOUT ...?!
JUST TALKING'S NOT GONNA GET US ANY-WHERE!
WE'LL HAVE TO WALK AROUND AND SEARCH FOR HIM! WE DON'T HAVE ANY OTHER CHOICE!
LET'S GO!
WAAH WAAH
!!!
LOOK, EDDIE! COOL, RIGHT?!

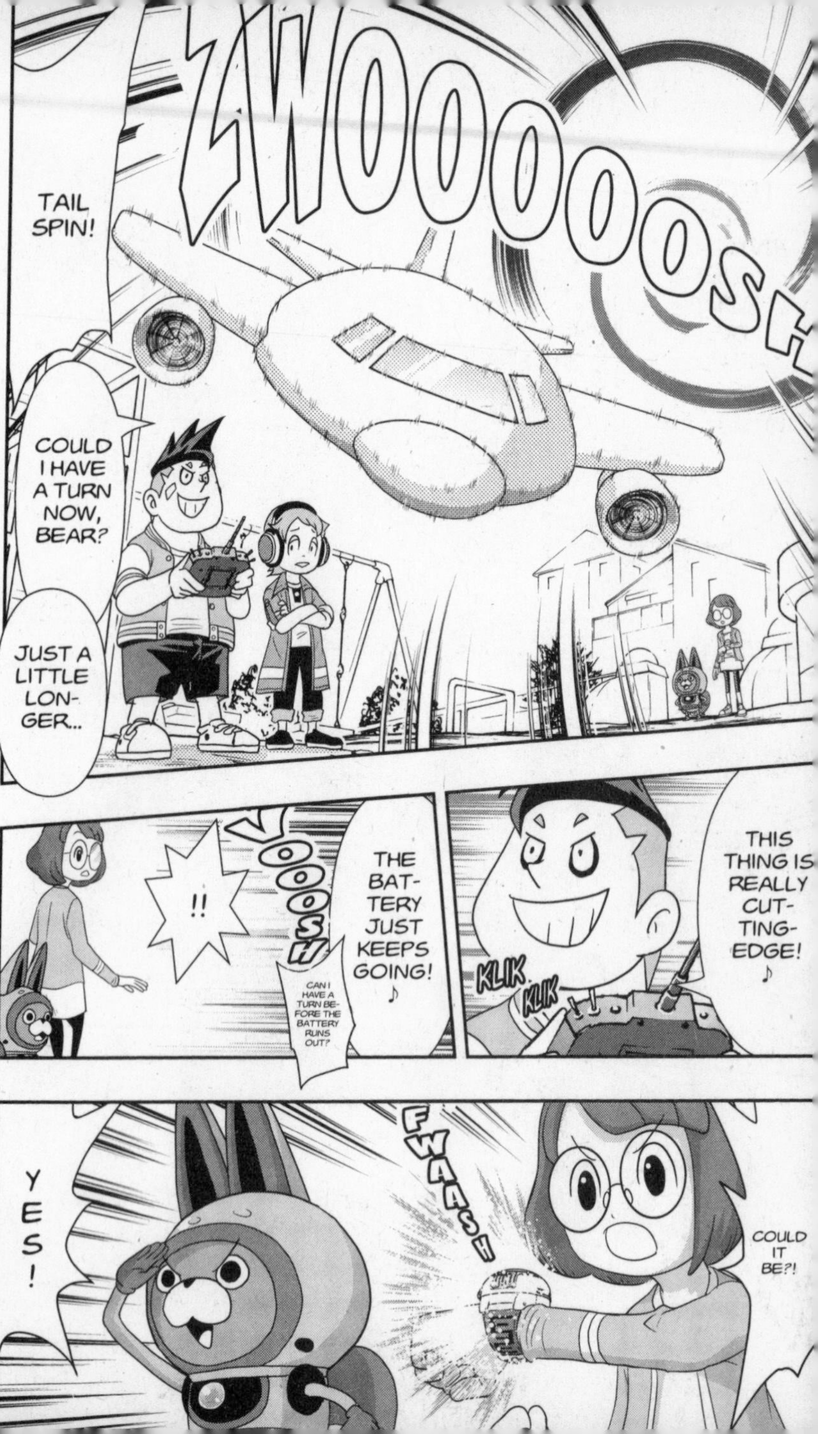
ZWOOOOOOSH
TAIL SPIN!
COULD I HAVE A TURN NOW, BEAR?
JUST A LITTLE LONGER...
THIS THING IS REALLY CUTTING-EDGE! ♪
KLIK KLIK
THE BATTERY JUST KEEPS GOING! ♪
WOOOOSH
!!
CAN I HAVE A TURN BEFORE THE BATTERY RUNS OUT?
COULD IT BE?!
FWAASH
YES!

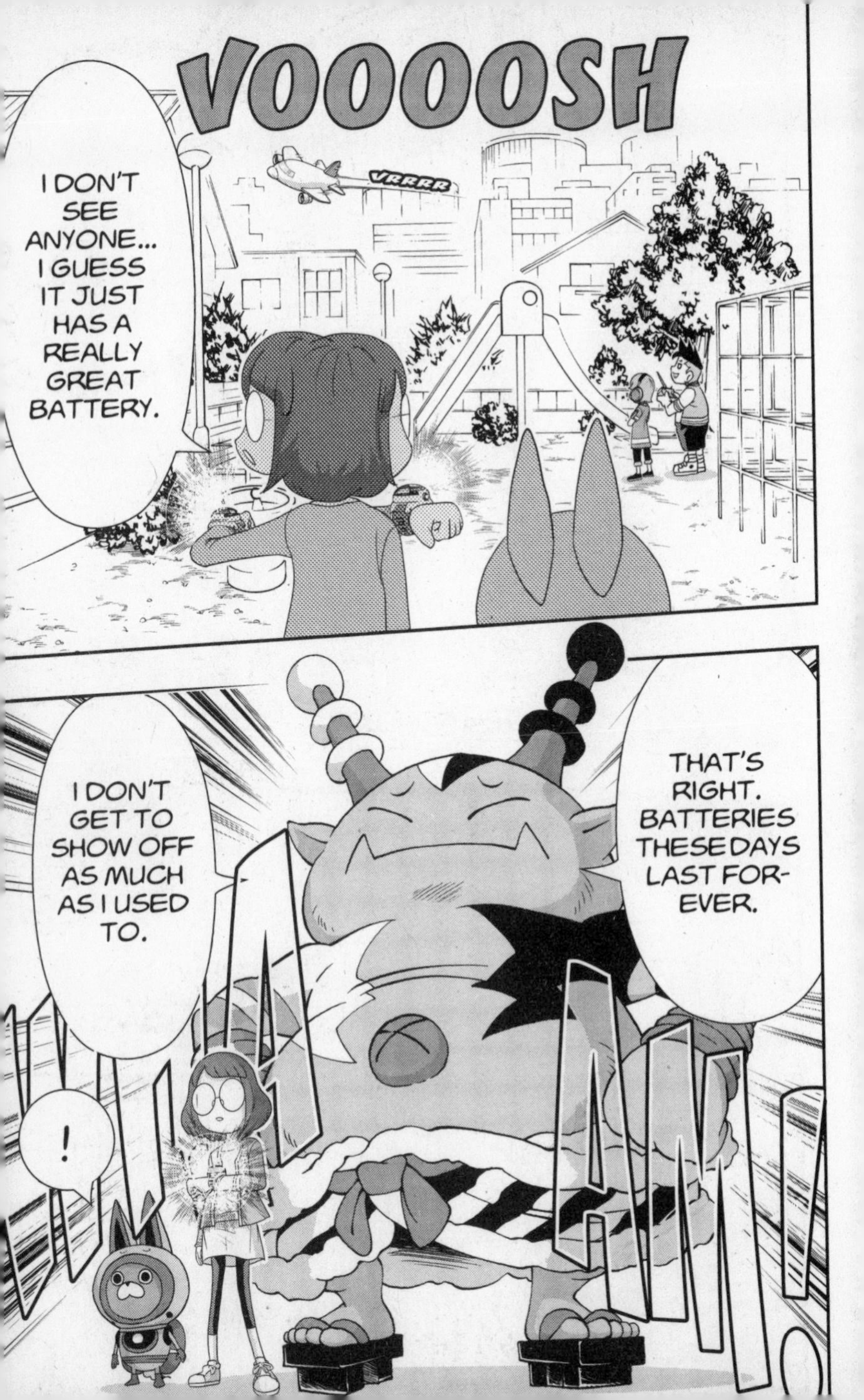
VOOOOSH
VRRRR
I DON'T SEE ANYONE... I GUESS IT JUST HAS A REALLY GREAT BATTERY.
THAT'S RIGHT. BATTERIES THESE DAYS LAST FOR-EVER.
I DON'T GET TO SHOW OFF AS MUCH AS I USED TO.
!

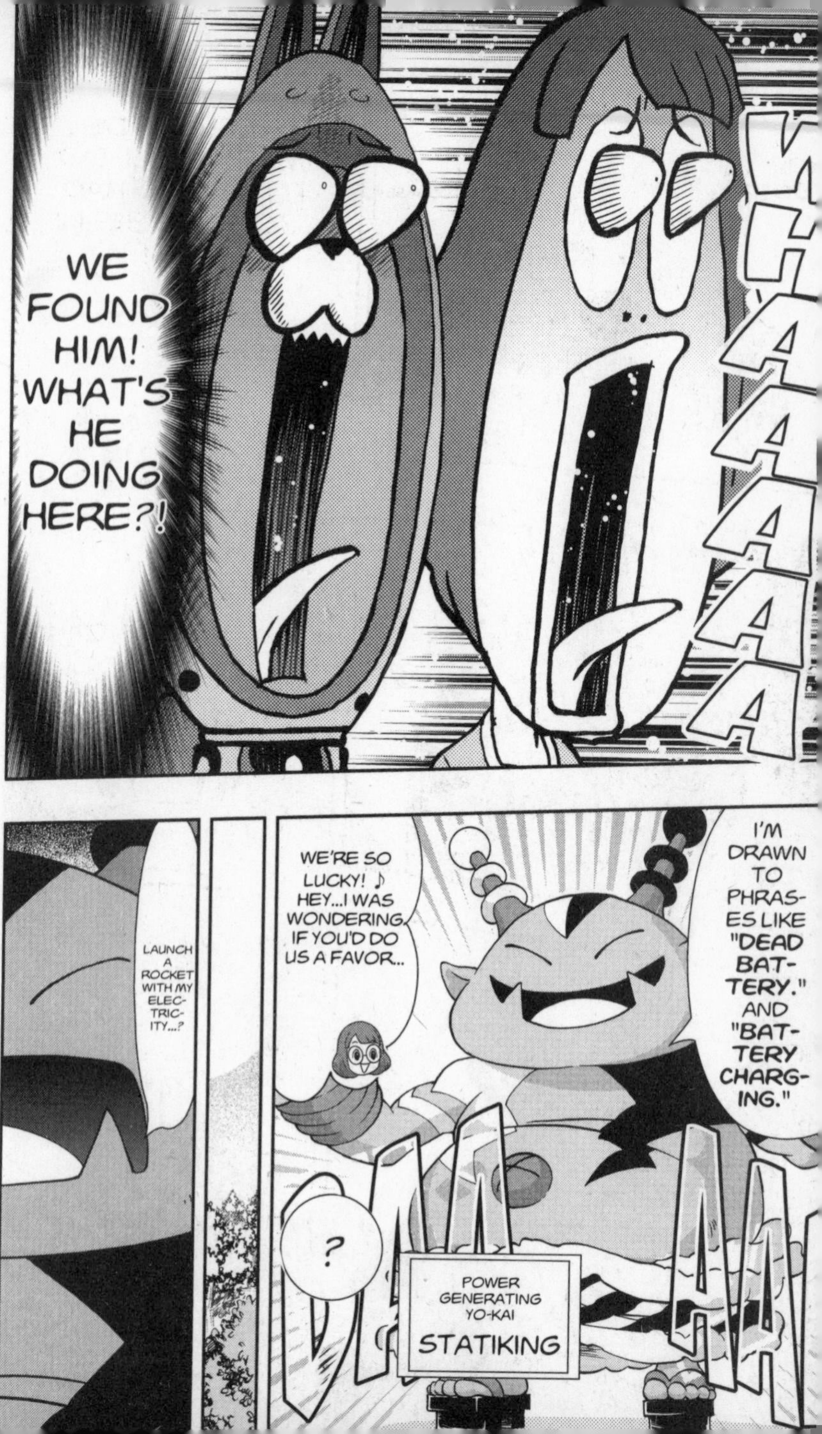
WHAAAAAA
WE FOUND HIM! WHAT'S HE DOING HERE?!
I'M DRAWN TO PHRASES LIKE "DEAD BATTERY." AND "BATTERY CHARGING."
WE'RE SO LUCKY! ♪ HEY...I WAS WONDERING IF YOU'D DO US A FAVOR...
?
POWER GENERATING YO-KAI
STATIKING
LAUNCH A ROCKET WITH MY ELECTRICITY...?

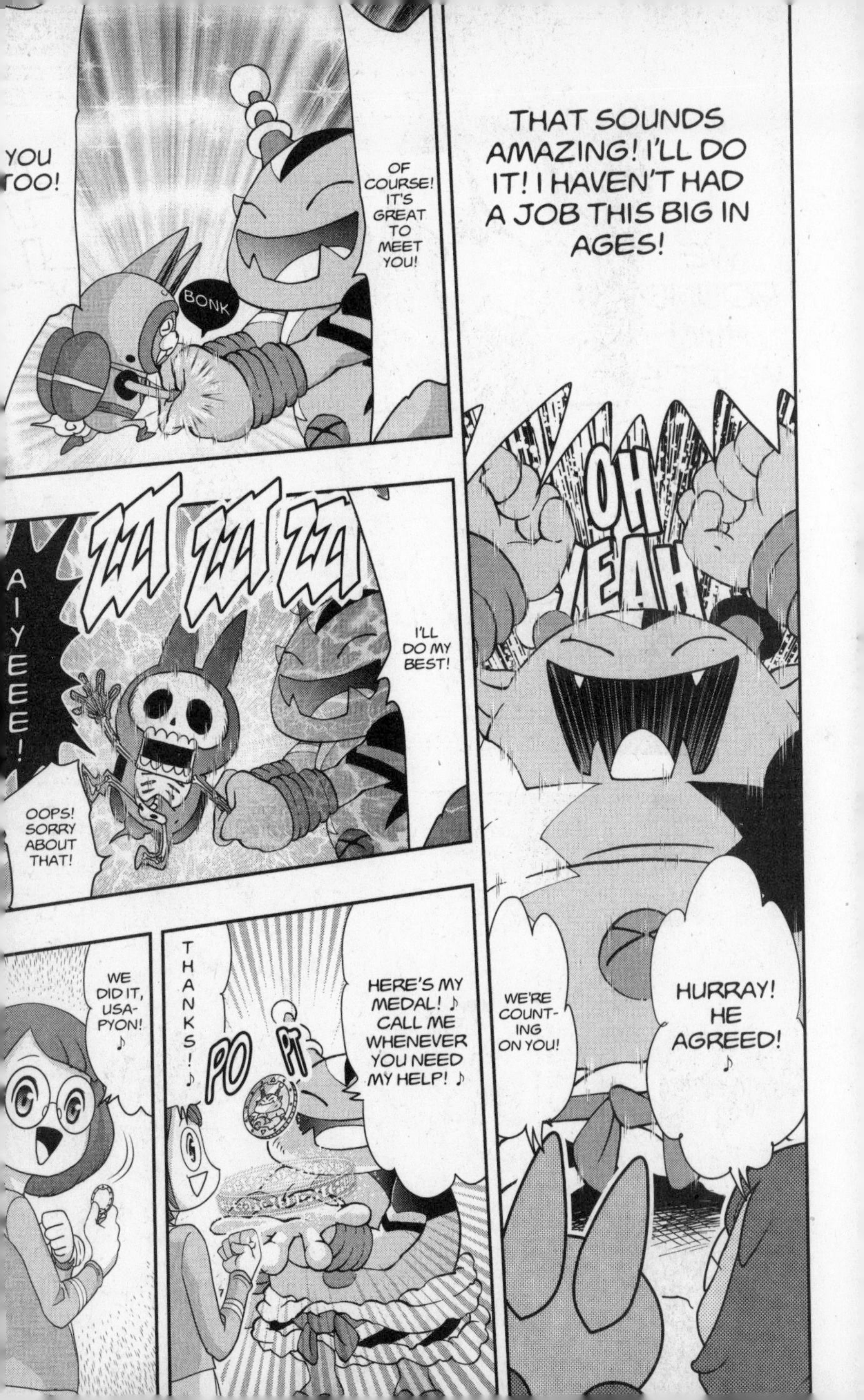
THAT SOUNDS AMAZING! I'LL DO IT! I HAVEN'T HAD A JOB THIS BIG IN AGES!
OH YEAH
HURRAY! HE AGREED! ♪
WE'RE COUNTING ON YOU!
OF COURSE! IT'S GREAT TO MEET YOU!
YOU TOO!
BONK
ZZT ZZT ZZA
I'LL DO MY BEST!
AIYEEE!
OOPS! SORRY ABOUT THAT!
HERE'S MY MEDAL! ♪ CALL ME WHENEVER YOU NEED MY HELP! ♪
PO PT
THANKS! ♪
WE DID IT, USAPYON! ♪

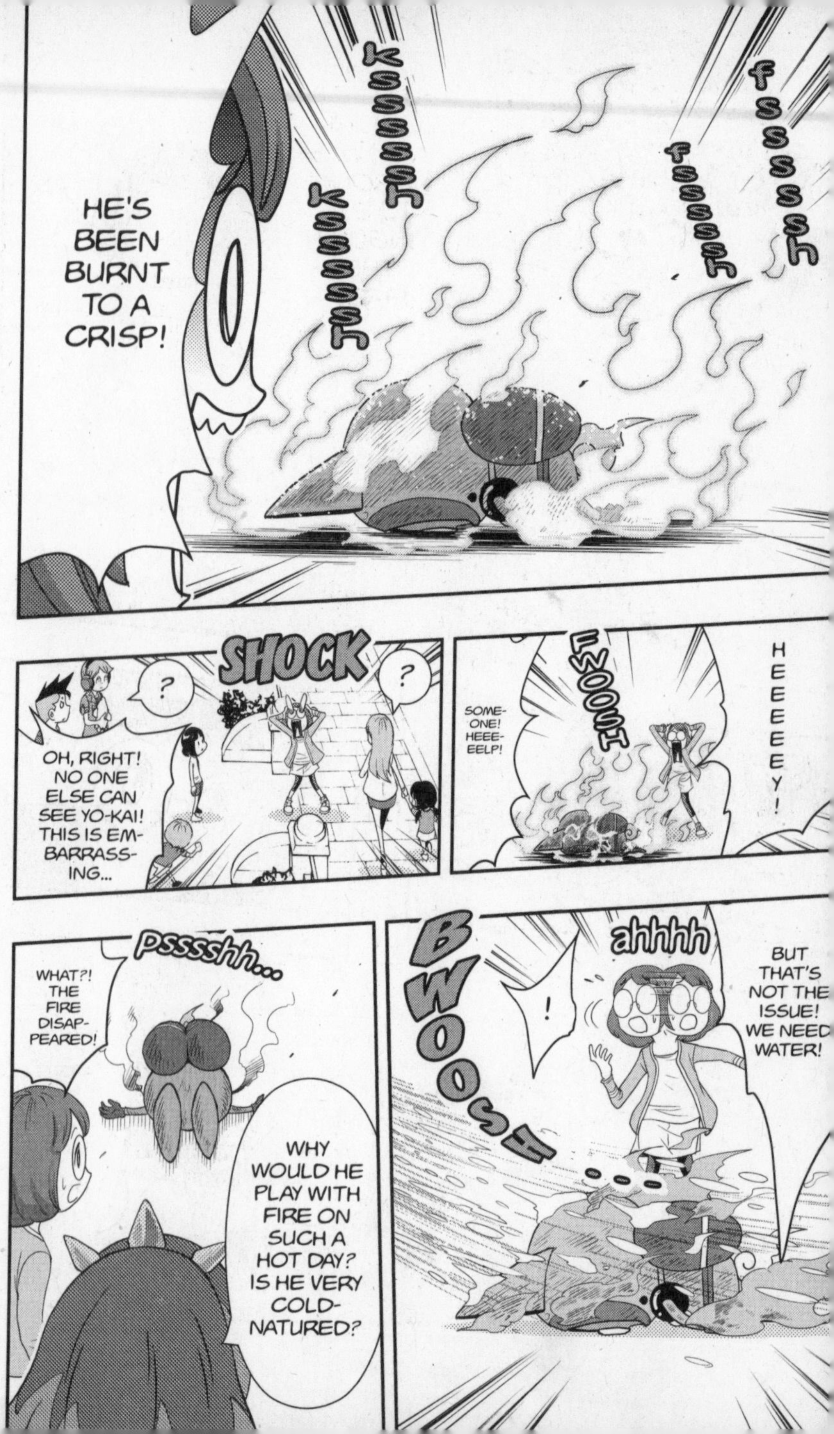
fssssh
fssssh
kssssh
ksssssh
HE'S BEEN BURNT TO A CRISP!
HEEEEEEY!
FWOOSH
SOME-ONE! HEEE-EELP!
SHOCK
?
?
OH, RIGHT! NO ONE ELSE CAN SEE YO-KAI! THIS IS EM-BARRASS-ING...
BUT THAT'S NOT THE ISSUE! WE NEED WATER!
ahhhh
!
BWOOOSH...
pssssh...
WHAT?! THE FIRE DISAP-PEARED!
WHY WOULD HE PLAY WITH FIRE ON SUCH A HOT DAY? IS HE VERY COLD-NATURED?

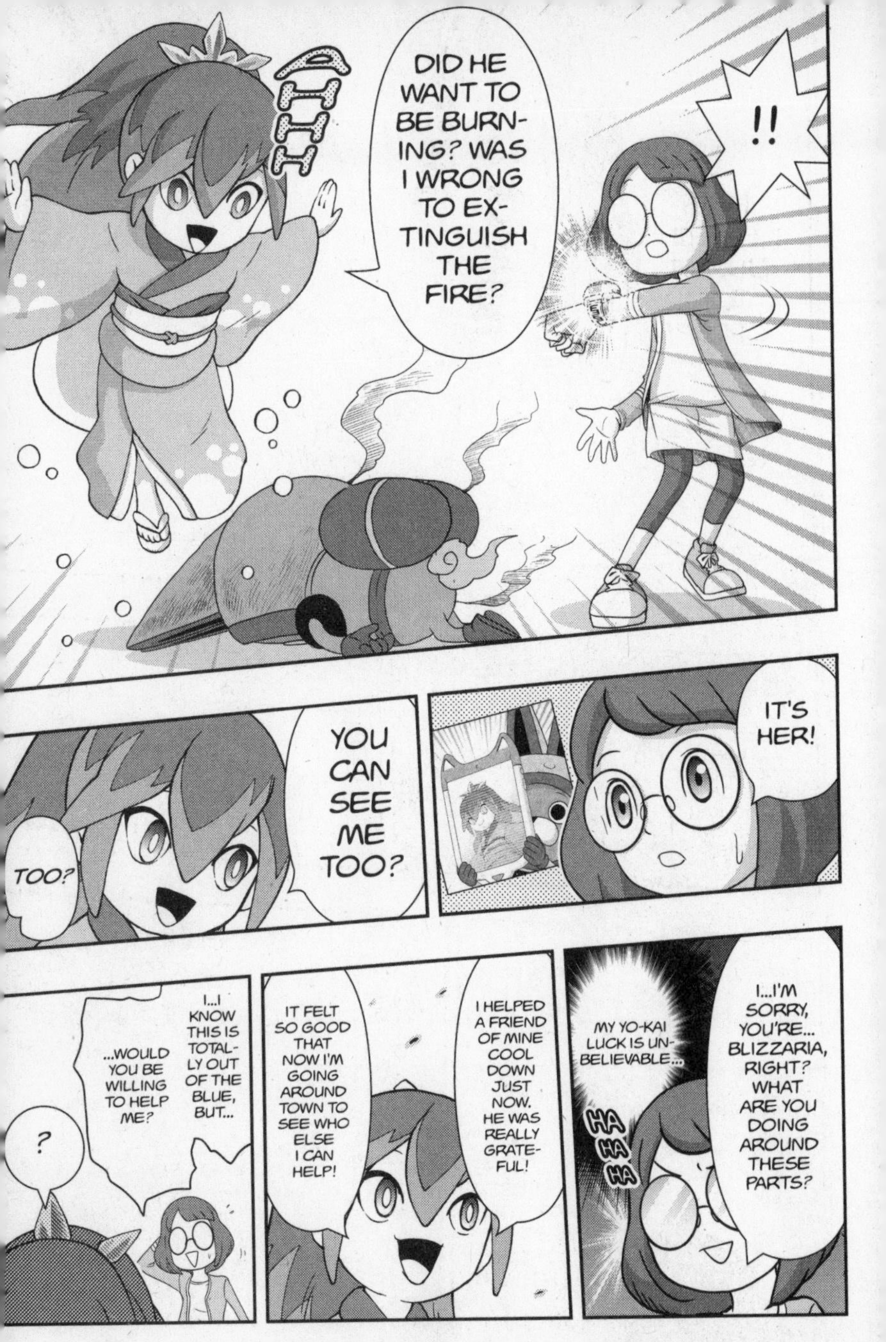
!!
DID HE WANT TO BE BURN-ING? WAS I WRONG TO EX-TINGUISH THE FIRE?
AHHH
IT'S HER!
YOU CAN SEE ME TOO?
TOO?
I...I'M SORRY, YOU'RE... BLIZZARIA, RIGHT? WHAT ARE YOU DOING AROUND THESE PARTS?
MY YO-KAI LUCK IS UN-BELIEVABLE...
HA HA HA
I HELPED A FRIEND OF MINE COOL DOWN JUST NOW. HE WAS REALLY GRATE-FUL!
IT FELT SO GOOD THAT NOW I'M GOING AROUND TOWN TO SEE WHO ELSE I CAN HELP!
I...I KNOW THIS IS TOTAL-LY OUT OF THE BLUE, BUT...
...WOULD YOU BE WILLING TO HELP ME?
?

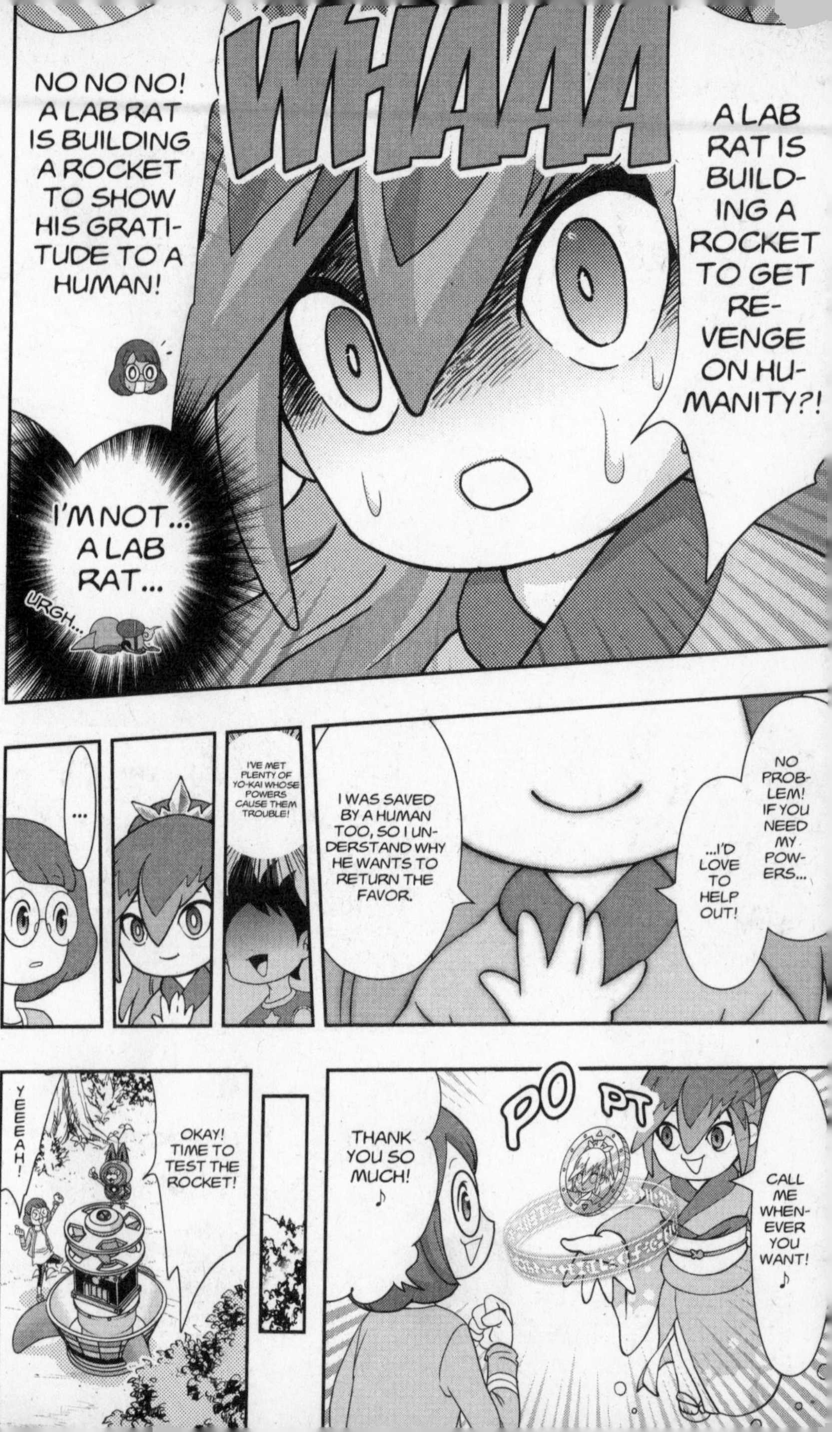
WHAAAA
A LAB RAT IS BUILDING A ROCKET TO GET REVENGE ON HUMANITY?!
NO NO NO! A LAB RAT IS BUILDING A ROCKET TO SHOW HIS GRATITUDE TO A HUMAN!
I'M NOT... A LAB RAT...
URGH...
NO PROBLEM! IF YOU NEED MY POWERS...
...I'D LOVE TO HELP OUT!
I WAS SAVED BY A HUMAN TOO, SO I UNDERSTAND WHY HE WANTS TO RETURN THE FAVOR.
I'VE MET PLENTY OF YO-KAI WHOSE POWERS CAUSE THEM TROUBLE!
...
POPT
CALL ME WHENEVER YOU WANT! ♪
THANK YOU SO MUCH! ♪
OKAY! TIME TO TEST THE ROCKET!
YEEEEAH!

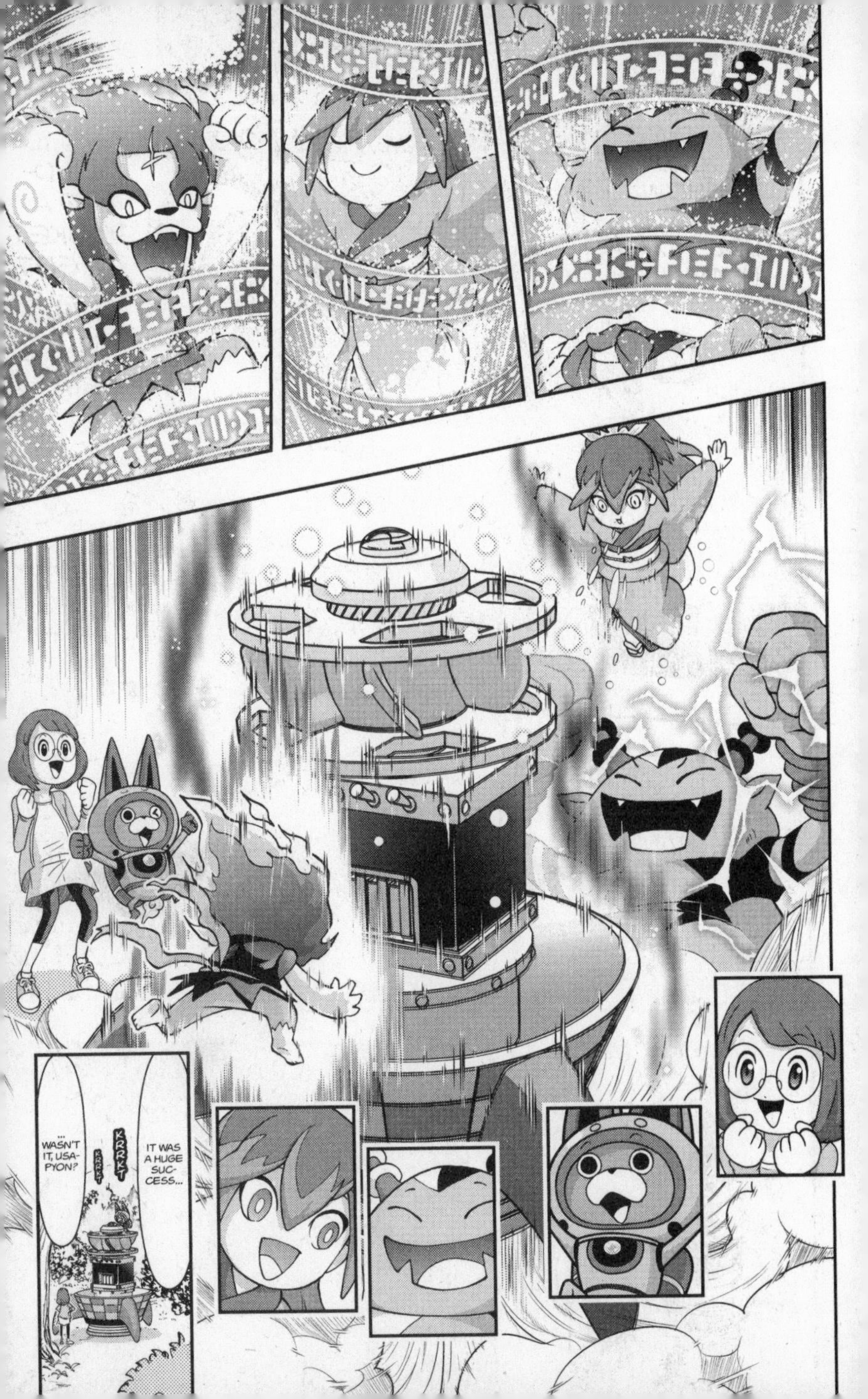
IT WAS A HUGE SUCCESS...
KRRKT
KRRKT
...WASN'T IT, USA-PYON?

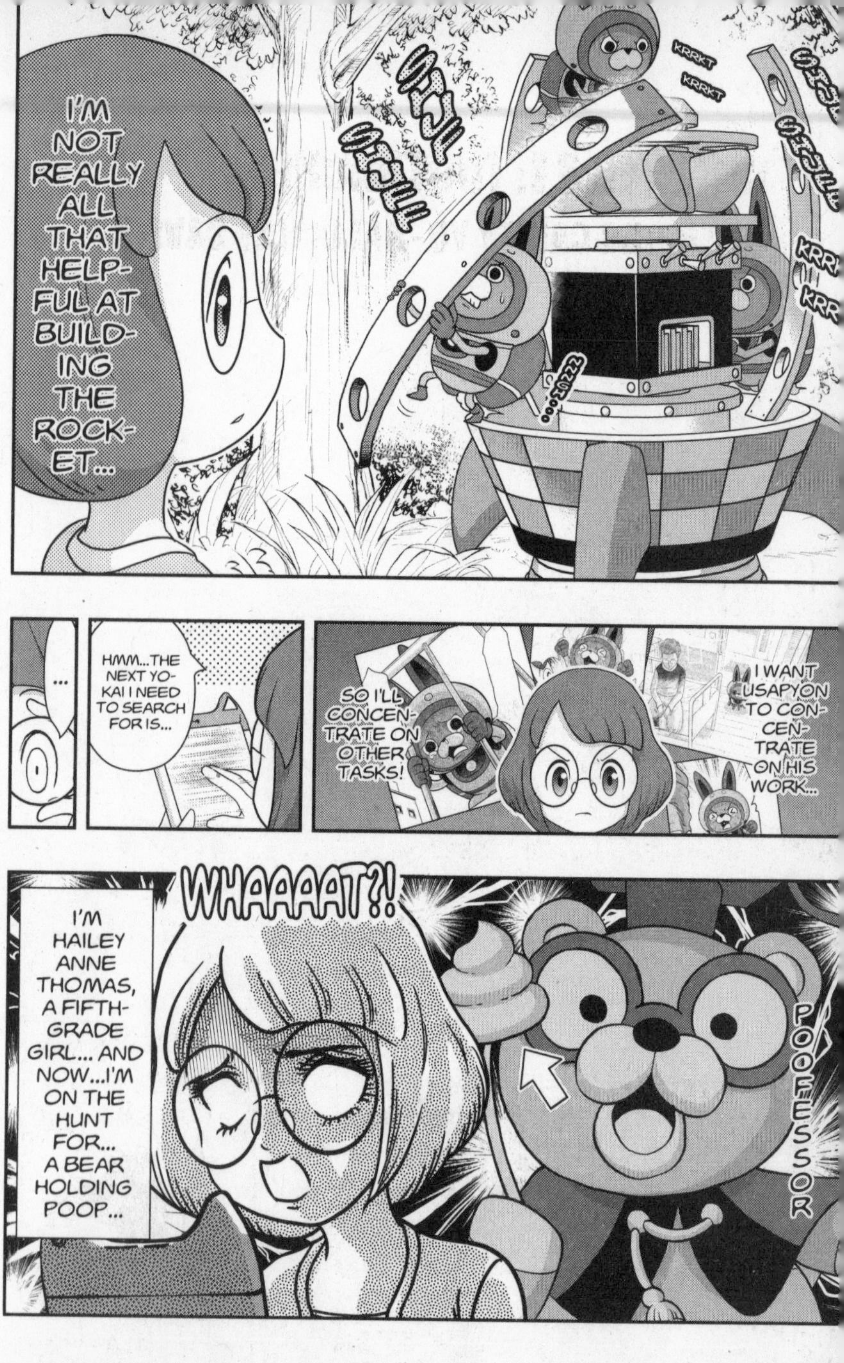
KRRKT
KRRKT
KRR KRR
I'M NOT REALLY ALL THAT HELPFUL AT BUILDING THE ROCKET...
I WANT USAPYON TO CONCENTRATE ON HIS WORK...
SO I'LL CONCENTRATE ON OTHER TASKS!
HMM...THE NEXT YOKAI I NEED TO SEARCH FOR IS...
...
POOFESSOR
WHAAAAT?!
I'M HAILEY ANNE THOMAS, A FIFTH-GRADE GIRL... AND NOW...I'M ON THE HUNT FOR... A BEAR HOLDING POOP...

CHAPTER 81: TOOTHACHE!!
FEATURING CAVITY YO-KAI COUNT CAVITY

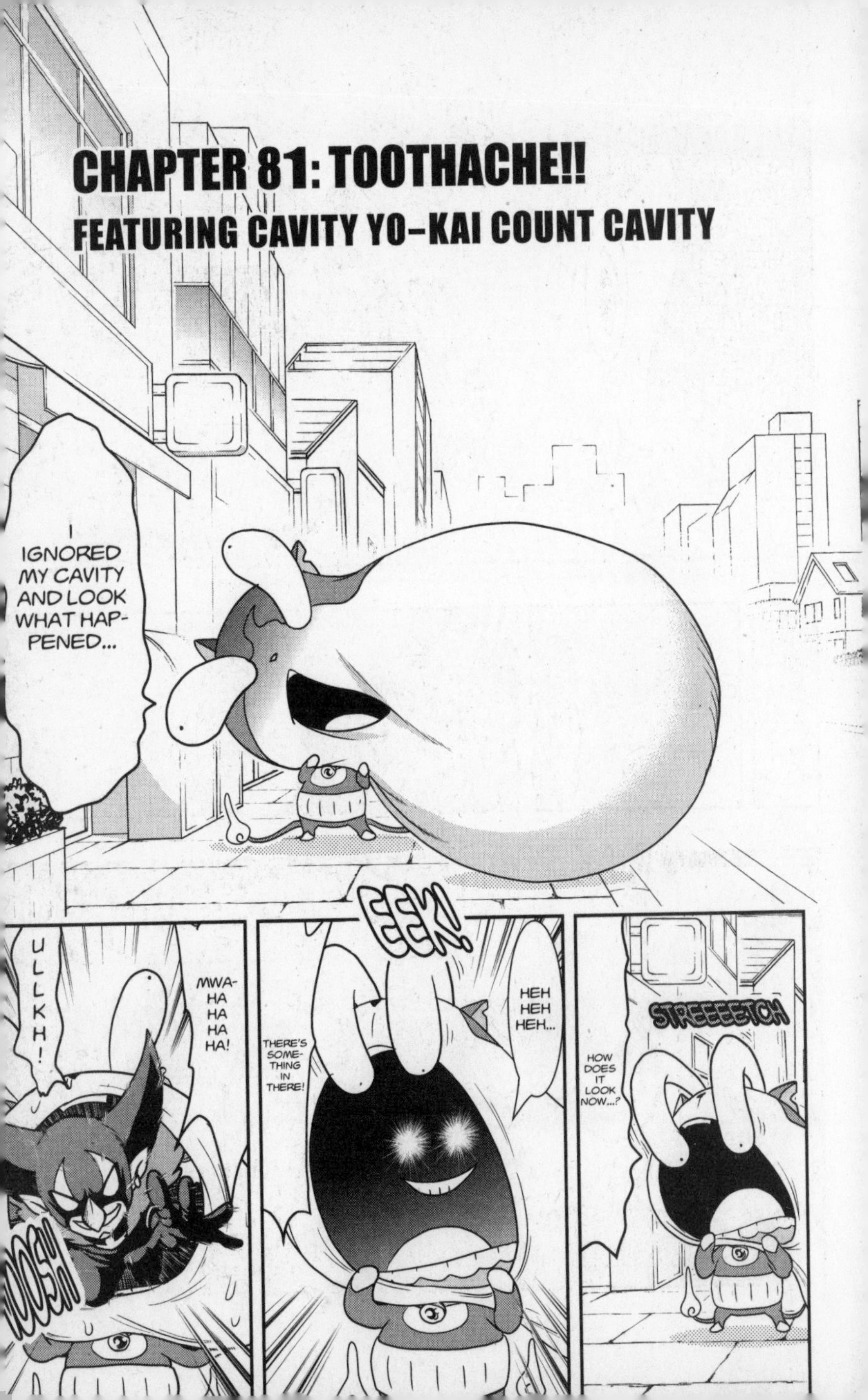
I IGNORED MY CAVITY AND LOOK WHAT HAP-PENED...
STREEEEETCH
HOW DOES IT LOOK NOW...?
EEK!
HEH HEH HEH...
THERE'S SOME-THING IN THERE!
MWA-HA HA HA HA!
ULLKH!

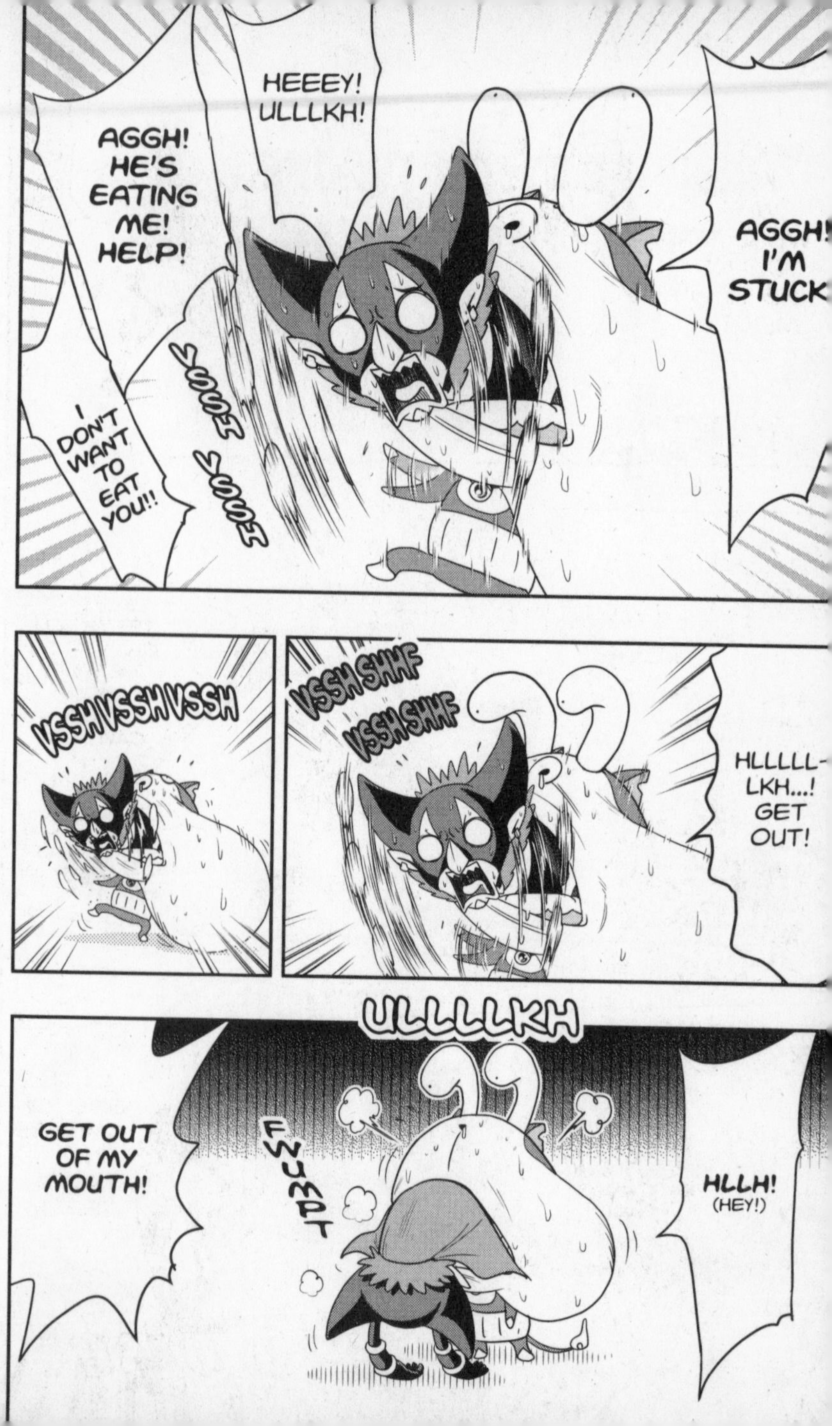
AGGH! I'M STUCK!
HEEEY! ULLLKH!
AGGH! HE'S EATING ME! HELP!
VSSH VSSH
I DON'T WANT TO EAT YOU!!
VSSH SHHF
VSSH SHHF
HLLLLL-LKH...! GET OUT!
VSSHVSSHVSSH
ULLLLKH
HLLH! (HEY!)
FWUMPT
GET OUT OF MY MOUTH!

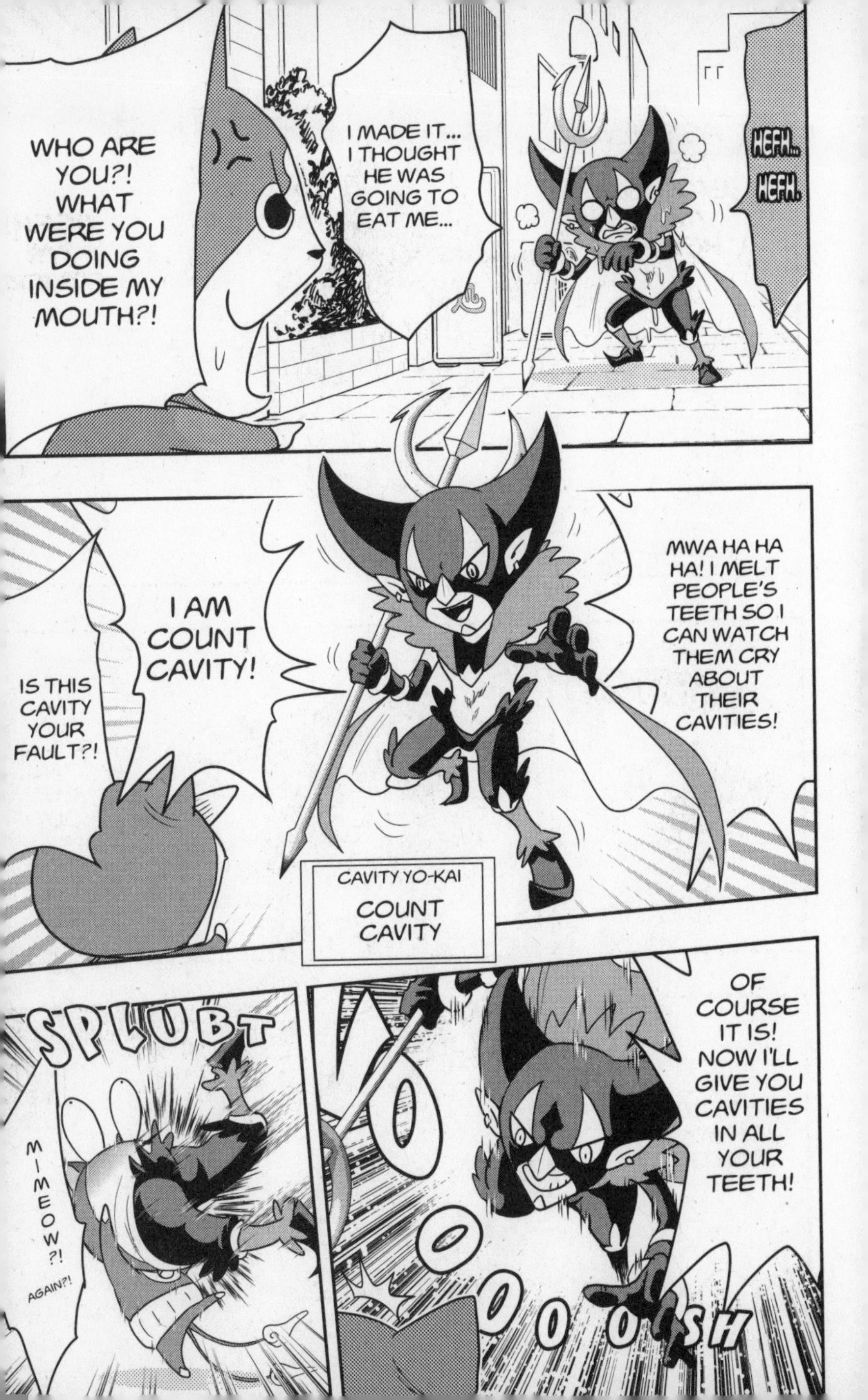
HEFH... HEFH.
I MADE IT... I THOUGHT HE WAS GOING TO EAT ME...
WHO ARE YOU?! WHAT WERE YOU DOING INSIDE MY MOUTH?!
MWA HA HA HA! I MELT PEOPLE'S TEETH SO I CAN WATCH THEM CRY ABOUT THEIR CAVITIES!
I AM COUNT CAVITY!
IS THIS CAVITY YOUR FAULT?!
CAVITY YO-KAI
COUNT CAVITY
OF COURSE IT IS! NOW I'LL GIVE YOU CAVITIES IN ALL YOUR TEETH!
OOOOOOOSH
SPLUBT
MIMEOW?!
AGAIN?!

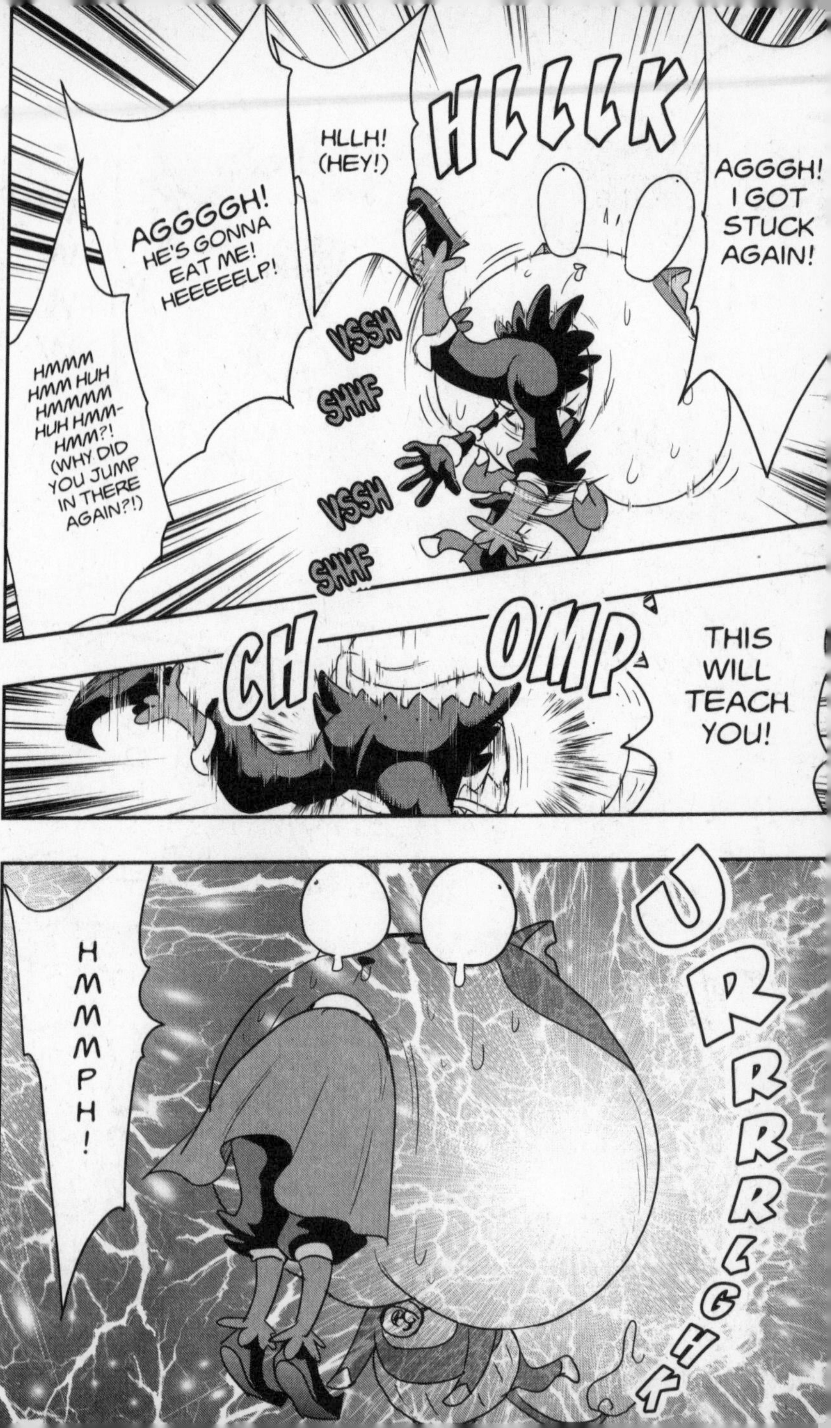
AGGGH! I GOT STUCK AGAIN!
HLLLK
HLLH! (HEY!)
AGGGGH! HE'S GONNA EAT ME! HEEEEELP!
VSSH
SHHF
VSSH
SHHF
HMMM HMM HUH HMMMM HUH HMM-HMM?! (WHY DID YOU JUMP IN THERE AGAIN?!)
THIS WILL TEACH YOU!
CHOMP
URRRRLGHK
HMMMPH!

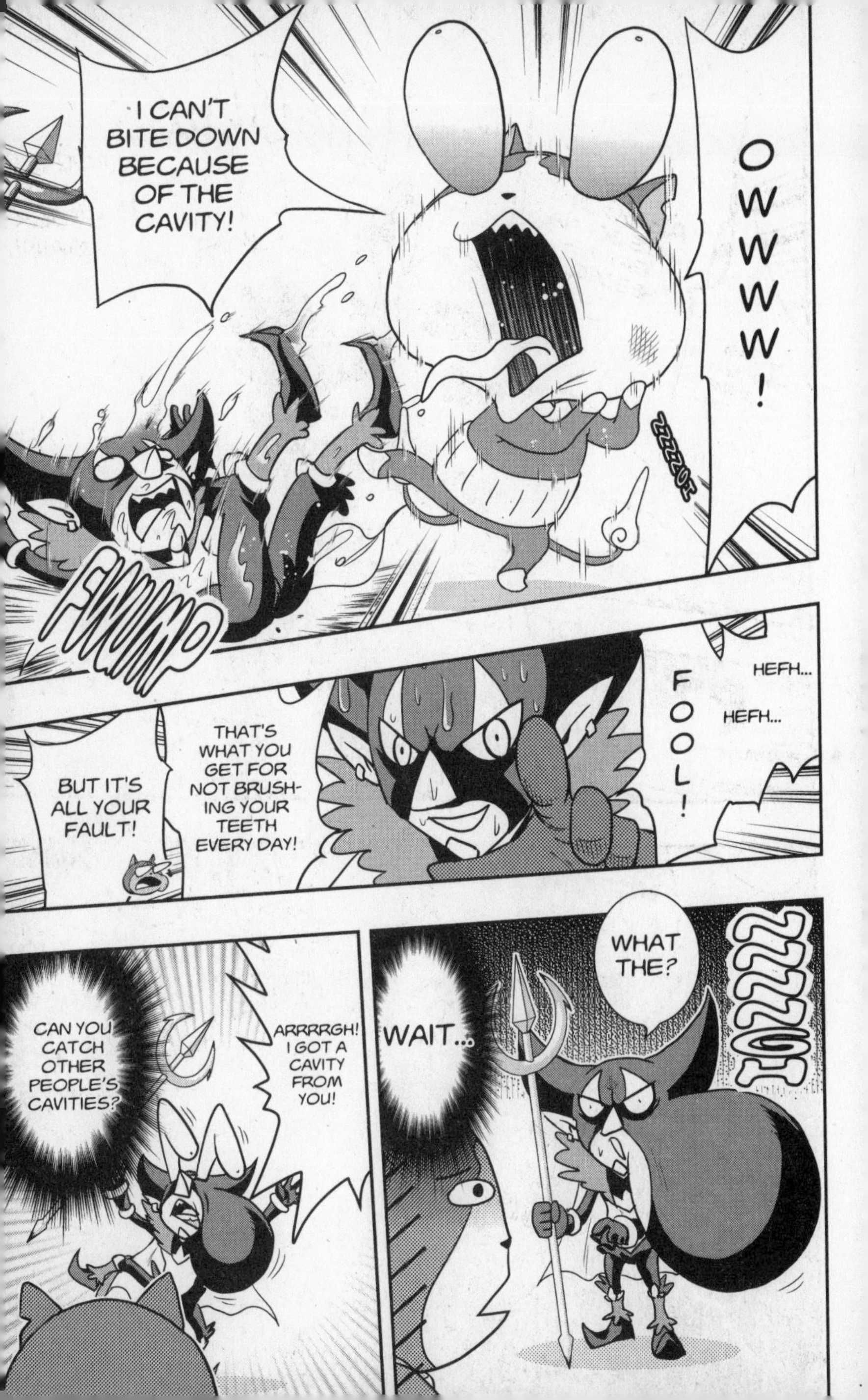
OWWWW!
I CAN'T BITE DOWN BECAUSE OF THE CAVITY!
ZZZZOT
FWUMP
HEFH... HEFH...
FOOL!
THAT'S WHAT YOU GET FOR NOT BRUSHING YOUR TEETH EVERY DAY!
BUT IT'S ALL YOUR FAULT!
ZZZZOT
WHAT THE?
WAIT...
ARRRRGH! I GOT A CAVITY FROM YOU!
CAN YOU CATCH OTHER PEOPLE'S CAVITIES?

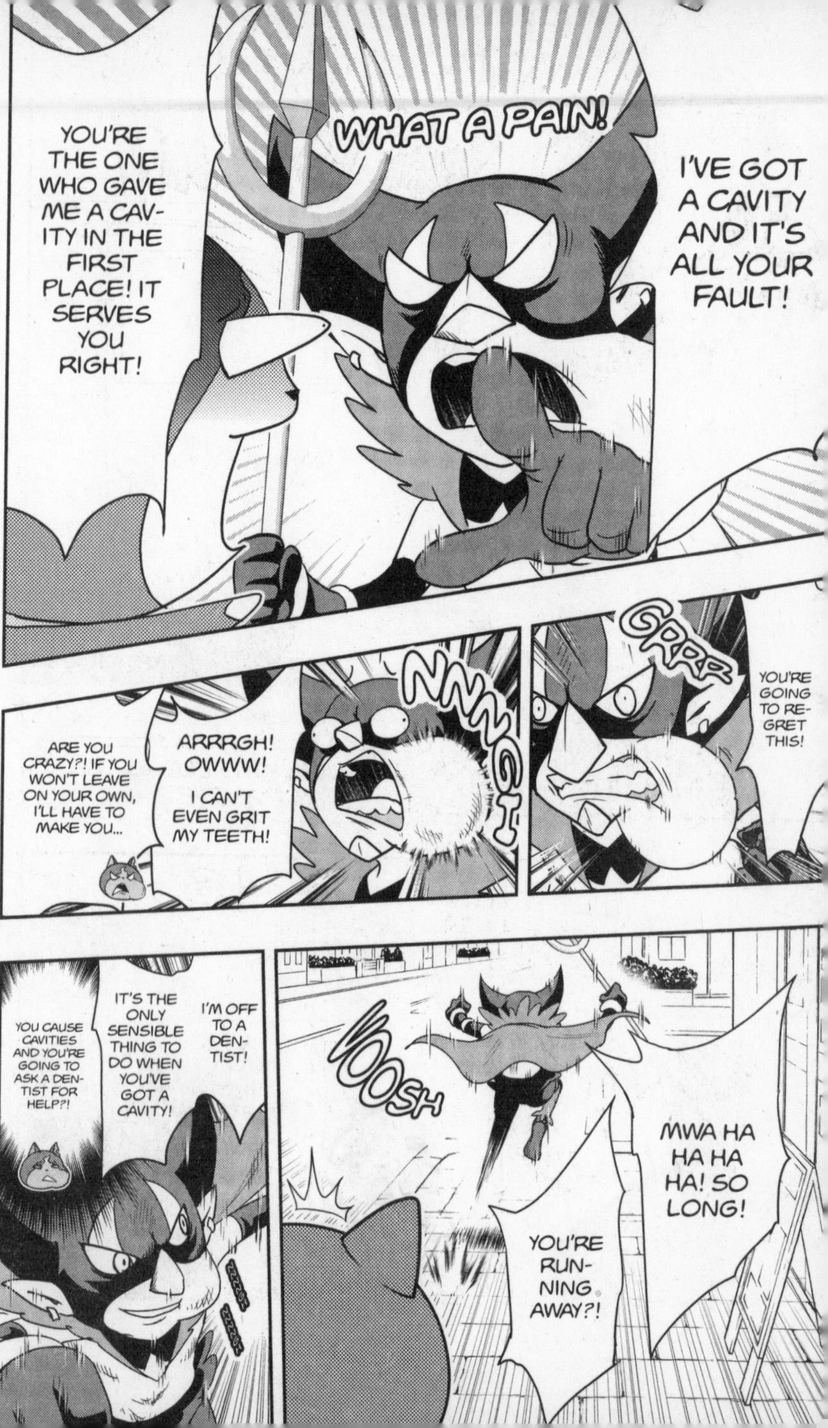
WHAT A PAIN!
I'VE GOT A CAVITY AND IT'S ALL YOUR FAULT!
YOU'RE THE ONE WHO GAVE ME A CAV-ITY IN THE FIRST PLACE! IT SERVES YOU RIGHT!
GRRR
YOU'RE GOING TO RE-GRET THIS!
NNNNG!
ARRRGH! OWWW!
I CAN'T EVEN GRIT MY TEETH!
ARE YOU CRAZY?! IF YOU WON'T LEAVE ON YOUR OWN, I'LL HAVE TO MAKE YOU...
WOOSH
MWA HA HA HA HA! SO LONG!
YOU'RE RUN-NING AWAY?!
I'M OFF TO A DEN-TIST!
IT'S THE ONLY SENSIBLE THING TO DO WHEN YOU'VE GOT A CAVITY!
YOU CAUSE CAVITIES AND YOU'RE GOING TO ASK A DEN-TIST FOR HELP?!

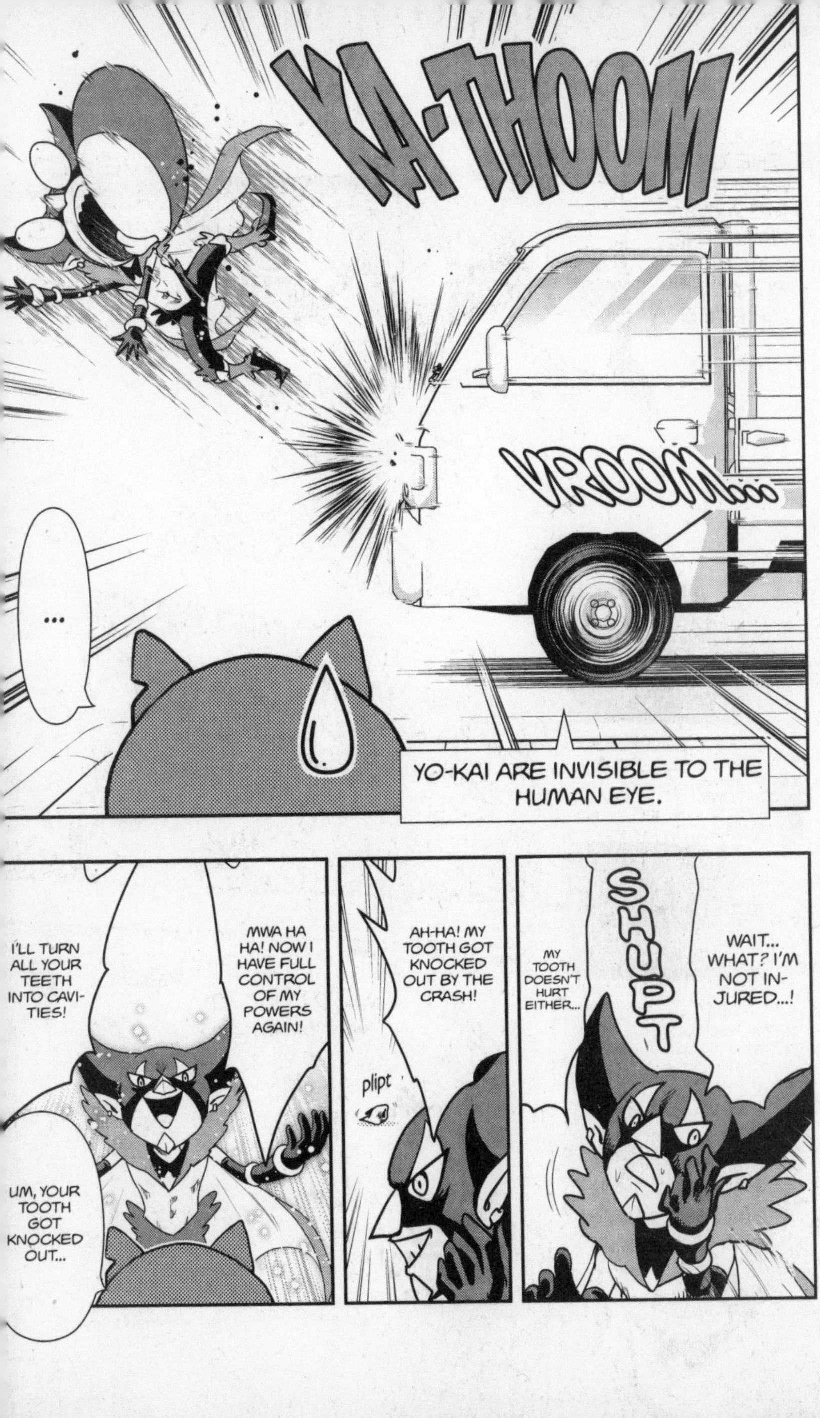
KA-THOOM
VROOM...
...
YO-KAI ARE INVISIBLE TO THE HUMAN EYE.
SHUPT
WAIT... WHAT? I'M NOT INJURED...!
MY TOOTH DOESN'T HURT EITHER...
AH-HA! MY TOOTH GOT KNOCKED OUT BY THE CRASH!
plipt
MWA HA HA! NOW I HAVE FULL CONTROL OF MY POWERS AGAIN!
I'LL TURN ALL YOUR TEETH INTO CAVITIES!
UM, YOUR TOOTH GOT KNOCKED OUT...

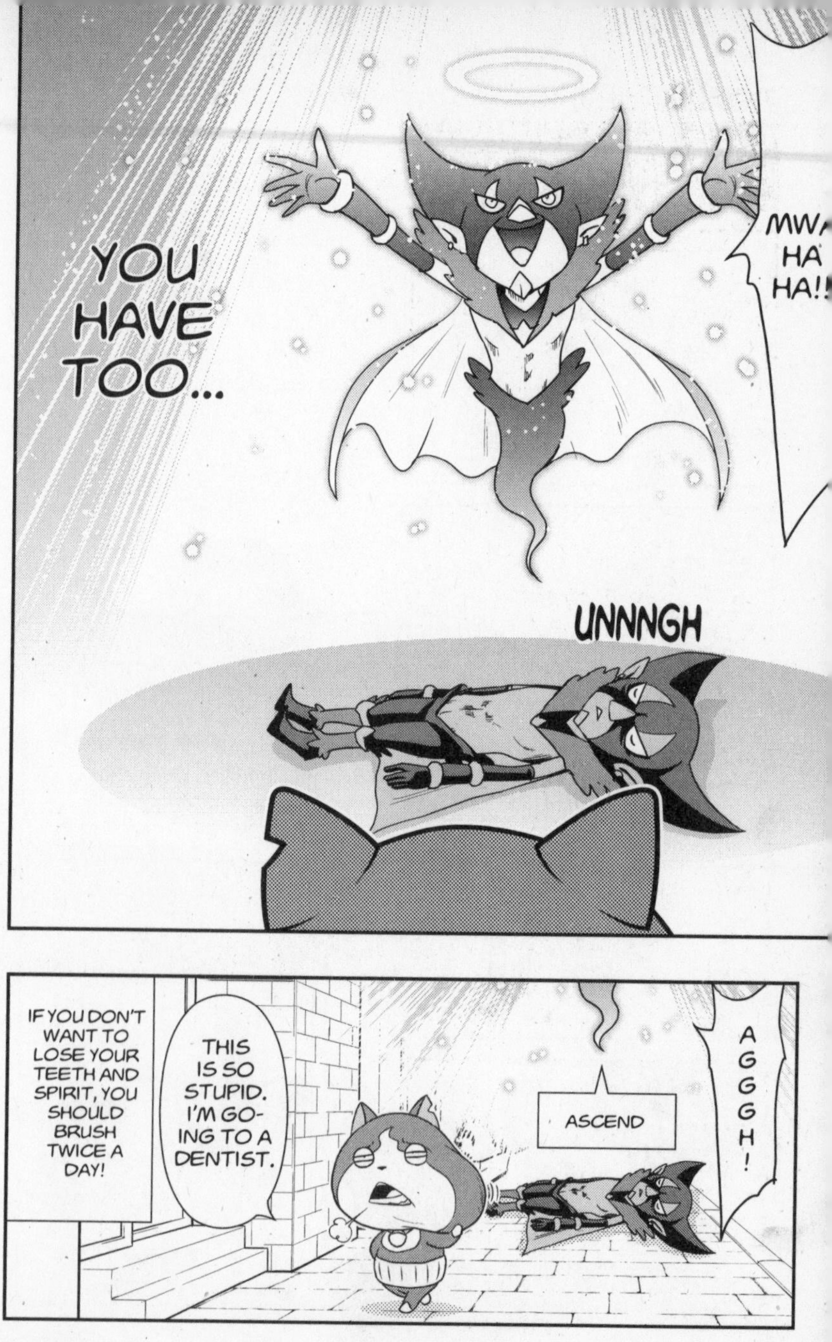
MWA HA HA!!
YOU HAVE TOO...
UNNNGH
AGGGH!
ASCEND
THIS IS SO STUPID. I'M GO-ING TO A DENTIST.
IF YOU DON'T WANT TO LOSE YOUR TEETH AND SPIRIT, YOU SHOULD BRUSH TWICE A DAY!

DENTAL TREATMENT

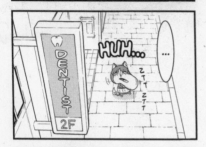

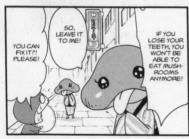

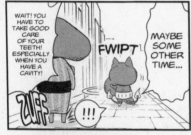

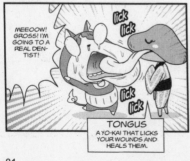

...
HUH...
ZTT ZTT
DENTIST 2F
MAYBE SOME OTHER TIME...
FWIPT
WAIT! YOU HAVE TO TAKE GOOD CARE OF YOUR TEETH! ESPECIALLY WHEN YOU HAVE A CAVITY!
!!!
ZUFF
IF YOU LOSE YOUR TEETH, YOU WON'T BE ABLE TO EAT MUSH-ROOMS ANYMORE!
SO, LEAVE IT TO ME!
YOU CAN FIX IT?! PLEASE!
lick lick
MEEOOW! GROSS! I'M GOING TO A REAL DEN-TIST!
lick lick
TONGUS
A YO-KAI THAT LICKS YOUR WOUNDS AND HEALS THEM.

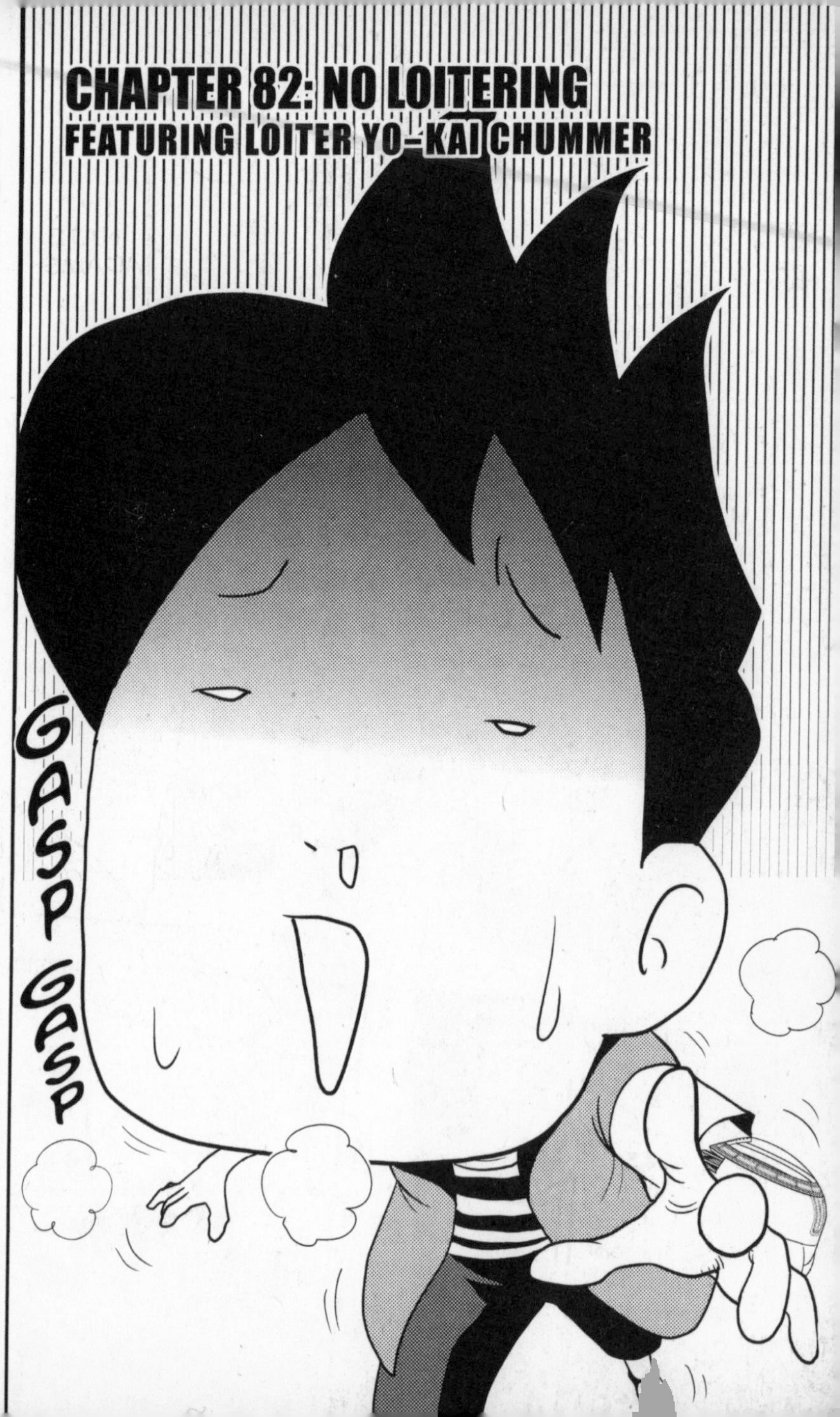
CHAPTER 82: NO LOITERING
FEATURING LOITER YO-KAI CHUMMER
GASP GASP

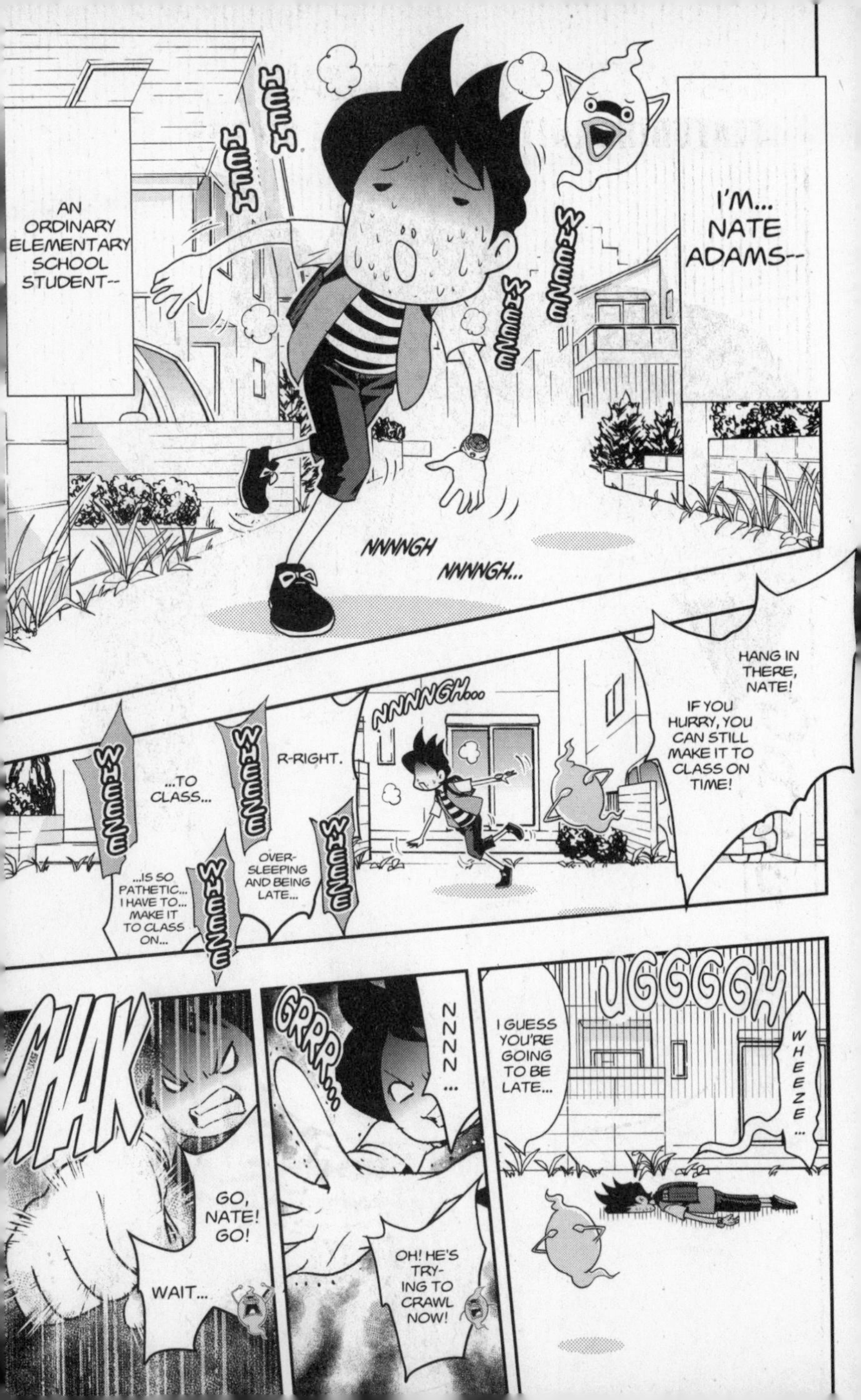
I'M... NATE ADAMS--
WHEEZE
HEH
HEH
WHEEZE
AN ORDINARY ELEMENTARY SCHOOL STUDENT--
NNNNGH
NNNNGH...
HANG IN THERE, NATE!
IF YOU HURRY, YOU CAN STILL MAKE IT TO CLASS ON TIME!
NNNNGH...
R-RIGHT.
WHEEZE
OVER-SLEEPING AND BEING LATE...
WHEEZE
...TO CLASS...
WHEEZE
...IS SO PATHETIC... I HAVE TO... MAKE IT TO CLASS ON...
WHEEZE
UGGGGH
WHEEZE...
I GUESS YOU'RE GOING TO BE LATE...
GRRR...
NNNN...
OH! HE'S TRY-ING TO CRAWL NOW!
CHAK
GO, NATE! GO!
WAIT...

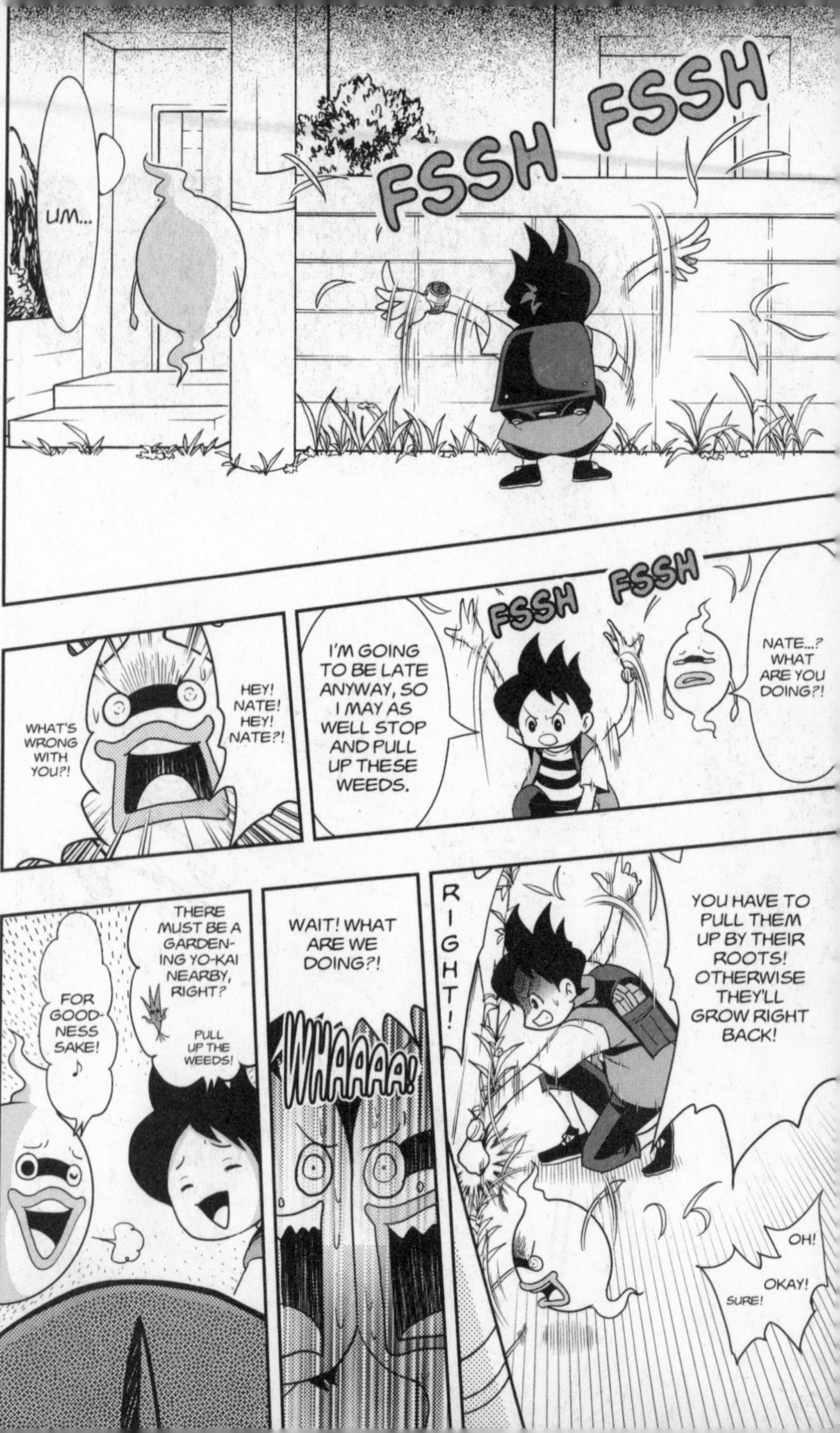
FSSH FSSH
UM...
FSSH FSSH
NATE...? WHAT ARE YOU DOING?!
I'M GOING TO BE LATE ANYWAY, SO I MAY AS WELL STOP AND PULL UP THESE WEEDS.
HEY! NATE! HEY! NATE?!
WHAT'S WRONG WITH YOU?!
YOU HAVE TO PULL THEM UP BY THEIR ROOTS! OTHERWISE THEY'LL GROW RIGHT BACK!
RIGHT!
OH!
OKAY!
SURE!
WAIT! WHAT ARE WE DOING?!
WHAAAAA!
THERE MUST BE A GARDEN-ING YO-KAI NEARBY, RIGHT?
PULL UP THE WEEDS!
FOR GOOD-NESS SAKE! ♪

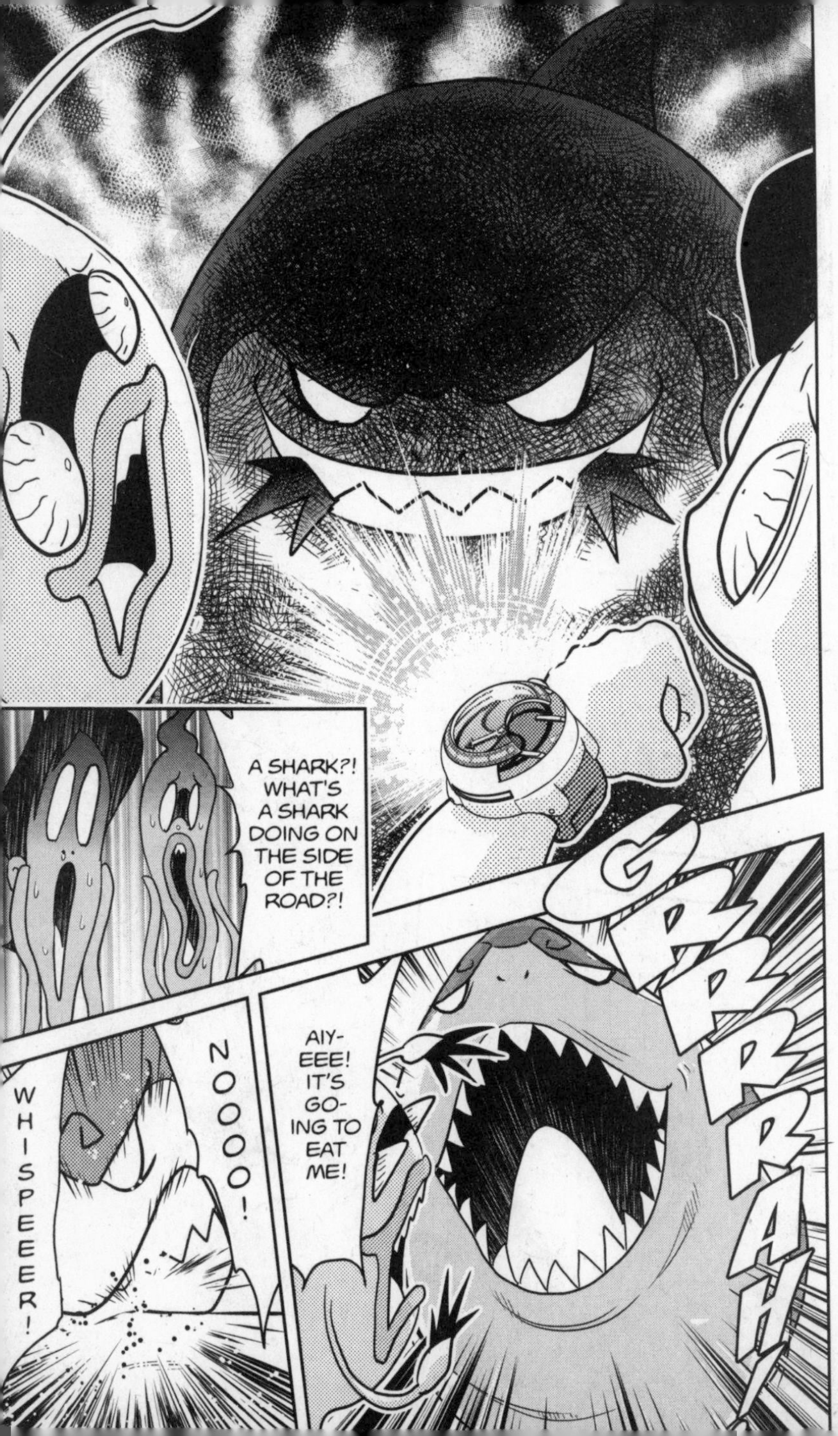
A SHARK?! WHAT'S A SHARK DOING ON THE SIDE OF THE ROAD?!
GRRRRAH!
AIY-EEE! IT'S GO-ING TO EAT ME!
NOOOO!
WHISPEEER!

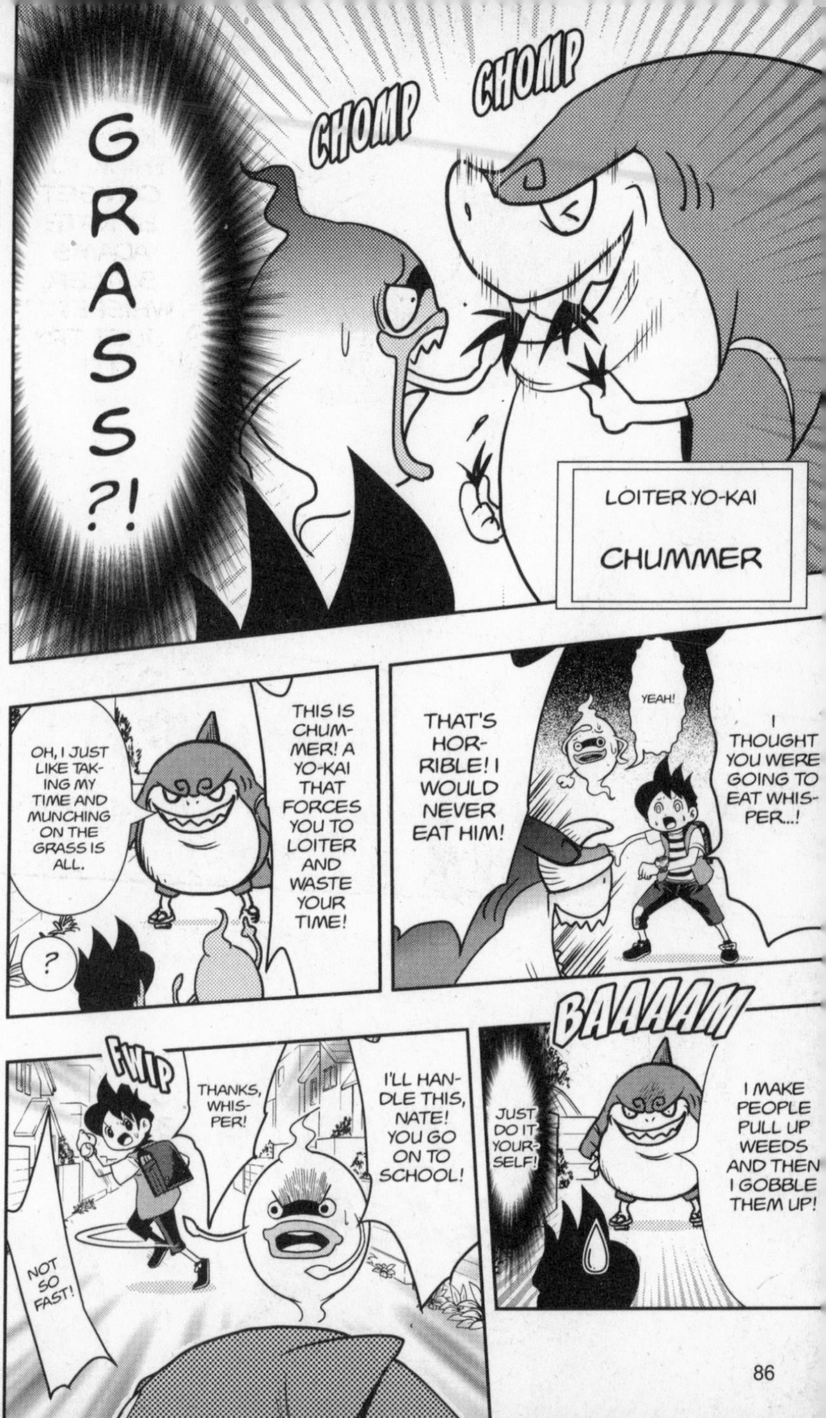
CHOMP
CHOMP
GRASS?!
LOITER YO-KAI
CHUMMER
I THOUGHT YOU WERE GOING TO EAT WHISPER...!
YEAH!
THAT'S HORRIBLE! I WOULD NEVER EAT HIM!
THIS IS CHUMMER! A YO-KAI THAT FORCES YOU TO LOITER AND WASTE YOUR TIME!
OH, I JUST LIKE TAKING MY TIME AND MUNCHING ON THE GRASS IS ALL.
?
BAAAAM
I MAKE PEOPLE PULL UP WEEDS AND THEN I GOBBLE THEM UP!
JUST DO IT YOURSELF!
I'LL HANDLE THIS, NATE! YOU GO ON TO SCHOOL!
THANKS, WHISPER!
FWIP
NOT SO FAST!

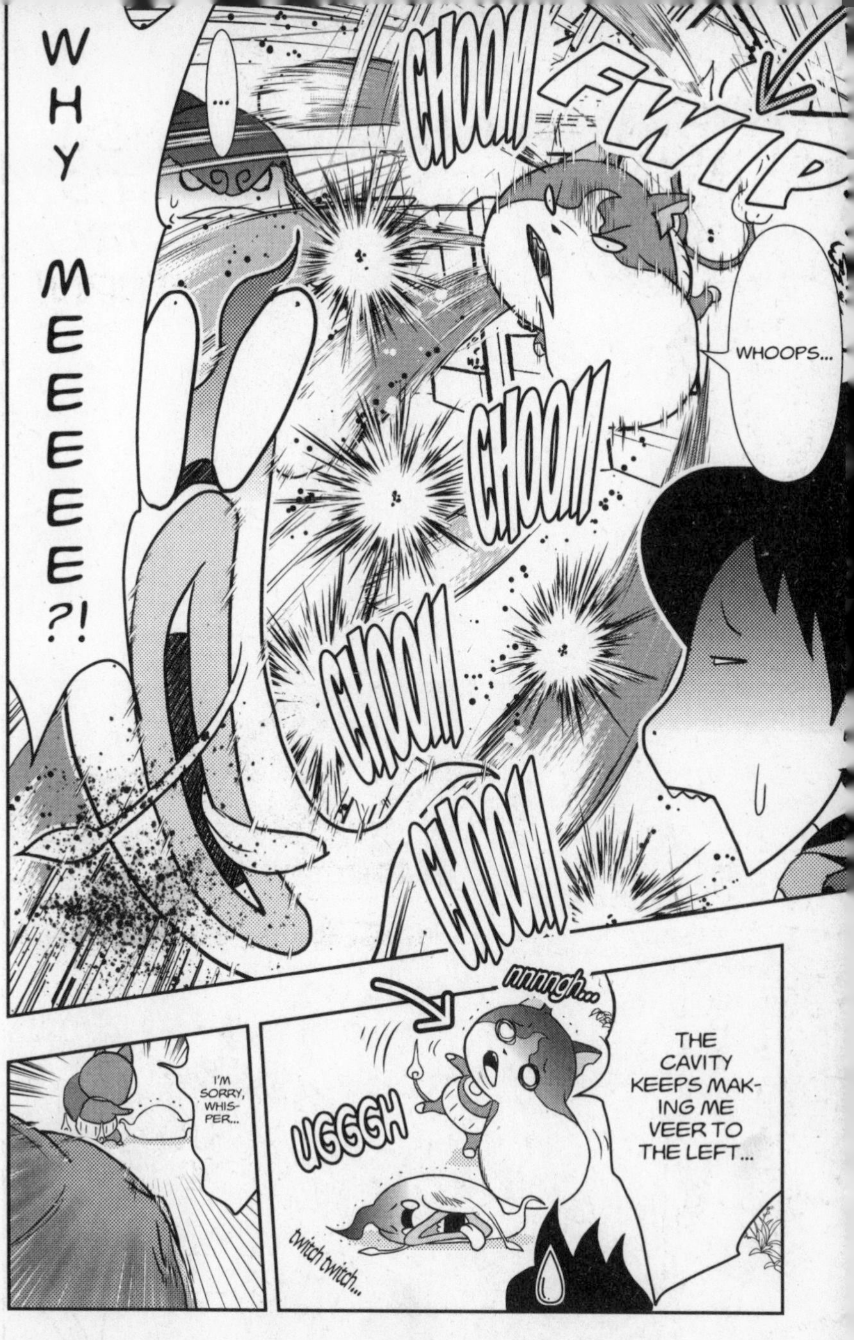
FWIP
CHOOM
WHOOPS...
...
CHOOM
CHOOM
CHOOM
CHOOM
WHY MEEEEEE?!
nnnngh...
THE CAVITY KEEPS MAKING ME VEER TO THE LEFT...
UGGGH
twitch twitch...
I'M SORRY, WHISPER...

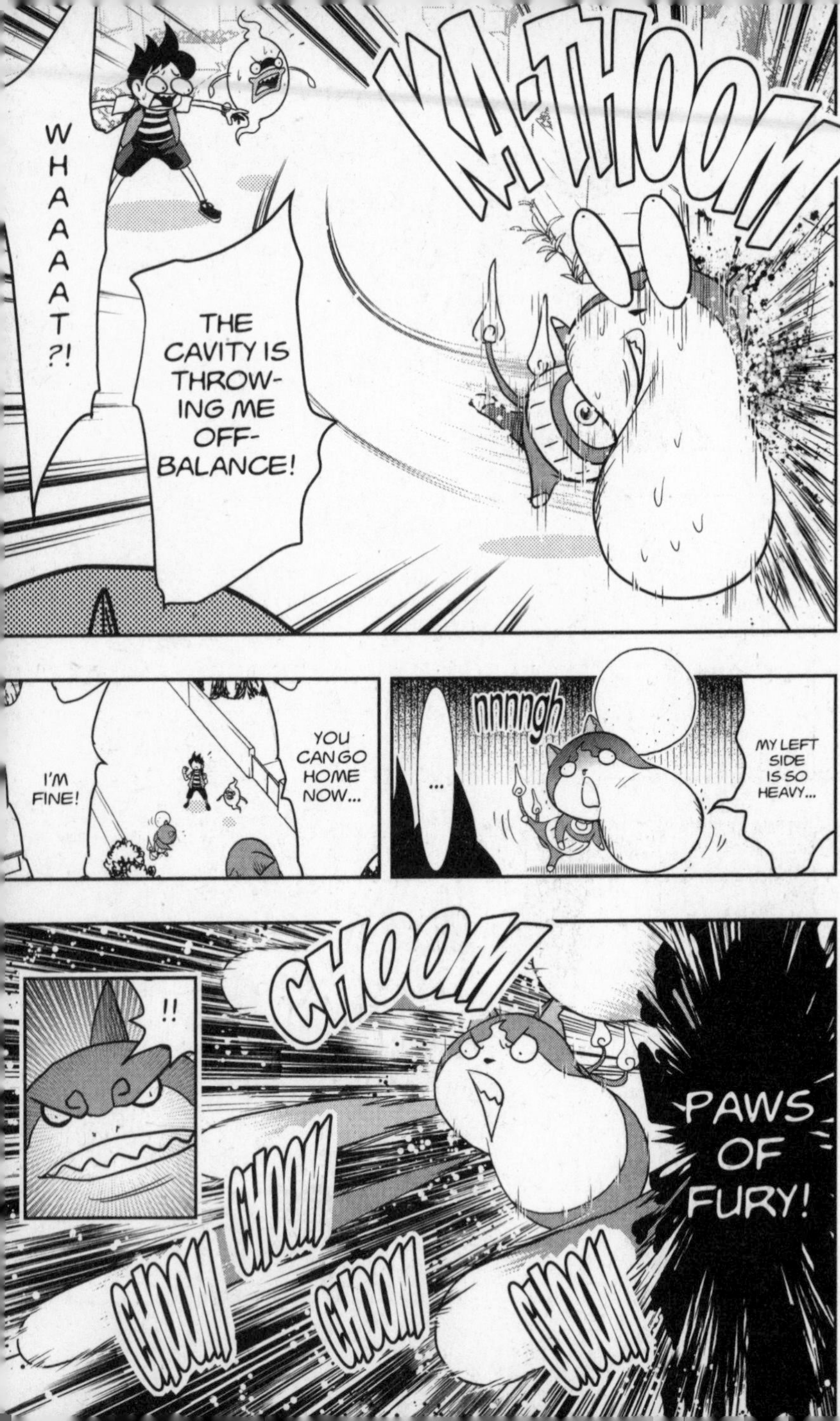

KA-THOOM
THE CAVITY IS THROWING ME OFF-BALANCE!
WHAAAAAT?!
nnnngh
MY LEFT SIDE IS SO HEAVY...
...
YOU CAN GO HOME NOW...
I'M FINE!
CHOOM
PAWS OF FURY!
!!
CHOOM
CHOOM
CHOOM
CHOOM
CHOOM

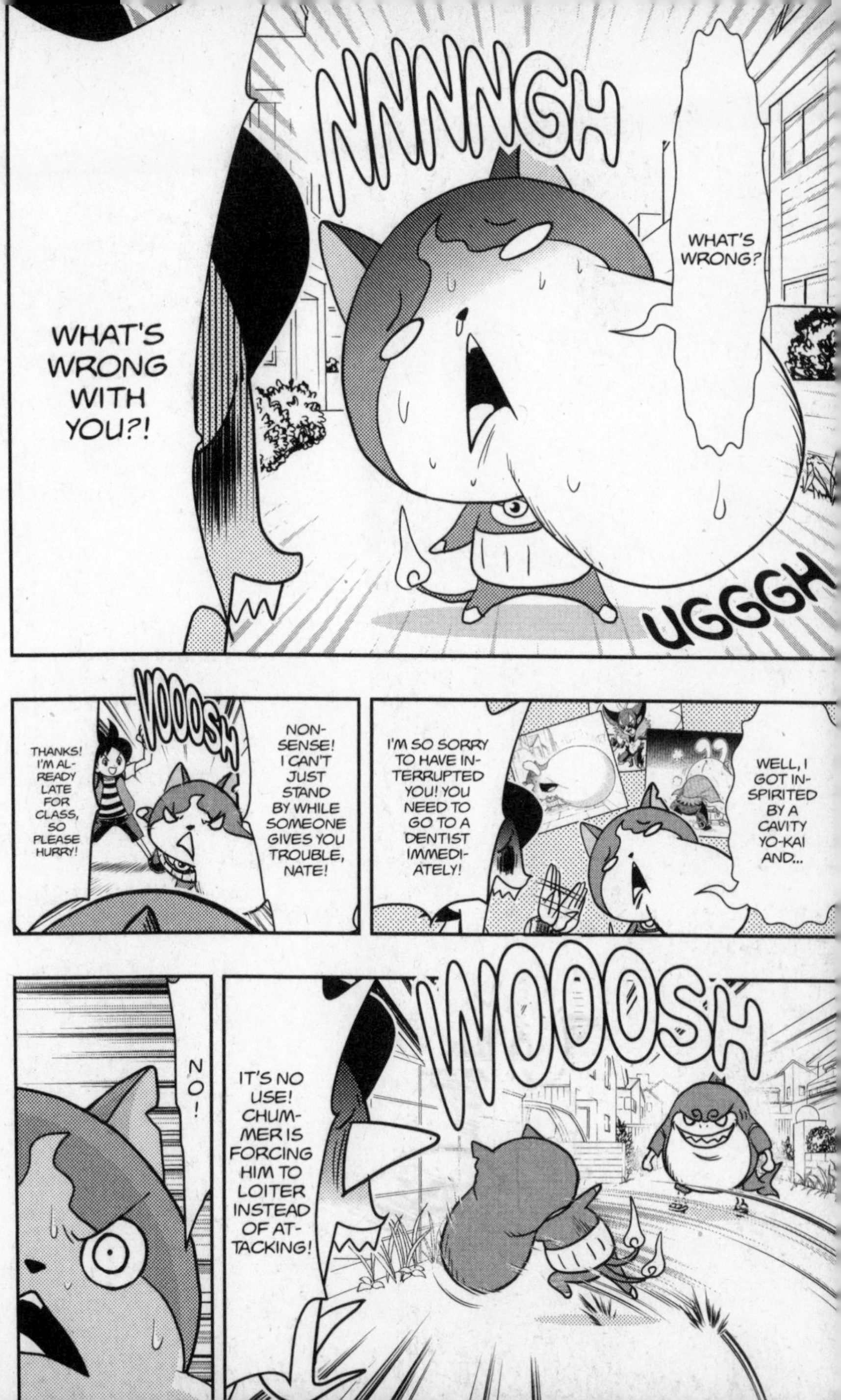
WHAT'S WRONG?
NNNNGH
WHAT'S WRONG WITH YOU?!
UGGGH
WELL, I GOT INSPIRITED BY A CAVITY YO-KAI AND...
I'M SO SORRY TO HAVE INTERRUPTED YOU! YOU NEED TO GO TO A DENTIST IMMEDIATELY!
NONSENSE! I CAN'T JUST STAND BY WHILE SOMEONE GIVES YOU TROUBLE, NATE!
WOOOSH
THANKS! I'M ALREADY LATE FOR CLASS, SO PLEASE HURRY!
WOOOSH
IT'S NO USE! CHUMMER IS FORCING HIM TO LOITER INSTEAD OF ATTACKING!
NO!

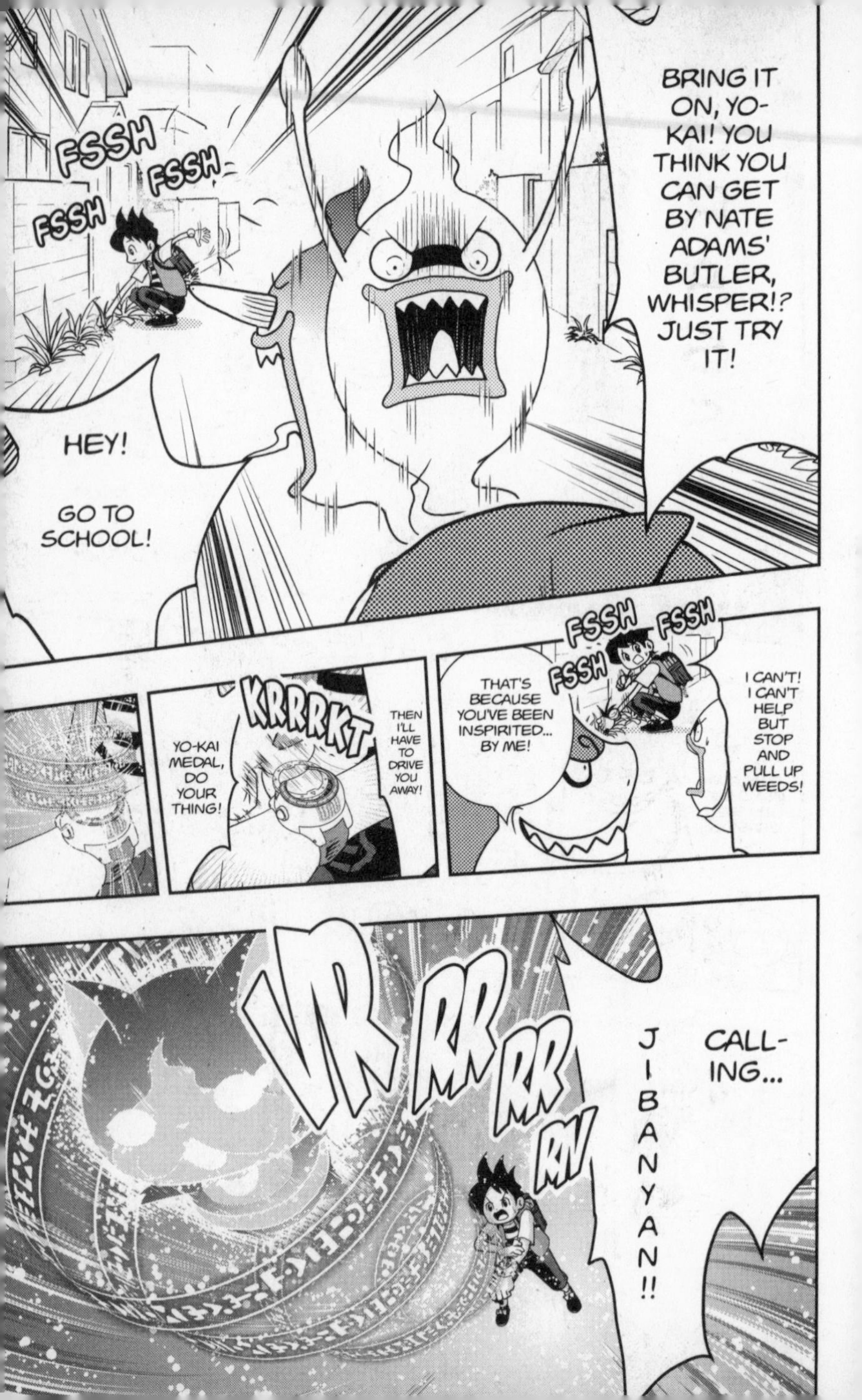
BRING IT ON, YO-KAI! YOU THINK YOU CAN GET BY NATE ADAMS' BUTLER, WHISPER!? JUST TRY IT!
FSSH
FSSH
FSSH
HEY!
GO TO SCHOOL!
I CAN'T! I CAN'T HELP BUT STOP AND PULL UP WEEDS!
FSSH
FSSH
FSSH
THAT'S BECAUSE YOU'VE BEEN INSPIRITED... BY ME!
THEN I'LL HAVE TO DRIVE YOU AWAY!
KRRRKT
YO-KAI MEDAL, DO YOUR THING!
CALLING...
JIBANYAN!!
VRRRRRRV

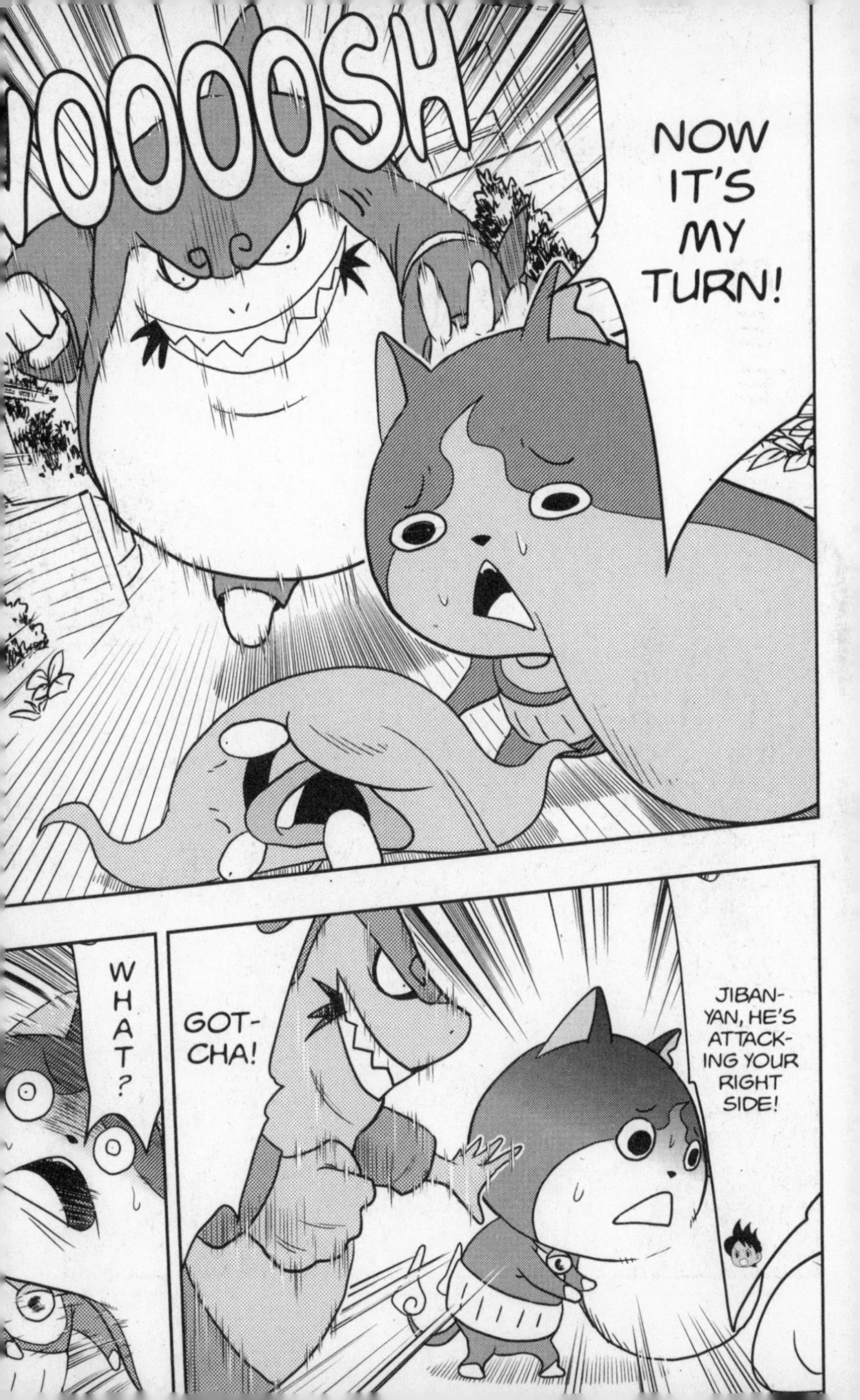
WOOOOSH
NOW IT'S MY TURN!
JIBAN-YAN, HE'S ATTACK-ING YOUR RIGHT SIDE!
GOT-CHA!
WHAT?

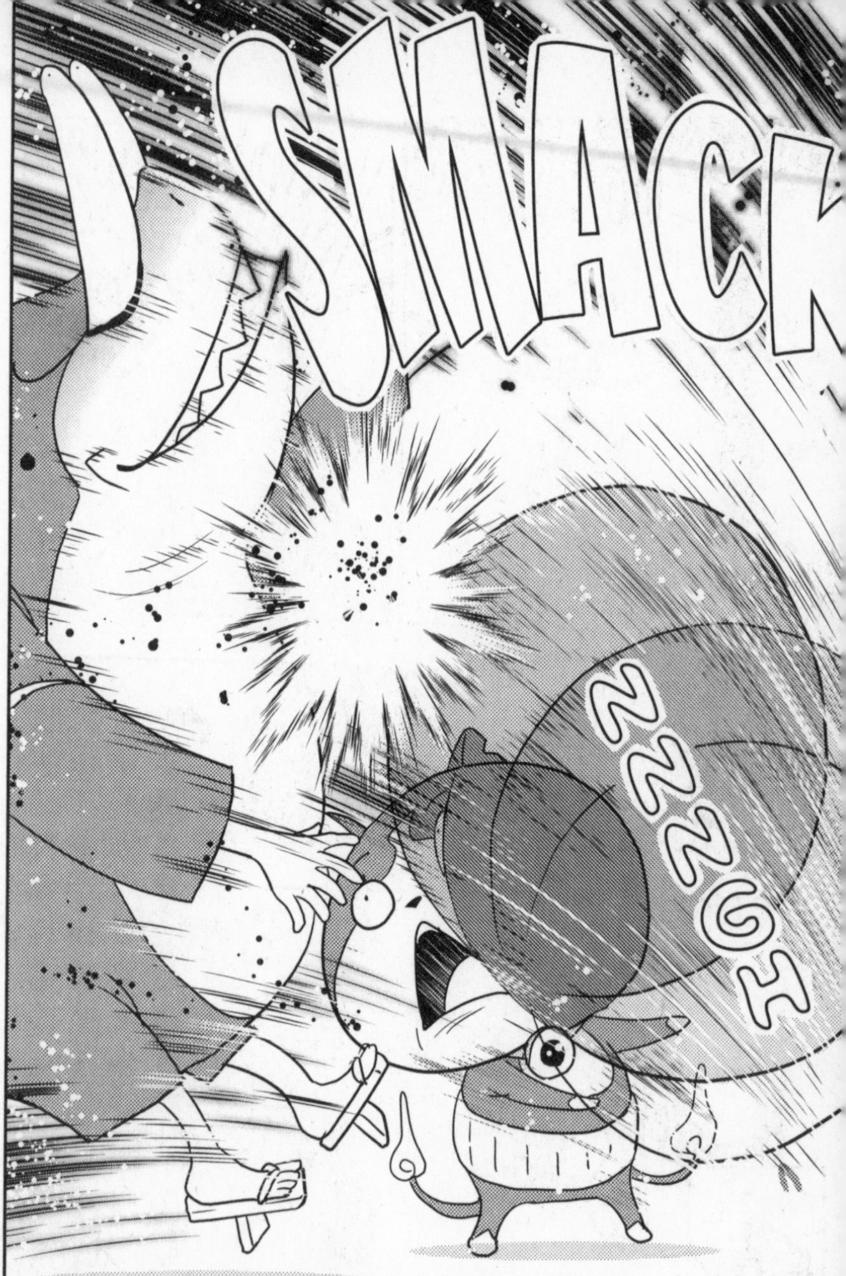
SMACK
NNNGH

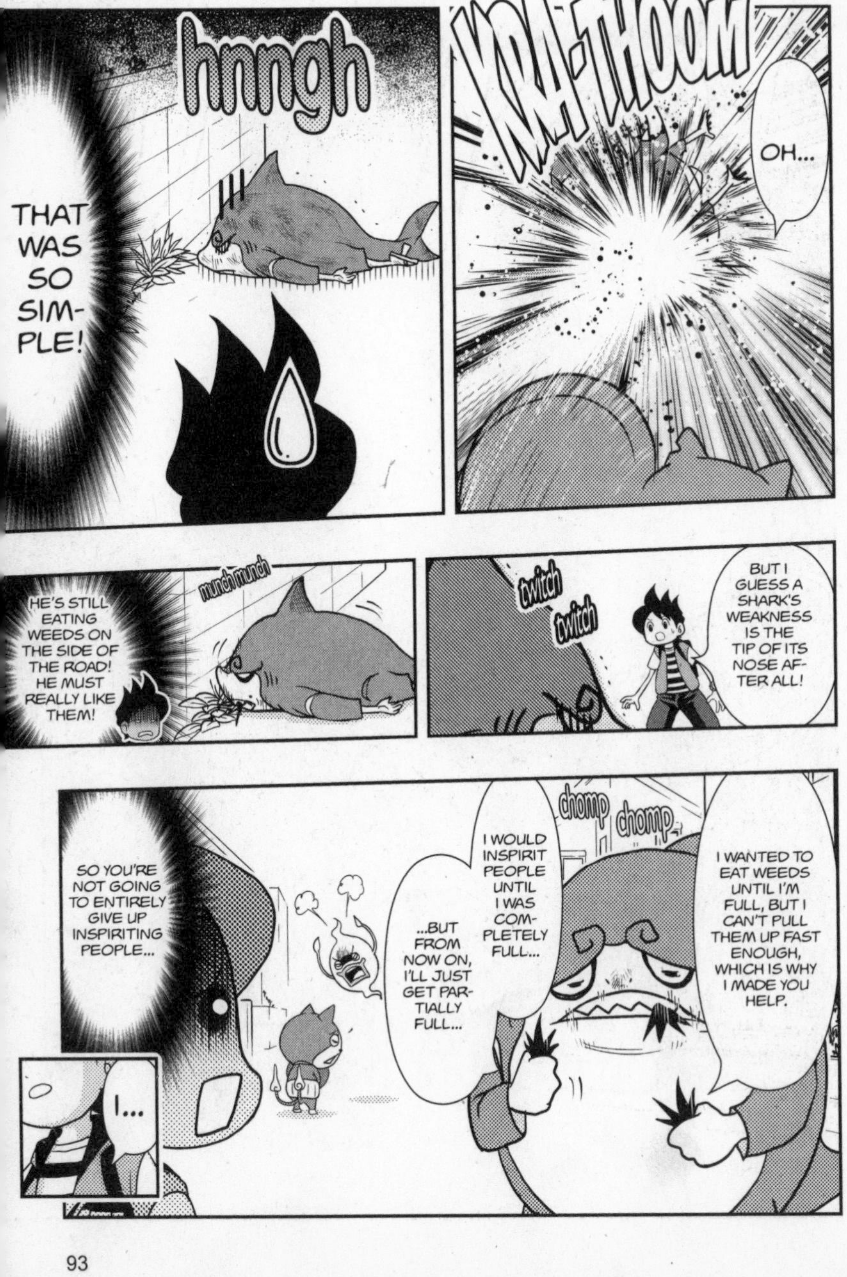
KRA-THOOM
OH...
hnngh
THAT WAS SO SIMPLE!
twitch twitch
BUT I GUESS A SHARK'S WEAKNESS IS THE TIP OF ITS NOSE AFTER ALL!
munch munch
HE'S STILL EATING WEEDS ON THE SIDE OF THE ROAD! HE MUST REALLY LIKE THEM!
chomp chomp
I WANTED TO EAT WEEDS UNTIL I'M FULL, BUT I CAN'T PULL THEM UP FAST ENOUGH, WHICH IS WHY I MADE YOU HELP.
I WOULD INSPIRIT PEOPLE UNTIL I WAS COMPLETELY FULL...
...BUT FROM NOW ON, I'LL JUST GET PARTIALLY FULL...
SO YOU'RE NOT GOING TO ENTIRELY GIVE UP INSPIRITING PEOPLE...
I...

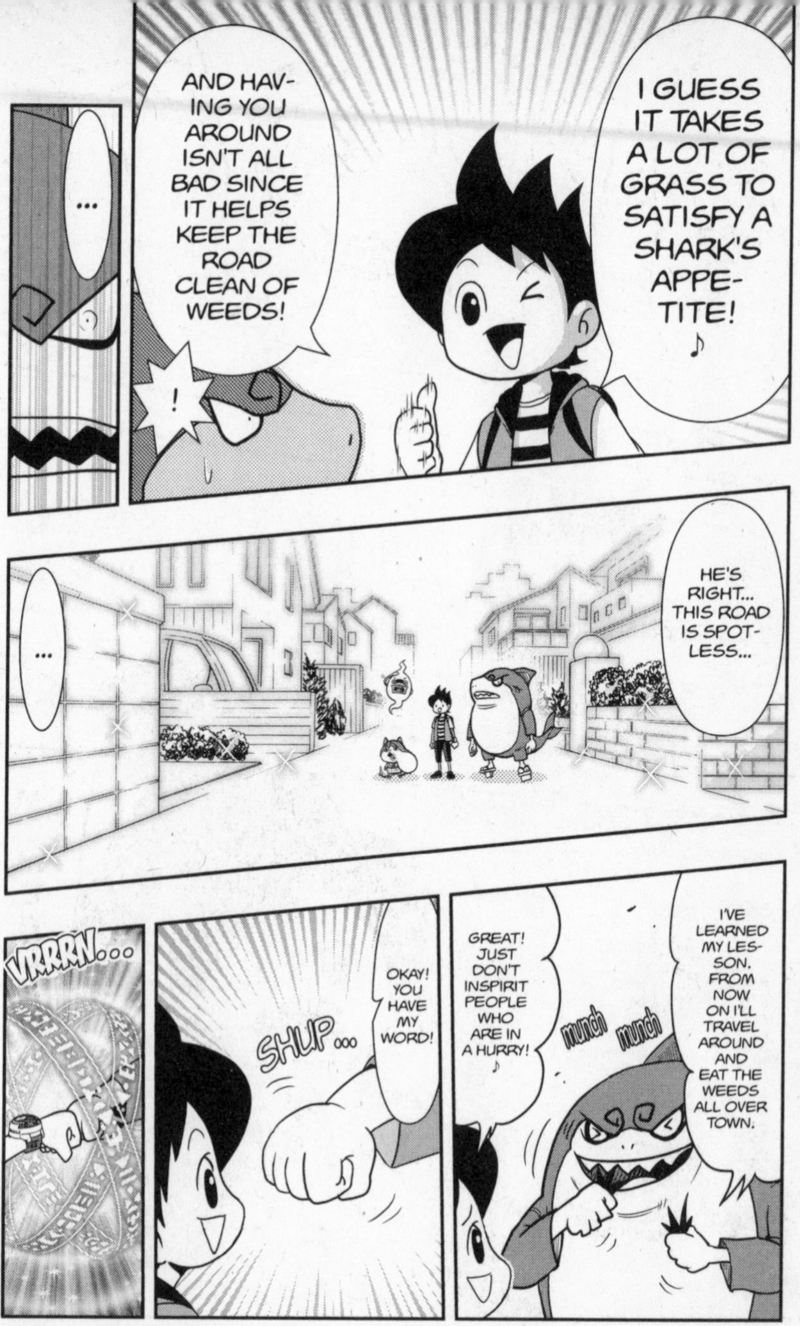

I GUESS IT TAKES A LOT OF GRASS TO SATISFY A SHARK'S APPE-TITE! ♪
AND HAV-ING YOU AROUND ISN'T ALL BAD SINCE IT HELPS KEEP THE ROAD CLEAN OF WEEDS!
!
...
HE'S RIGHT... THIS ROAD IS SPOT-LESS...
...
I'VE LEARNED MY LES-SON. FROM NOW ON I'LL TRAVEL AROUND AND EAT THE WEEDS ALL OVER TOWN.
munch munch
GREAT! JUST DON'T INSPIRIT PEOPLE WHO ARE IN A HURRY! ♪
OKAY! YOU HAVE MY WORD!
SHUP...
VRRRN...

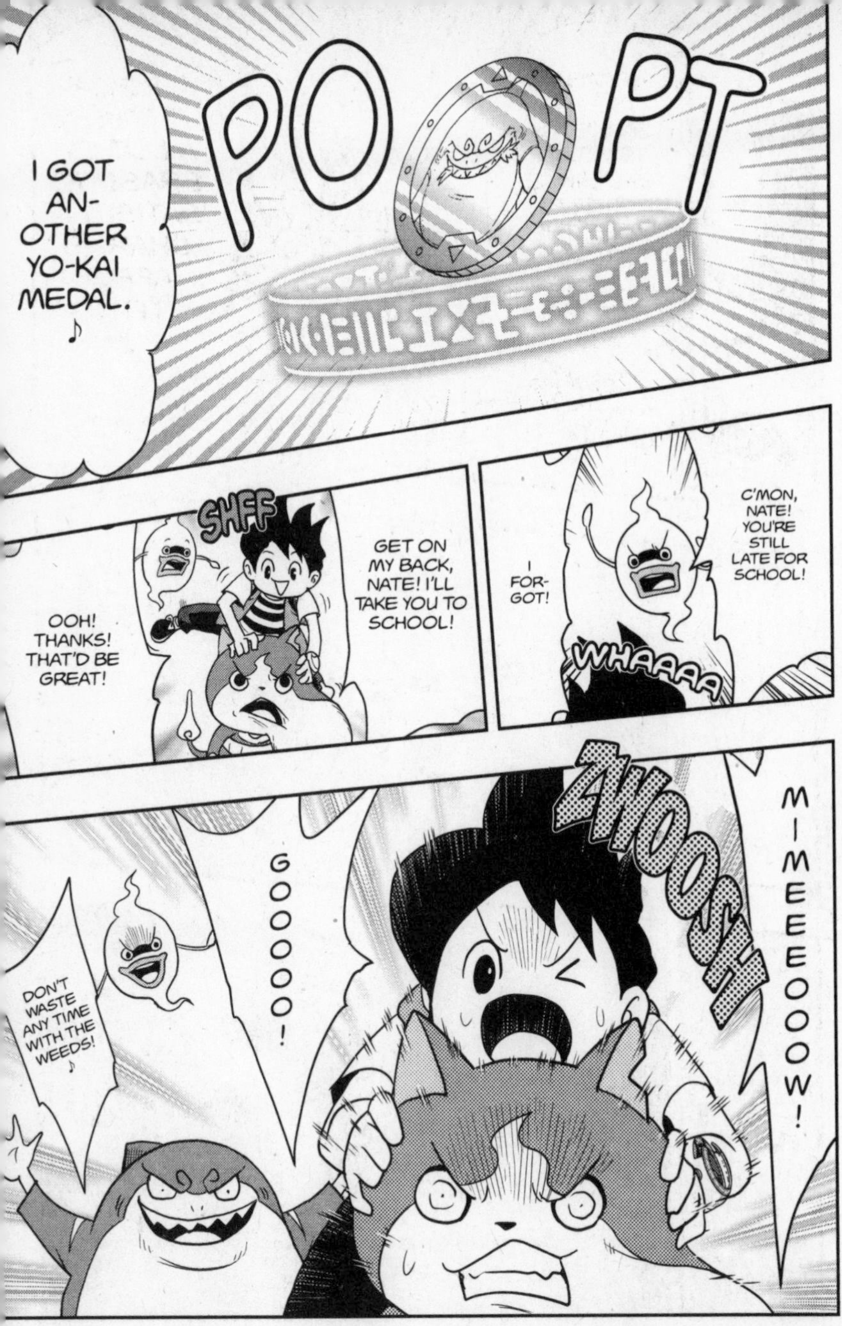
POOPT
I GOT AN-OTHER YO-KAI MEDAL. ♪
C'MON, NATE! YOU'RE STILL LATE FOR SCHOOL!
I FOR-GOT!
WHAAAAA
SHFF
GET ON MY BACK, NATE! I'LL TAKE YOU TO SCHOOL!
OOH! THANKS! THAT'D BE GREAT!
ZWOOSH
MIMEEEOOOOW!
GOOOOOO!
DON'T WASTE ANY TIME WITH THE WEEDS! ♪

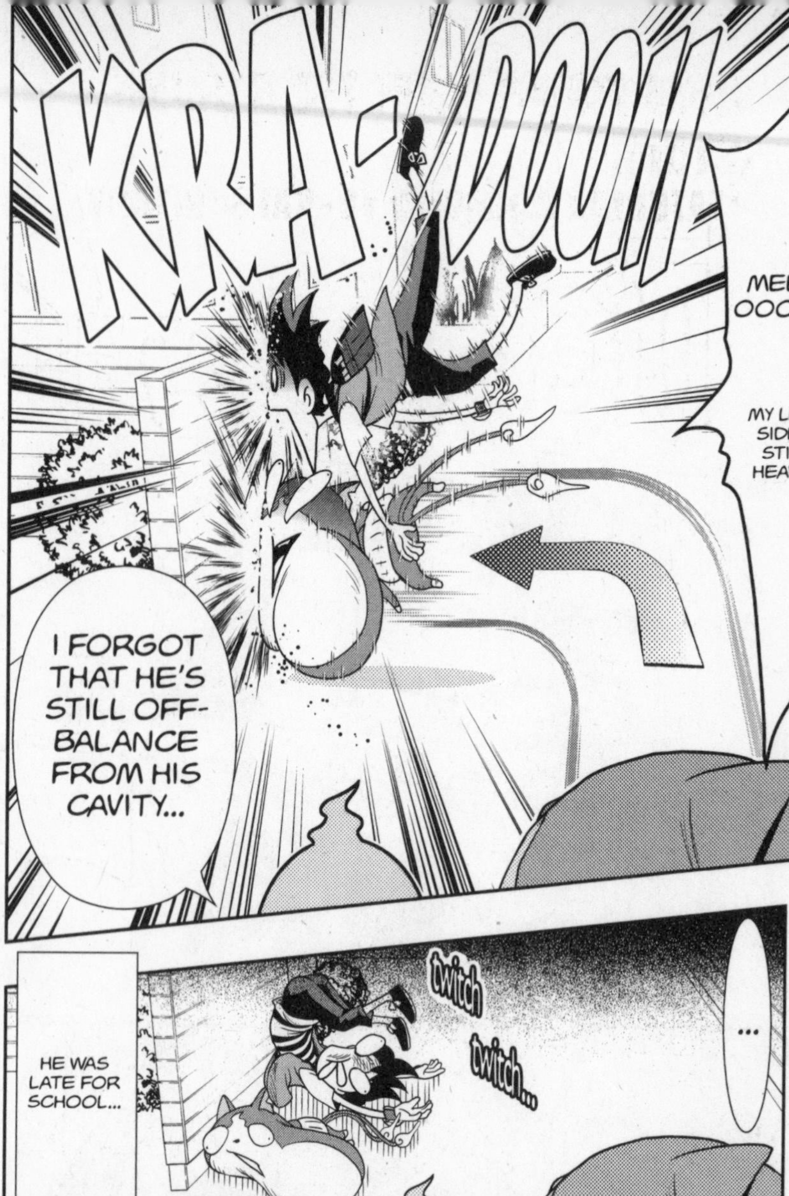
KRA-DOOOM
MEE-OOOW!
MY LEFT SIDE'S STILL HEAVY...
I FORGOT THAT HE'S STILL OFF-BALANCE FROM HIS CAVITY...
...
twitch
twitch...
HE WAS LATE FOR SCHOOL...

NATE ADAMS'S CURRENT NUMBER OF YO-KAI FRIENDS: 56

CHAPTER 83: MAKE THE ITCHING STOP!!
FEATURING MOSQUITO YO-KAI SCRITCHY

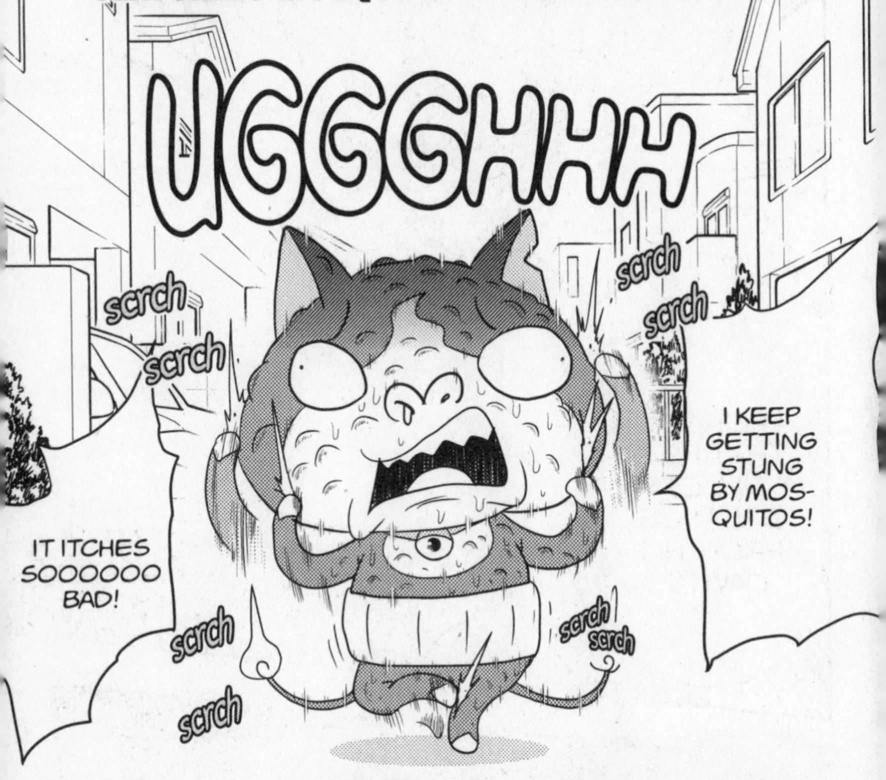
UGGGHHH
scrch
scrch
scrch
scrch
I KEEP GETTING STUNG BY MOS-QUITOS!
IT ITCHES SOOOOOO BAD!
scrch
scrch
scrch
scrch

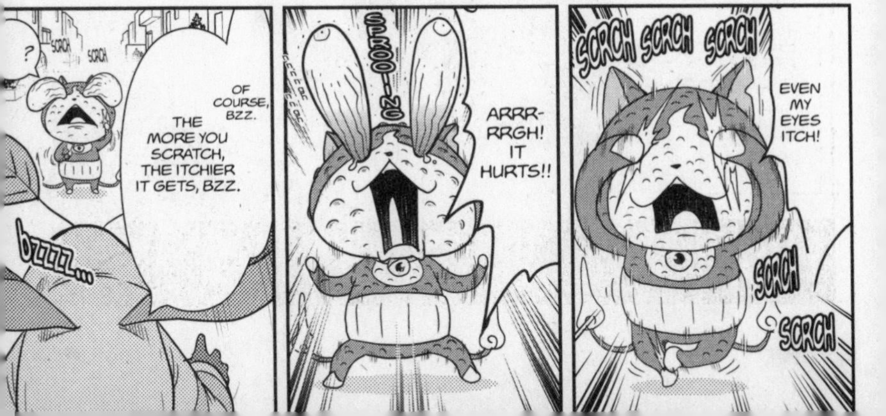
SCRCH SCRCH SCRCH
EVEN MY EYES ITCH!
SCRCH
SCRCH
ARRR-RRGH! IT HURTS!!
SCRCH
SCRCH
?
OF COURSE, BZZ.
THE MORE YOU SCRATCH, THE ITCHIER IT GETS, BZZ.
bzzzz...

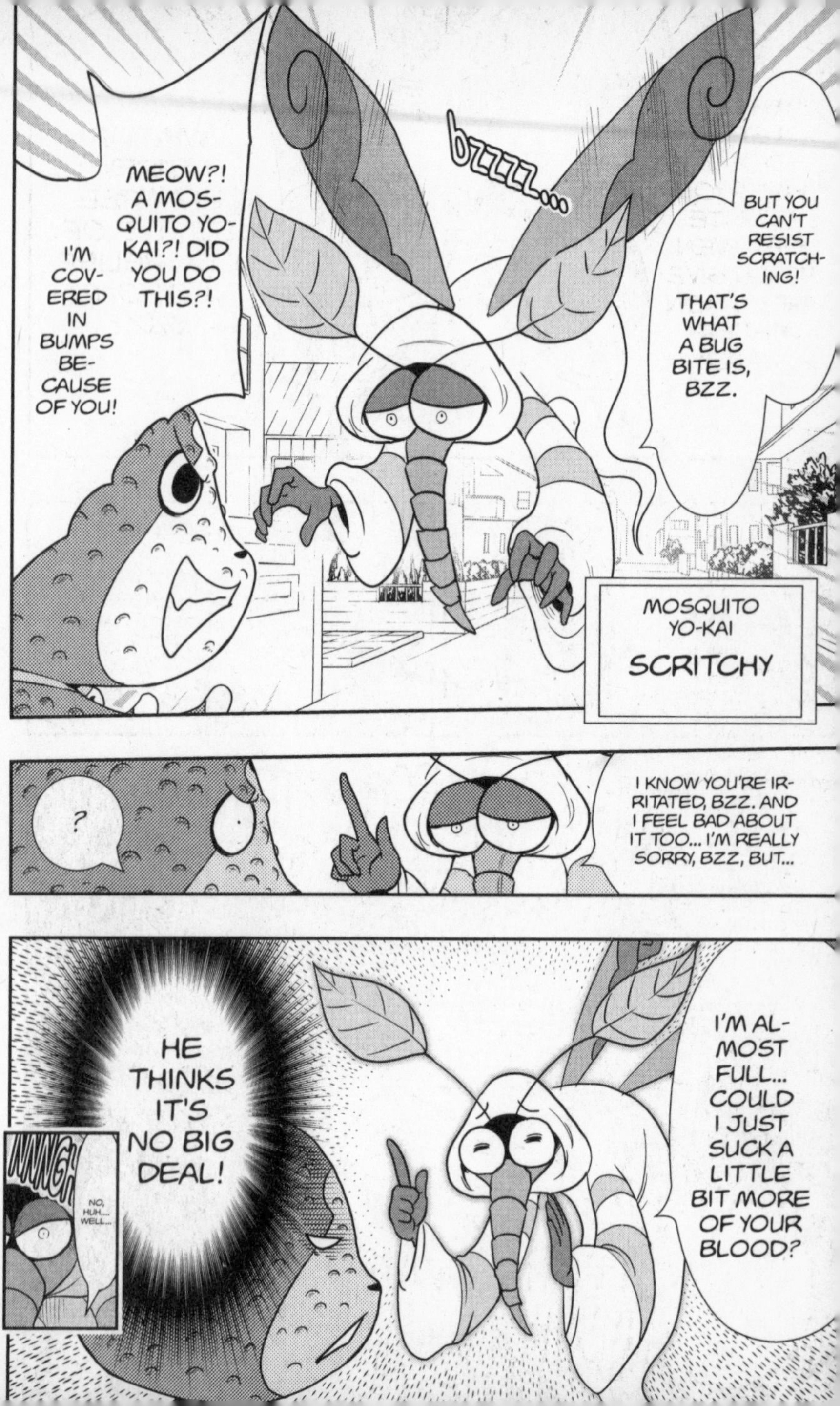
MEOW?! A MOS-QUITO YO-KAI?! DID YOU DO THIS?!
I'M COV-ERED IN BUMPS BE-CAUSE OF YOU!
bzzzzz...
BUT YOU CAN'T RESIST SCRATCH-ING!
THAT'S WHAT A BUG BITE IS, BZZ.
MOSQUITO YO-KAI
SCRITCHY
I KNOW YOU'RE IR-RITATED, BZZ. AND I FEEL BAD ABOUT IT TOO... I'M REALLY SORRY, BZZ, BUT...
?
I'M AL-MOST FULL... COULD I JUST SUCK A LITTLE BIT MORE OF YOUR BLOOD?
HE THINKS IT'S NO BIG DEAL!
NNNGH
NO, HUH... WELL...

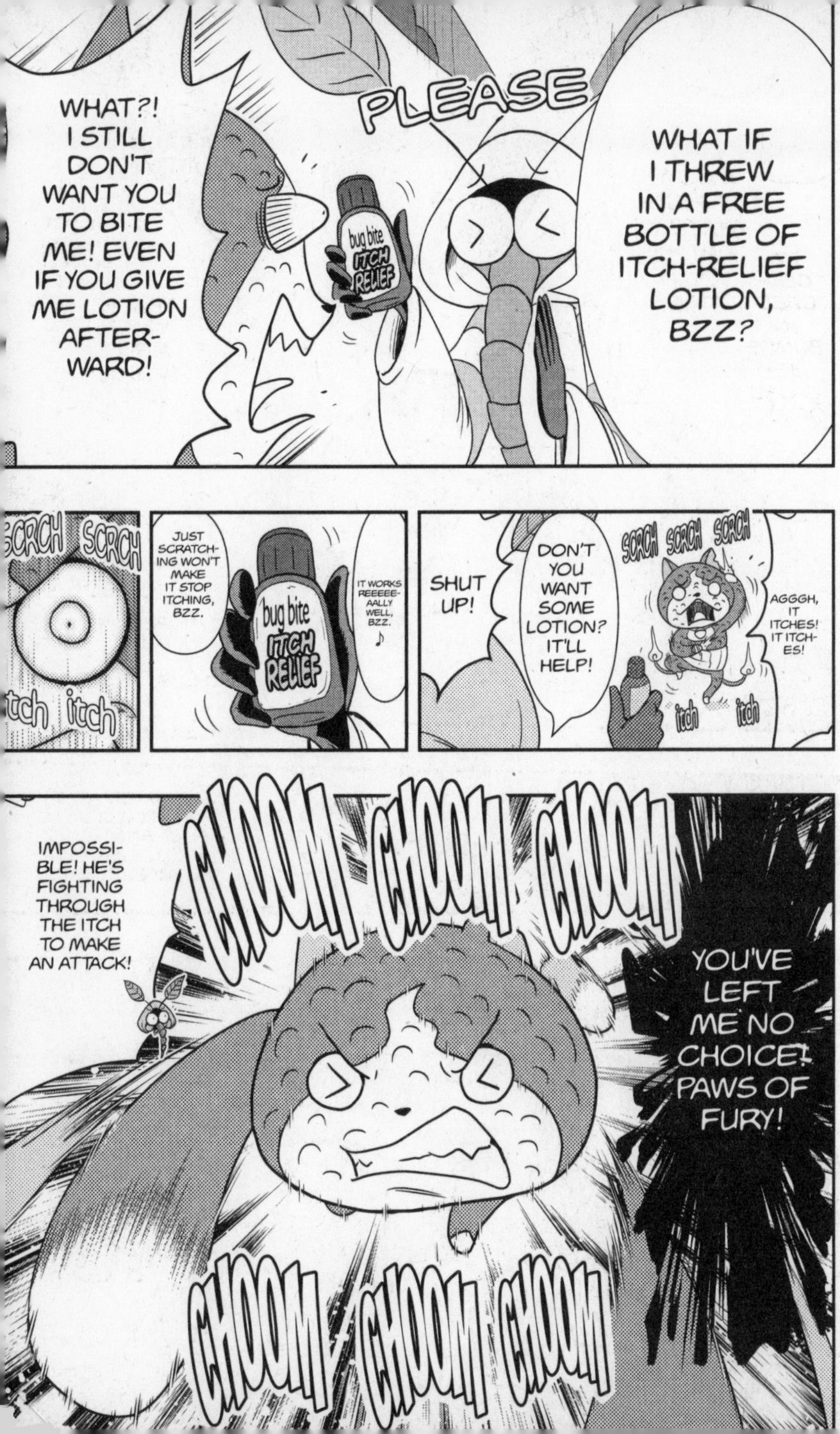
WHAT IF I THREW IN A FREE BOTTLE OF ITCH-RELIEF LOTION, BZZ?
PLEASE
bug bite ITCH RELIEF
WHAT?! I STILL DON'T WANT YOU TO BITE ME! EVEN IF YOU GIVE ME LOTION AFTERWARD!
AGGGH, IT ITCHES! IT ITCHES!
SCRCH SCRCH SCRCH
DON'T YOU WANT SOME LOTION? IT'LL HELP!
SHUT UP!
itch itch
IT WORKS REEEEEAALLY WELL, BZZ. ♪
bug bite ITCH RELIEF
JUST SCRATCHING WON'T MAKE IT STOP ITCHING, BZZ.
SCRCH SCRCH
itch
YOU'VE LEFT ME NO CHOICE! PAWS OF FURY!
CHOOM CHOOM CHOOM
IMPOSSIBLE! HE'S FIGHTING THROUGH THE ITCH TO MAKE AN ATTACK!
CHOOM CHOOM CHOOM

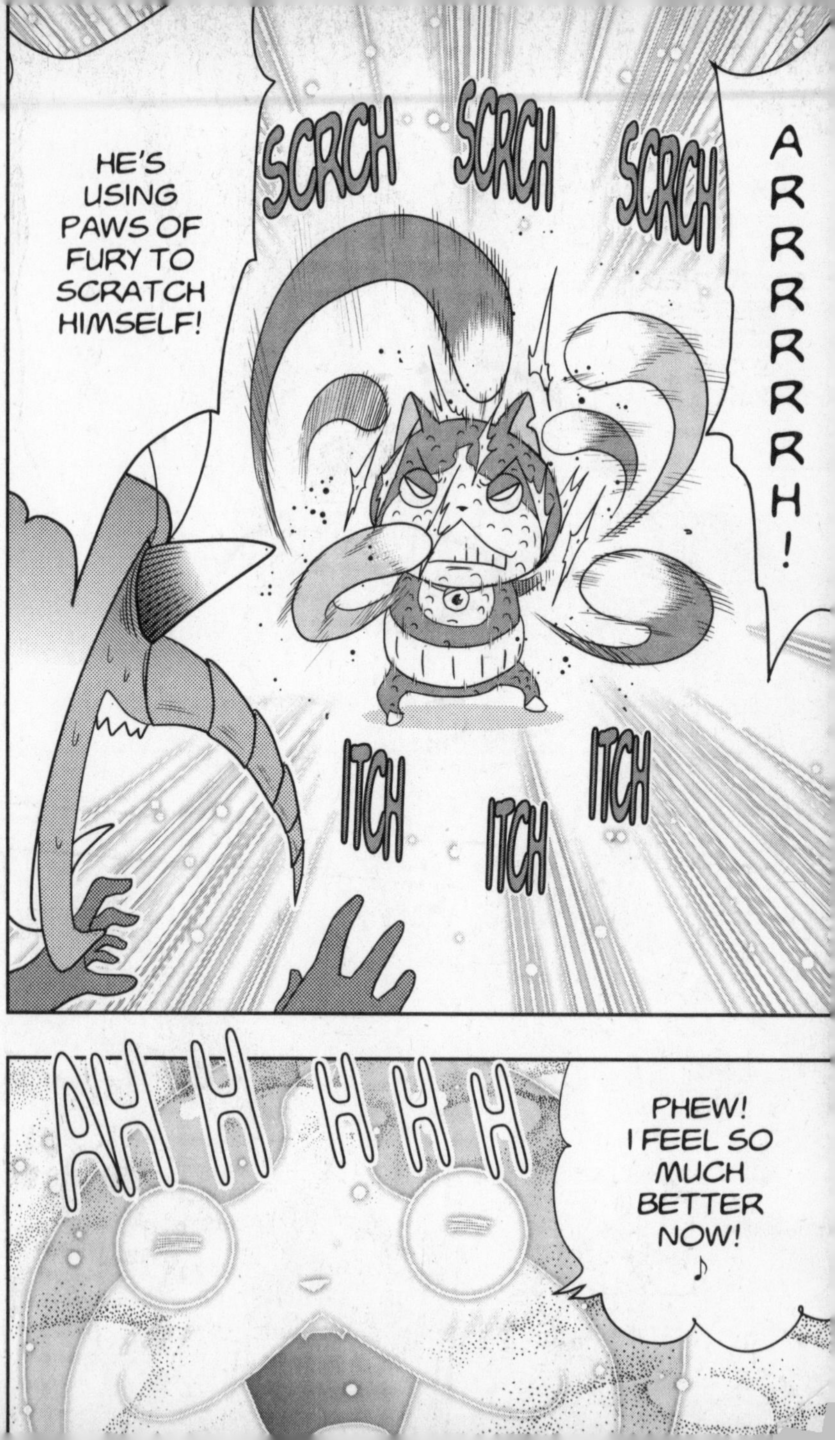
ARRRRRRH!
SCRCH SCRCH SCRCH
ITCH ITCH ITCH
HE'S USING PAWS OF FURY TO SCRATCH HIMSELF!
PHEW! I FEEL SO MUCH BETTER NOW! ♪
AHHHHHH

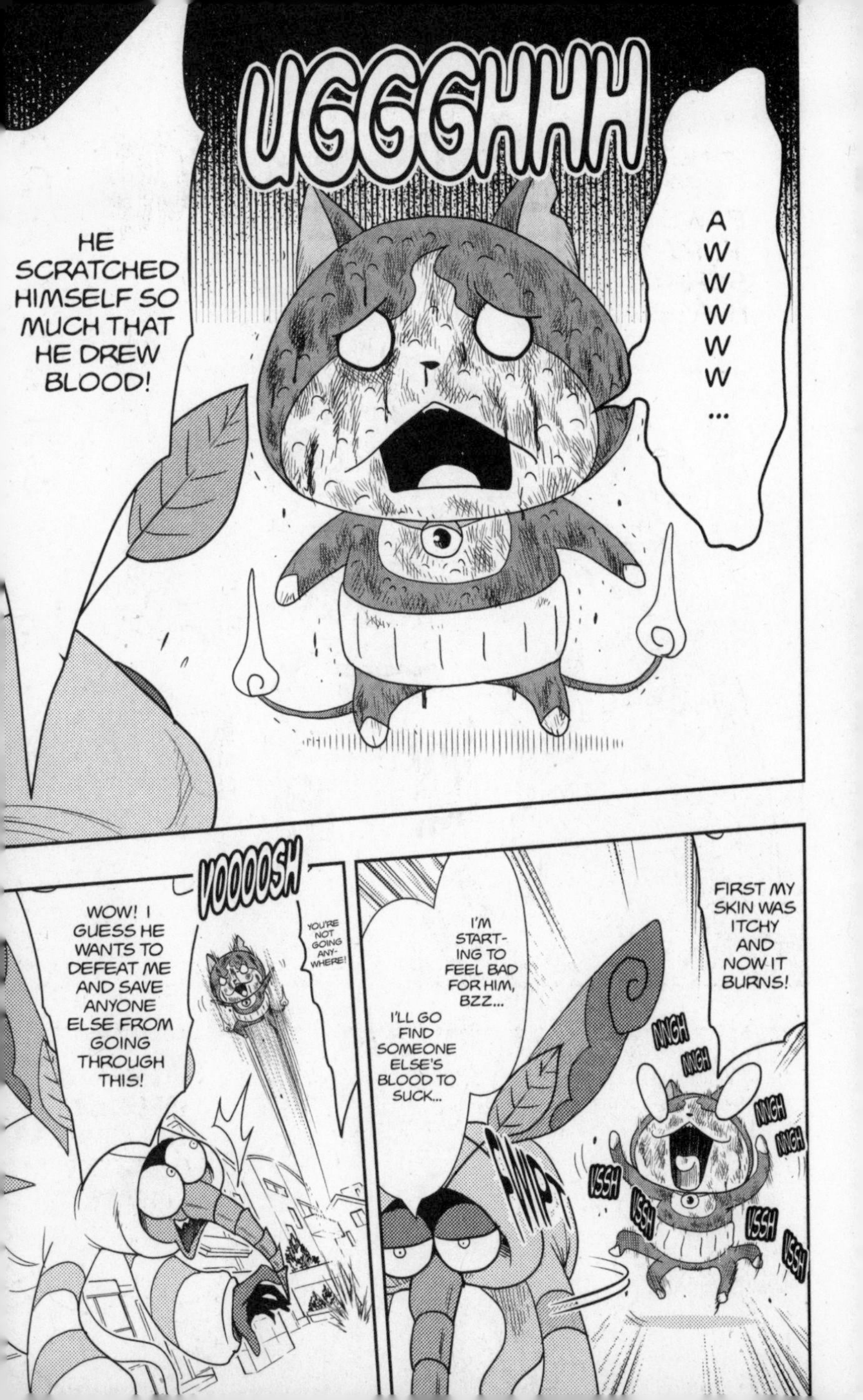
UGGGHHH
AWWWWWW...
HE SCRATCHED HIMSELF SO MUCH THAT HE DREW BLOOD!
FIRST MY SKIN WAS ITCHY AND NOW IT BURNS!
NNGH
NNGH
NNGH
NNGH
ISSH
ISSH
ISSH
ISSH
I'M STARTING TO FEEL BAD FOR HIM, BZZ...
I'LL GO FIND SOMEONE ELSE'S BLOOD TO SUCK...
VOOOOSH
YOU'RE NOT GOING ANYWHERE!
WOW! I GUESS HE WANTS TO DEFEAT ME AND SAVE ANYONE ELSE FROM GOING THROUGH THIS!

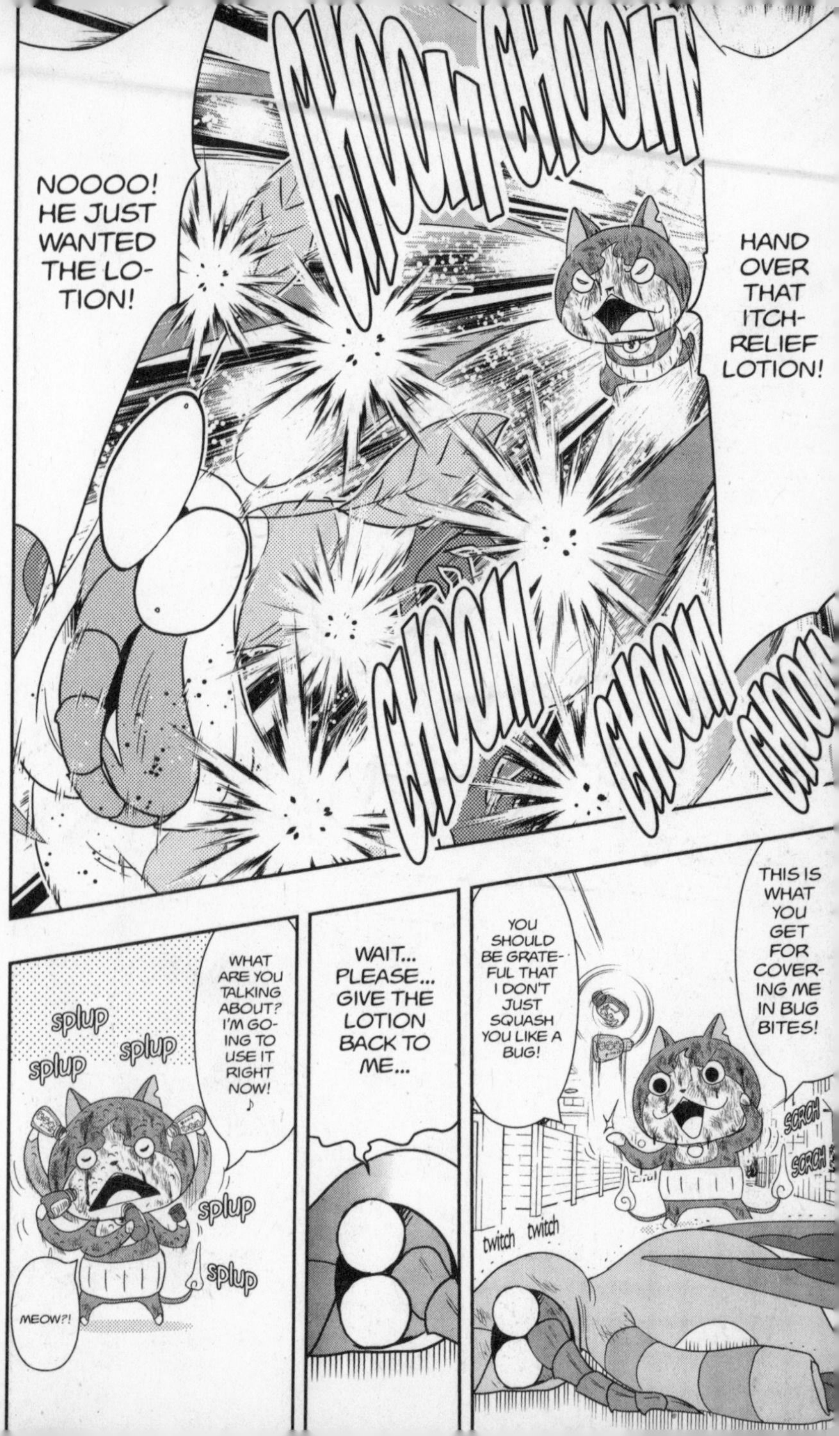
HAND OVER THAT ITCH-RELIEF LOTION!
CHOOM CHOOM
NOOOO! HE JUST WANTED THE LO-TION!
CHOOM
CHOOM
CHOOM
THIS IS WHAT YOU GET FOR COVER-ING ME IN BUG BITES!
YOU SHOULD BE GRATE-FUL THAT I DON'T JUST SQUASH YOU LIKE A BUG!
SCRCH
SCRCH
twitch twitch
WAIT... PLEASE... GIVE THE LOTION BACK TO ME...
WHAT ARE YOU TALKING ABOUT? I'M GO-ING TO USE IT RIGHT NOW! ♪
splup
splup
splup
splup
splup
MEOW?!

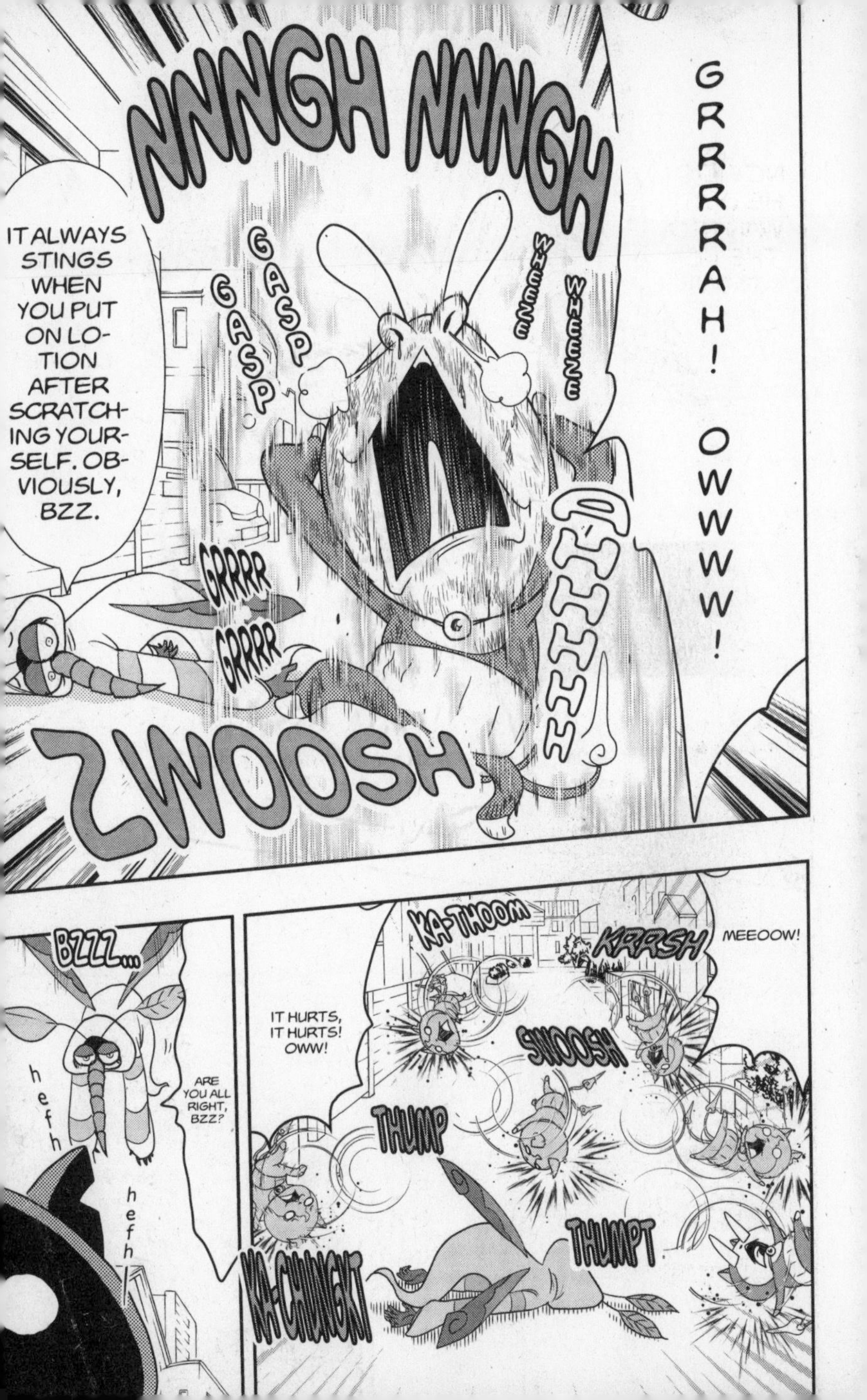
GRRRRAH! OWWWWW!
NNNGH NNNGH
WHEEENE WHEEENE
GASP GASP
IT ALWAYS STINGS WHEN YOU PUT ON LO-TION AFTER SCRATCH-ING YOUR-SELF. OB-VIOUSLY, BZZ.
HIIII!
GRRRR GRRRR
ZWOOSH
MEEOOW!
KRRSH
KA-THOOM
IT HURTS, IT HURTS! OWW!
SNOOSH
THUMP
THUMPT
KA-CHUNGKT
BZZZ...
ARE YOU ALL RIGHT, BZZ?
hefh hefh

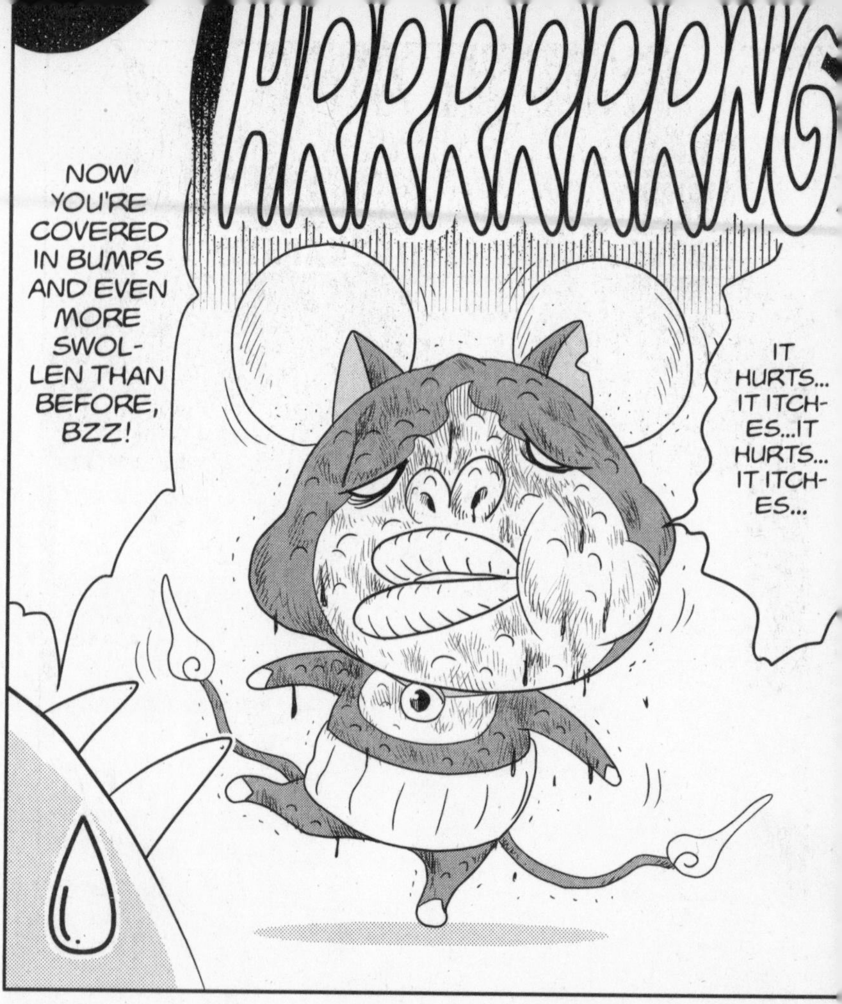
HRRRRRRNG
IT HURTS... IT ITCHES...IT HURTS... IT ITCHES...
NOW YOU'RE COVERED IN BUMPS AND EVEN MORE SWOLLEN THAN BEFORE, BZZ!

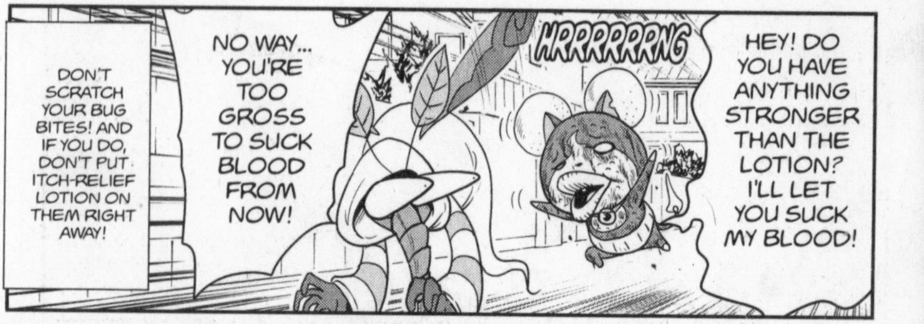
HEY! DO YOU HAVE ANYTHING STRONGER THAN THE LOTION? I'LL LET YOU SUCK MY BLOOD!
HRRRRRRNG
NO WAY... YOU'RE TOO GROSS TO SUCK BLOOD FROM NOW!
DON'T SCRATCH YOUR BUG BITES! AND IF YOU DO, DON'T PUT ITCH-RELIEF LOTION ON THEM RIGHT AWAY!

CHAPTER 84: WORKING UP A SWEAT

FEATURING SWEATY YO-KAI SWELTON

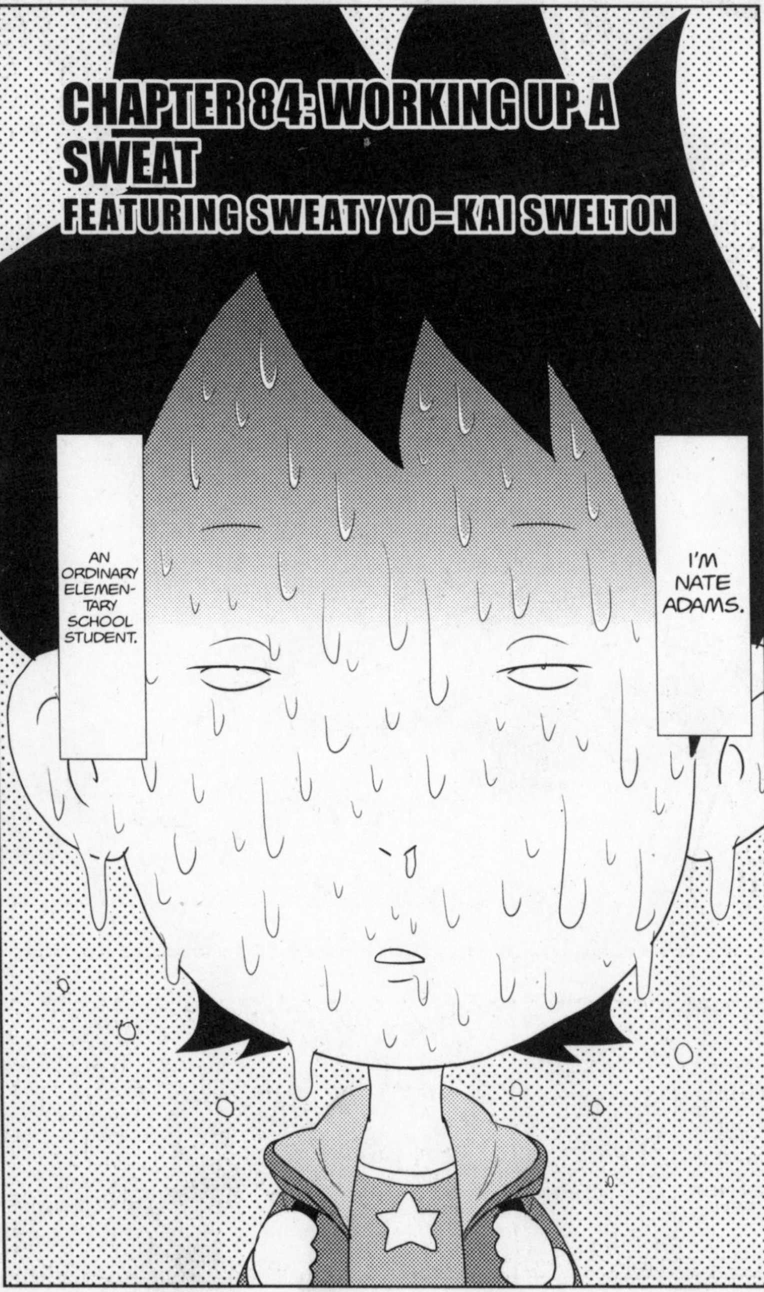

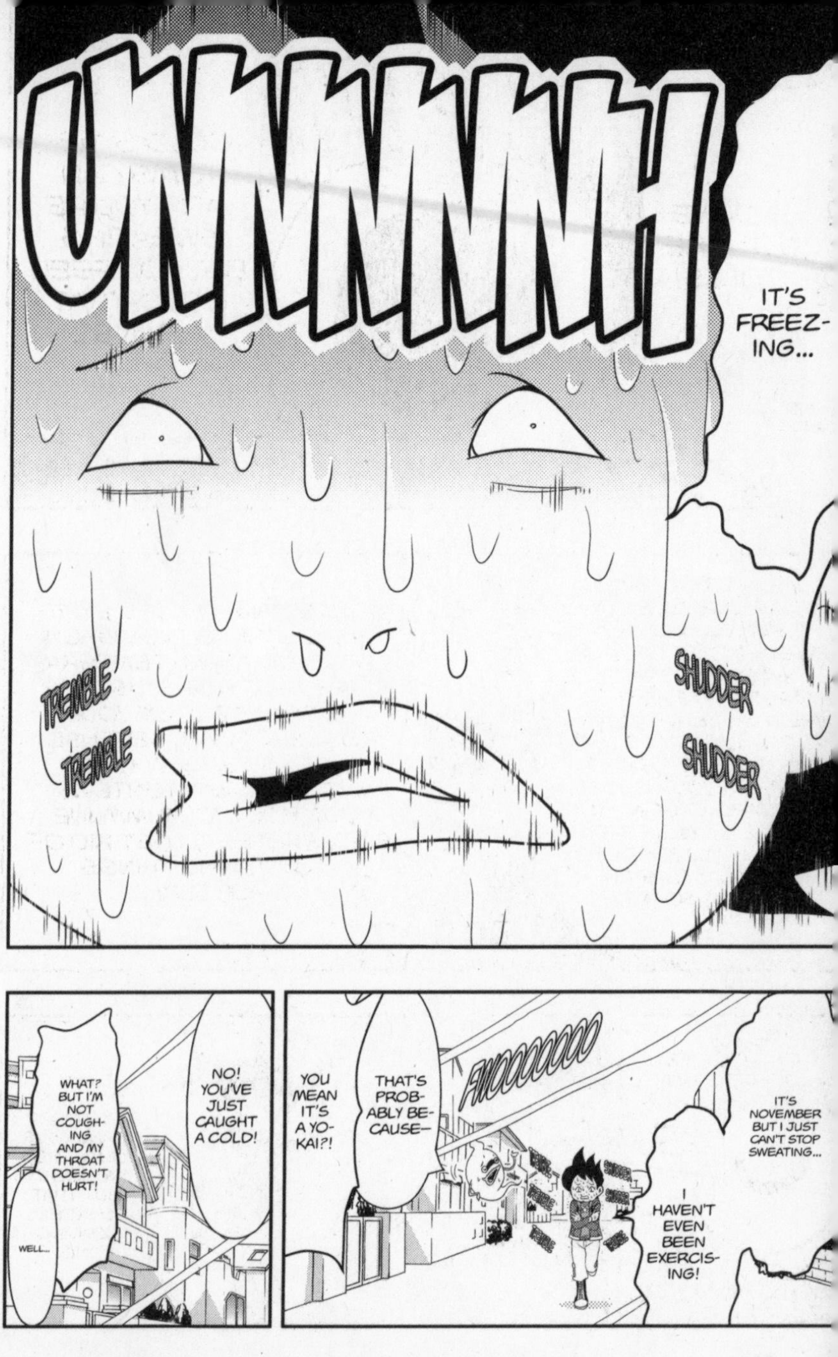
UNNNNNNH
IT'S FREEZ-ING...
SHUDDER
SHUDDER
TREMBLE
TREMBLE
IT'S NOVEMBER BUT I JUST CAN'T STOP SWEATING...
I HAVEN'T EVEN BEEN EXERCIS-ING!
FWOOOOOOOO
THAT'S PROB-ABLY BE-CAUSE—
YOU MEAN IT'S A YO-KAI?!
NO! YOU'VE JUST CAUGHT A COLD!
WHAT? BUT I'M NOT COUGH-ING AND MY THROAT DOESN'T HURT!
WELL...

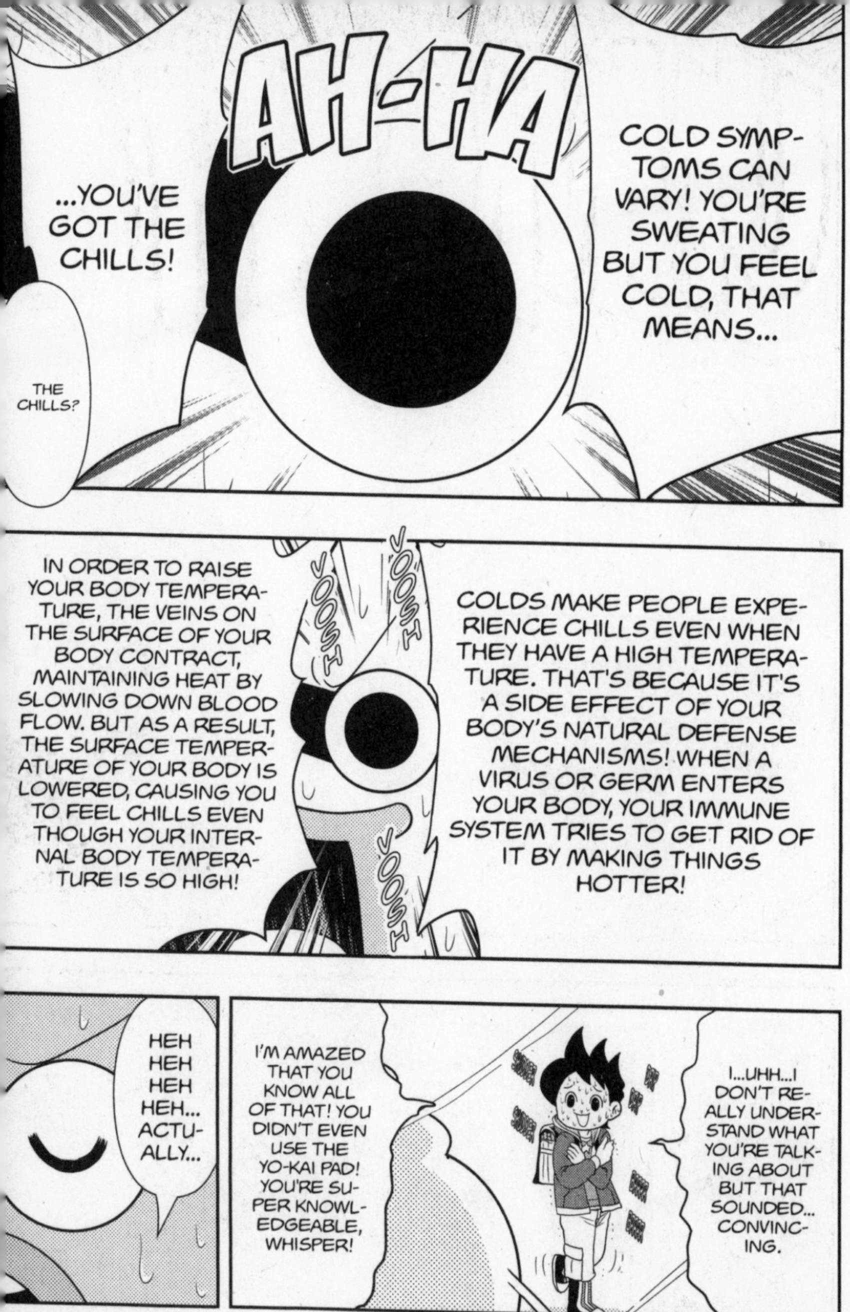
AH-HA
COLD SYMPTOMS CAN VARY! YOU'RE SWEATING BUT YOU FEEL COLD, THAT MEANS...
...YOU'VE GOT THE CHILLS!
THE CHILLS?
COLDS MAKE PEOPLE EXPERIENCE CHILLS EVEN WHEN THEY HAVE A HIGH TEMPERATURE. THAT'S BECAUSE IT'S A SIDE EFFECT OF YOUR BODY'S NATURAL DEFENSE MECHANISMS! WHEN A VIRUS OR GERM ENTERS YOUR BODY, YOUR IMMUNE SYSTEM TRIES TO GET RID OF IT BY MAKING THINGS HOTTER!
IN ORDER TO RAISE YOUR BODY TEMPERATURE, THE VEINS ON THE SURFACE OF YOUR BODY CONTRACT, MAINTAINING HEAT BY SLOWING DOWN BLOOD FLOW. BUT AS A RESULT, THE SURFACE TEMPERATURE OF YOUR BODY IS LOWERED, CAUSING YOU TO FEEL CHILLS EVEN THOUGH YOUR INTERNAL BODY TEMPERATURE IS SO HIGH!
VOOM
VOOM
VOOM
I...UHH...I DON'T REALLY UNDERSTAND WHAT YOU'RE TALKING ABOUT BUT THAT SOUNDED... CONVINCING.
I'M AMAZED THAT YOU KNOW ALL OF THAT! YOU DIDN'T EVEN USE THE YO-KAI PAD! YOU'RE SUPER KNOWLEDGEABLE, WHISPER!
HEH HEH HEH HEH... ACTUALLY...

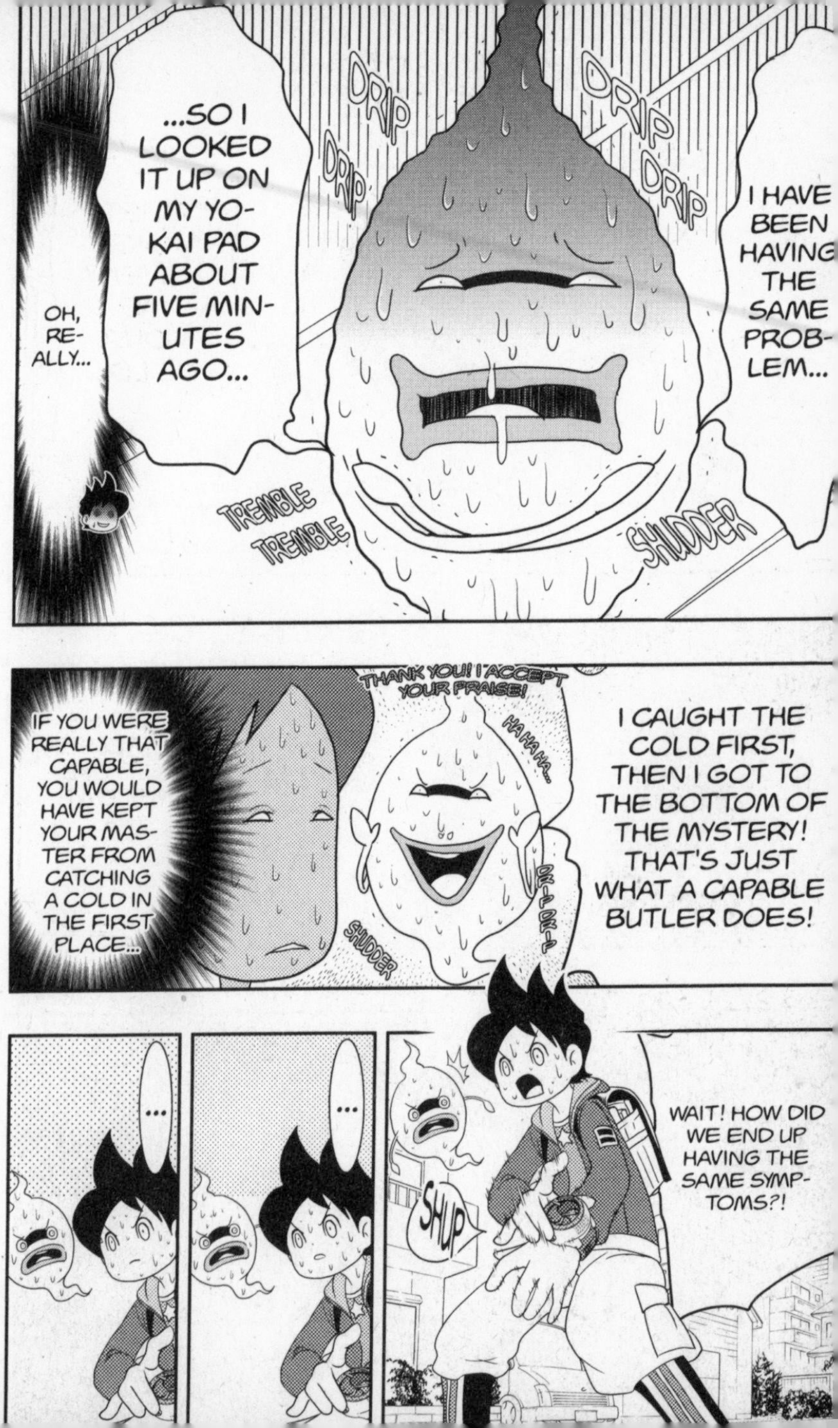
DRIP DRIP
DRIP DRIP
I HAVE BEEN HAVING THE SAME PROBLEM...
...SO I LOOKED IT UP ON MY YO-KAI PAD ABOUT FIVE MINUTES AGO...
OH, REALLY...
SHUDDER
TREMBLE TREMBLE
I CAUGHT THE COLD FIRST, THEN I GOT TO THE BOTTOM OF THE MYSTERY! THAT'S JUST WHAT A CAPABLE BUTLER DOES!
THANK YOU! I ACCEPT YOUR PRAISE!
HA HA HA...
DRIP DRIP
SHUDDER
IF YOU WERE REALLY THAT CAPABLE, YOU WOULD HAVE KEPT YOUR MASTER FROM CATCHING A COLD IN THE FIRST PLACE...
WAIT! HOW DID WE END UP HAVING THE SAME SYMPTOMS?!
SHUP
...
...

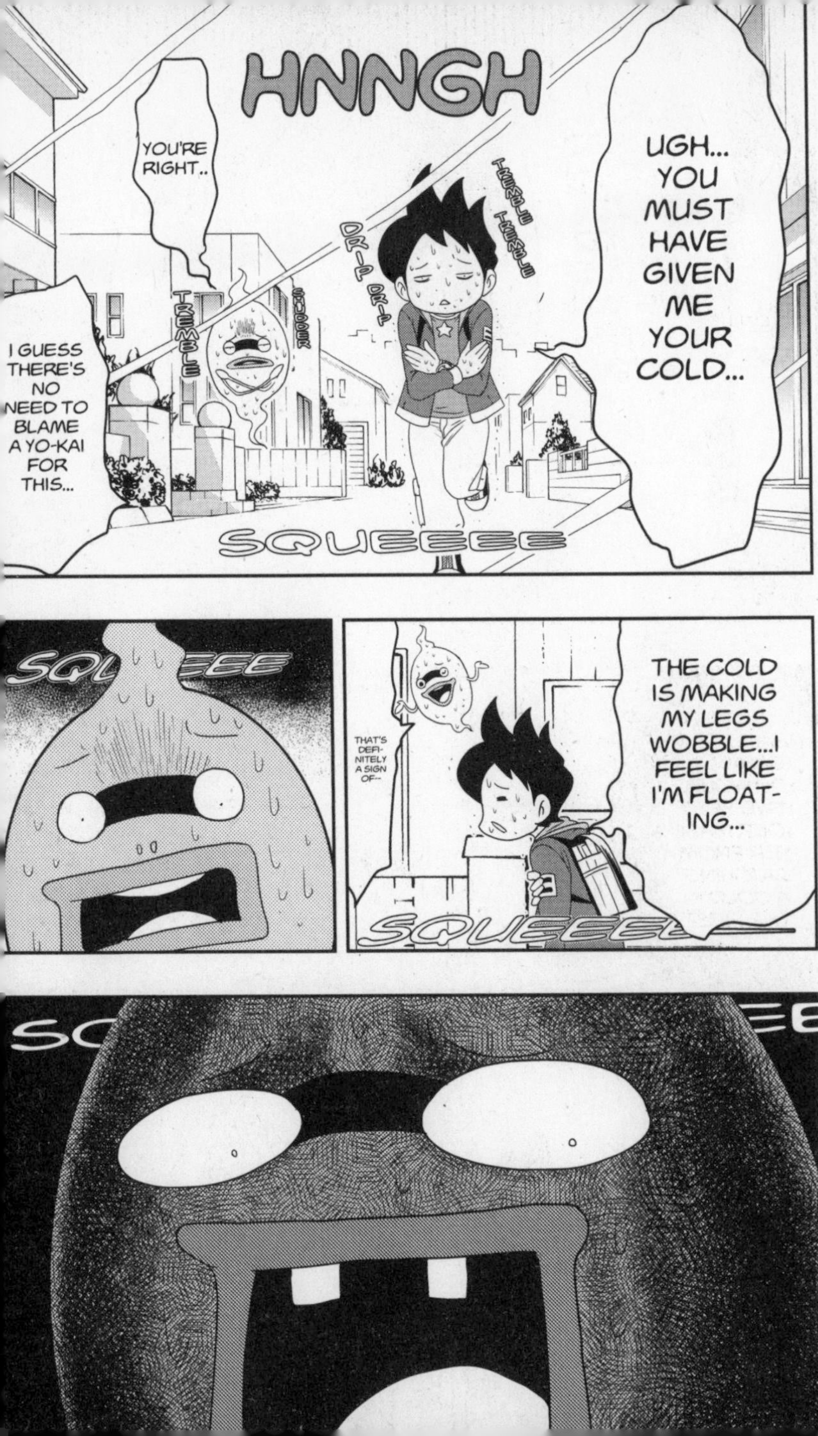
HNNGH
UGH... YOU MUST HAVE GIVEN ME YOUR COLD...
TREMBLE TREMBLE
DRIP DRIP
SHUDDER
TREMBLE
YOU'RE RIGHT..
I GUESS THERE'S NO NEED TO BLAME A YO-KAI FOR THIS...
SQUEEEE
THE COLD IS MAKING MY LEGS WOBBLE...I FEEL LIKE I'M FLOAT-ING...
THAT'S DEFI-NITELY A SIGN OF--
SQUEEEE
SQUEEEE
SC
EE

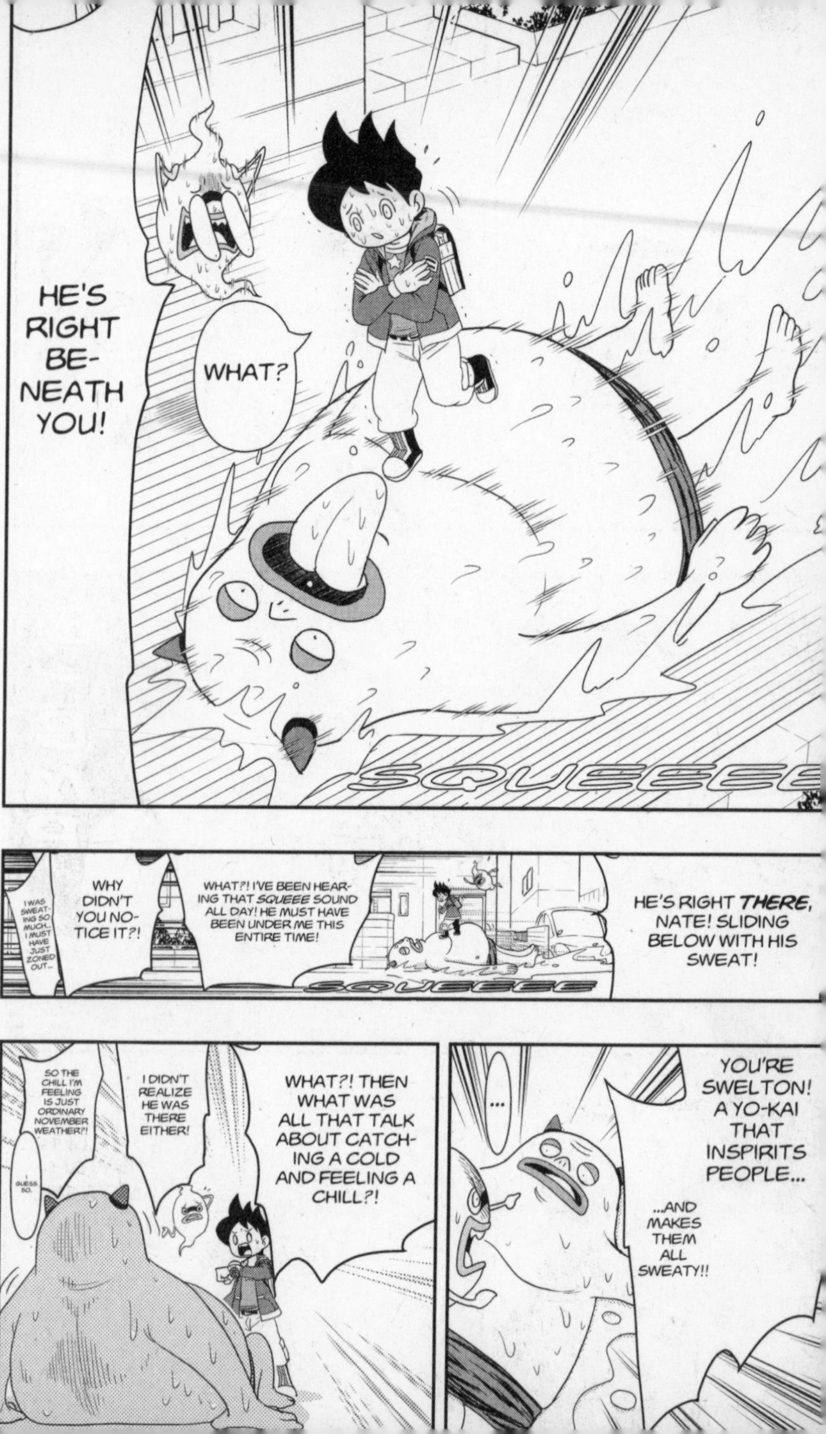
WHAT?
HE'S RIGHT BE-NEATH YOU!
SQUEEEE
HE'S RIGHT *THERE*, NATE! SLIDING BELOW WITH HIS SWEAT!
WHAT?! I'VE BEEN HEARING THAT *SQUEEE* SOUND ALL DAY! HE MUST HAVE BEEN UNDER ME THIS ENTIRE TIME!
WHY DIDN'T YOU NOTICE IT?!
I WAS SWEATING SO MUCH... I MUST HAVE JUST ZONED OUT...
SQUEEEE
YOU'RE SWELTON! A YO-KAI THAT INSPIRITS PEOPLE...
...
...AND MAKES THEM ALL SWEATY!!
WHAT?! THEN WHAT WAS ALL THAT TALK ABOUT CATCHING A COLD AND FEELING A CHILL?!
I DIDN'T REALIZE HE WAS THERE EITHER!
SO THE CHILL I'M FEELING IS JUST ORDINARY NOVEMBER WEATHER?!
I GUESS SO.

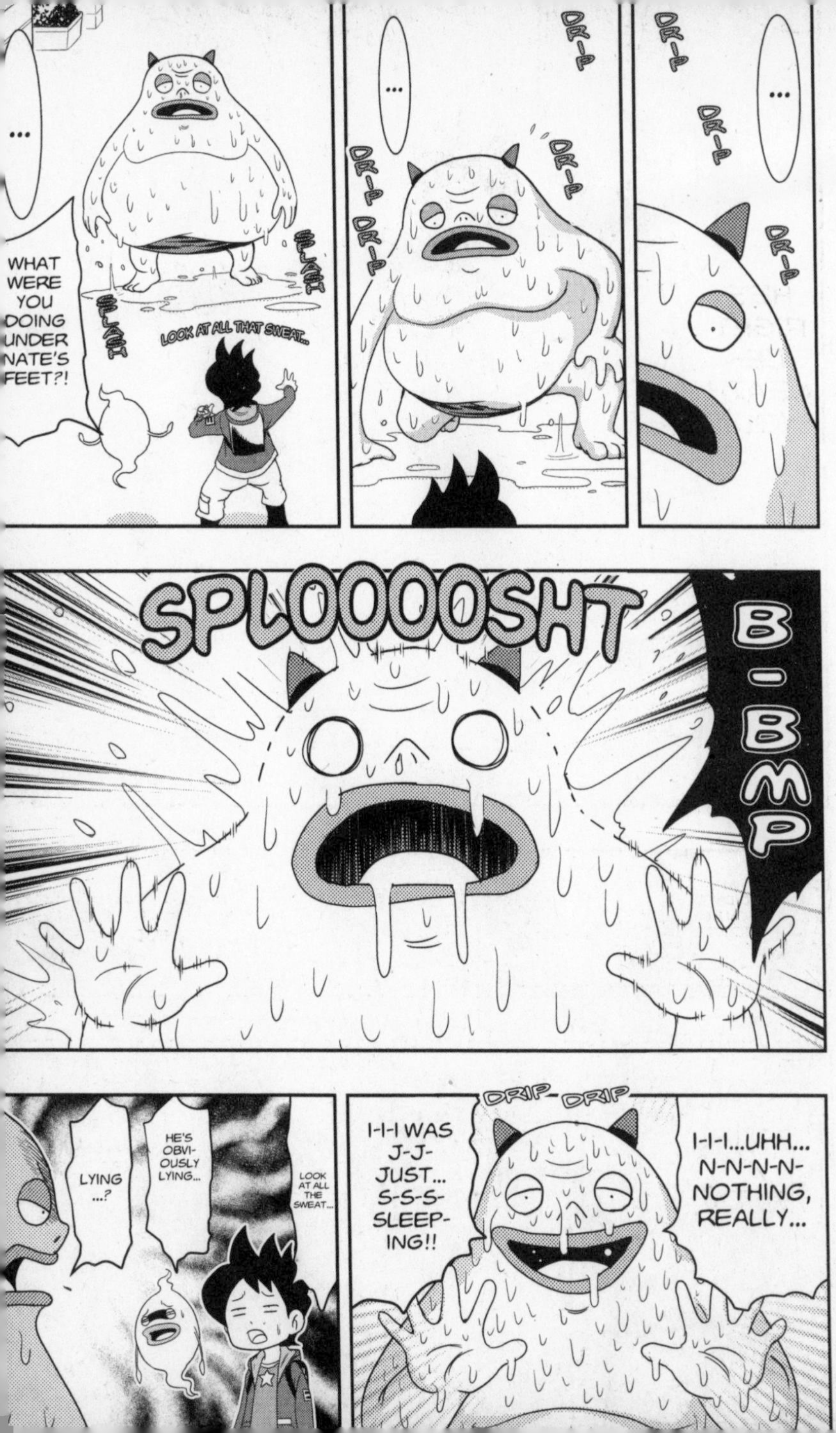
…
DRIP
DRIP
DRIP
…
DRIP
DRIP DRIP
DRIP
…
SPLASH
SPLASH
LOOK AT ALL THAT SWEAT...
WHAT WERE YOU DOING UNDER NATE'S FEET?!
B-B-BMP
SPLOOOOSHT
DRIP DRIP
I-I-I...UHH... N-N-N-N-NOTHING, REALLY...
I-I-I WAS J-J-JUST... S-S-S-SLEEPING!!
LOOK AT ALL THE SWEAT...
HE'S OBVIOUSLY LYING...
LYING ...?

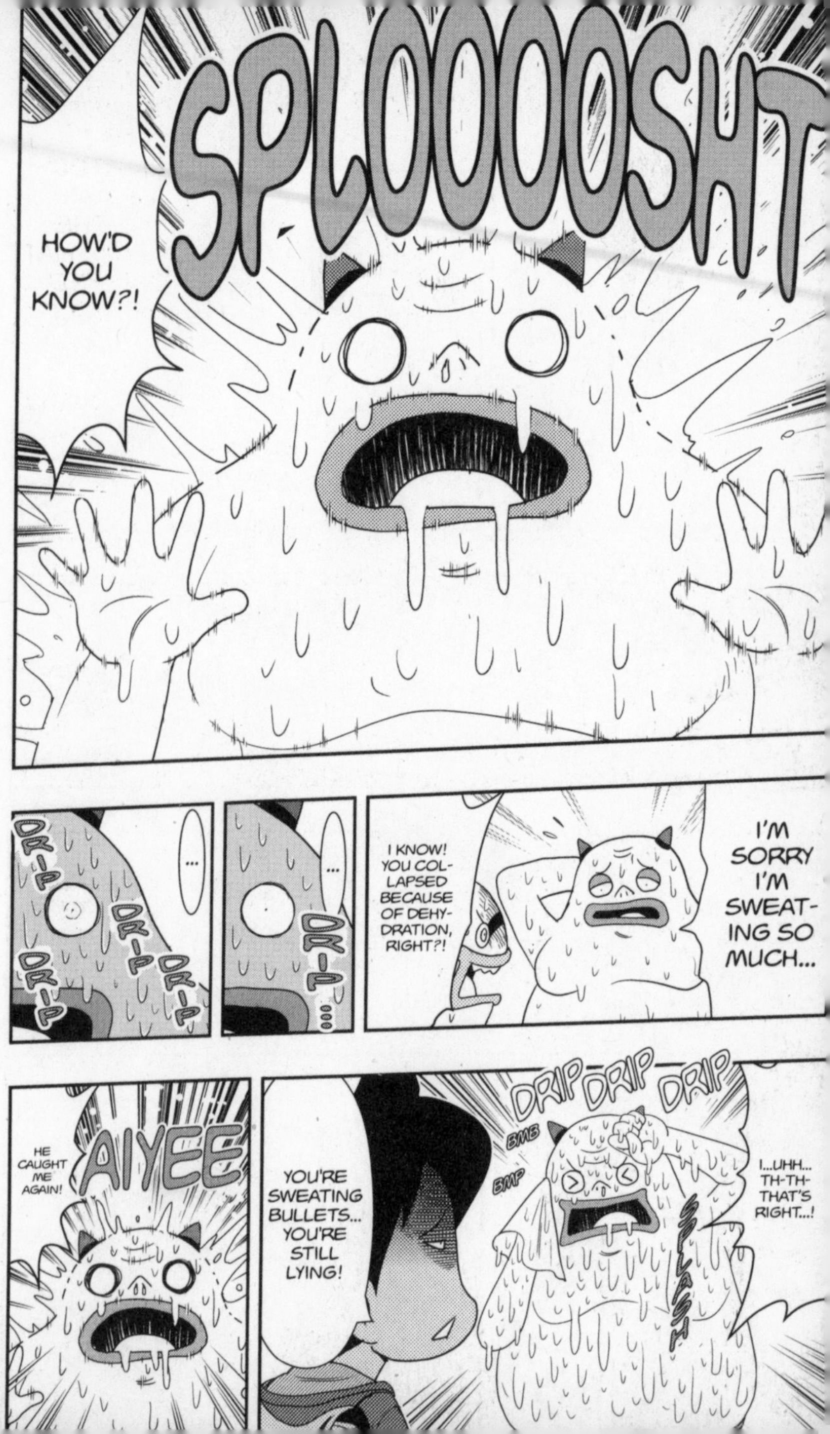
SPLOOOOSHT
HOW'D YOU KNOW?!
I'M SORRY I'M SWEATING SO MUCH...
I KNOW! YOU COL-LAPSED BECAUSE OF DEHY-DRATION, RIGHT?!
...
DRIP...
...
DRIP
DRIP
DRIP
DRIP
DRIP DRIP DRIP
I...UHH... TH-TH-THAT'S RIGHT...!
BMB
BMP
YOU'RE SWEATING BULLETS... YOU'RE STILL LYING!
AIYEE
HE CAUGHT ME AGAIN!

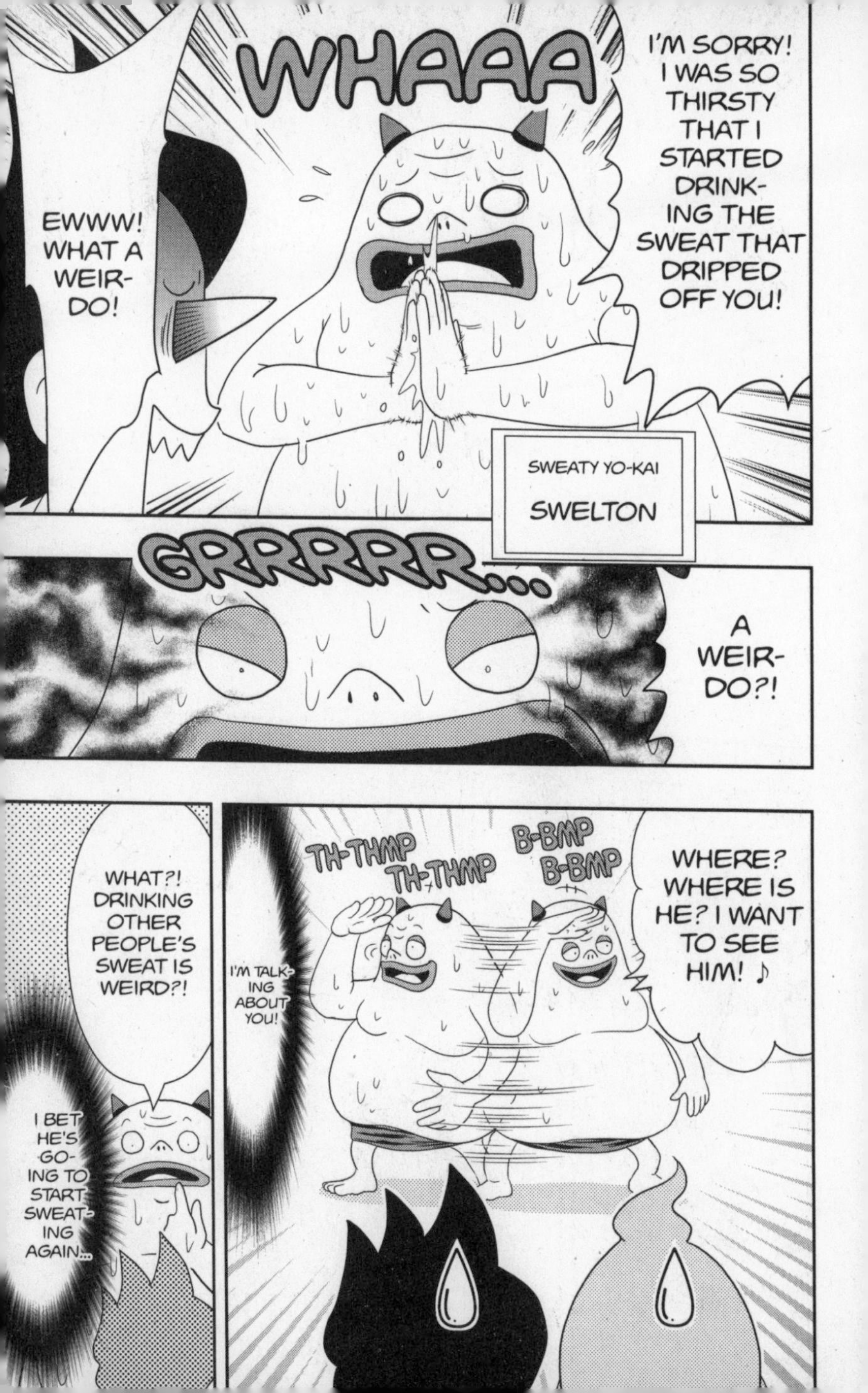
I'M SORRY! I WAS SO THIRSTY THAT I STARTED DRINKING THE SWEAT THAT DRIPPED OFF YOU!
WHAAA
EWWW! WHAT A WEIRDO!
SWEATY YO-KAI
SWELTON
A WEIRDO?!
GRRRRR...
WHERE? WHERE IS HE? I WANT TO SEE HIM! ♪
B-BMP B-BMP
TH-THMP TH-THMP
I'M TALKING ABOUT YOU!
WHAT?! DRINKING OTHER PEOPLE'S SWEAT IS WEIRD?!
I BET HE'S GOING TO START SWEATING AGAIN...

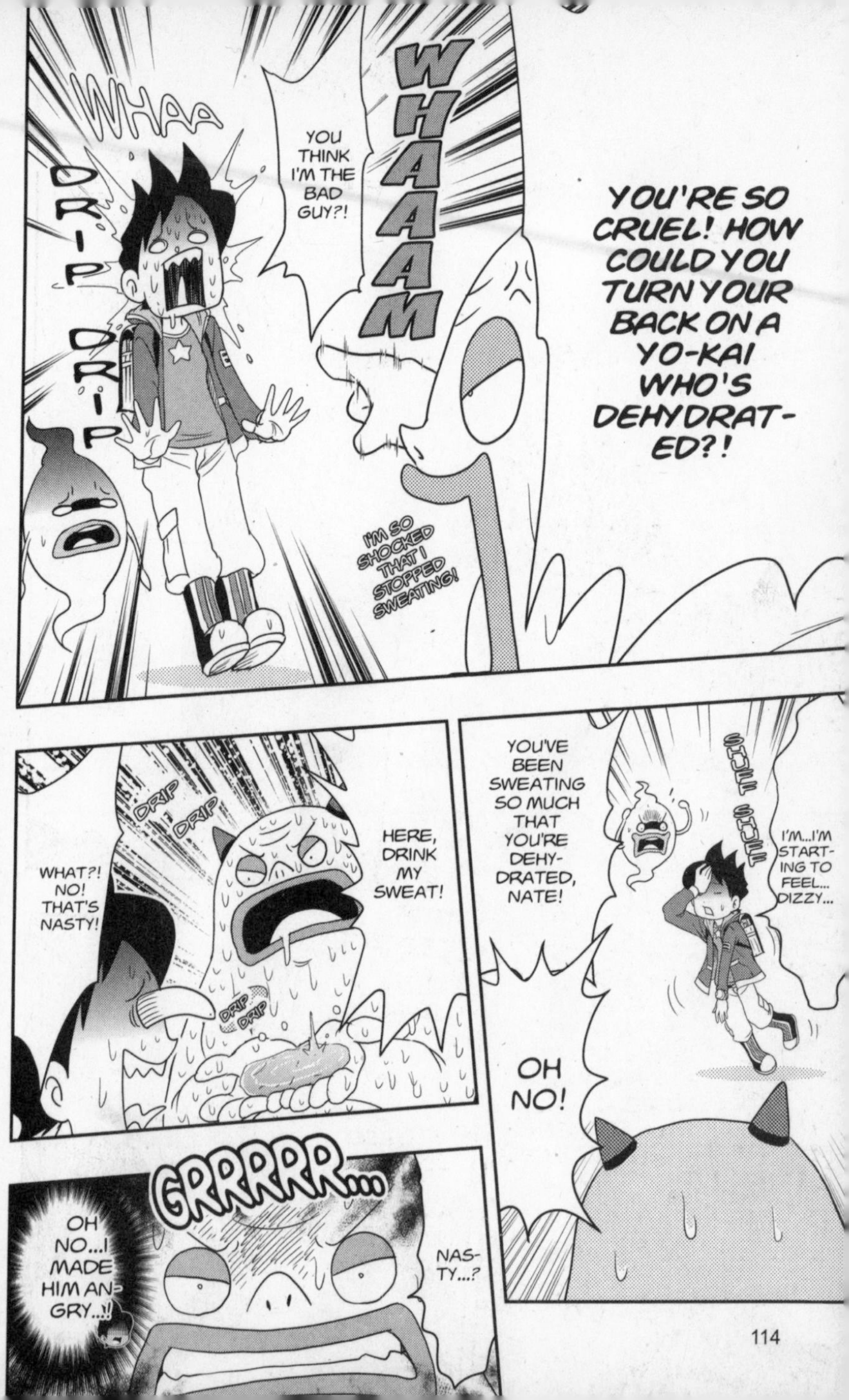
YOU'RE SO CRUEL! HOW COULD YOU TURN YOUR BACK ON A YO-KAI WHO'S DEHYDRAT-ED?!
WHAAAAM
YOU THINK I'M THE BAD GUY?!
WHAA
DRIP DRIP
I'M SO SHOCKED THAT I STOPPED SWEATING!
I'M...I'M START-ING TO FEEL... DIZZY...
SHUFF SHUFF
YOU'VE BEEN SWEATING SO MUCH THAT YOU'RE DEHY-DRATED, NATE!
OH NO!
HERE, DRINK MY SWEAT!
WHAT?! NO! THAT'S NASTY!
DRIP DRIP
DRIP DRIP
GRRRRR...
NAS-TY...?
OH NO...I MADE HIM AN-GRY...!

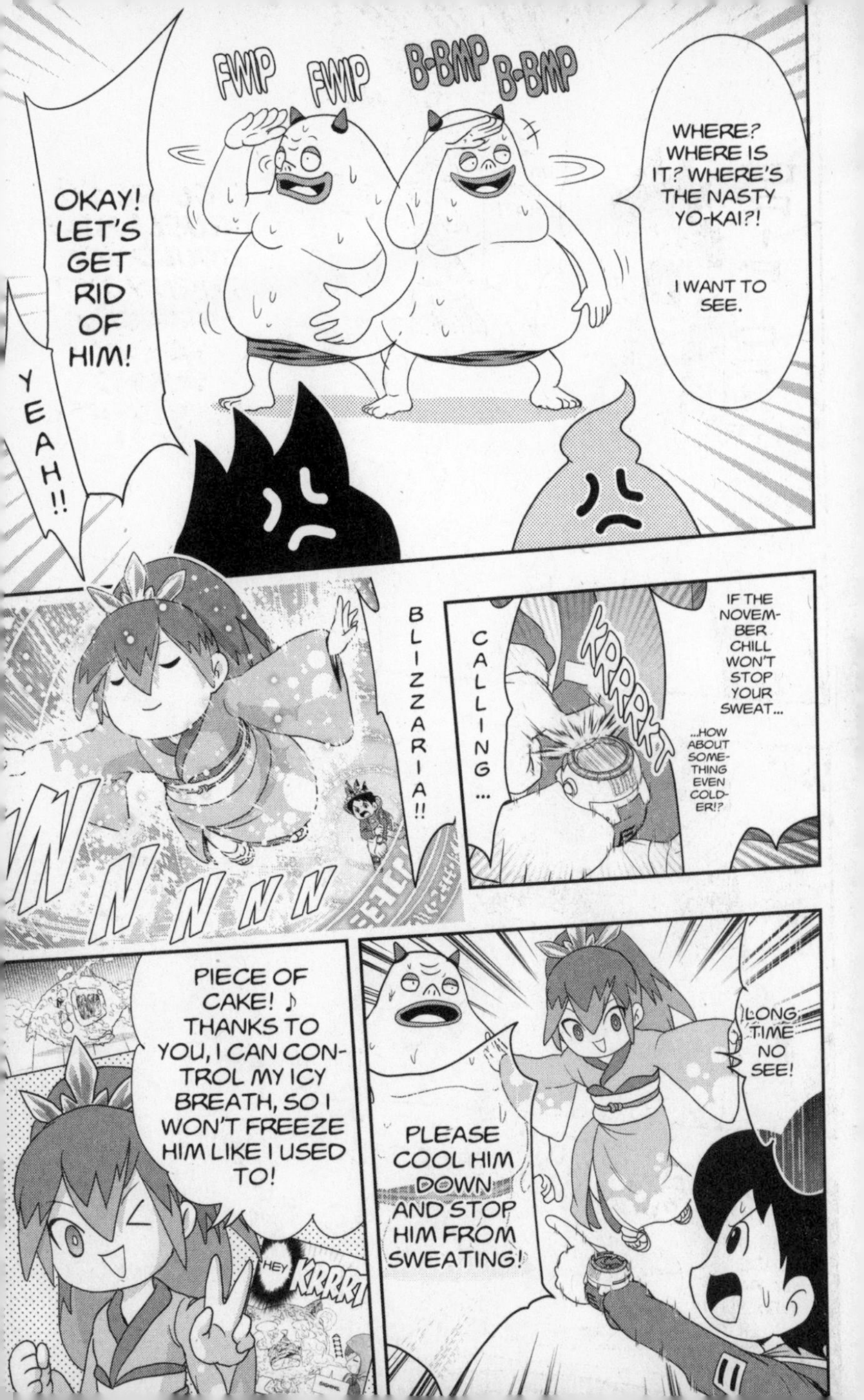
WHERE? WHERE IS IT? WHERE'S THE NASTY YO-KAI?!
I WANT TO SEE.
B-BMP B-BMP
FWIP FWIP
OKAY! LET'S GET RID OF HIM!
YEAH!!
IF THE NOVEM-BER CHILL WON'T STOP YOUR SWEAT...
...HOW ABOUT SOME-THING EVEN COLD-ER!?
KRRRKT
CALLING...
BLIZZARIA!!
NNNNN
LONG TIME NO SEE!
PLEASE COOL HIM DOWN AND STOP HIM FROM SWEATING!
PIECE OF CAKE! ♪ THANKS TO YOU, I CAN CON-TROL MY ICY BREATH, SO I WON'T FREEZE HIM LIKE I USED TO!
HEY
KRRRT

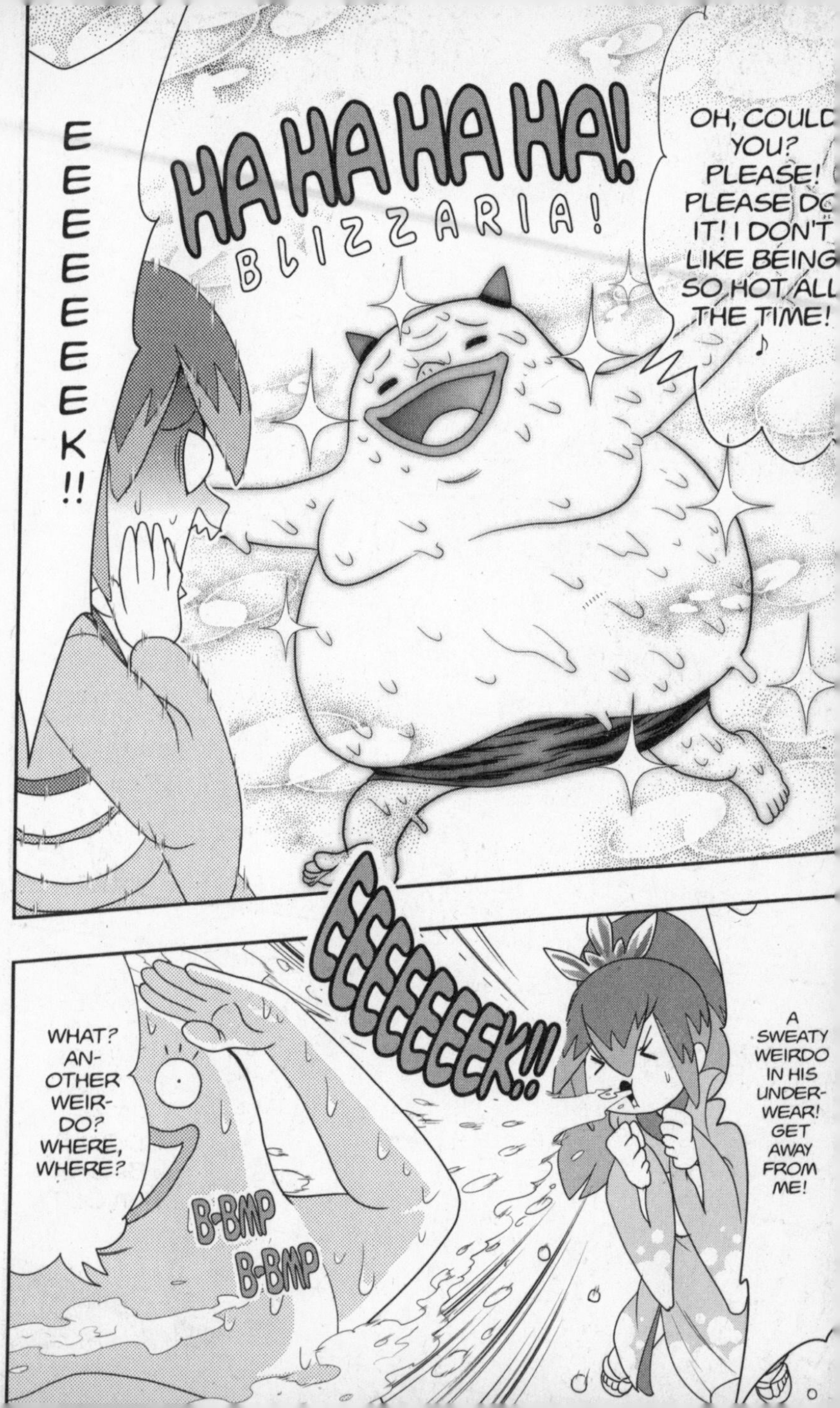
OH, COULD YOU? PLEASE! PLEASE DO IT! I DON'T LIKE BEING SO HOT ALL THE TIME! ♪
HA HA HA HA HA!
BLIZZARIA!
EEEEEEEEEK!!
A SWEATY WEIRDO IN HIS UNDER-WEAR! GET AWAY FROM ME!
EEEEEEEEK!!
WHAT? AN-OTHER WEIR-DO? WHERE, WHERE?
B-BMP
B-BMP

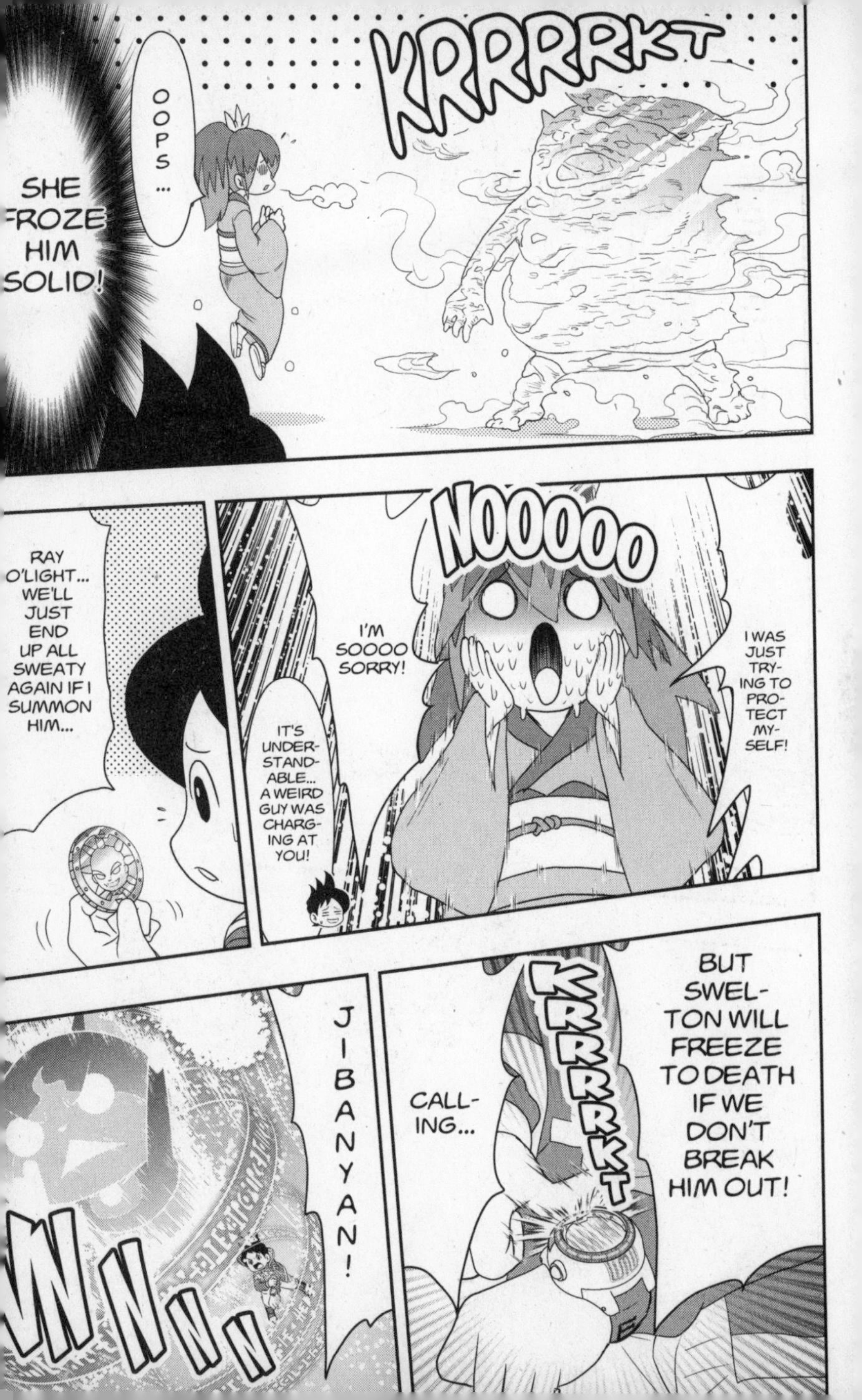
KRRRRKT
OOPS...
SHE FROZE HIM SOLID!
NOOOOO
I WAS JUST TRYING TO PROTECT MYSELF!
I'M SOOOO SORRY!
IT'S UNDERSTANDABLE... A WEIRD GUY WAS CHARGING AT YOU!
RAY O'LIGHT... WE'LL JUST END UP ALL SWEATY AGAIN IF I SUMMON HIM...
BUT SWELTON WILL FREEZE TO DEATH IF WE DON'T BREAK HIM OUT!
KRRRRKT
CALLING...
JIBANYAN!
NNNN

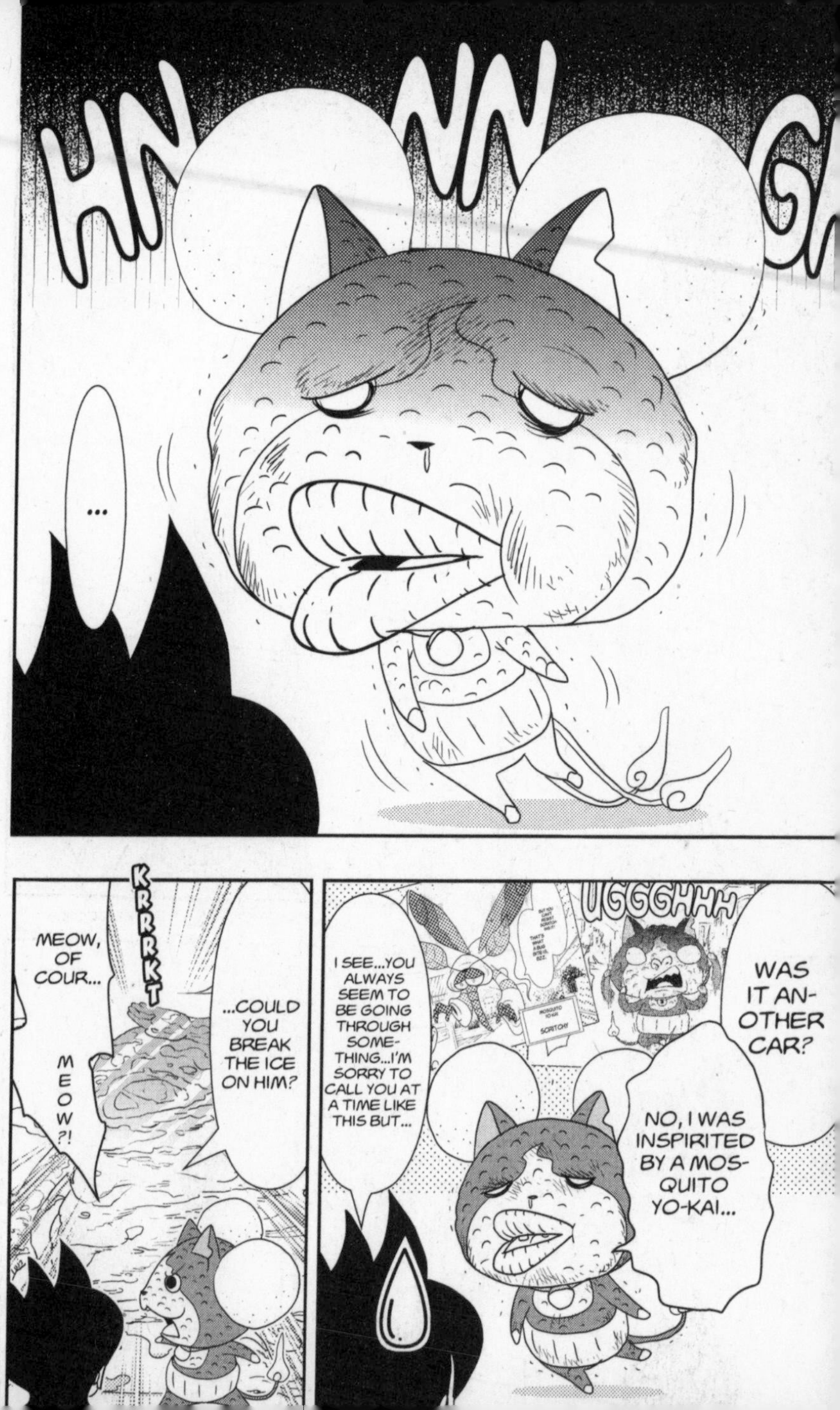
HNNNG
...
UGGGHHH
WAS IT AN-OTHER CAR?
NO, I WAS INSPIRITED BY A MOS-QUITO YO-KAI...
I SEE...YOU ALWAYS SEEM TO BE GOING THROUGH SOME-THING...I'M SORRY TO CALL YOU AT A TIME LIKE THIS BUT...
...COULD YOU BREAK THE ICE ON HIM?
KRRRKT
MEOW, OF COUR...
MEOW?!

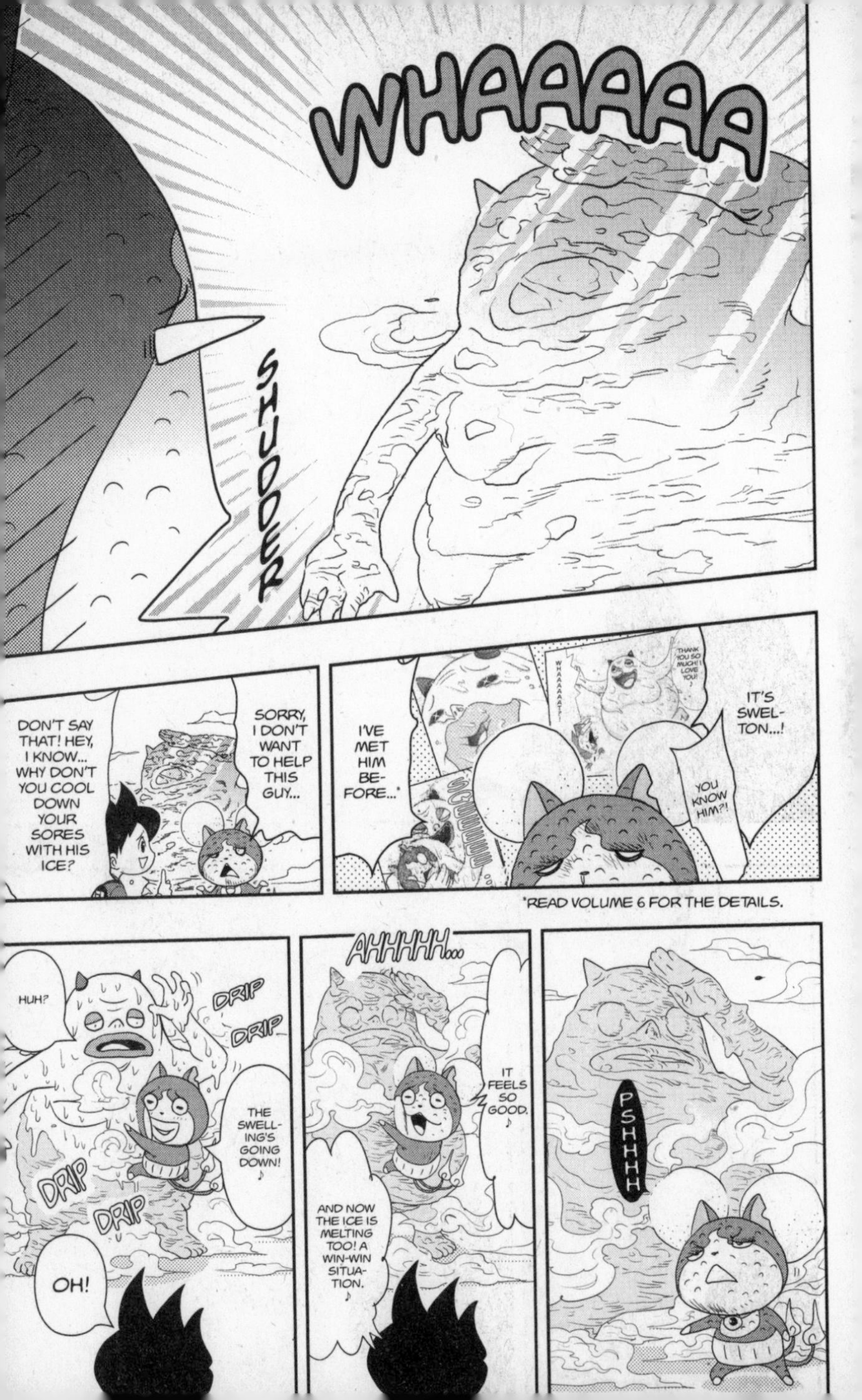
WHAAAAAA
SHUDDER
THANK YOU SO MUCH! I LOVE YOU! ♪
WHAAAAAAT?!
IT'S SWEL-TON...!
YOU KNOW HIM?!
I'VE MET HIM BE-FORE...*
SORRY, I DON'T WANT TO HELP THIS GUY...
DON'T SAY THAT! HEY, I KNOW... WHY DON'T YOU COOL DOWN YOUR SORES WITH HIS ICE?
*READ VOLUME 6 FOR THE DETAILS.
PSHHHH
AHHHHH...
IT FEELS SO GOOD. ♪
AND NOW THE ICE IS MELTING TOO! A WIN-WIN SITUA-TION. ♪
HUH?
DRIP
DRIP
THE SWELL-ING'S GOING DOWN! ♪
DRIP
DRIP
OH!

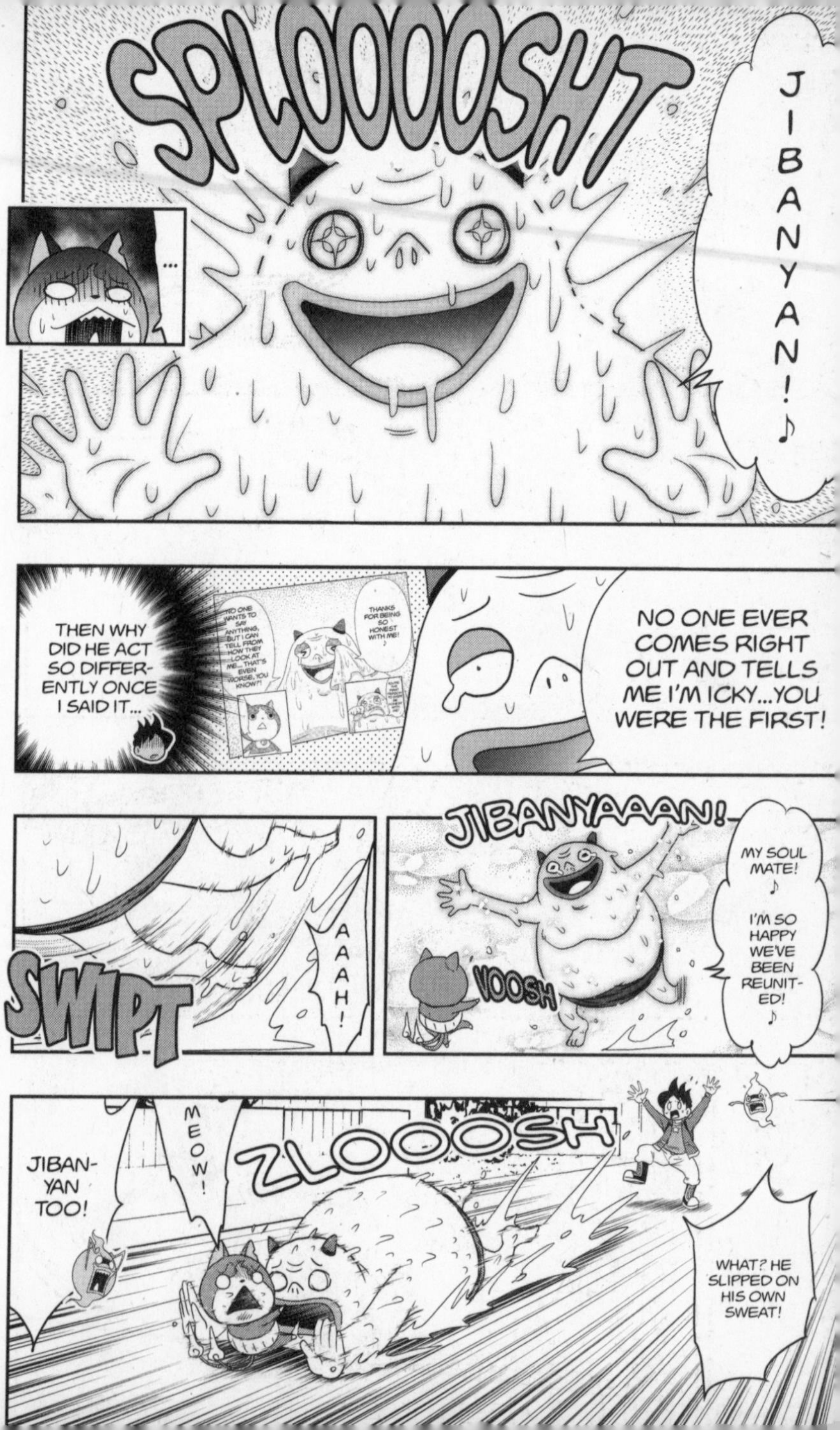
SPLOOOSHT
JIBANYAN! ♪
...
NO ONE EVER COMES RIGHT OUT AND TELLS ME I'M ICKY...YOU WERE THE FIRST!
THANKS FOR BEING SO HONEST WITH ME! ♪
NO ONE WANTS TO SAY ANYTHING, BUT I CAN TELL FROM HOW THEY LOOK AT ME... THAT'S EVEN WORSE, YOU KNOW?!
THEN WHY DID HE ACT SO DIFFERENTLY ONCE I SAID IT...
JIBANYAAAN!
MY SOUL MATE! ♪
I'M SO HAPPY WE'VE BEEN REUNITED! ♪
VOOSH
AAAAH!
SWIPT
WHAT? HE SLIPPED ON HIS OWN SWEAT!
ZLOOOSH
MEOW!
JIBANYAN TOO!

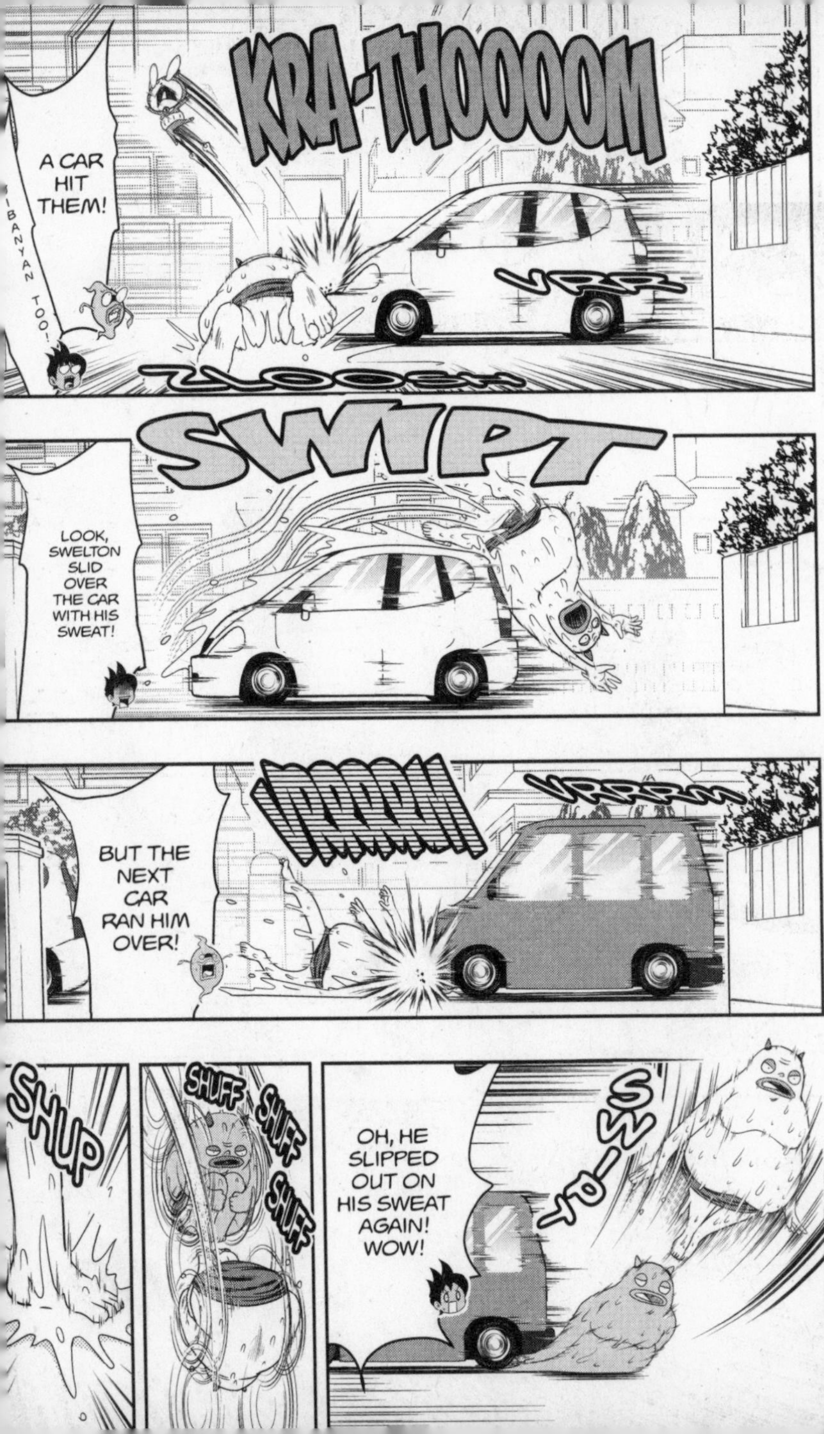
KRA-THOOOOM
VRR
A CAR HIT THEM!
IBANYAN TOO!
ZLOOSH
SWIPT
LOOK, SWELTON SLID OVER THE CAR WITH HIS SWEAT!
VRRRM
VRRRRM
BUT THE NEXT CAR RAN HIM OVER!
SW-OT
OH, HE SLIPPED OUT ON HIS SWEAT AGAIN! WOW!
SHUFF
SHUFF
SHUFF
SHUP

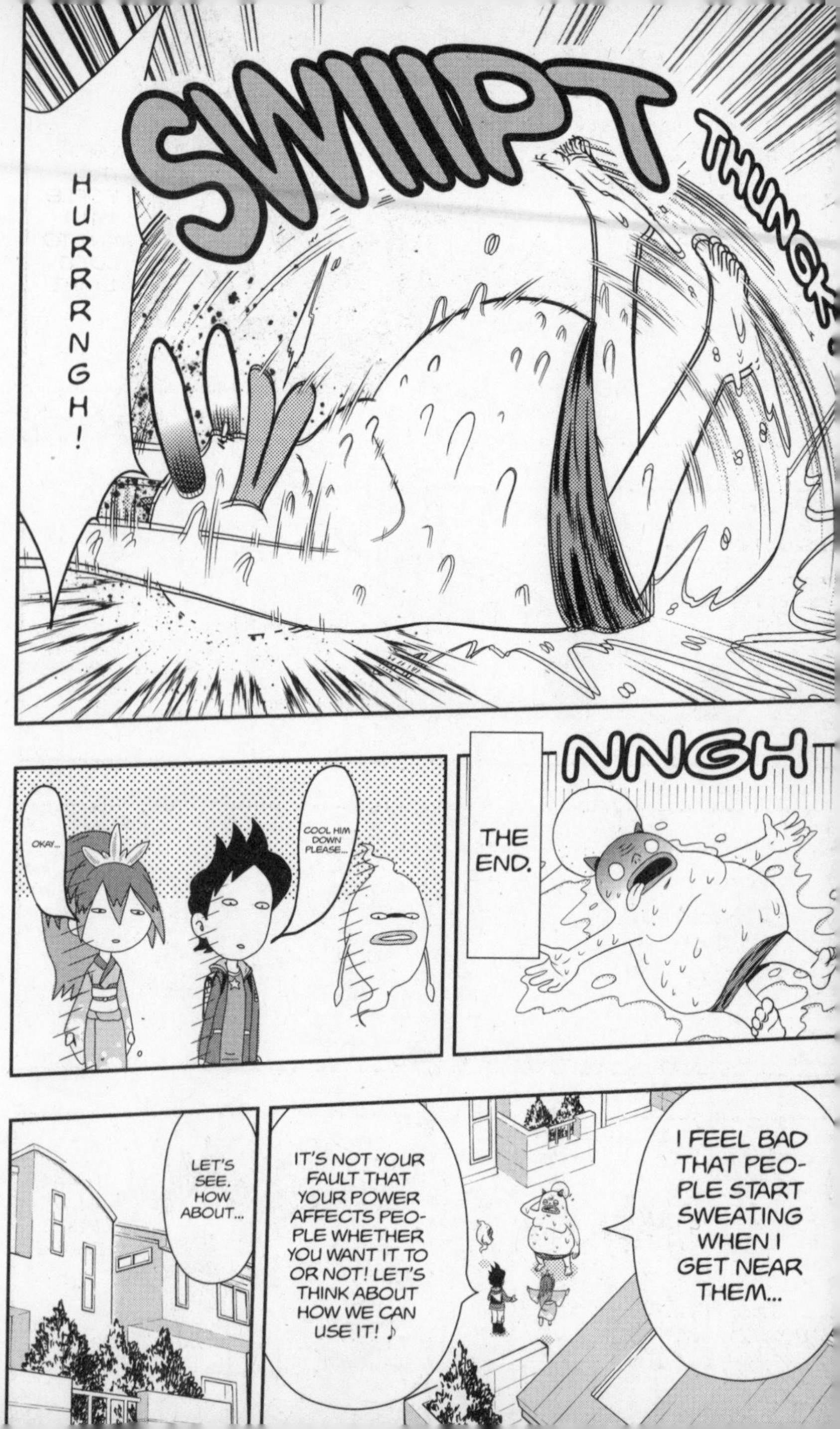
SWIIPT
THUNGK!
HURRRNGH!
NNGH
THE END.
COOL HIM DOWN PLEASE...
OKAY...
I FEEL BAD THAT PEOPLE START SWEATING WHEN I GET NEAR THEM...
IT'S NOT YOUR FAULT THAT YOUR POWER AFFECTS PEOPLE WHETHER YOU WANT IT TO OR NOT! LET'S THINK ABOUT HOW WE CAN USE IT! ♪
LET'S SEE. HOW ABOUT...

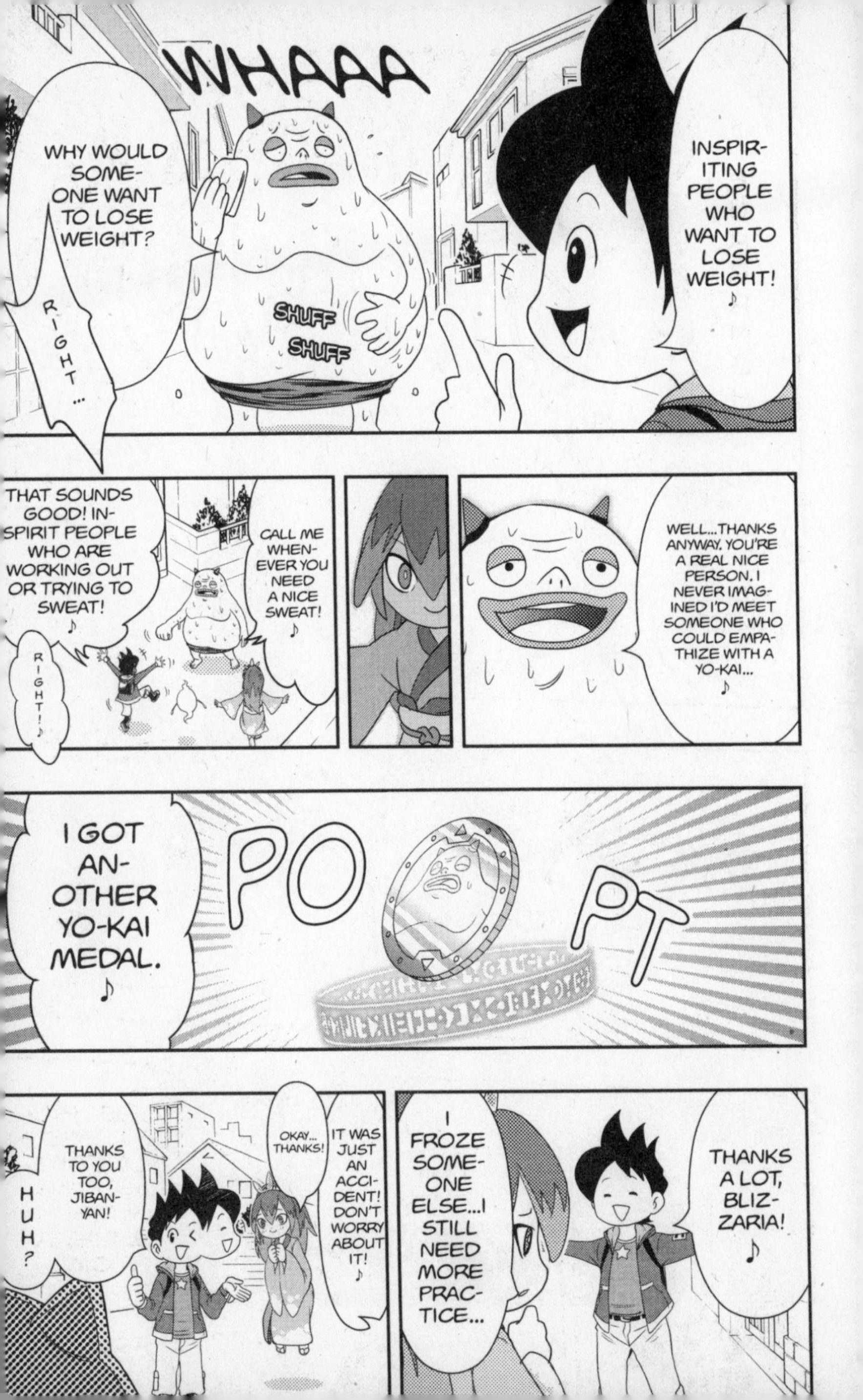
INSPIRITING PEOPLE WHO WANT TO LOSE WEIGHT! ♪
WHAAA
SHUFF SHUFF
WHY WOULD SOMEONE WANT TO LOSE WEIGHT?
RIGHT...
WELL...THANKS ANYWAY. YOU'RE A REAL NICE PERSON. I NEVER IMAGINED I'D MEET SOMEONE WHO COULD EMPATHIZE WITH A YO-KAI... ♪
CALL ME WHENEVER YOU NEED A NICE SWEAT! ♪
THAT SOUNDS GOOD! INSPIRIT PEOPLE WHO ARE WORKING OUT OR TRYING TO SWEAT! ♪
RIGHT!♪
POOPT
I GOT ANOTHER YO-KAI MEDAL. ♪
THANKS A LOT, BLIZZARIA! ♪
I FROZE SOMEONE ELSE...I STILL NEED MORE PRACTICE...
IT WAS JUST AN ACCIDENT! DON'T WORRY ABOUT IT! ♪
OKAY... THANKS!
THANKS TO YOU TOO, JIBANYAN!
HUH?

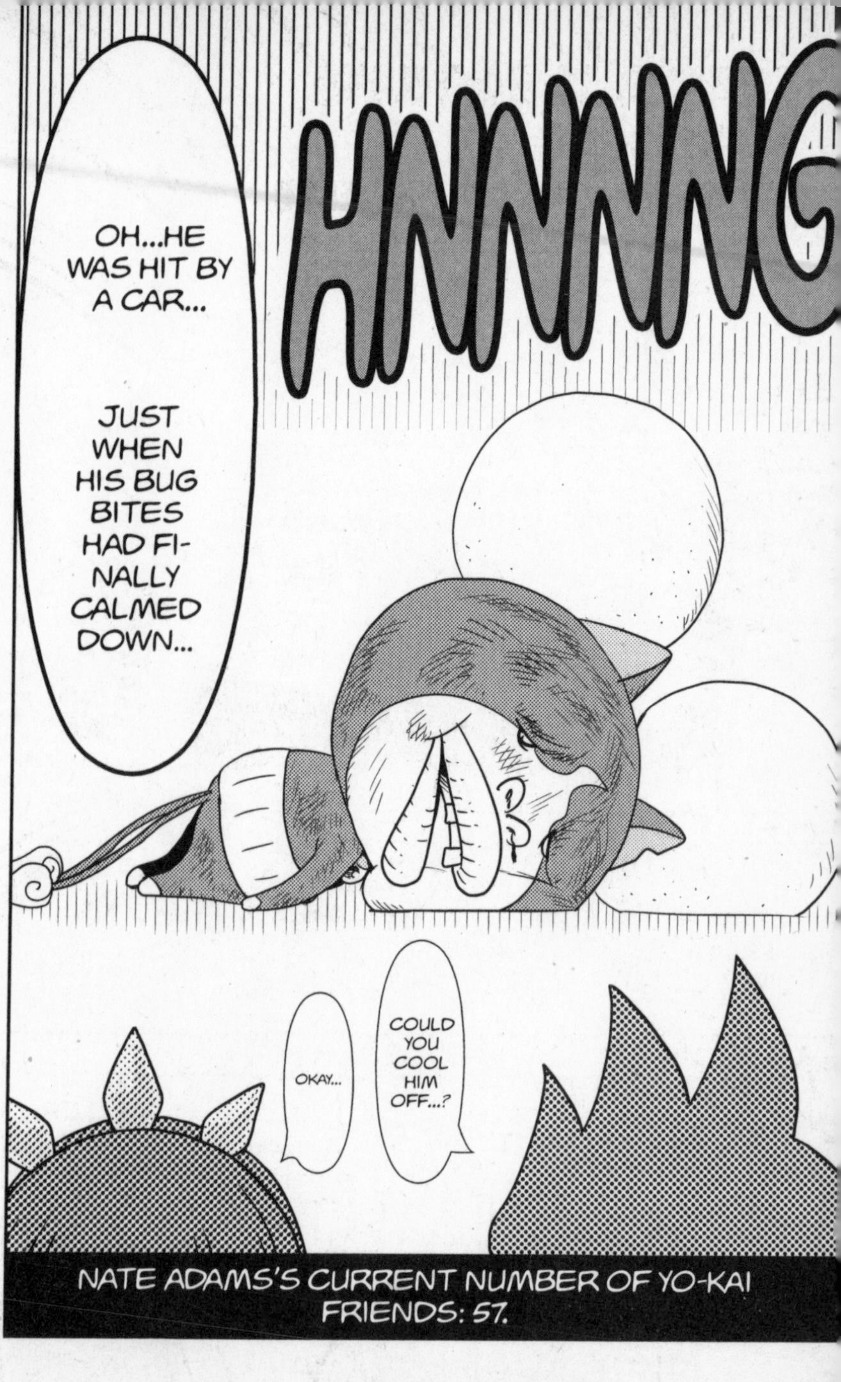
HNNNG
OH...HE WAS HIT BY A CAR...
JUST WHEN HIS BUG BITES HAD FI-NALLY CALMED DOWN...
COULD YOU COOL HIM OFF...?
OKAY...
NATE ADAMS'S CURRENT NUMBER OF YO-KAI FRIENDS: 57.

CHAPTER 85: HIGH WIND WARNING?!
FEATURING WINDY YO-KAI TENGU

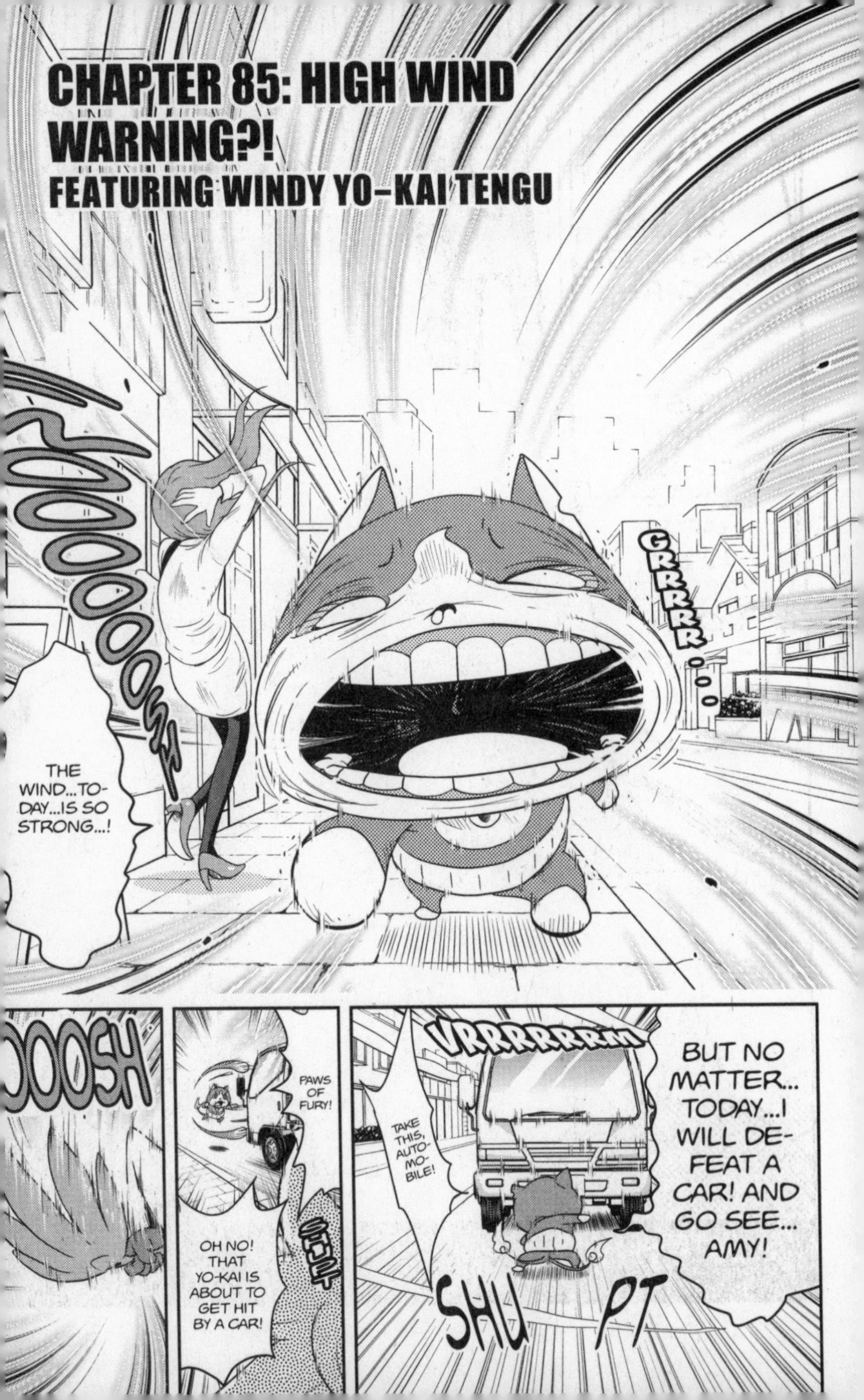
GRRRRR
THE WIND...TO-DAY...IS SO STRONG...!
VRRRRRRM
BUT NO MATTER... TODAY...I WILL DE-FEAT A CAR! AND GO SEE... AMY!
TAKE THIS, AUTO-MOBILE!
SHU PT
PAWS OF FURY!
OH NO! THAT YO-KAI IS ABOUT TO GET HIT BY A CAR!

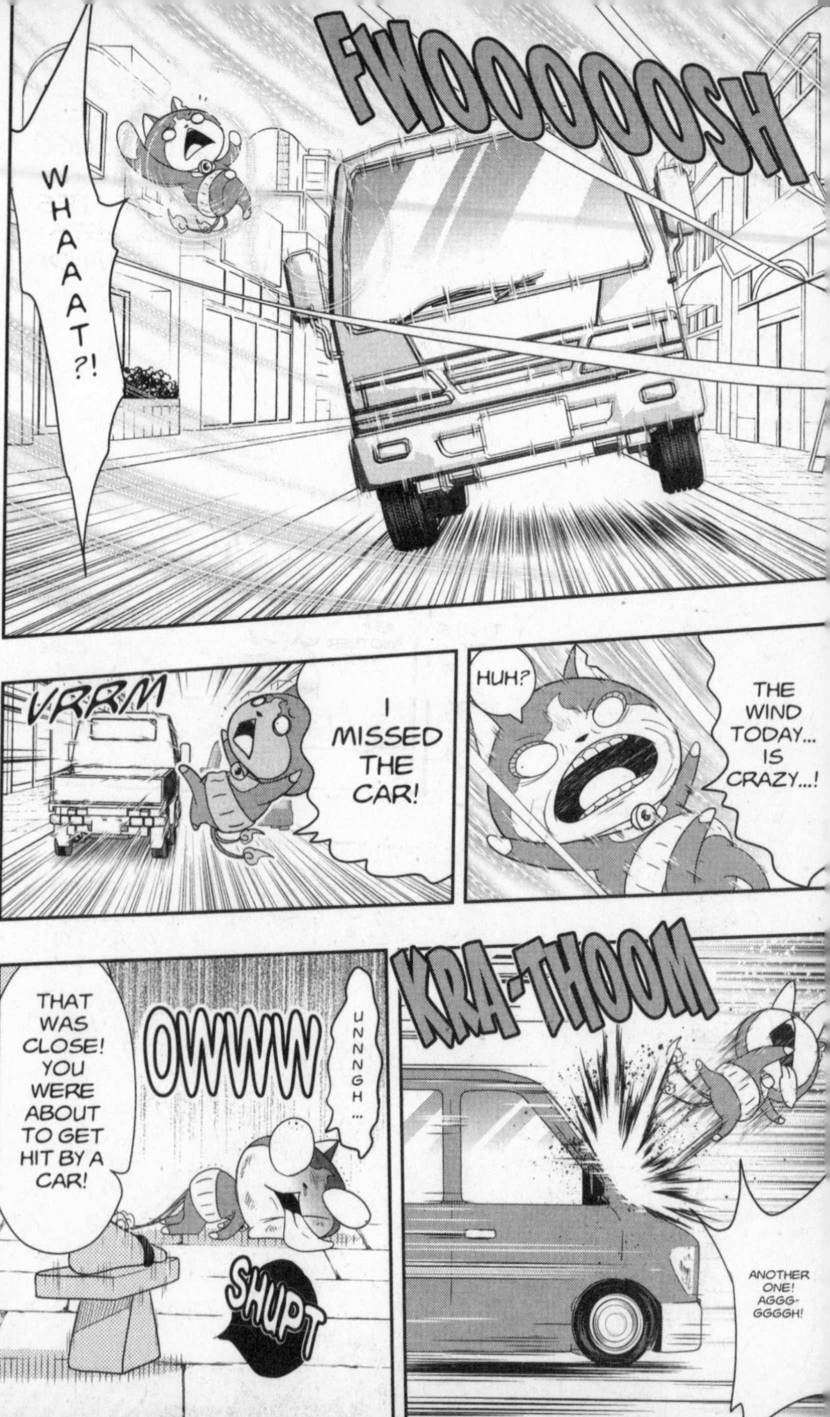
FWOOOOOOSH
WHAAAAT?!
HUH?
THE WIND TODAY... IS CRAZY...!
VRRM
I MISSED THE CAR!
KRA-THOOM
ANOTHER ONE! AGGG-GGGGH!
UNNNGH...
OWWW
THAT WAS CLOSE! YOU WERE ABOUT TO GET HIT BY A CAR!
SHUPT

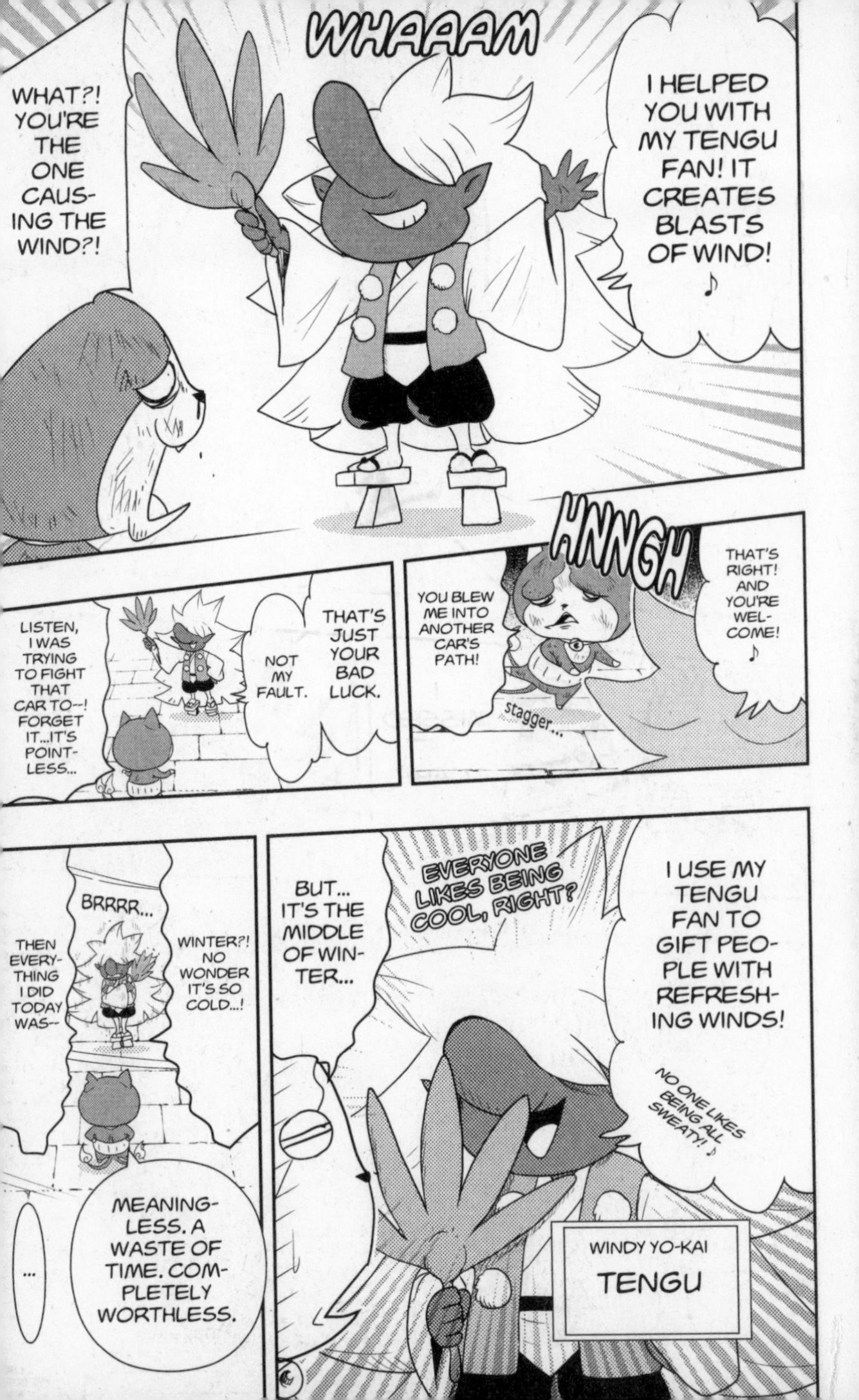
WHAAAM
I HELPED YOU WITH MY TENGU FAN! IT CREATES BLASTS OF WIND! ♪
WHAT?! YOU'RE THE ONE CAUSING THE WIND?!
HNNGH
THAT'S RIGHT! AND YOU'RE WELCOME! ♪
YOU BLEW ME INTO ANOTHER CAR'S PATH!
stagger...
THAT'S JUST YOUR BAD LUCK.
NOT MY FAULT.
LISTEN, I WAS TRYING TO FIGHT THAT CAR TO--! FORGET IT...IT'S POINTLESS...
I USE MY TENGU FAN TO GIFT PEOPLE WITH REFRESHING WINDS!
EVERYONE LIKES BEING COOL, RIGHT?
BUT... IT'S THE MIDDLE OF WINTER...
NO ONE LIKES BEING ALL SWEATY! ♪
WINDY YO-KAI
TENGU
BRRRR...
WINTER?! NO WONDER IT'S SO COLD...!
THEN EVERYTHING I DID TODAY WAS--
MEANINGLESS. A WASTE OF TIME. COMPLETELY WORTHLESS.
...

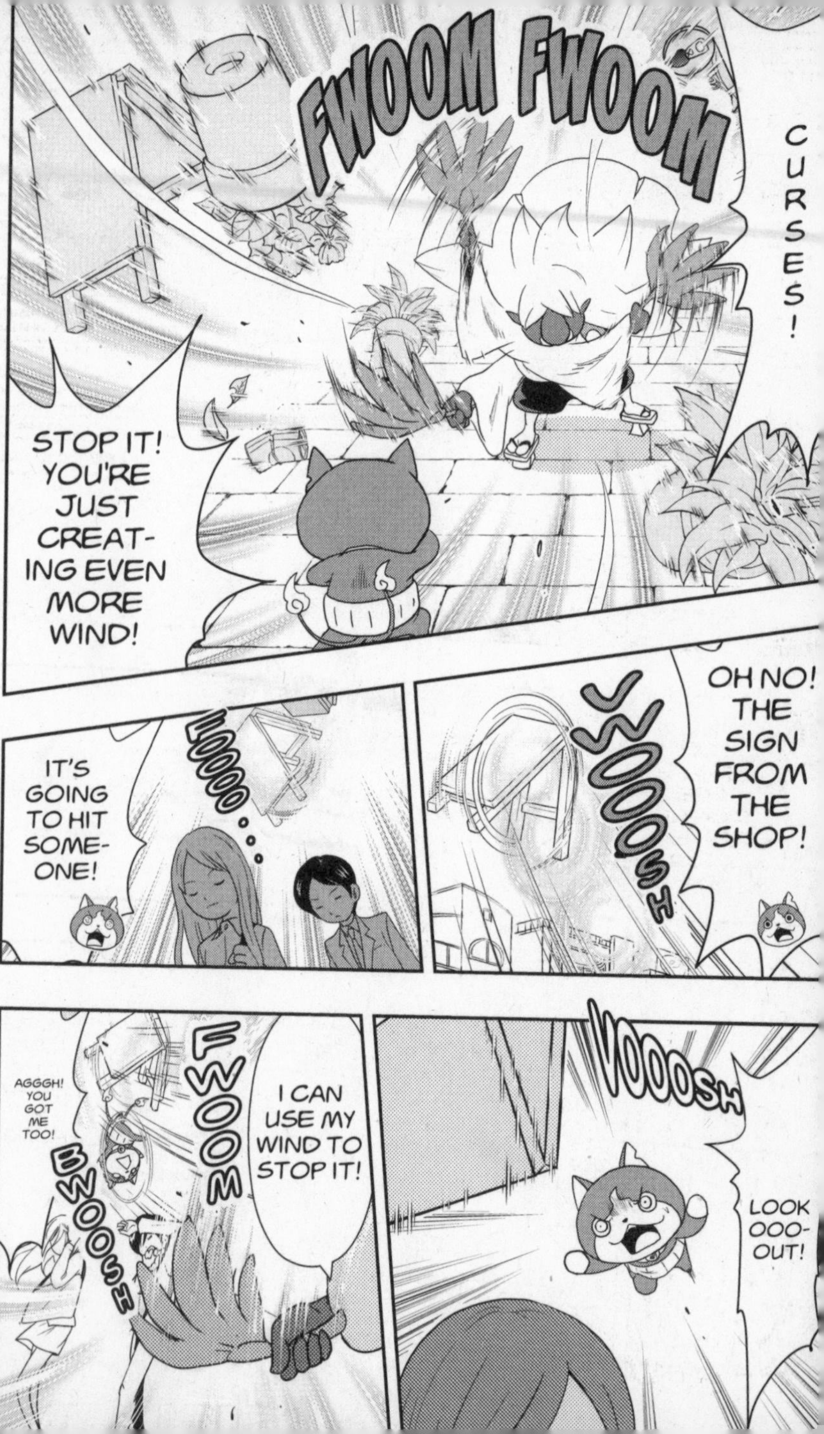
CURSES!
FWOOM FWOOM
STOP IT! YOU'RE JUST CREAT-ING EVEN MORE WIND!
OH NO! THE SIGN FROM THE SHOP!
VWOOOSH
LOOOO...
IT'S GOING TO HIT SOME-ONE!
VOOOSH
LOOK OOO-OUT!
FWOOOM
I CAN USE MY WIND TO STOP IT!
AGGGH! YOU GOT ME TOO!
BWOOSH

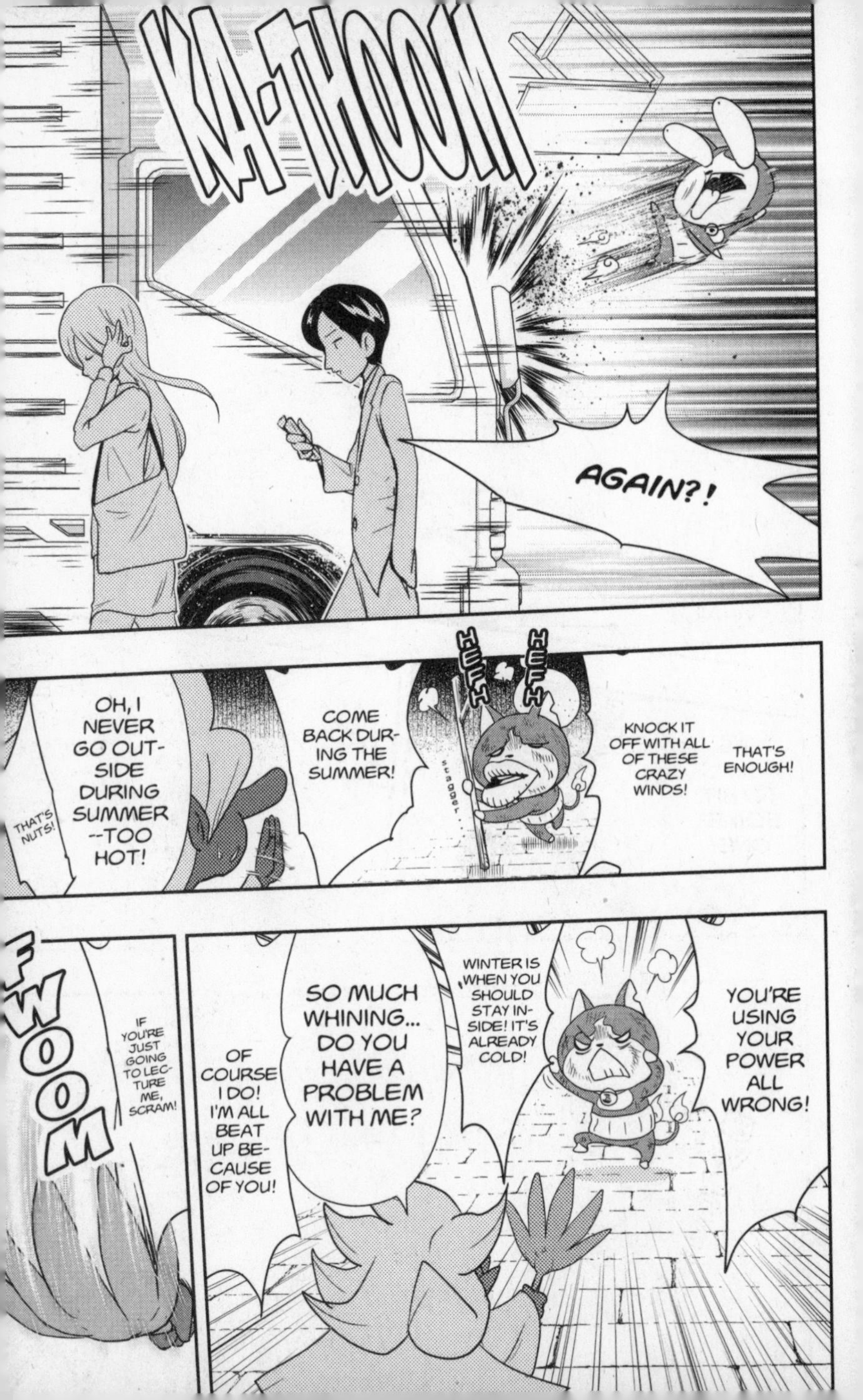
KA-THOOM
AGAIN?!
THAT'S ENOUGH!
KNOCK IT OFF WITH ALL OF THESE CRAZY WINDS!
HEFH HEFH
stagger
COME BACK DURING THE SUMMER!
OH, I NEVER GO OUTSIDE DURING SUMMER --TOO HOT!
THAT'S NUTS!
YOU'RE USING YOUR POWER ALL WRONG!
WINTER IS WHEN YOU SHOULD STAY INSIDE! IT'S ALREADY COLD!
SO MUCH WHINING... DO YOU HAVE A PROBLEM WITH ME?
OF COURSE I DO! I'M ALL BEAT UP BECAUSE OF YOU!
IF YOU'RE JUST GOING TO LECTURE ME, SCRAM!
FWOOM

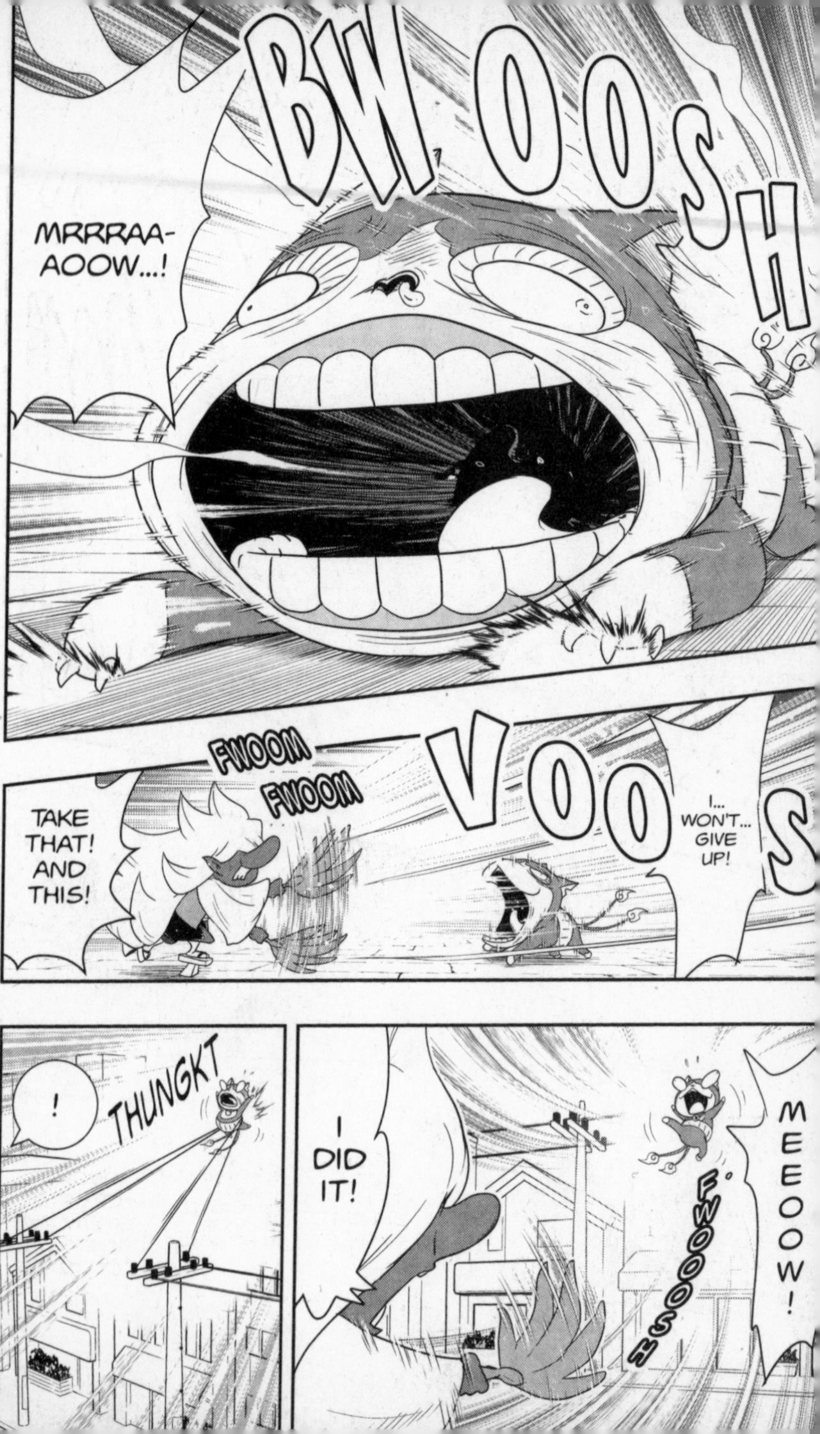
BWOOSH
MRRRAA-AOOW...!
VOOS
I... WON'T... GIVE UP!
FWOOM FWOOM
TAKE THAT! AND THIS!
MEEOOOW!
FWOOOOSH
I DID IT!
THUNGKT
!

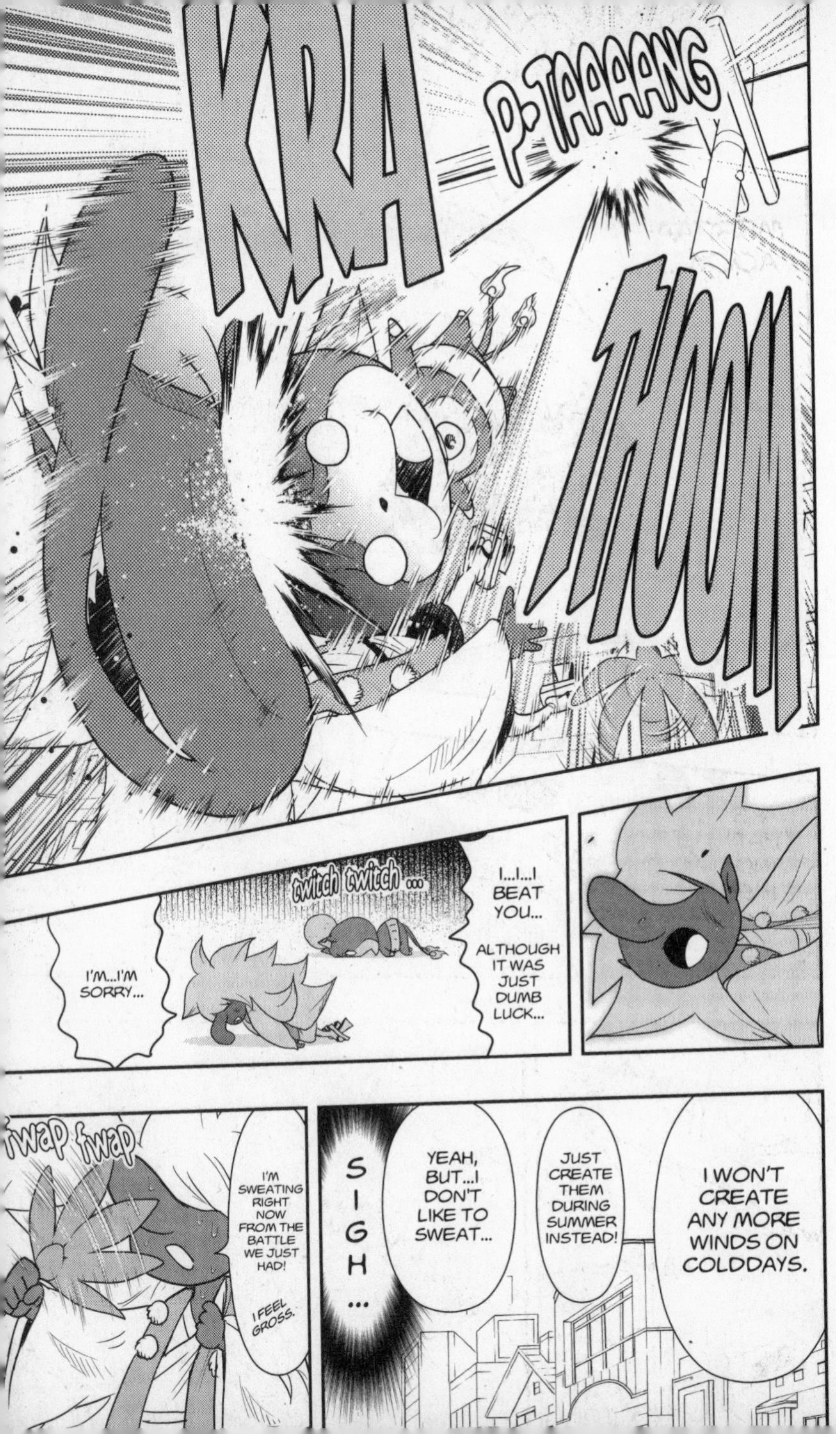
P-TAAAANG
KRA
THOOM
I...I...I BEAT YOU...
ALTHOUGH IT WAS JUST DUMB LUCK...
twitch twitch ...
I'M...I'M SORRY...
I WON'T CREATE ANY MORE WINDS ON COLDDAYS.
JUST CREATE THEM DURING SUMMER INSTEAD!
YEAH, BUT...I DON'T LIKE TO SWEAT...
SIGH...
I'M SWEATING RIGHT NOW FROM THE BATTLE WE JUST HAD!
I FEEL GROSS.
fwap fwap

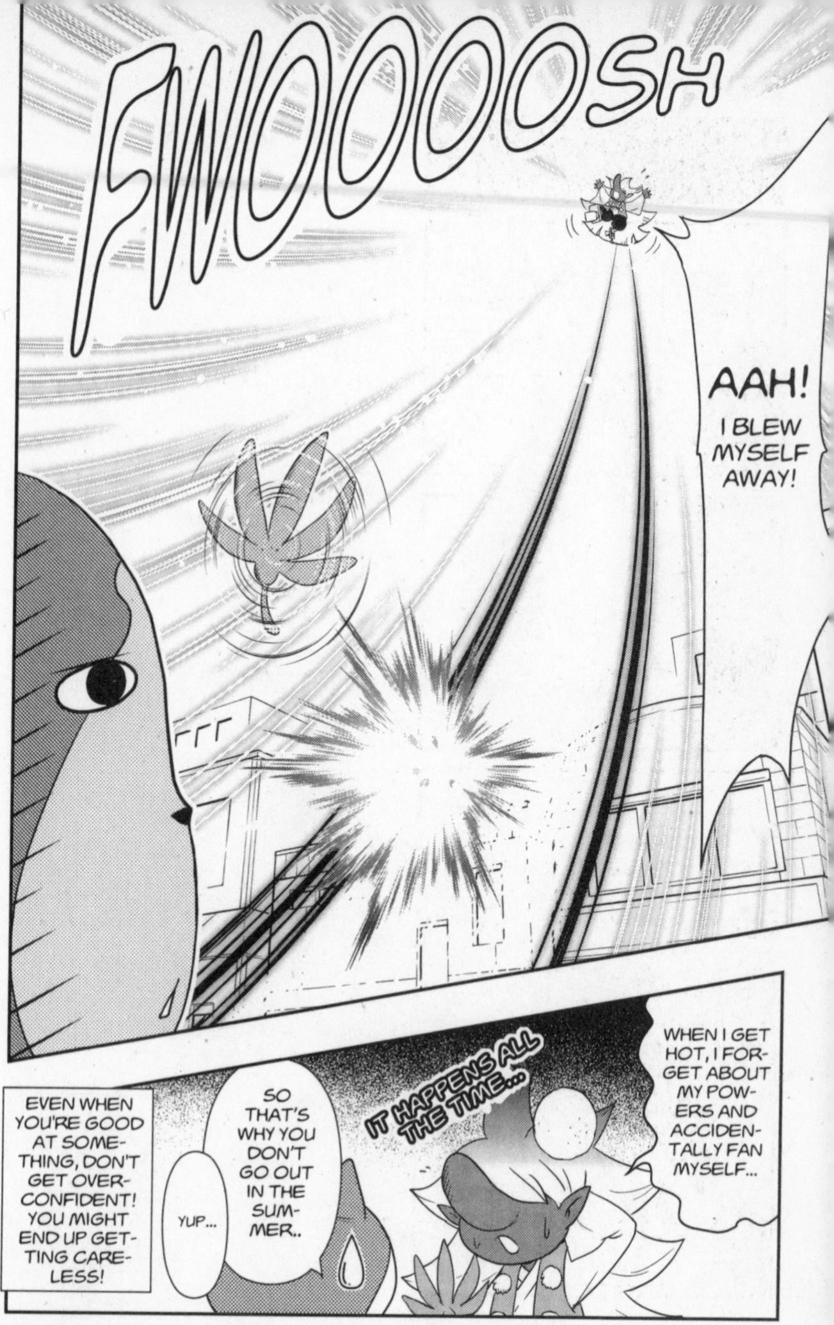
FWOOOOSH
AAH! I BLEW MYSELF AWAY!
WHEN I GET HOT, I FORGET ABOUT MY POWERS AND ACCIDENTALLY FAN MYSELF...
IT HAPPENS ALL THE TIME...
SO THAT'S WHY YOU DON'T GO OUT IN THE SUMMER..
YUP...
EVEN WHEN YOU'RE GOOD AT SOMETHING, DON'T GET OVERCONFIDENT! YOU MIGHT END UP GETTING CARELESS!

SWEAT

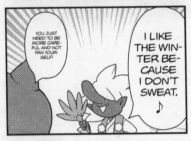

I LIKE THE WINTER BECAUSE I DON'T SWEAT. ♪
YOU JUST NEED TO BE MORE CAREFUL AND NOT FAN YOURSELF!
I DON'T EVER EXERCISE...
...AND I'VE BEEN TRAINING MYSELF NOT TO SWEAT. ♪
THEN TRAIN YOURSELF TO NOT USE YOUR FAN!
HEY, JIBANYAN! ♪
BUT IN THE WINTER...
UH-OH...
FWOOOOSH
?
WHOOPS...
SWELTON
HE FANNED HIMSELF.

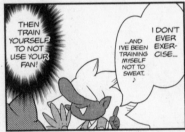

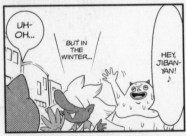

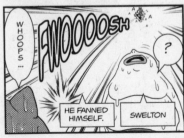

SWELTON VS. BLIZZARIA

MY SOUL MATE! ♬
VOOOSH
QUIT FOLLOWING ME AROUND!
AHHH! BLIZ-ZARIA! HELP ME!
I DON'T WANT TO SWEAT!!
WHAT...? BUT THE ONLY THING I CAN DO IS...
FREEZE THINGS!
KRRRKT
FWOOOH
AGGGH! MY SOUL-MATE!
I...I...I WON'T SWEAT, BUT I'M...GOING TO FREEZE...TO DEATH...
I'LL MAKE HIM SWEAT TO MELT THE ICE!
DRIP DRIP
ARRGH! NOW I'M SWEATY AGAIN!
SPLOT SPLOT
LEAVE IT TO ME! I'LL FREEZE ALL OF YOUR SWEAT!
FWOOH
DRIP DRIP SPLOT SPLOT
I WON'T GIVE UP!
UGGGH
HEFH HEFH
ALL THE CHANGING TEMPERATURES GAVE HIM A COLD!
WHOOPS.
SORRY.

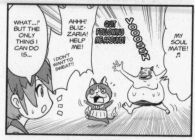

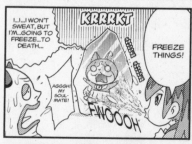

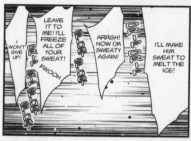

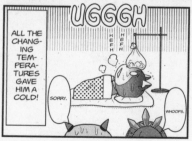

CHAPTER 86: ONLY SEVEN PAGES
FEATURING PRICKLY YO-KAI THORNYAN

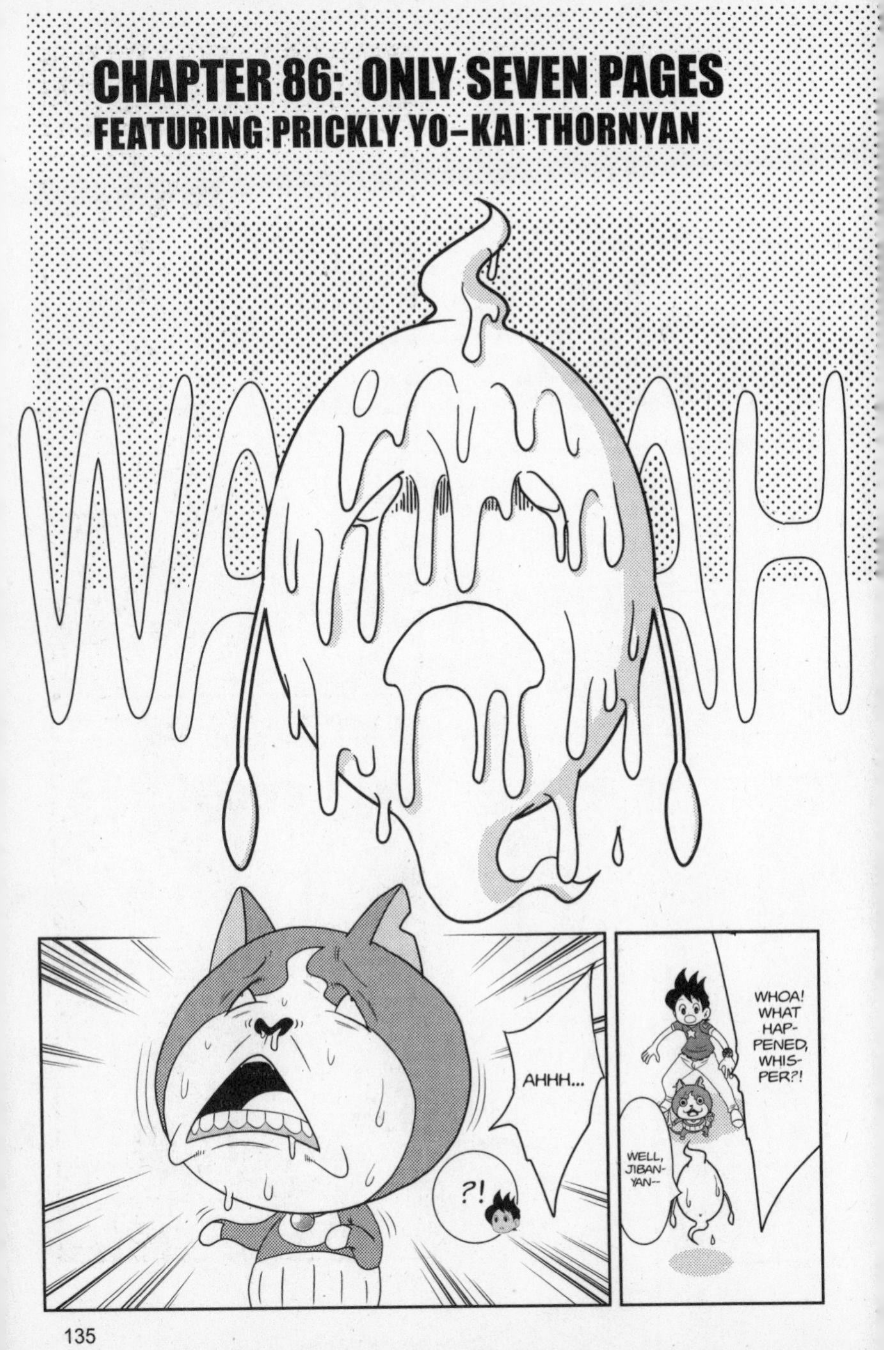
WHOA! WHAT HAP-PENED, WHIS-PER?!
WELL, JIBAN-YAN--
AHHH...
?!

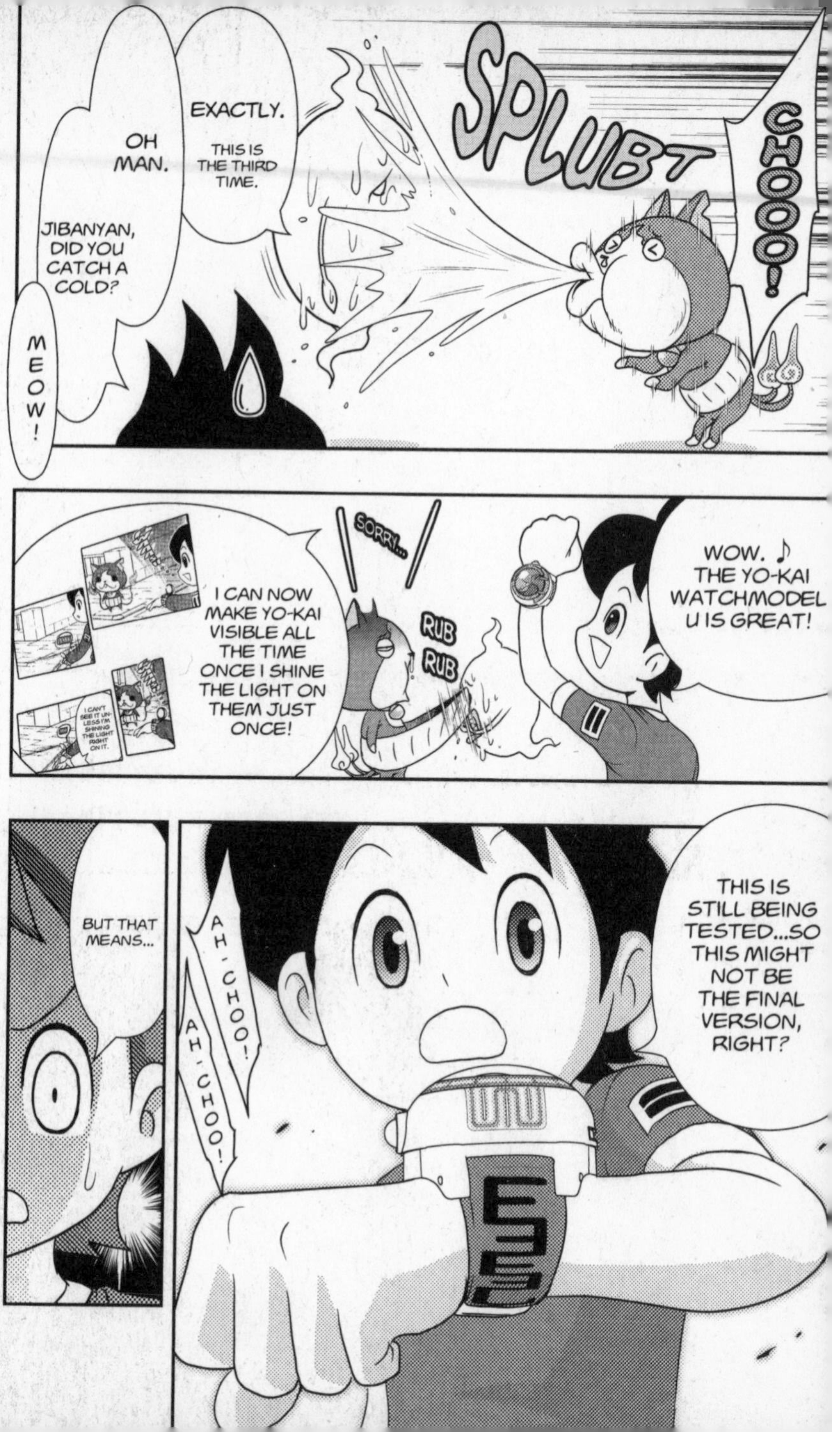
CHOOOO!
SPLUBT
EXACTLY.
THIS IS THE THIRD TIME.
OH MAN.
JIBANYAN, DID YOU CATCH A COLD?
MEOW!
WOW. ♪ THE YO-KAI WATCH MODEL U IS GREAT!
RUB RUB
SORRY...
I CAN NOW MAKE YO-KAI VISIBLE ALL THE TIME ONCE I SHINE THE LIGHT ON THEM JUST ONCE!
I CAN'T SEE IT UNLESS I'M SHINING THE LIGHT RIGHT ON IT.
THIS IS STILL BEING TESTED...SO THIS MIGHT NOT BE THE FINAL VERSION, RIGHT?
AH-CHOO!
AH-CHOO!
BUT THAT MEANS...

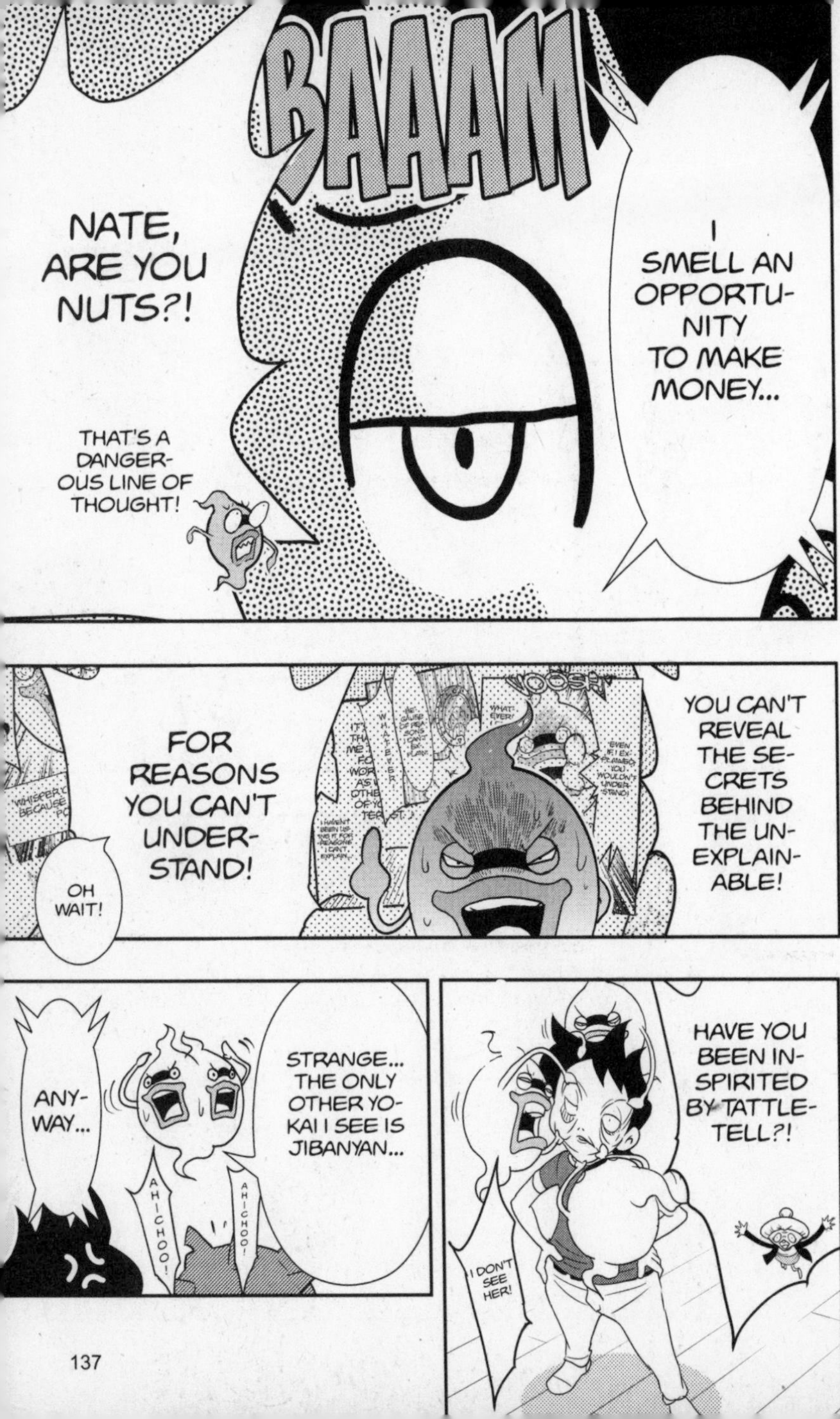
BAAAM
I SMELL AN OPPORTUNITY TO MAKE MONEY...
NATE, ARE YOU NUTS?!
THAT'S A DANGEROUS LINE OF THOUGHT!
YOU CAN'T REVEAL THE SECRETS BEHIND THE UNEXPLAINABLE!
FOR REASONS YOU CAN'T UNDERSTAND!
OH WAIT!
HAVE YOU BEEN INSPIRITED BY TATTLETELL?!
I DON'T SEE HER!
STRANGE... THE ONLY OTHER YOKAI I SEE IS JIBANYAN...
AHICHOO!
AHICHOO!
ANYWAY...

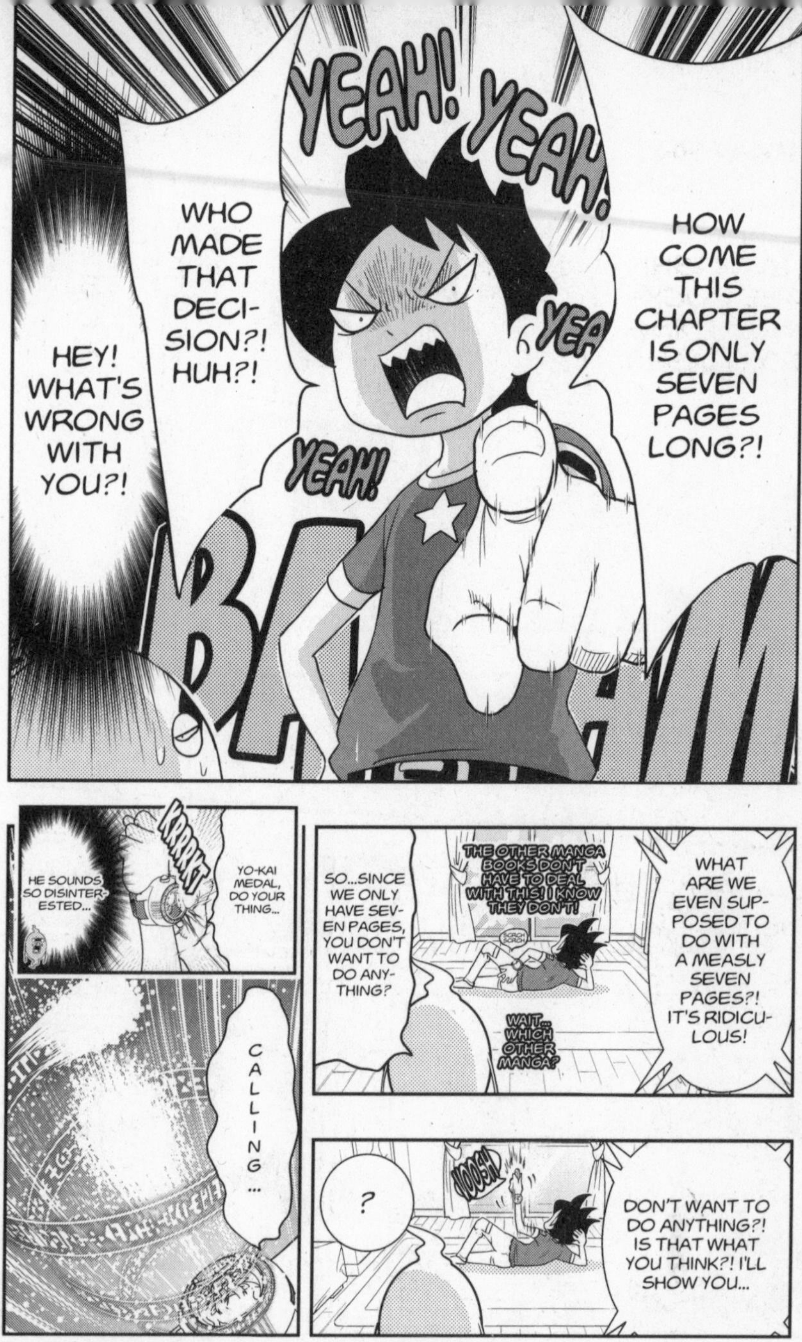
YEAH! YEAH!
HOW COME THIS CHAPTER IS ONLY SEVEN PAGES LONG?!
YEA
WHO MADE THAT DECISION?! HUH?!
YEAH!
HEY! WHAT'S WRONG WITH YOU?!
WHAT ARE WE EVEN SUPPOSED TO DO WITH A MEASLY SEVEN PAGES?! IT'S RIDICULOUS!
THE OTHER MANGA BOOKS DON'T HAVE TO DEAL WITH THIS! I KNOW THEY DON'T!
WAIT... WHICH OTHER MANGA?
SO...SINCE WE ONLY HAVE SEVEN PAGES, YOU DON'T WANT TO DO ANYTHING?
DON'T WANT TO DO ANYTHING?! IS THAT WHAT YOU THINK?! I'LL SHOW YOU...
WOOSH
?
YO-KAI MEDAL, DO YOUR THING...
KRRRKT
HE SOUNDS SO DISINTERESTED...
CALLING...

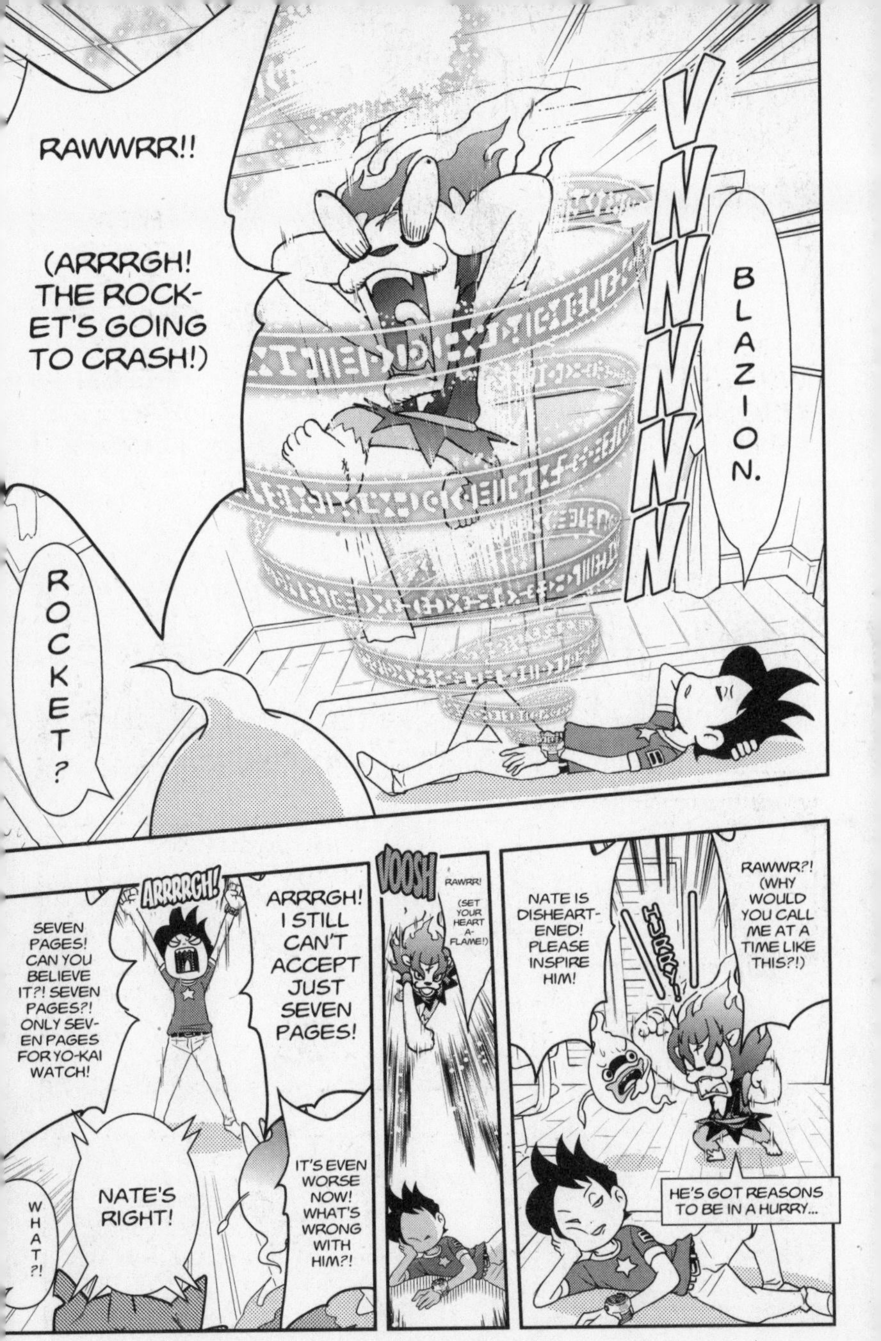
VNNNNNN
BLAZION.
RAWWRR!!
(ARRRGH! THE ROCKET'S GOING TO CRASH!)
ROCKET?
RAWWR?! (WHY WOULD YOU CALL ME AT A TIME LIKE THIS?!)
NATE IS DISHEARTENED! PLEASE INSPIRE HIM!
HE'S GOT REASONS TO BE IN A HURRY...
VOOSH
RAWRR! (SET YOUR HEART A-FLAME!)
IT'S EVEN WORSE NOW! WHAT'S WRONG WITH HIM?!
ARRRGH! I STILL CAN'T ACCEPT JUST SEVEN PAGES!
ARRRRGH!
SEVEN PAGES! CAN YOU BELIEVE IT?! SEVEN PAGES?! ONLY SEVEN PAGES FOR YO-KAI WATCH!
NATE'S RIGHT!
WHAT?!

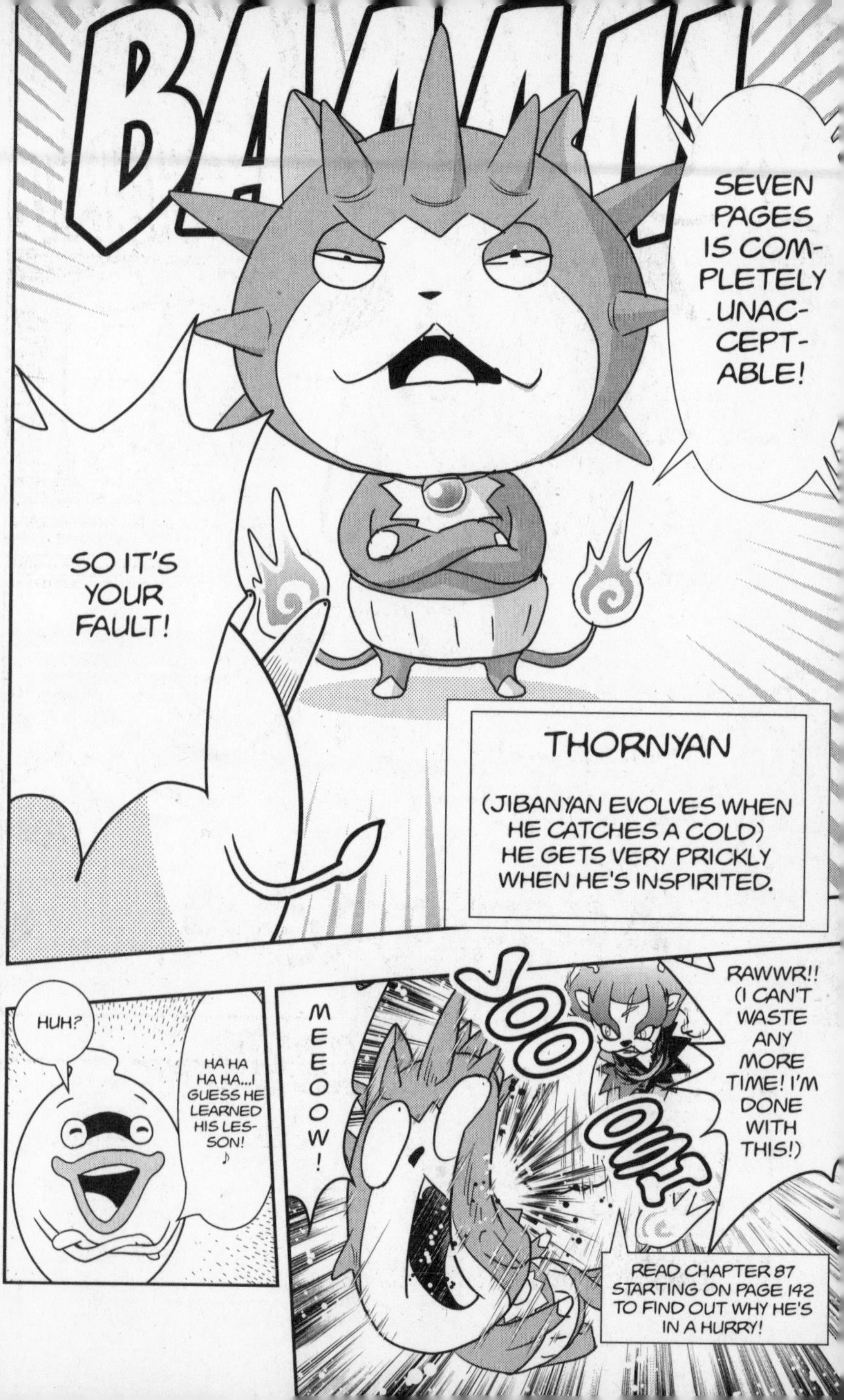
SEVEN PAGES IS COMPLETELY UNACCEPTABLE!
SO IT'S YOUR FAULT!
THORNYAN
(JIBANYAN EVOLVES WHEN HE CATCHES A COLD) HE GETS VERY PRICKLY WHEN HE'S INSPIRITED.
RAWWR!! (I CAN'T WASTE ANY MORE TIME! I'M DONE WITH THIS!)
MEEOOOW!
READ CHAPTER 87 STARTING ON PAGE 142 TO FIND OUT WHY HE'S IN A HURRY!
HUH?
HA HA HA HA...I GUESS HE LEARNED HIS LESSON! ♪

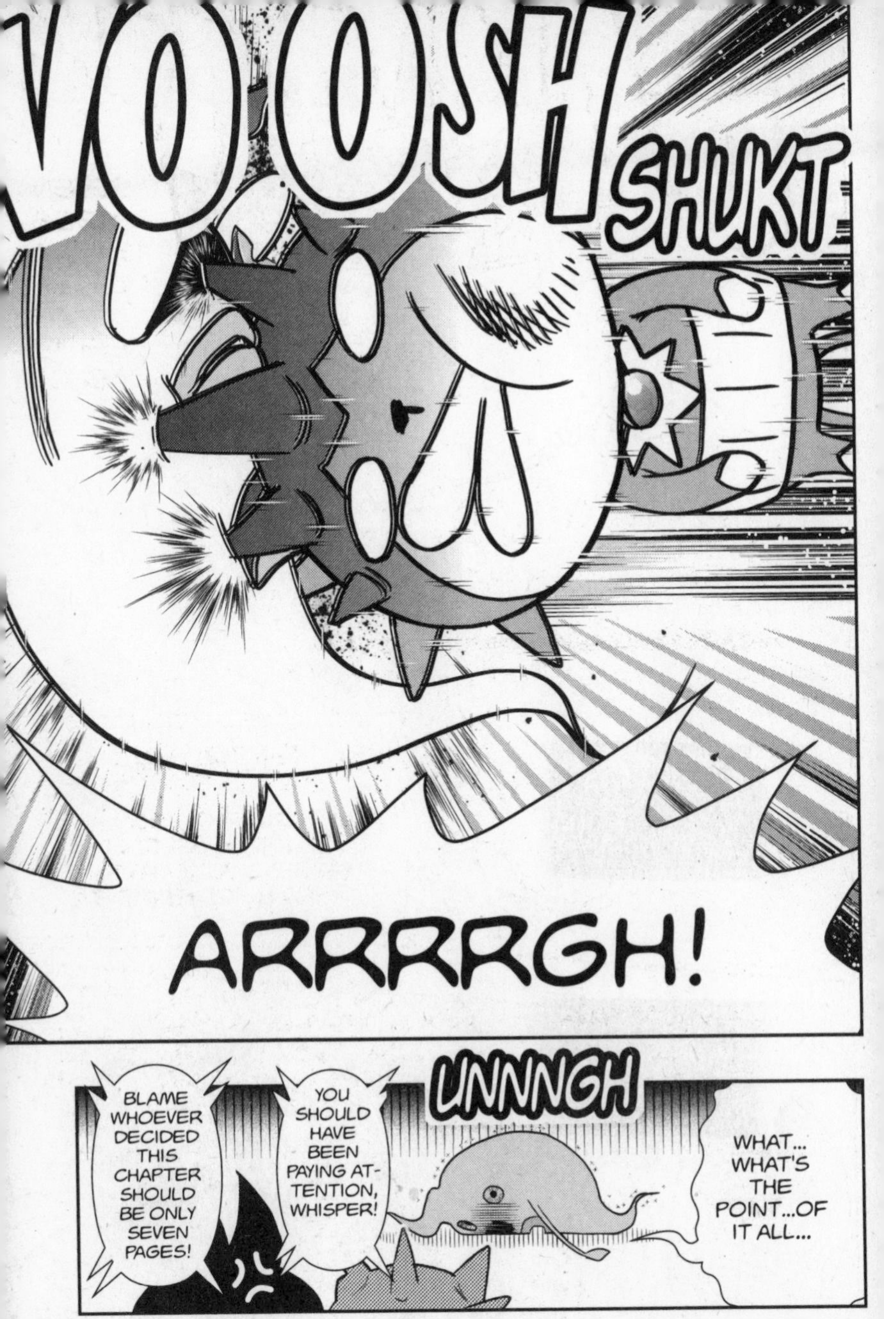
VOOSH
SHUKT
ARRRRGH!
WHAT... WHAT'S THE POINT...OF IT ALL...
UNNNGH
YOU SHOULD HAVE BEEN PAYING AT-TENTION, WHISPER!
BLAME WHOEVER DECIDED THIS CHAPTER SHOULD BE ONLY SEVEN PAGES!

CHAPTER 87: LAUNCH THE DREAM ROCKET!!

FEATURING TRIVIA YO-KAI POOFESSOR

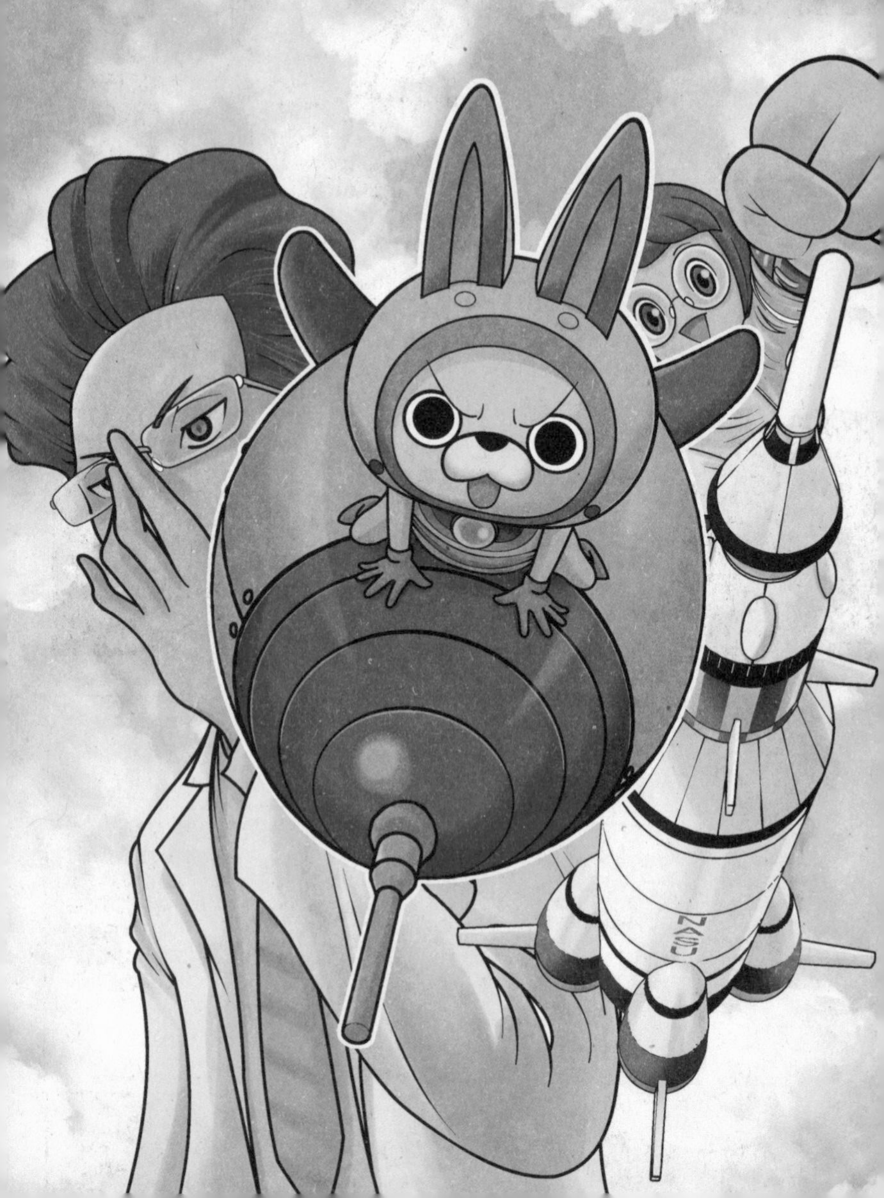
NASU

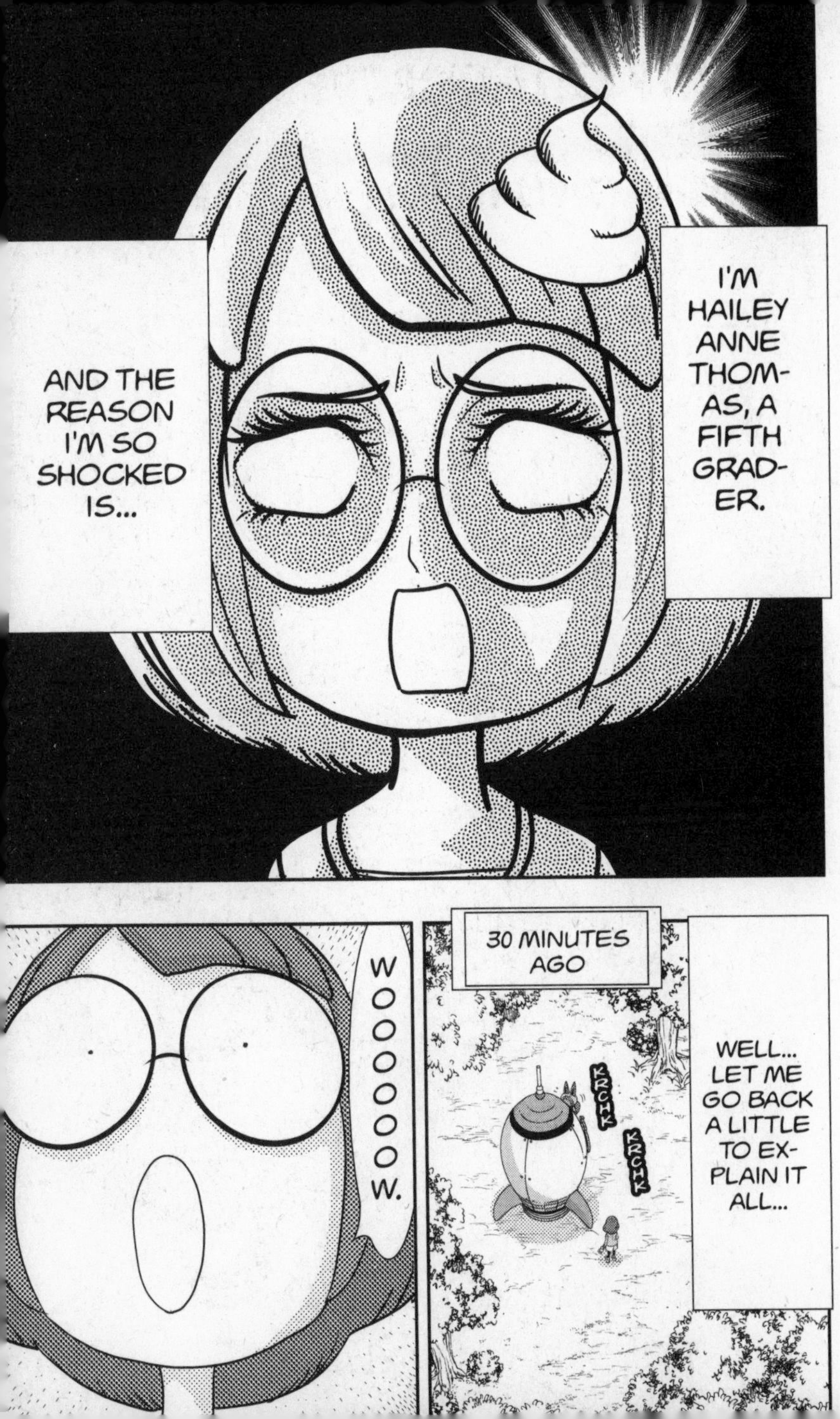
I'M HAILEY ANNE THOMAS, A FIFTH GRADER.
AND THE REASON I'M SO SHOCKED IS...
WELL... LET ME GO BACK A LITTLE TO EXPLAIN IT ALL...
30 MINUTES AGO
KRCHK
KRCHK
WOOOOOOOW.

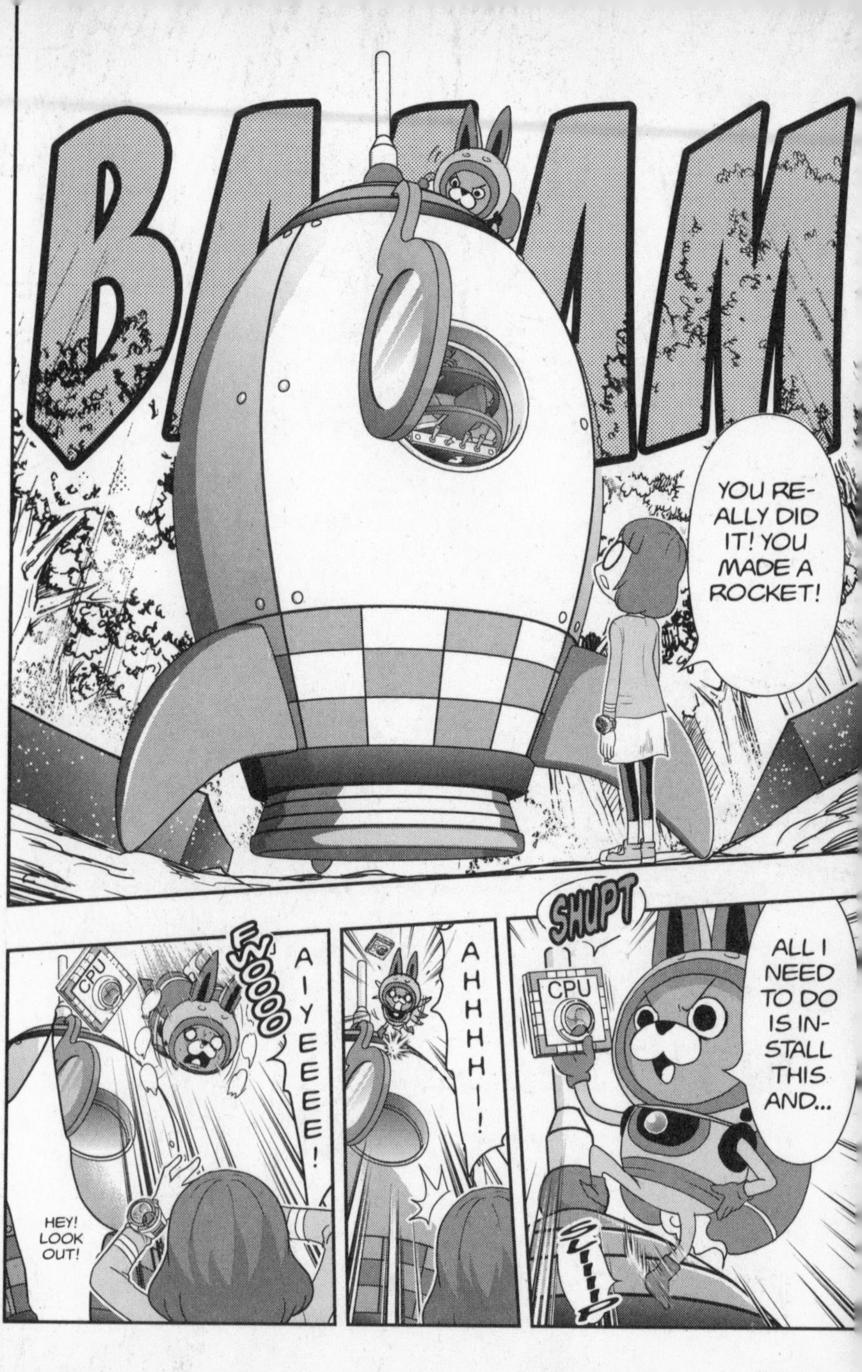
BAMM
YOU RE-
ALLY DID
IT! YOU
MADE A
ROCKET!
SHUPT
CPU
ALL I
NEED
TO DO
IS IN-
STALL
THIS
AND...
CPU
AHHHH!!
AIYEEEEE!
FWOOOO
CPU
HEY!
LOOK
OUT!

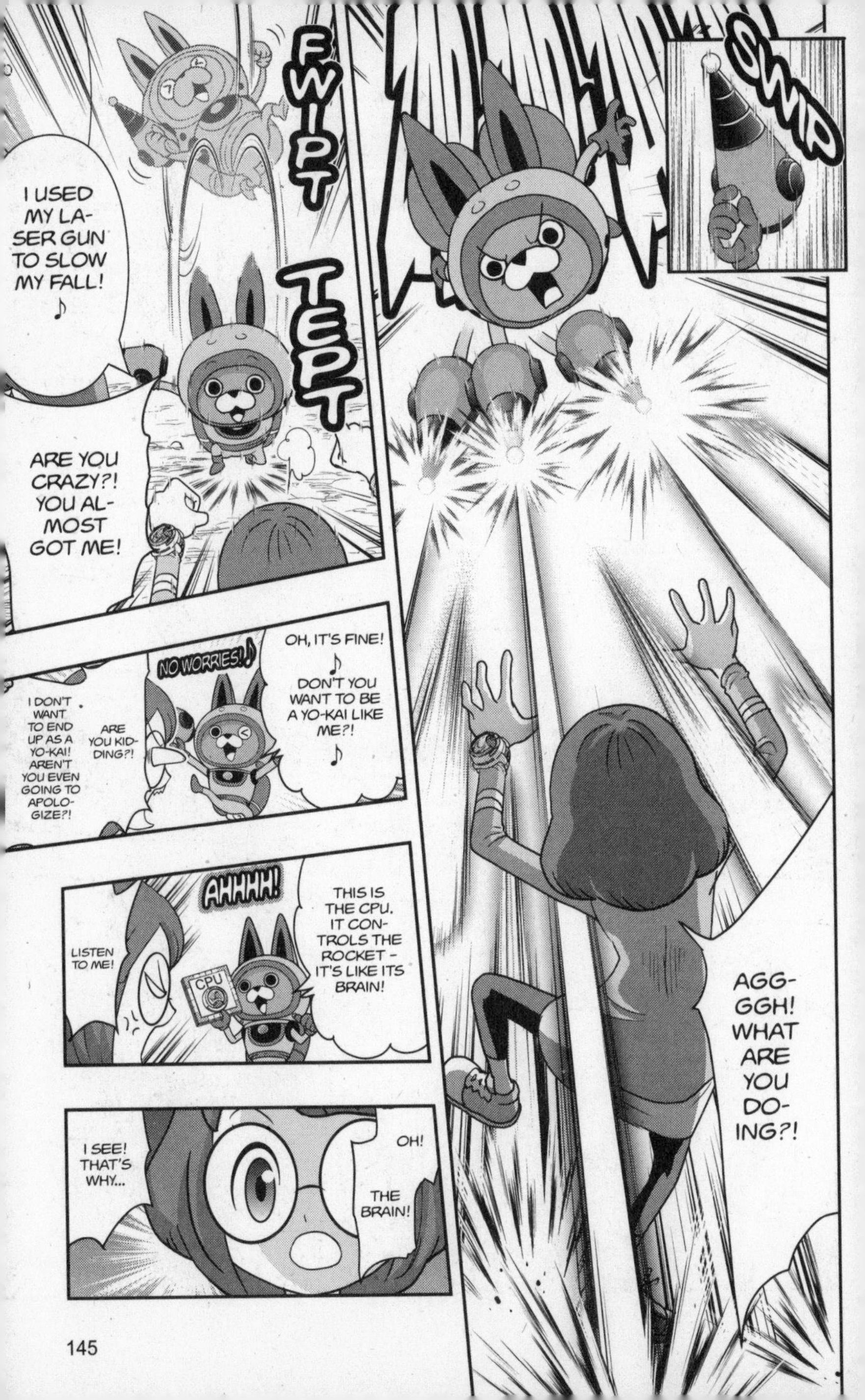
SWIP
AGG-
GGH!
WHAT
ARE
YOU
DO-
ING?!
FWIPT
TEPT
I USED
MY LA-
SER GUN
TO SLOW
MY FALL!
♪
ARE YOU
CRAZY?!
YOU AL-
MOST
GOT ME!
NO WORRIES!♪
OH, IT'S FINE!
♪
DON'T YOU
WANT TO BE
A YO-KAI LIKE
ME?!
♪
ARE
YOU KID-
DING?!
I DON'T
WANT
TO END
UP AS A
YO-KAI!
AREN'T
YOU EVEN
GOING TO
APOLO-
GIZE?!
AHHHH!
THIS IS
THE CPU.
IT CON-
TROLS THE
ROCKET -
IT'S LIKE ITS
BRAIN!
CPU
LISTEN
TO ME!
OH!
THE
BRAIN!
I SEE!
THAT'S
WHY...

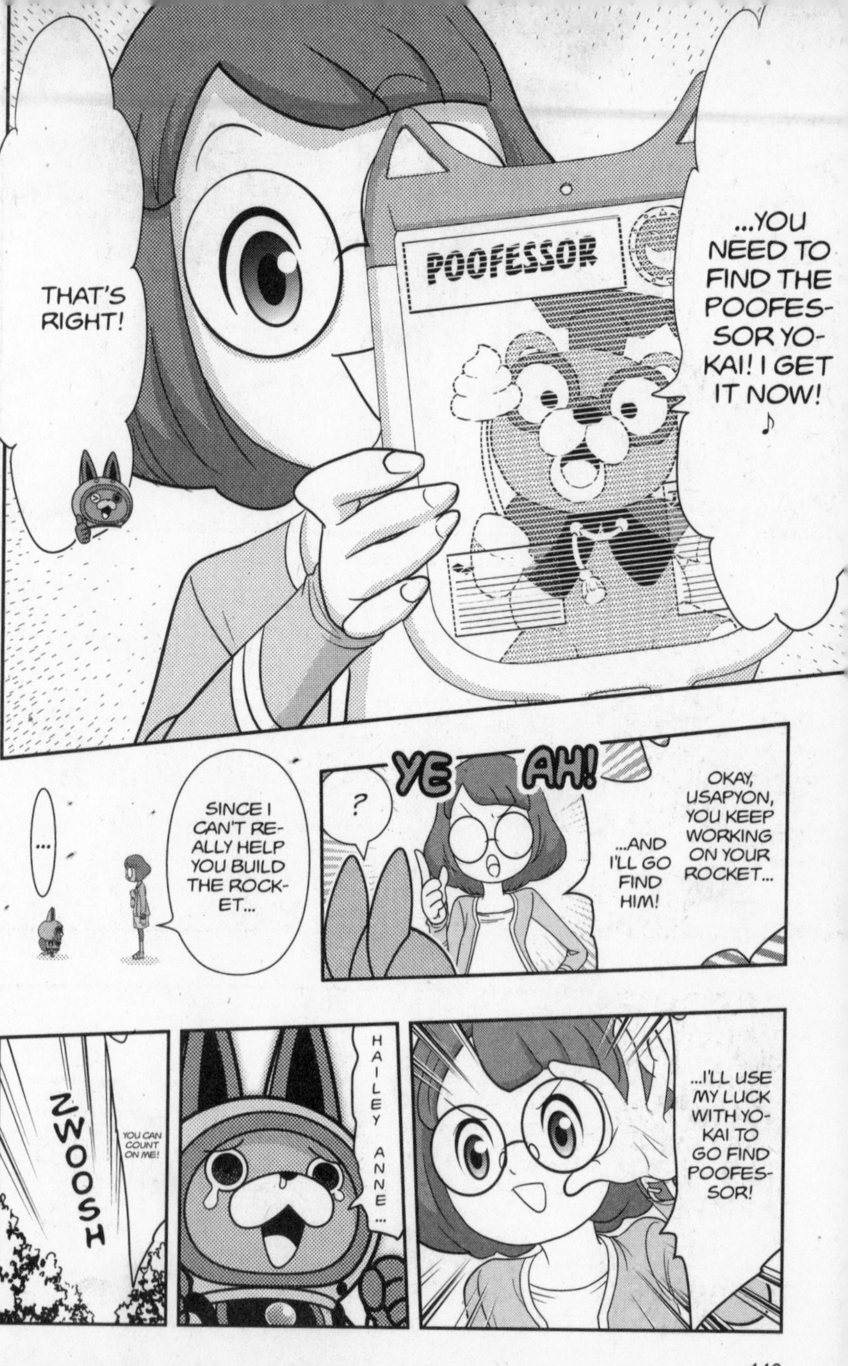
...YOU NEED TO FIND THE POOFES-SOR YO-KAI! I GET IT NOW! ♪
POOFESSOR
THAT'S RIGHT!
OKAY, USAPYON, YOU KEEP WORKING ON YOUR ROCKET...
...AND I'LL GO FIND HIM!
YE AH!
?
SINCE I CAN'T RE-ALLY HELP YOU BUILD THE ROCK-ET...
...
...I'LL USE MY LUCK WITH YO-KAI TO GO FIND POOFES-SOR!
HAILEY ANNE...
ZWOOSH
YOU CAN COUNT ON ME!

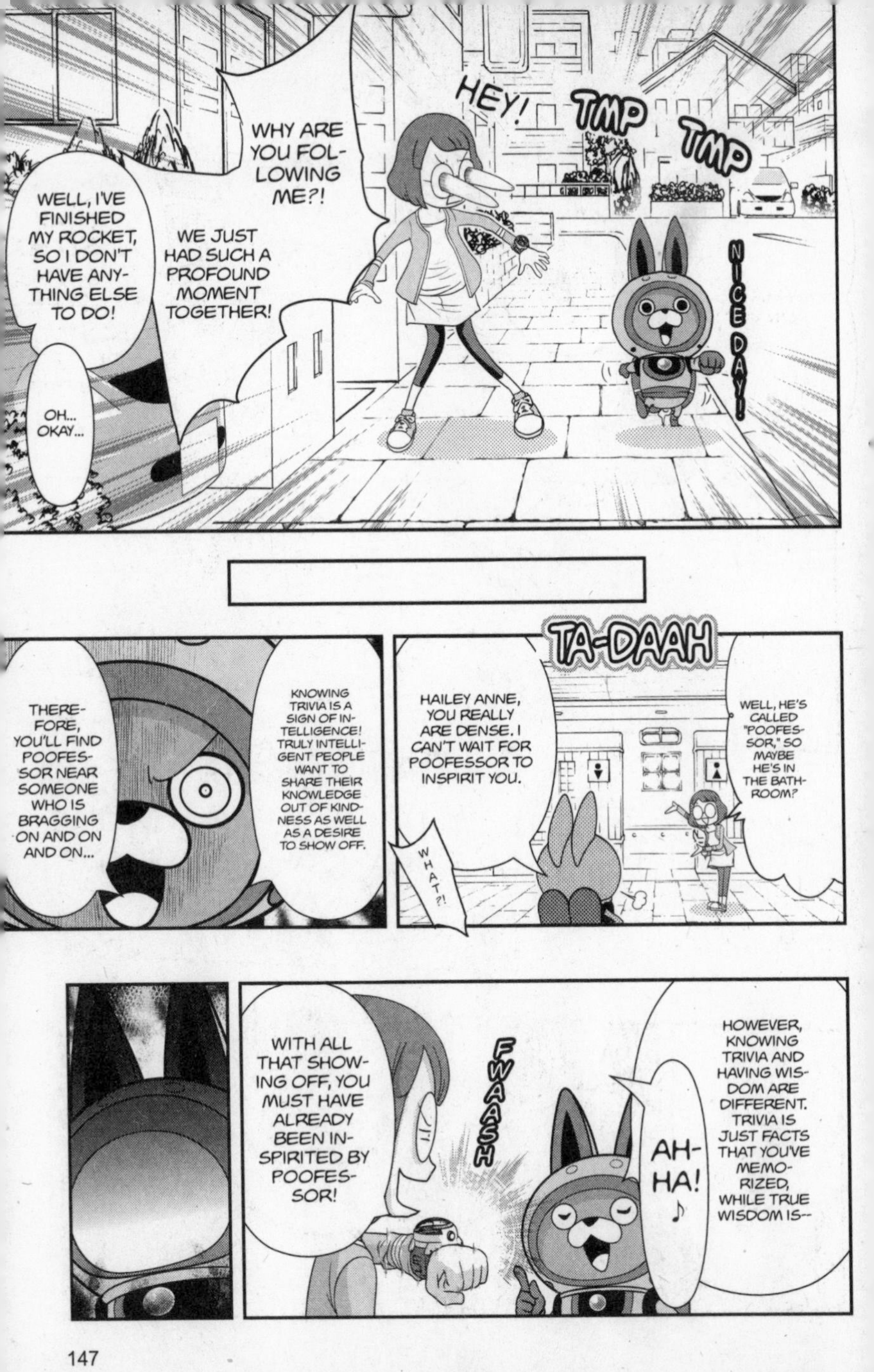
TMP TMP
NICE DAY!
HEY!
WHY ARE YOU FOL-LOWING ME?!
WE JUST HAD SUCH A PROFOUND MOMENT TOGETHER!
WELL, I'VE FINISHED MY ROCKET, SO I DON'T HAVE ANY-THING ELSE TO DO!
OH... OKAY...
TA-DAAH
WELL, HE'S CALLED "POOFES-SOR," SO MAYBE HE'S IN THE BATH-ROOM?
HAILEY ANNE, YOU REALLY ARE DENSE. I CAN'T WAIT FOR POOFESSOR TO INSPIRIT YOU.
WHAT?!
KNOWING TRIVIA IS A SIGN OF IN-TELLIGENCE! TRULY INTELLI-GENT PEOPLE WANT TO SHARE THEIR KNOWLEDGE OUT OF KIND-NESS AS WELL AS A DESIRE TO SHOW OFF.
THERE-FORE, YOU'LL FIND POOFES-SOR NEAR SOMEONE WHO IS BRAGGING ON AND ON AND ON...
HOWEVER, KNOWING TRIVIA AND HAVING WIS-DOM ARE DIFFERENT. TRIVIA IS JUST FACTS THAT YOU'VE MEMO-RIZED, WHILE TRUE WISDOM IS--
AH-HA! ♪
FWAASH
WITH ALL THAT SHOW-ING OFF, YOU MUST HAVE ALREADY BEEN IN-SPIRITED BY POOFES-SOR!

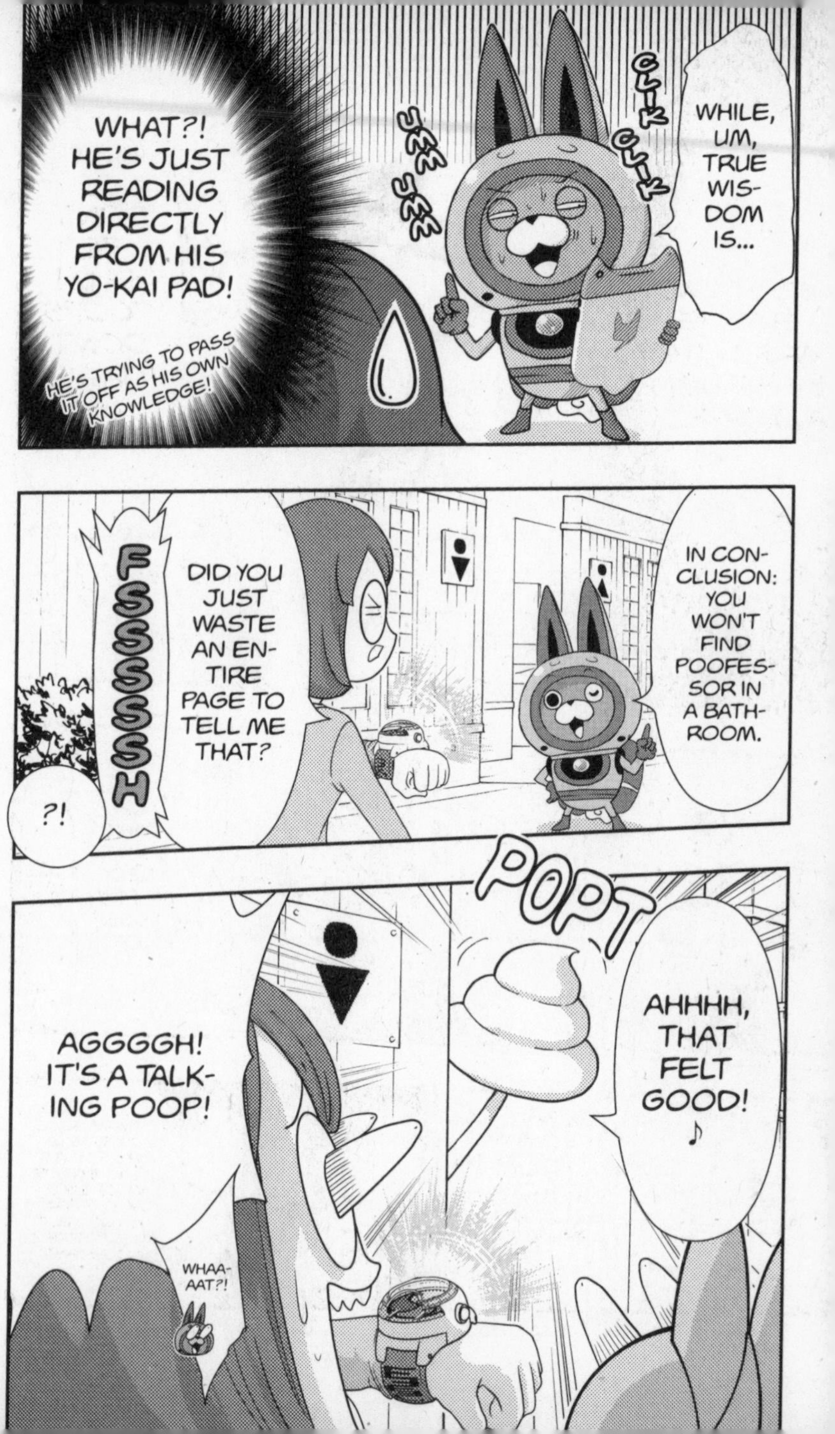

WHILE, UM, TRUE WISDOM IS...
CLIK CLIK
UMM UMM
WHAT?! HE'S JUST READING DIRECTLY FROM HIS YO-KAI PAD!
HE'S TRYING TO PASS IT OFF AS HIS OWN KNOWLEDGE!
IN CONCLUSION: YOU WON'T FIND POOFESSOR IN A BATHROOM.
DID YOU JUST WASTE AN ENTIRE PAGE TO TELL ME THAT?
FSSSSSH
?!
POPT
AHHHH, THAT FELT GOOD! ♪
AGGGGH! IT'S A TALKING POOP!
WHAA-AAT?!

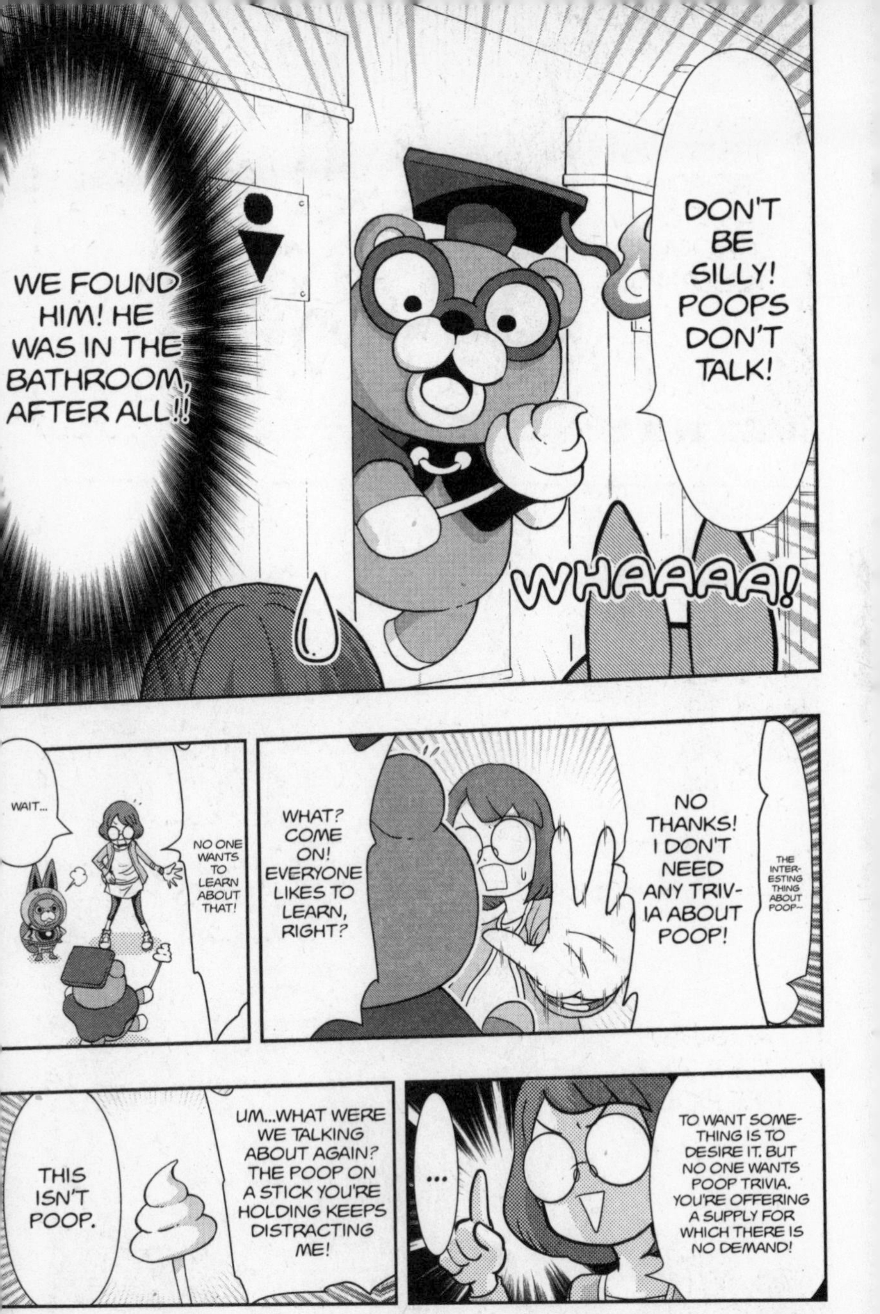
DON'T BE SILLY! POOPS DON'T TALK!
WE FOUND HIM! HE WAS IN THE BATHROOM, AFTER ALL!!
WHAAAAA!
THE INTER-ESTING THING ABOUT POOP~
NO THANKS! I DON'T NEED ANY TRIV-IA ABOUT POOP!
WHAT? COME ON! EVERYONE LIKES TO LEARN, RIGHT?
NO ONE WANTS TO LEARN ABOUT THAT!
WAIT...
TO WANT SOME-THING IS TO DESIRE IT. BUT NO ONE WANTS POOP TRIVIA. YOU'RE OFFERING A SUPPLY FOR WHICH THERE IS NO DEMAND!
...
UM...WHAT WERE WE TALKING ABOUT AGAIN? THE POOP ON A STICK YOU'RE HOLDING KEEPS DISTRACTING ME!
THIS ISN'T POOP.

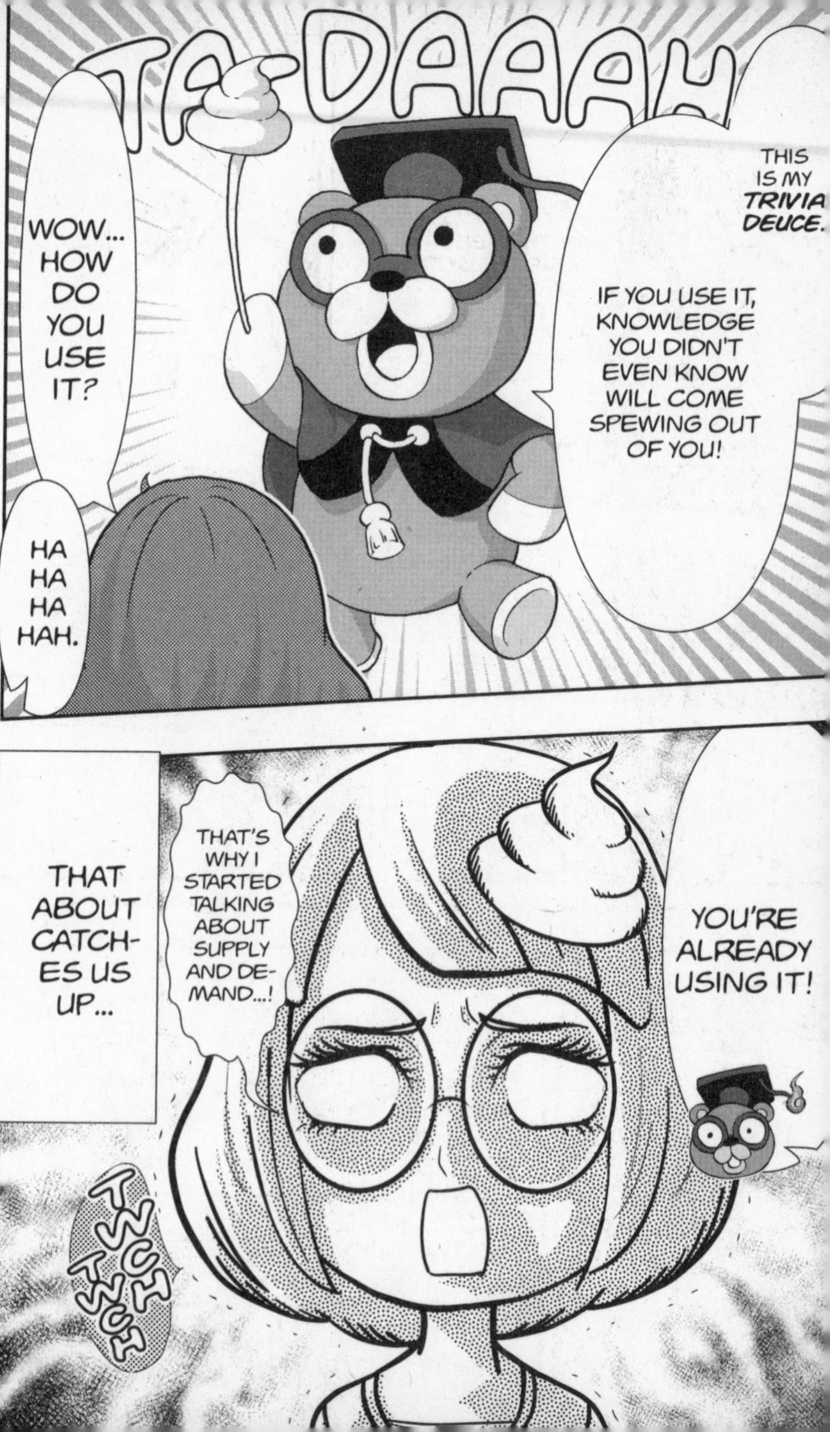
TA-DAAAAH
THIS IS MY *TRIVIA DEUCE.*
IF YOU USE IT, KNOWLEDGE YOU DIDN'T EVEN KNOW WILL COME SPEWING OUT OF YOU!
WOW... HOW DO YOU USE IT?
HA HA HA HAH.
YOU'RE ALREADY USING IT!
THAT'S WHY I STARTED TALKING ABOUT SUPPLY AND DE-MAND...!
THAT ABOUT CATCH-ES US UP...
TWITCH TWITCH

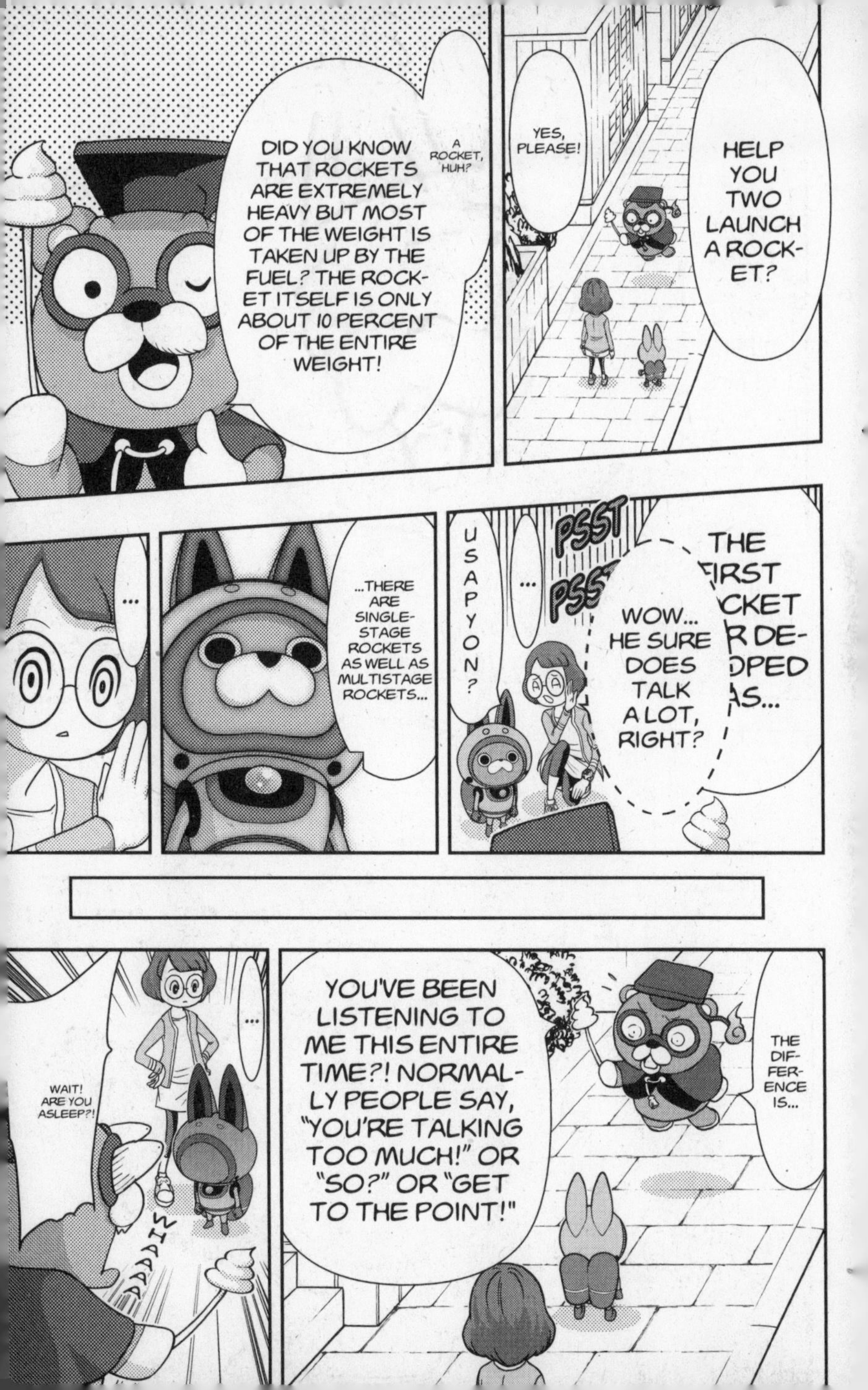
HELP YOU TWO LAUNCH A ROCK-ET?
YES, PLEASE!
A ROCKET, HUH?
DID YOU KNOW THAT ROCKETS ARE EXTREMELY HEAVY BUT MOST OF THE WEIGHT IS TAKEN UP BY THE FUEL? THE ROCK-ET ITSELF IS ONLY ABOUT 10 PERCENT OF THE ENTIRE WEIGHT!
PSSST
WOW... HE SURE DOES TALK A LOT, RIGHT?
...
USAPYON?
...THERE ARE SINGLE-STAGE ROCKETS AS WELL AS MULTISTAGE ROCKETS...
...
THE DIF-FER-ENCE IS...
YOU'VE BEEN LISTENING TO ME THIS ENTIRE TIME?! NORMAL-LY PEOPLE SAY, "YOU'RE TALKING TOO MUCH!" OR "SO?" OR "GET TO THE POINT!"
...
WAIT! ARE YOU ASLEEP?!
WHAAAA

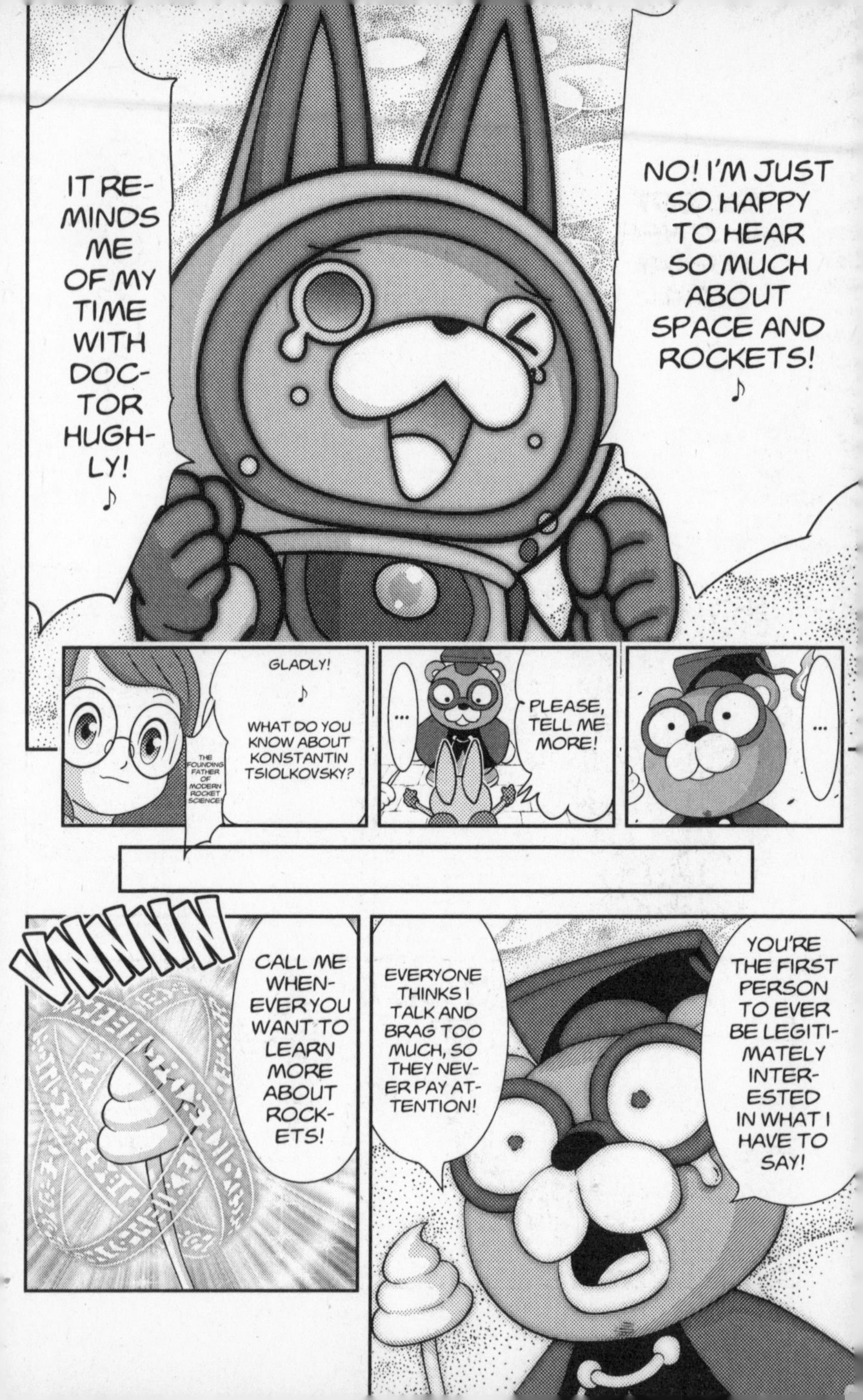
NO! I'M JUST SO HAPPY TO HEAR SO MUCH ABOUT SPACE AND ROCKETS! ♪
IT REMINDS ME OF MY TIME WITH DOCTOR HUGHLY! ♪
...
PLEASE, TELL ME MORE!
...
GLADLY! ♪ WHAT DO YOU KNOW ABOUT KONSTANTIN TSIOLKOVSKY?
THE FOUNDING FATHER OF MODERN ROCKET SCIENCE!
YOU'RE THE FIRST PERSON TO EVER BE LEGITIMATELY INTERESTED IN WHAT I HAVE TO SAY!
EVERYONE THINKS I TALK AND BRAG TOO MUCH, SO THEY NEVER PAY ATTENTION!
CALL ME WHENEVER YOU WANT TO LEARN MORE ABOUT ROCKETS!
VNNNNN

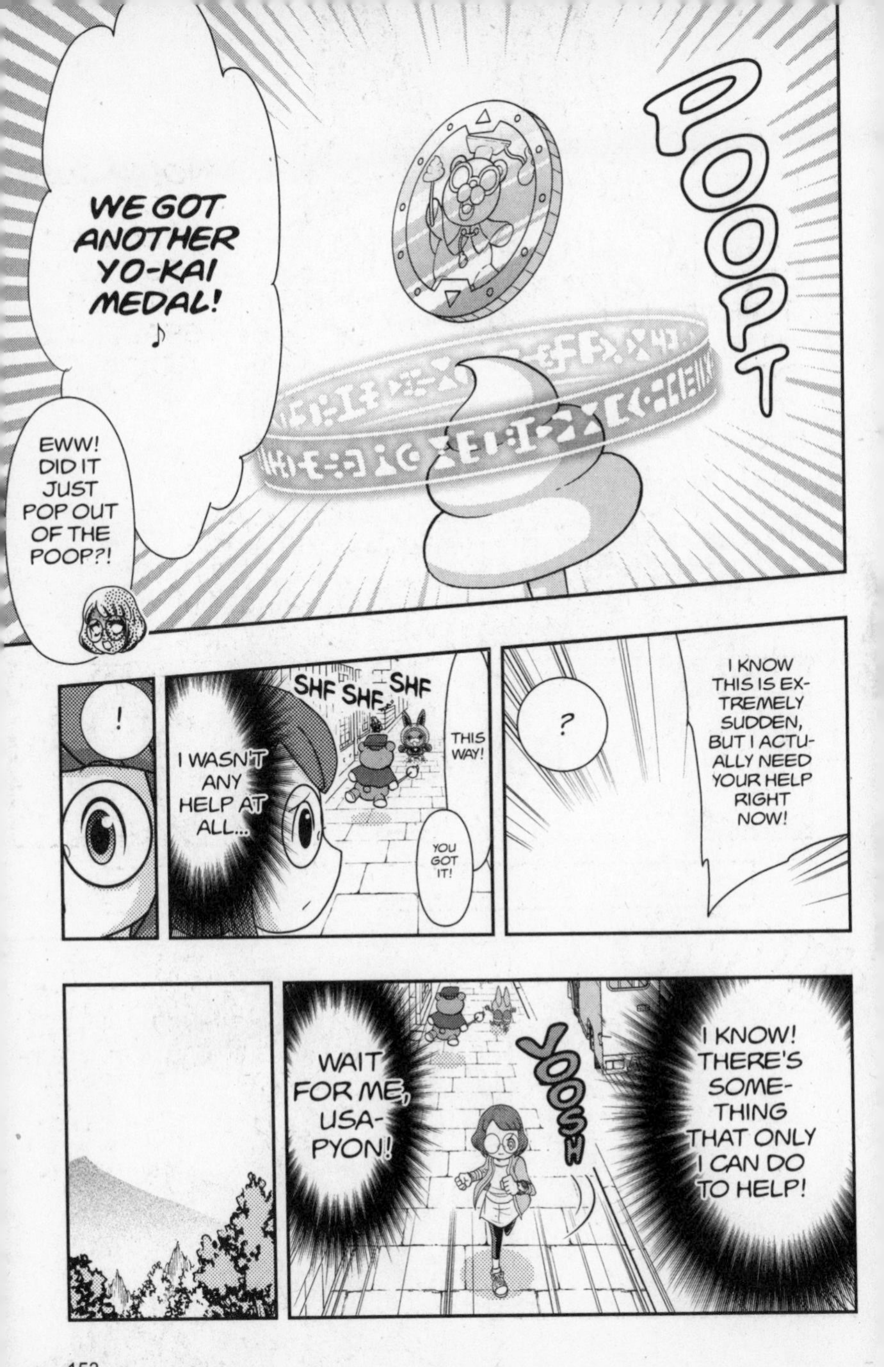
POOPT
WE GOT ANOTHER YO-KAI MEDAL! ♪
EWW! DID IT JUST POP OUT OF THE POOP?!
I KNOW THIS IS EX-TREMELY SUDDEN, BUT I ACTU-ALLY NEED YOUR HELP RIGHT NOW!
?
SHF SHF SHF
THIS WAY!
YOU GOT IT!
I WASN'T ANY HELP AT ALL...
!
I KNOW! THERE'S SOME-THING THAT ONLY I CAN DO TO HELP!
YOOSH
WAIT FOR ME, USA-PYON!

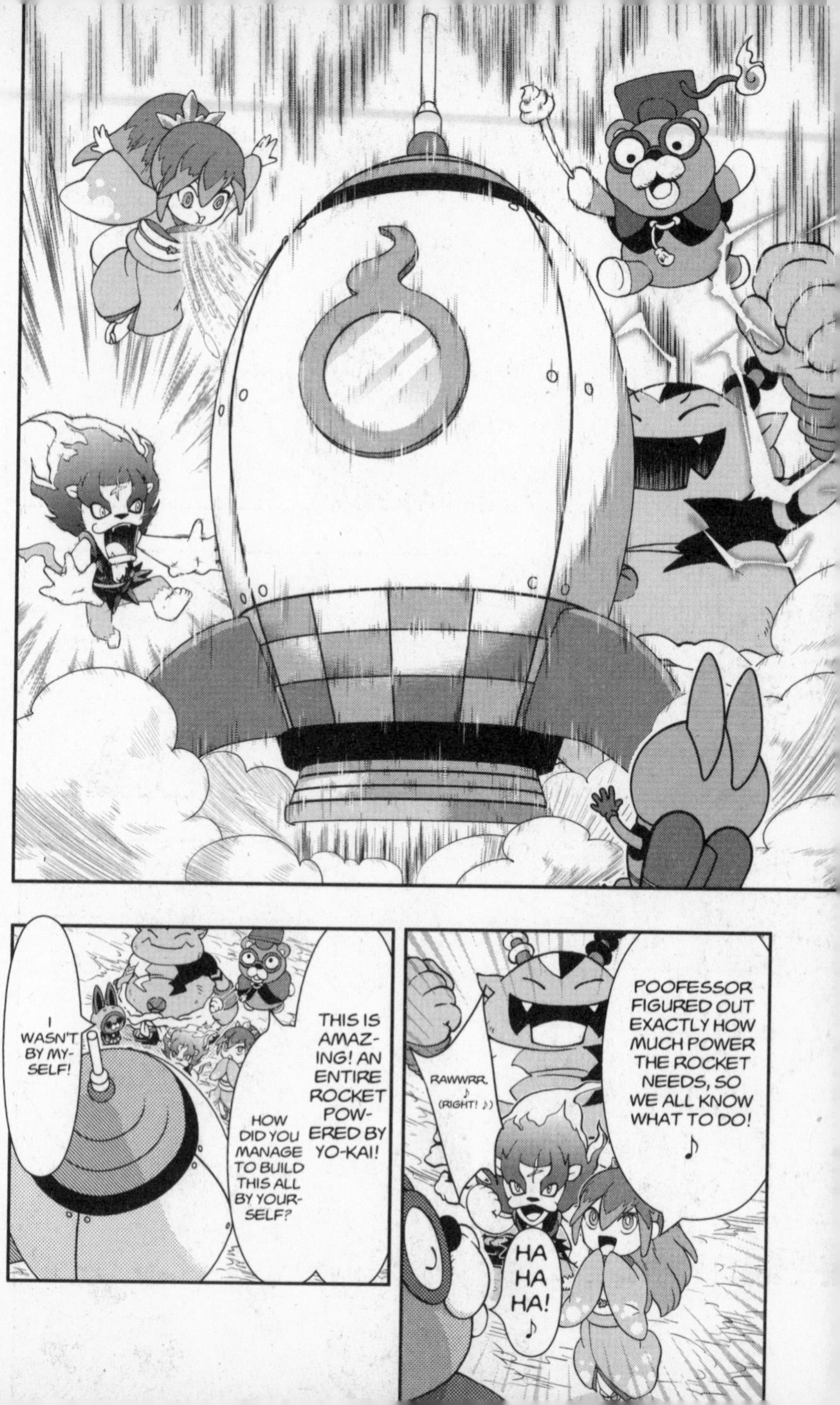
POOFESSOR FIGURED OUT EXACTLY HOW MUCH POWER THE ROCKET NEEDS, SO WE ALL KNOW WHAT TO DO! ♪
RAWWRR. ♪ (RIGHT! ♪)
HA HA HA! ♪
THIS IS AMAZING! AN ENTIRE ROCKET POWERED BY YO-KAI!
HOW DID YOU MANAGE TO BUILD THIS ALL BY YOURSELF?
I WASN'T BY MYSELF!

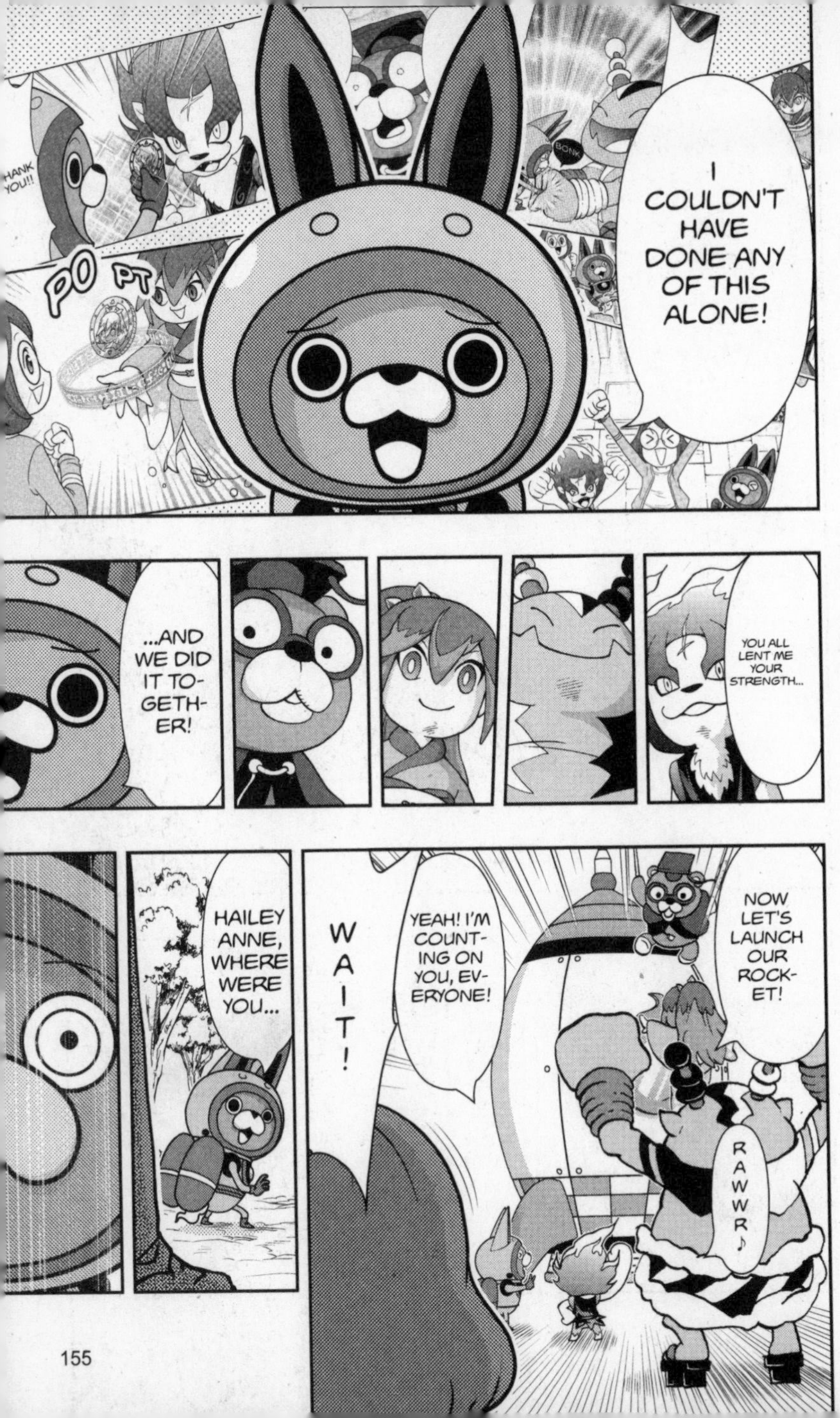

BONK
I COULDN'T HAVE DONE ANY OF THIS ALONE!
HANK YOU!!
PO PT
YOU ALL LENT ME YOUR STRENGTH...
...AND WE DID IT TO-GETH-ER!
NOW LET'S LAUNCH OUR ROCK-ET!
RAWWR♪
YEAH! I'M COUNT-ING ON YOU, EV-ERYONE!
WAIT!
HAILEY ANNE, WHERE WERE YOU...

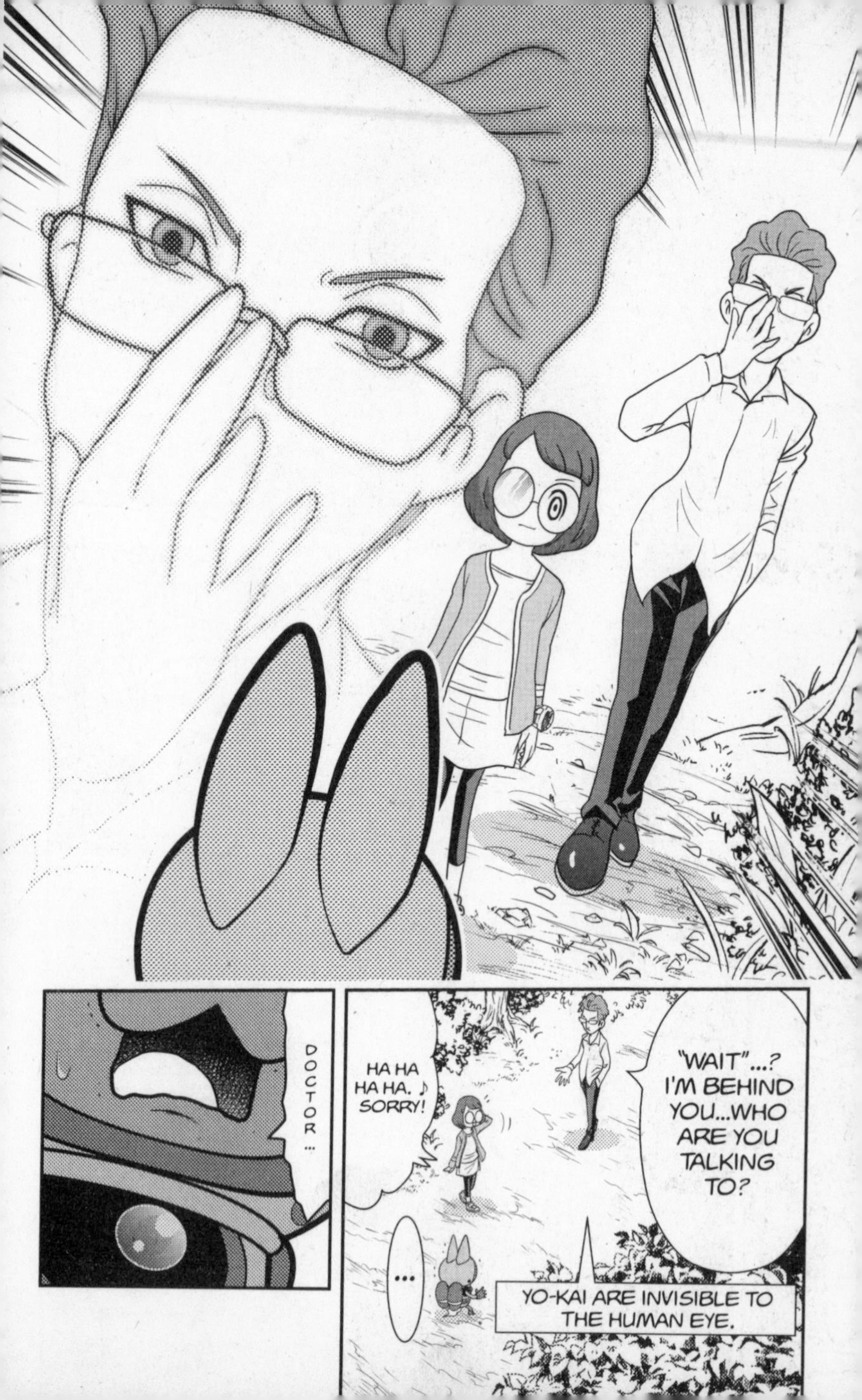
"WAIT"...? I'M BEHIND YOU...WHO ARE YOU TALKING TO?
HA HA HA HA. ♪ SORRY!
...
YO-KAI ARE INVISIBLE TO THE HUMAN EYE.
DOCTOR...

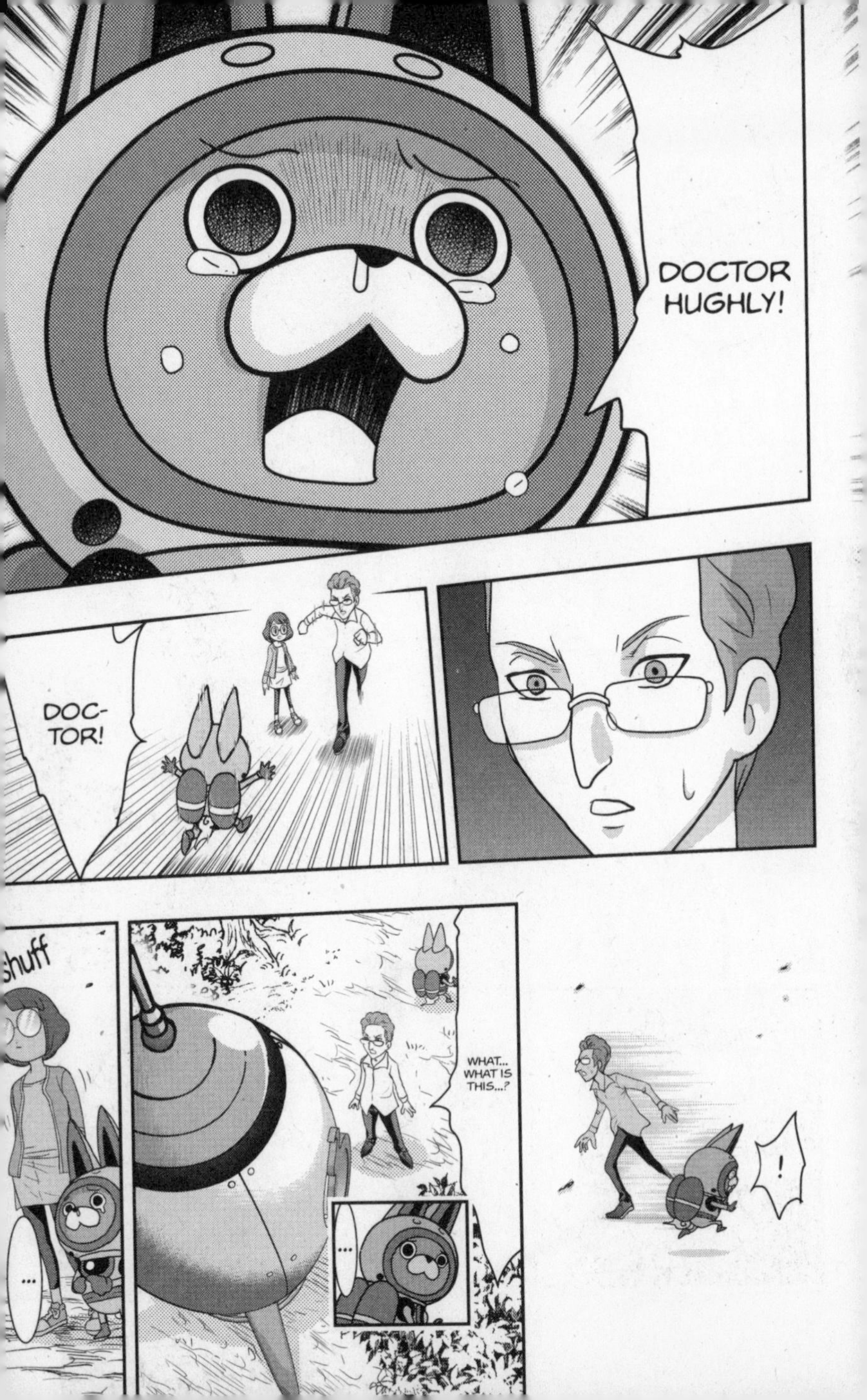
DOCTOR HUGHLY!
DOC-TOR!
!
WHAT... WHAT IS THIS...?
...
shuff
...

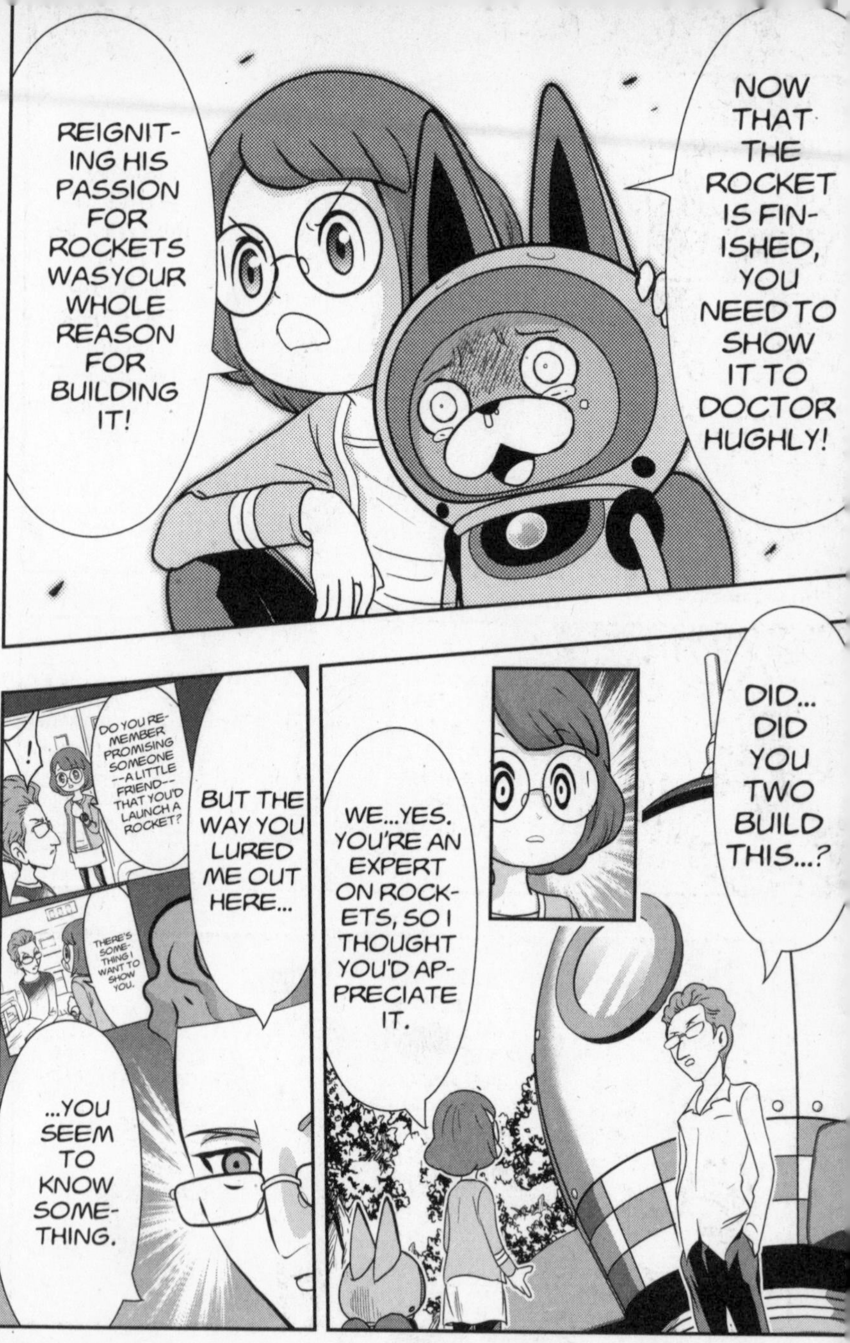
NOW THAT THE ROCKET IS FINISHED, YOU NEED TO SHOW IT TO DOCTOR HUGHLY!
REIGNITING HIS PASSION FOR ROCKETS WAS YOUR WHOLE REASON FOR BUILDING IT!
DID... DID YOU TWO BUILD THIS...?
WE...YES. YOU'RE AN EXPERT ON ROCKETS, SO I THOUGHT YOU'D APPRECIATE IT.
BUT THE WAY YOU LURED ME OUT HERE...
DO YOU REMEMBER PROMISING SOMEONE --A LITTLE FRIEND-- THAT YOU'D LAUNCH A ROCKET?
!
THERE'S SOMETHING I WANT TO SHOW YOU.
...YOU SEEM TO KNOW SOMETHING.

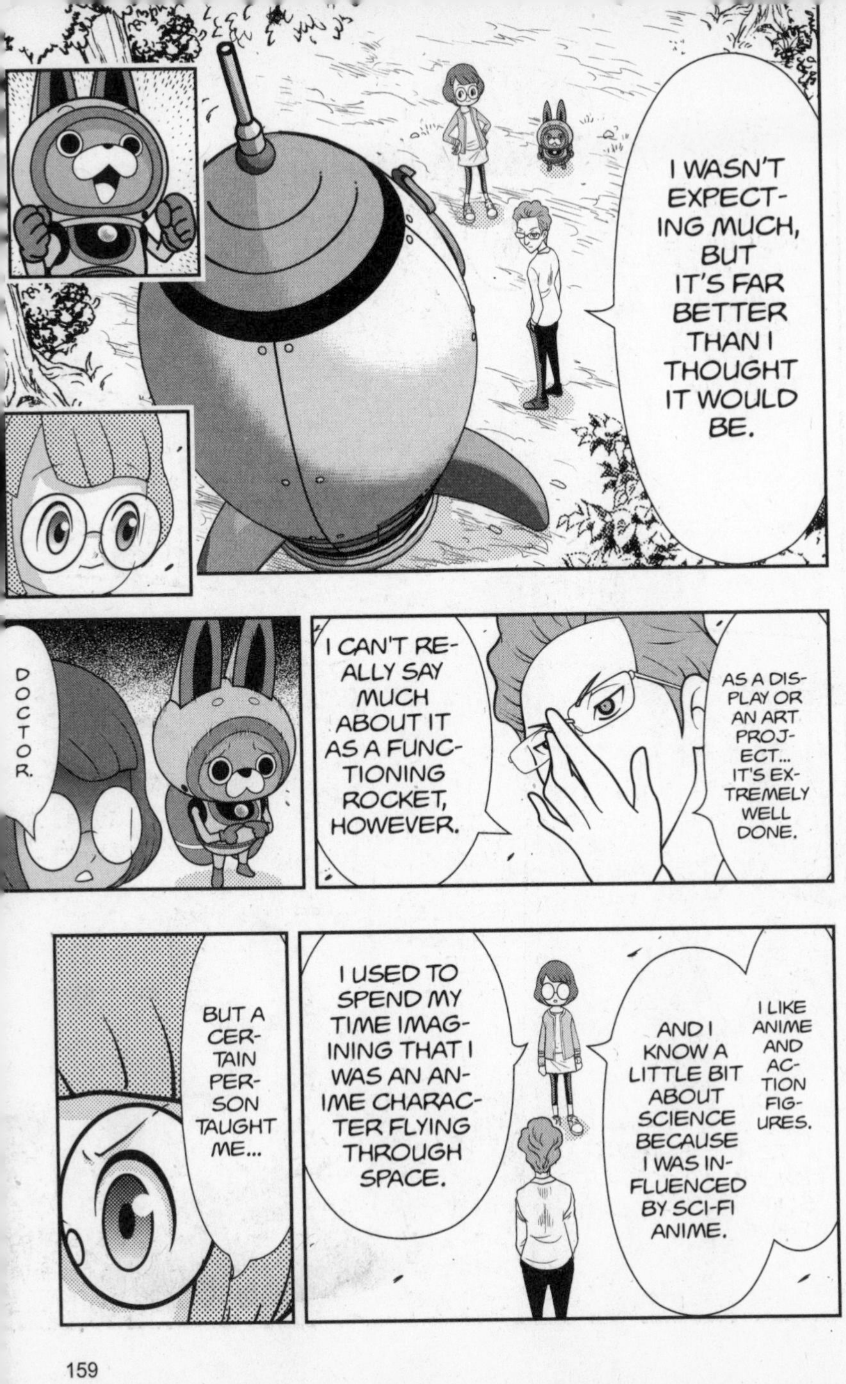
I WASN'T EXPECTING MUCH, BUT IT'S FAR BETTER THAN I THOUGHT IT WOULD BE.
AS A DISPLAY OR AN ART PROJECT... IT'S EXTREMELY WELL DONE.
I CAN'T REALLY SAY MUCH ABOUT IT AS A FUNCTIONING ROCKET, HOWEVER.
DOCTOR.
I LIKE ANIME AND ACTION FIGURES.
AND I KNOW A LITTLE BIT ABOUT SCIENCE BECAUSE I WAS INFLUENCED BY SCI-FI ANIME.
I USED TO SPEND MY TIME IMAGINING THAT I WAS AN ANIME CHARACTER FLYING THROUGH SPACE.
BUT A CERTAIN PERSON TAUGHT ME...

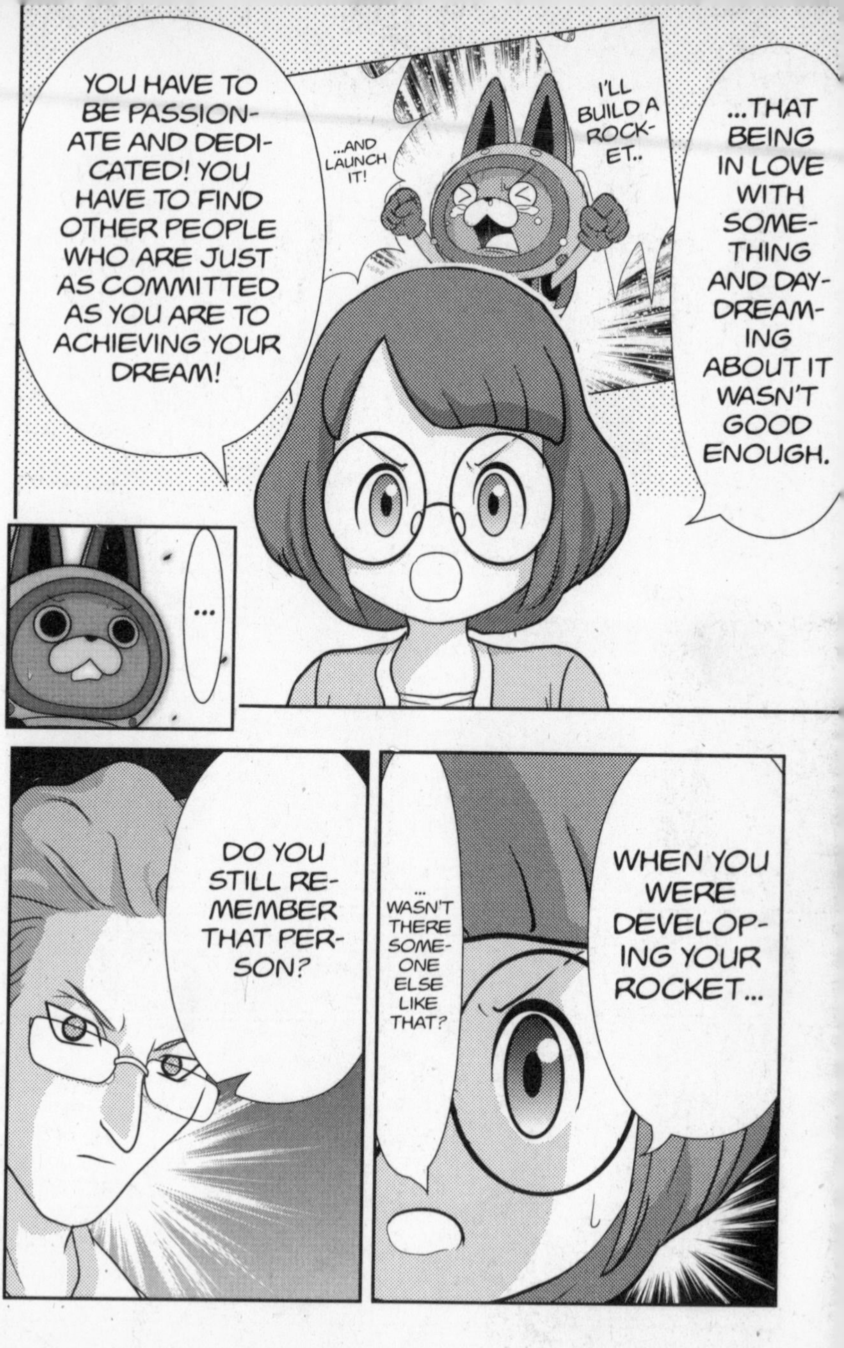
...THAT BEING IN LOVE WITH SOMETHING AND DAYDREAMING ABOUT IT WASN'T GOOD ENOUGH.
I'LL BUILD A ROCKET..
...AND LAUNCH IT!
YOU HAVE TO BE PASSIONATE AND DEDICATED! YOU HAVE TO FIND OTHER PEOPLE WHO ARE JUST AS COMMITTED AS YOU ARE TO ACHIEVING YOUR DREAM!
...
WHEN YOU WERE DEVELOPING YOUR ROCKET...
...WASN'T THERE SOMEONE ELSE LIKE THAT?
DO YOU STILL REMEMBER THAT PERSON?

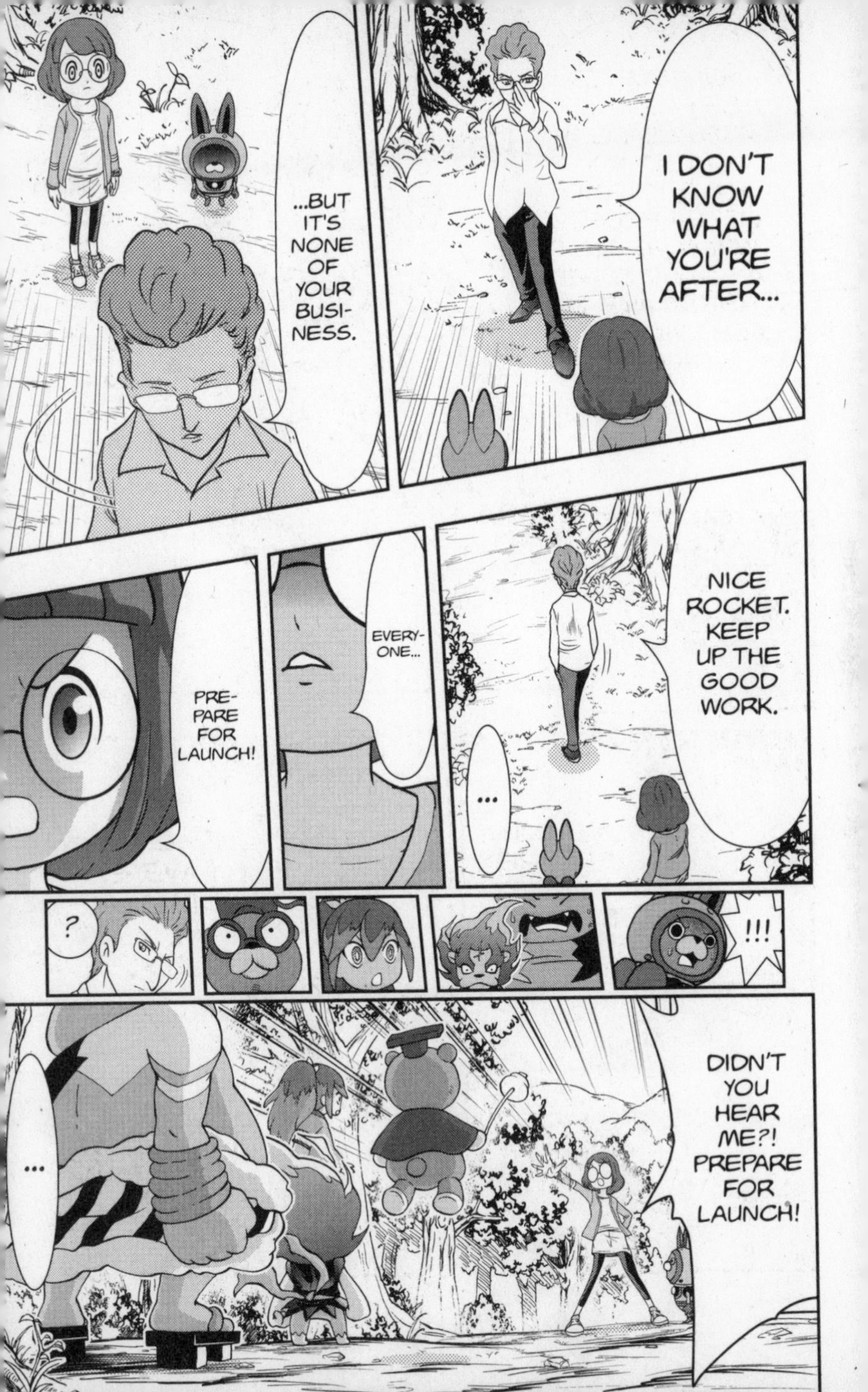
I DON'T KNOW WHAT YOU'RE AFTER...
...BUT IT'S NONE OF YOUR BUSI-NESS.
NICE ROCKET. KEEP UP THE GOOD WORK.
...
EVERY-ONE...
PRE-PARE FOR LAUNCH!
!!!
?
DIDN'T YOU HEAR ME?! PREPARE FOR LAUNCH!
...

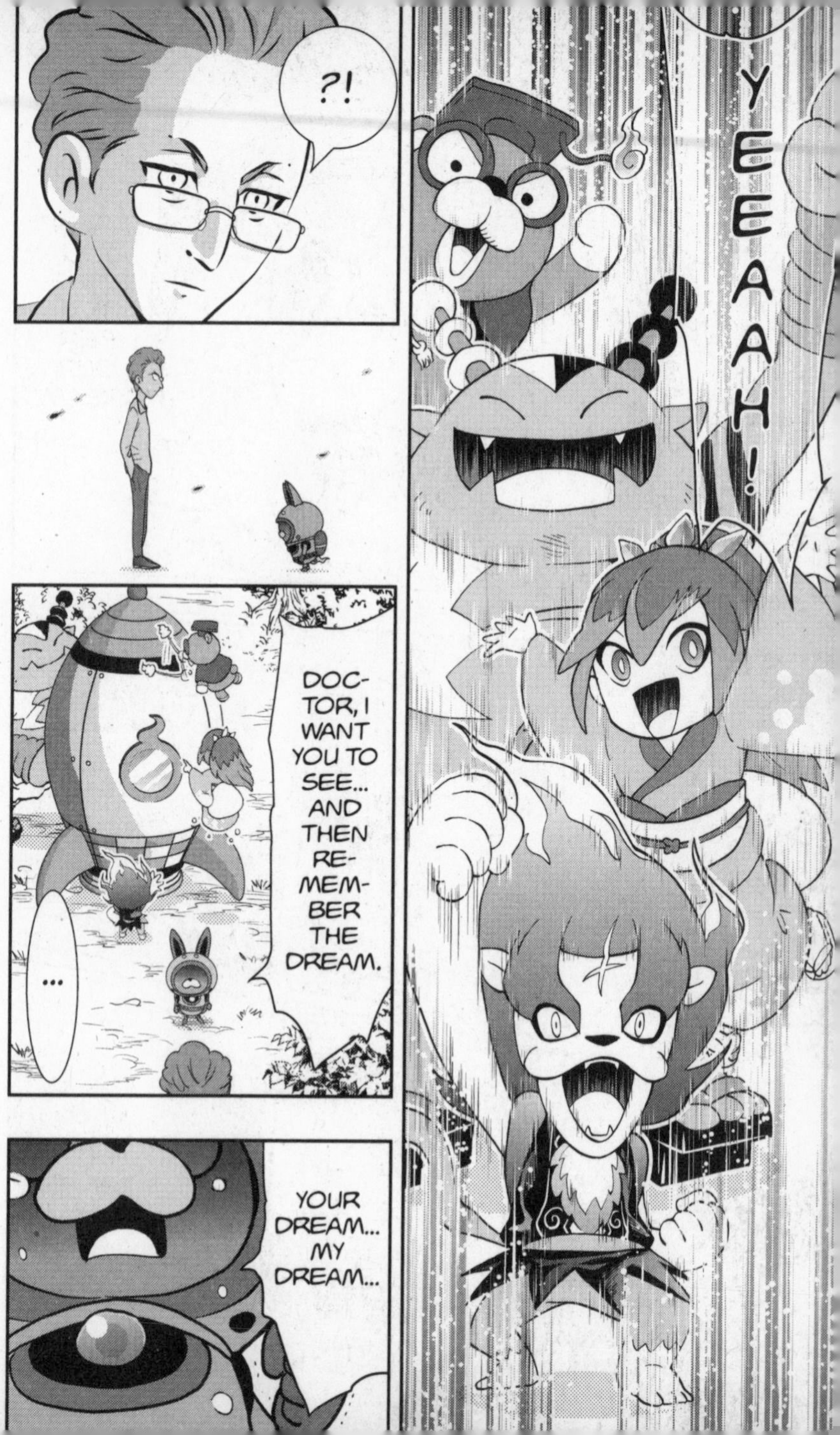
YEEAAAH!
?!
DOCTOR, I WANT YOU TO SEE... AND THEN REMEMBER THE DREAM.
...
YOUR DREAM... MY DREAM...

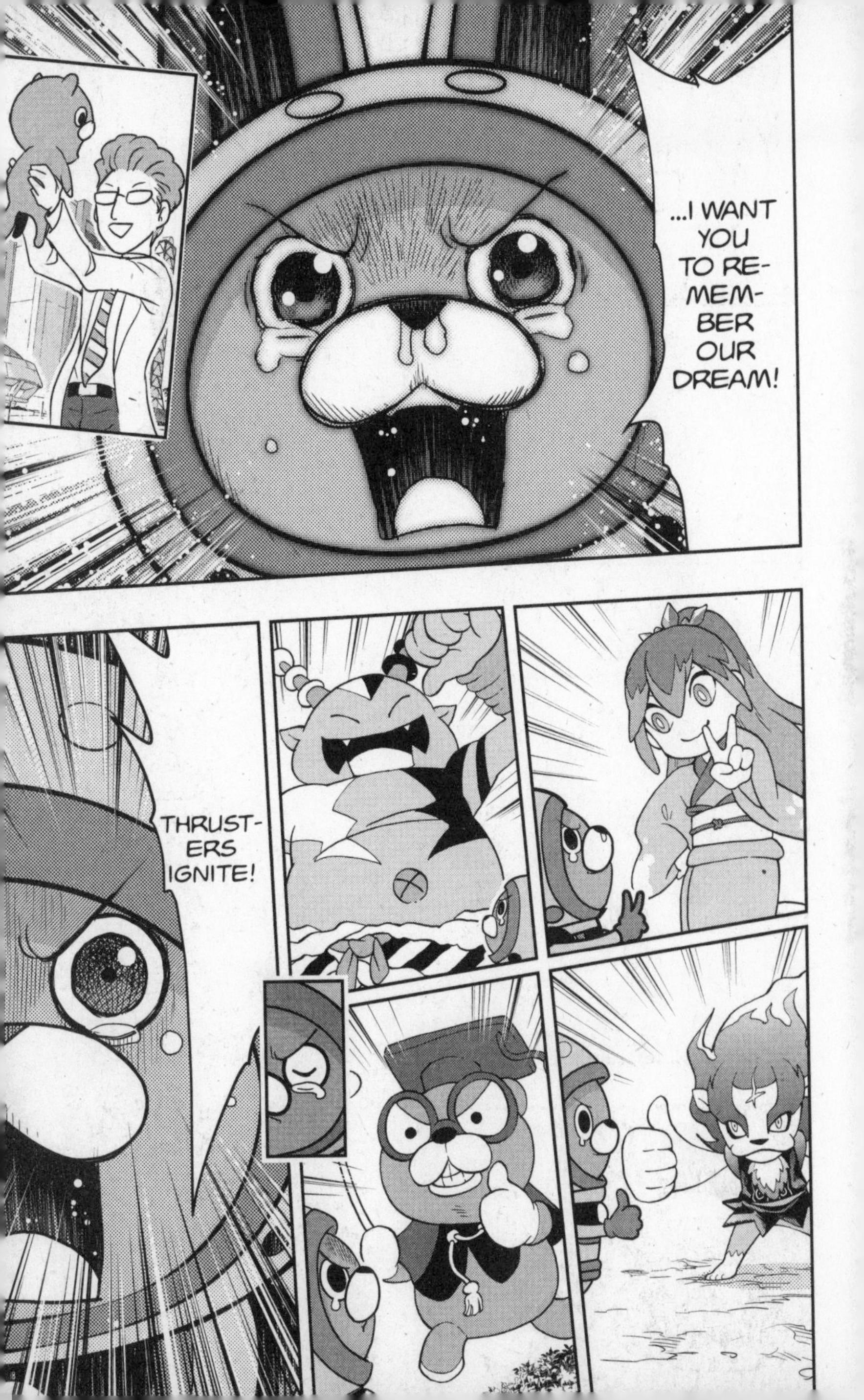
...I WANT YOU TO RE- MEM- BER OUR DREAM!
THRUST- ERS IGNITE!

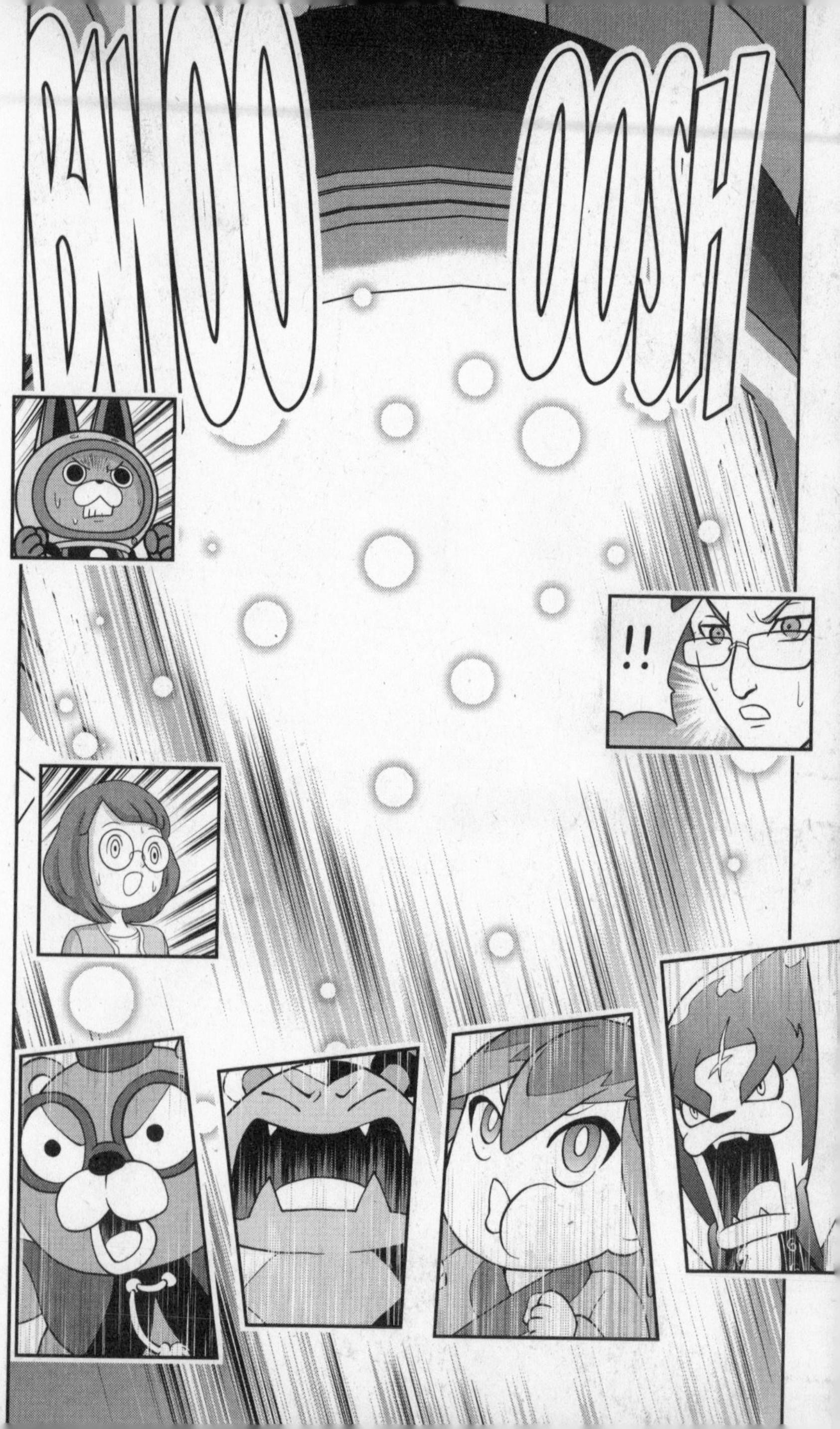
BAWOOO
OOSH
!!

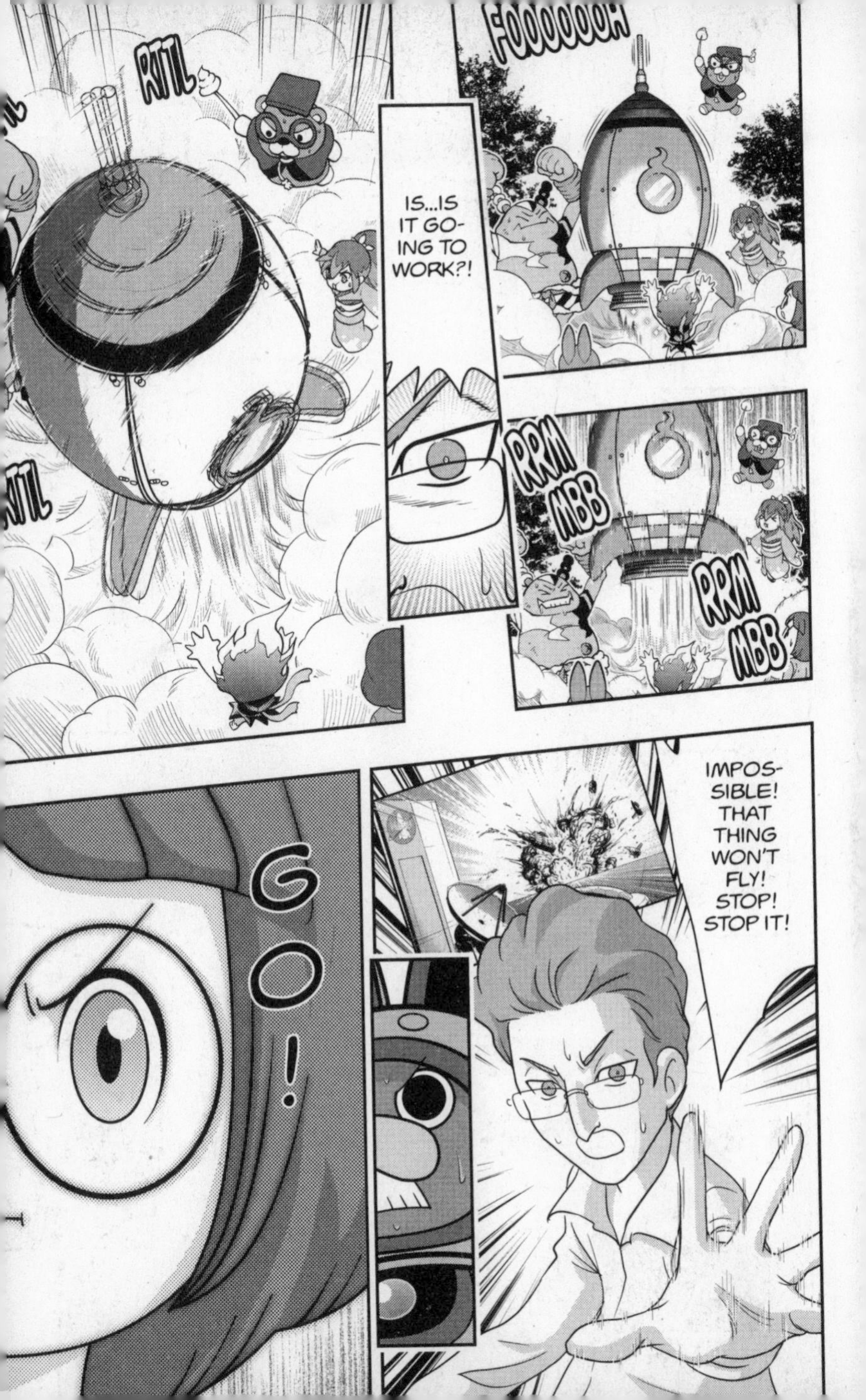
FOOOOOOH
RRM MBB
RRM MBB
IS...IS IT GO-ING TO WORK?!
RTTL
RTTL
IMPOS-SIBLE! THAT THING WON'T FLY! STOP! STOP IT!
GO!

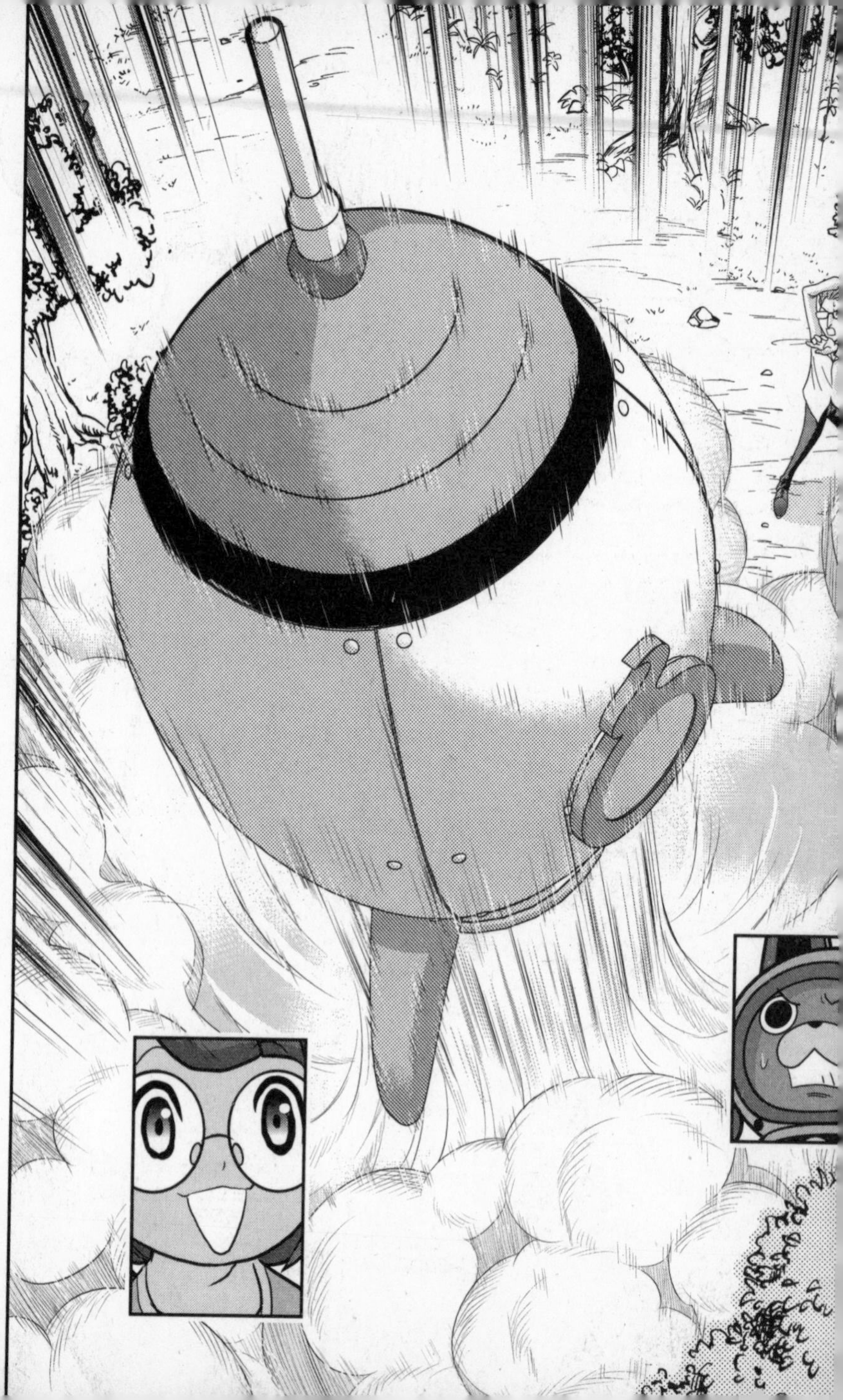

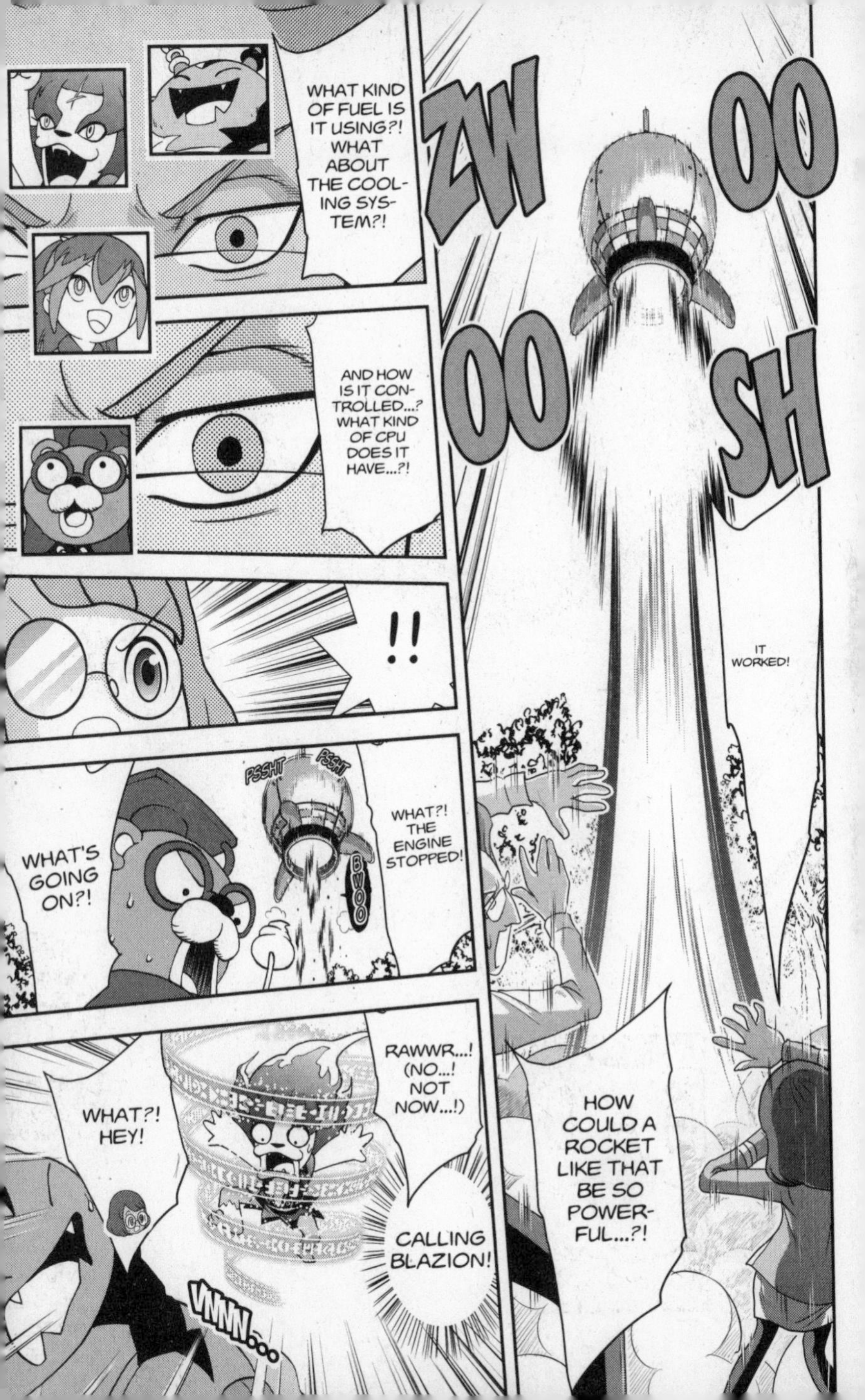
ZWOOOOSH
IT WORKED!
HOW COULD A ROCKET LIKE THAT BE SO POWERFUL...?!
WHAT KIND OF FUEL IS IT USING?! WHAT ABOUT THE COOLING SYSTEM?!
AND HOW IS IT CONTROLLED...? WHAT KIND OF CPU DOES IT HAVE...?!
!!
PSSHT
PSSHT
WHAT?! THE ENGINE STOPPED!
BWOO
WHAT'S GOING ON?!
RAWWR...! (NO...! NOT NOW...!)
CALLING BLAZION!
WHAT?! HEY!
VNNN...ooo

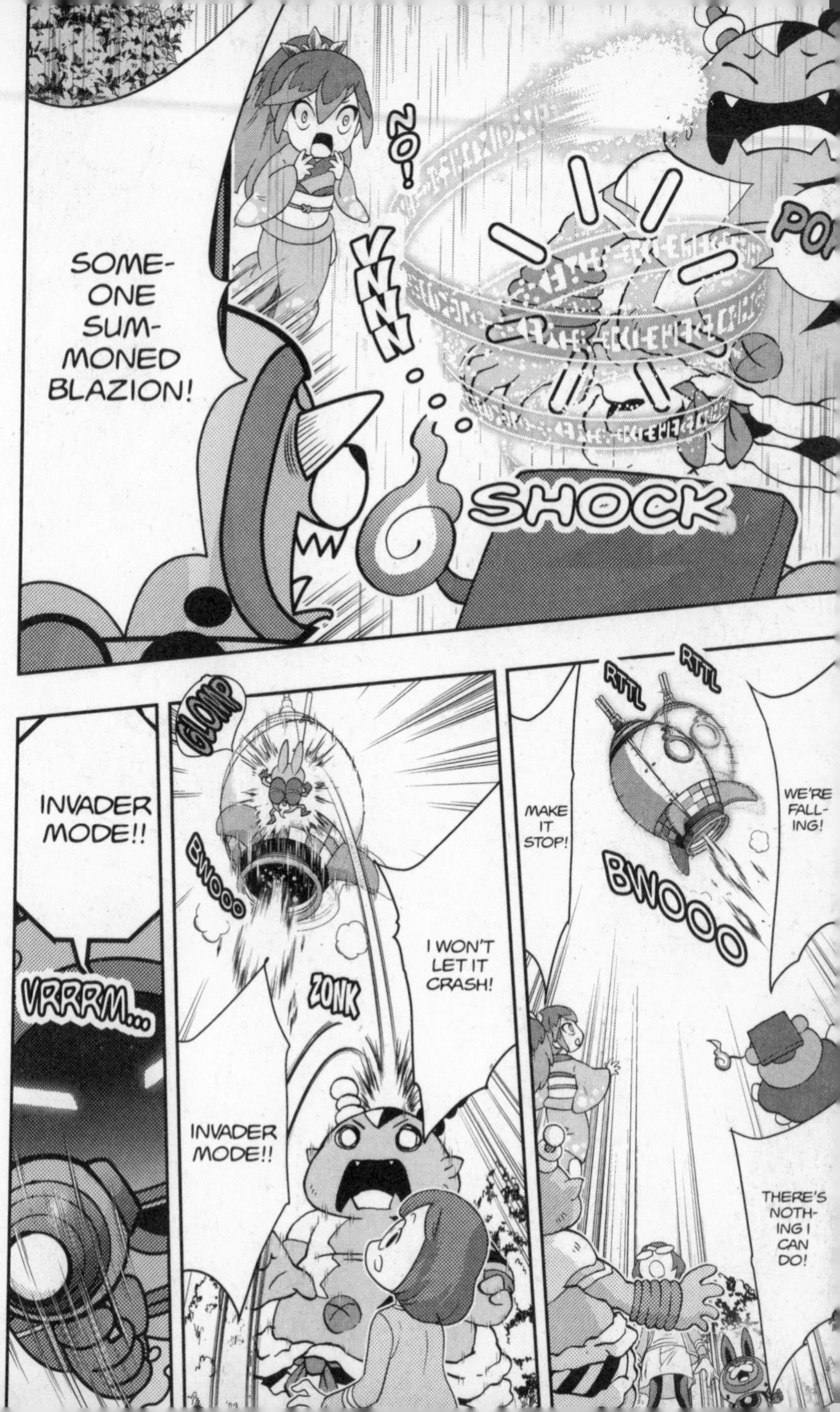

NO!
VNNN
SHOCK
SOME-
ONE
SUM-
MONED
BLAZION!
RTTL
RTTL
WE'RE
FALL-
ING!
MAKE
IT
STOP!
BWOOOO
THERE'S
NOTH-
ING I
CAN
DO!
GLOMP
BWOOO
I WON'T
LET IT
CRASH!
ZONK
INVADER
MODE!!
INVADER
MODE!!
VRRRM...

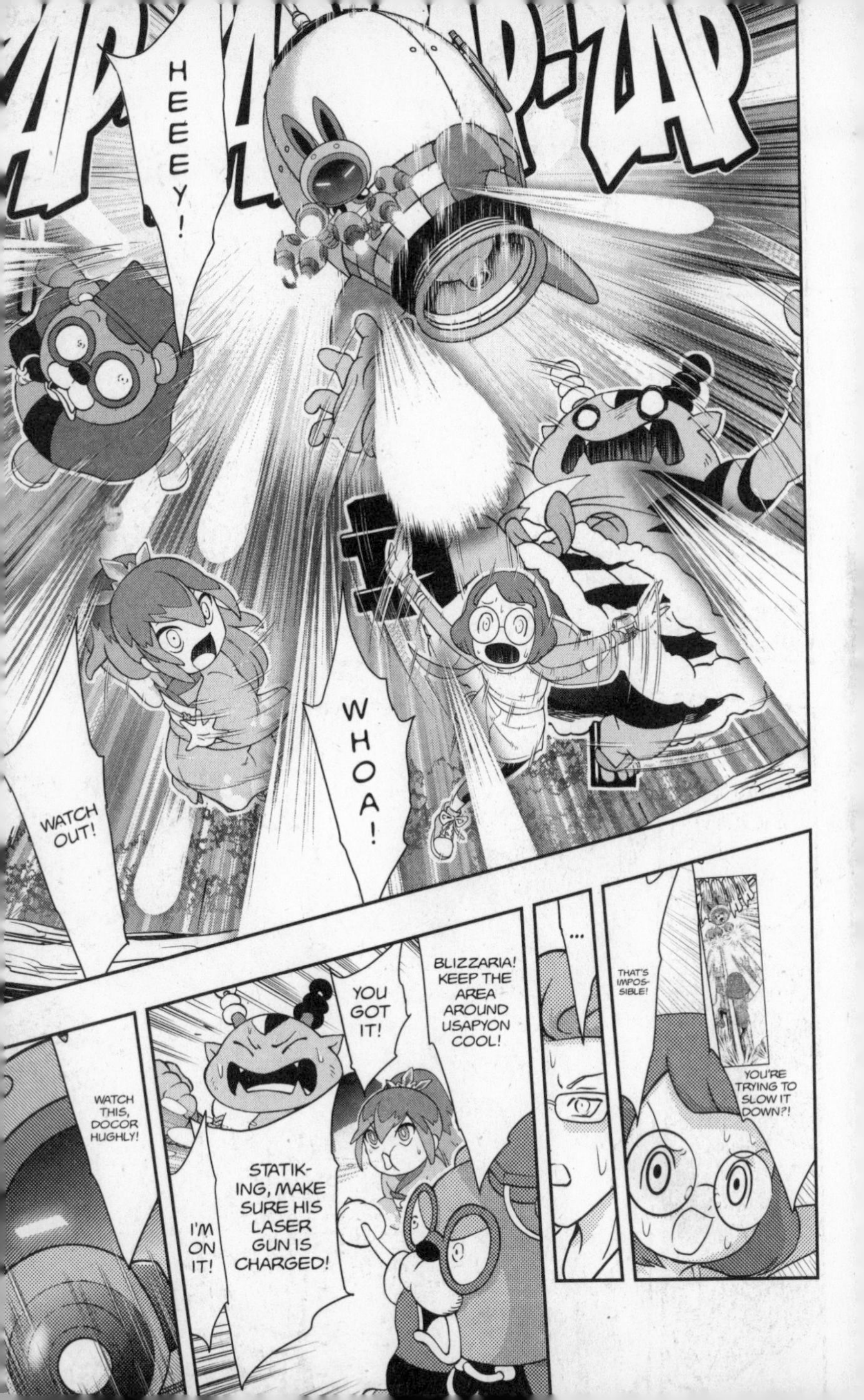
ZAP-ZAP
HEEEEY!
WHOA!
WATCH OUT!
THAT'S IMPOSSIBLE!
YOU'RE TRYING TO SLOW IT DOWN?!
...
BLIZZARIA! KEEP THE AREA AROUND USAPYON COOL!
YOU GOT IT!
STATIKING, MAKE SURE HIS LASER GUN IS CHARGED!
I'M ON IT!
WATCH THIS, DOCOR HUGHLY!

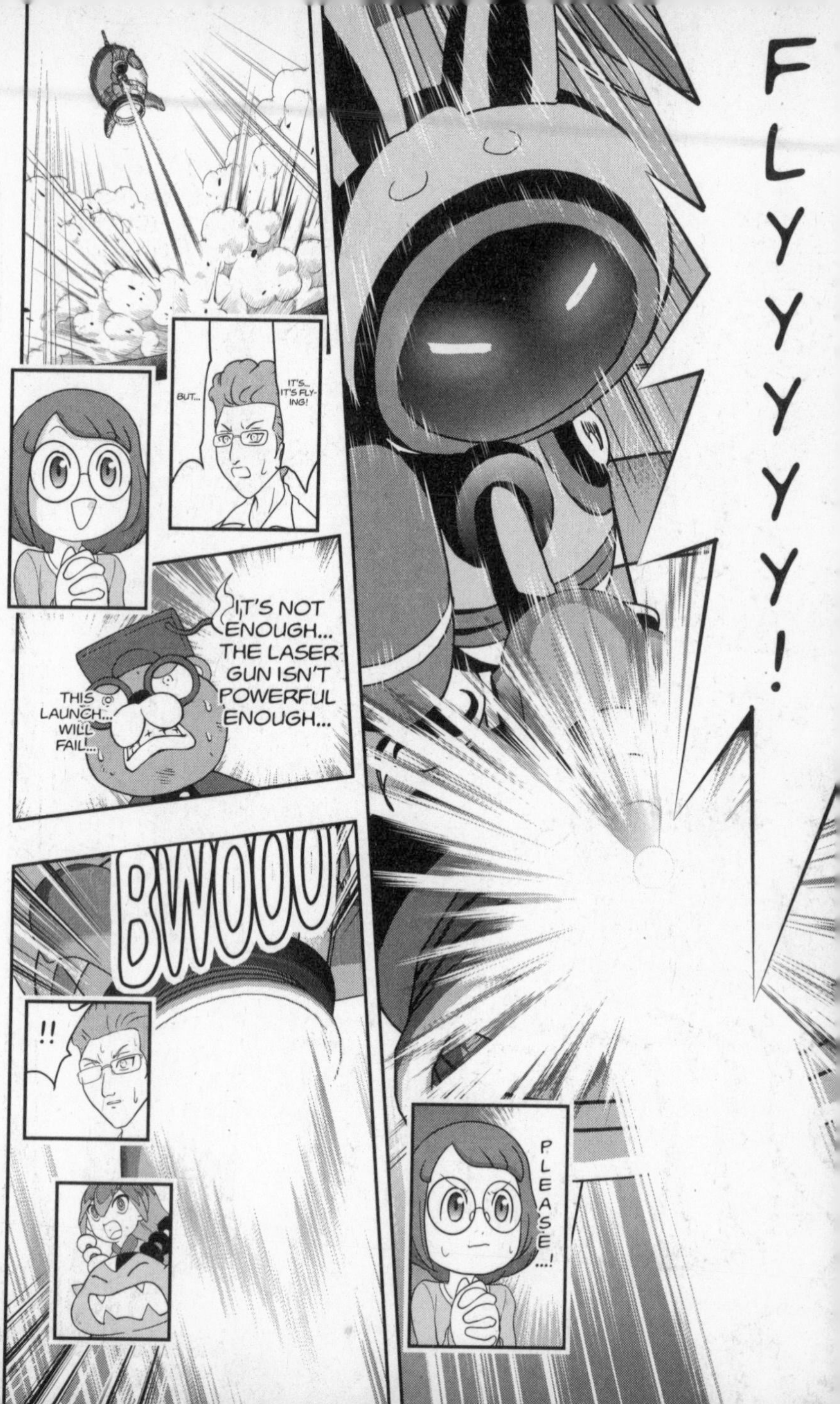
FLYYYY!
PLEASE...!
IT'S... IT'S FLYING!
BUT...
IT'S NOT ENOUGH... THE LASER GUN ISN'T POWERFUL ENOUGH...
THIS LAUNCH... WILL FAIL...
BWOOO
!!

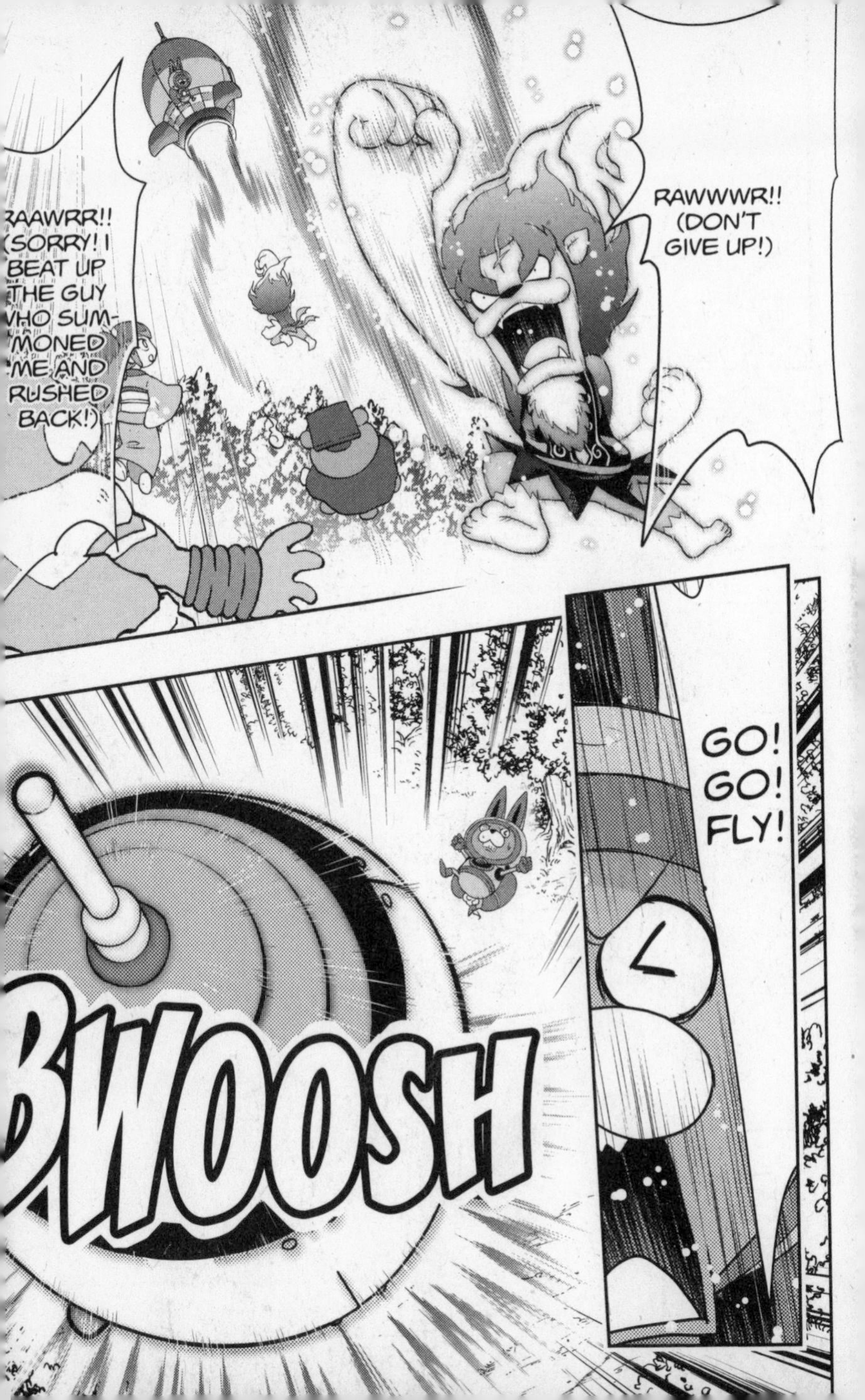
RAWWWR!! (DON'T GIVE UP!)
RAAWRR!! (SORRY! I BEAT UP THE GUY WHO SUM-MONED ME AND RUSHED BACK!)
GO! GO! FLY!
BWOOSH

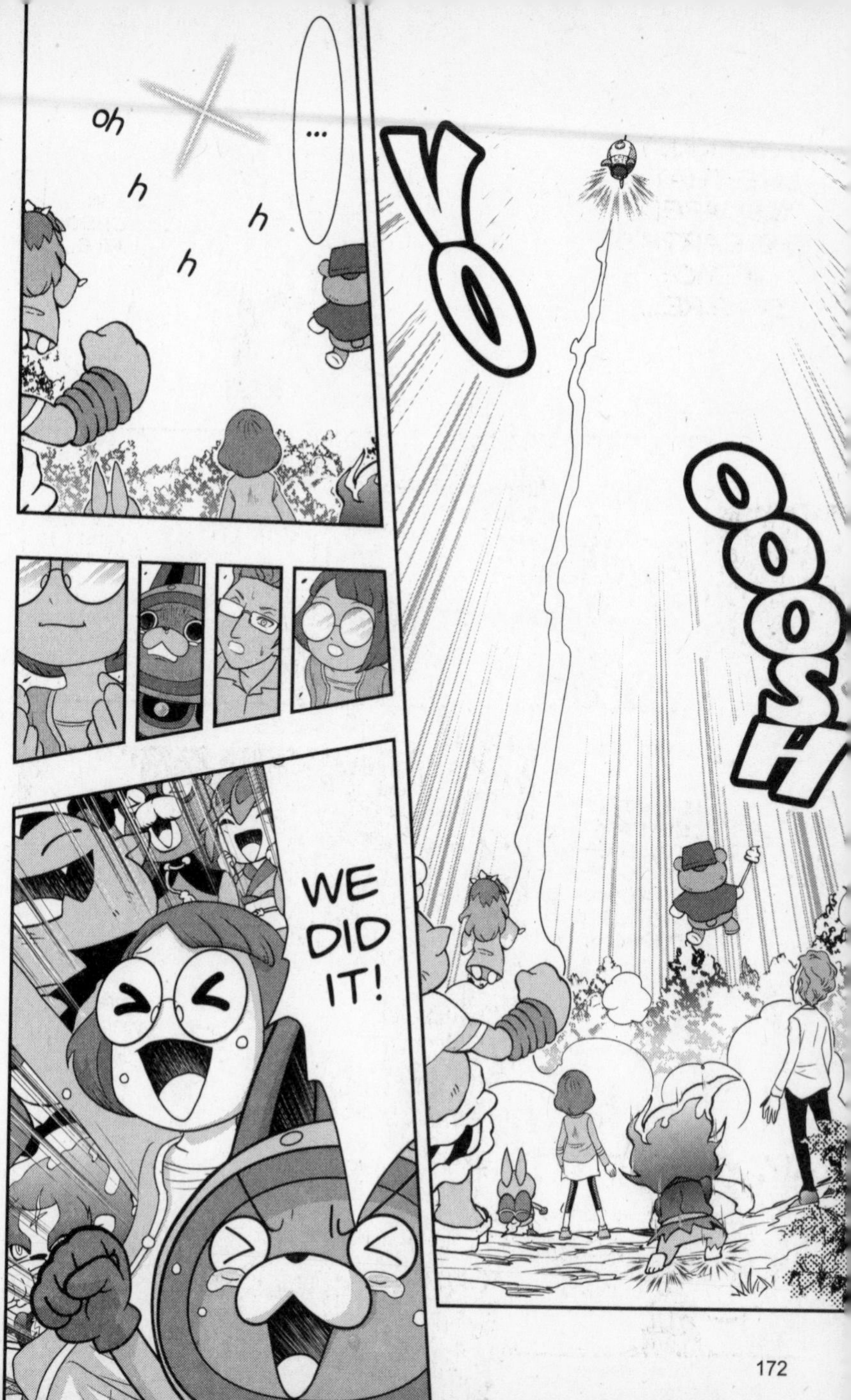
YOOOOOSH
...
oh
h
h
h
WE DID IT!

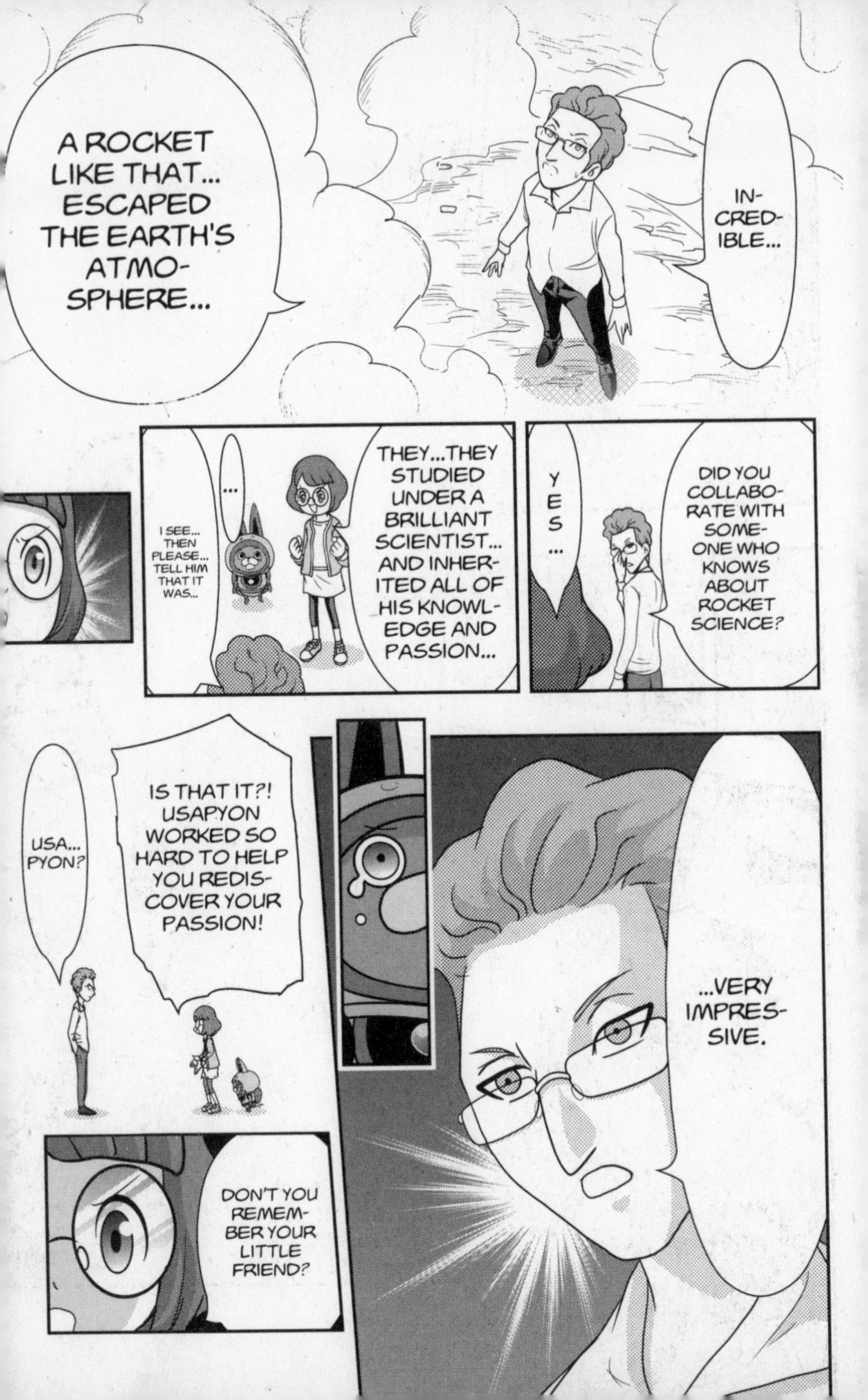
IN-CRED-IBLE...
A ROCKET LIKE THAT... ESCAPED THE EARTH'S ATMO-SPHERE...
DID YOU COLLABO-RATE WITH SOME-ONE WHO KNOWS ABOUT ROCKET SCIENCE?
YES...
THEY...THEY STUDIED UNDER A BRILLIANT SCIENTIST... AND INHER-ITED ALL OF HIS KNOWL-EDGE AND PASSION...
...
I SEE... THEN PLEASE... TELL HIM THAT IT WAS...
...VERY IMPRES-SIVE.
IS THAT IT?! USAPYON WORKED SO HARD TO HELP YOU REDIS-COVER YOUR PASSION!
USA... PYON?
DON'T YOU REMEM-BER YOUR LITTLE FRIEND?

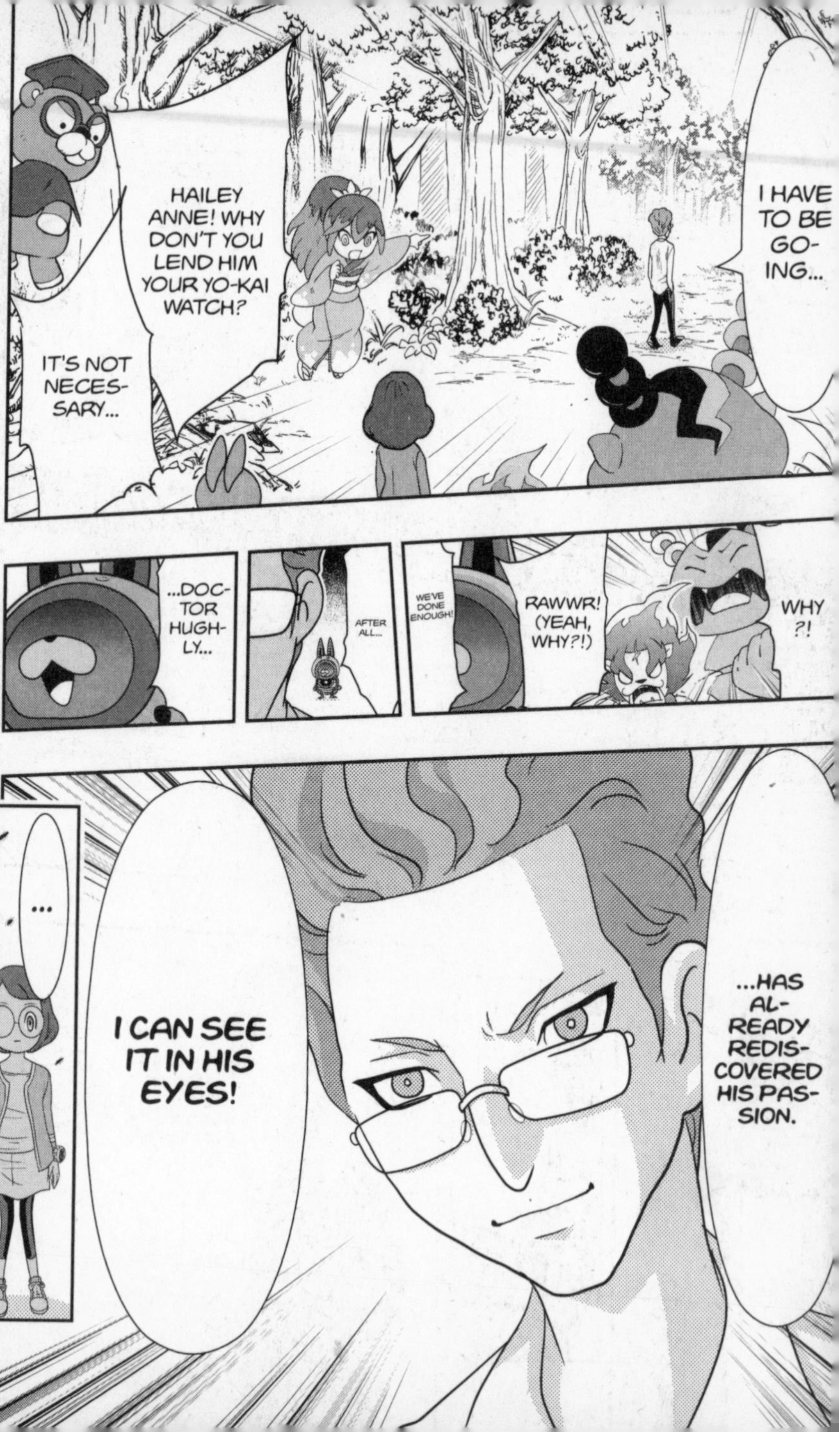

I HAVE TO BE GO-ING...
HAILEY ANNE! WHY DON'T YOU LEND HIM YOUR YO-KAI WATCH?
IT'S NOT NECES-SARY...
WHY?!
RAWWR! (YEAH, WHY?!)
WE'VE DONE ENOUGH!
AFTER ALL...
...DOC-TOR HUGH-LY...
...HAS AL-READY REDIS-COVERED HIS PAS-SION.
I CAN SEE IT IN HIS EYES!
...

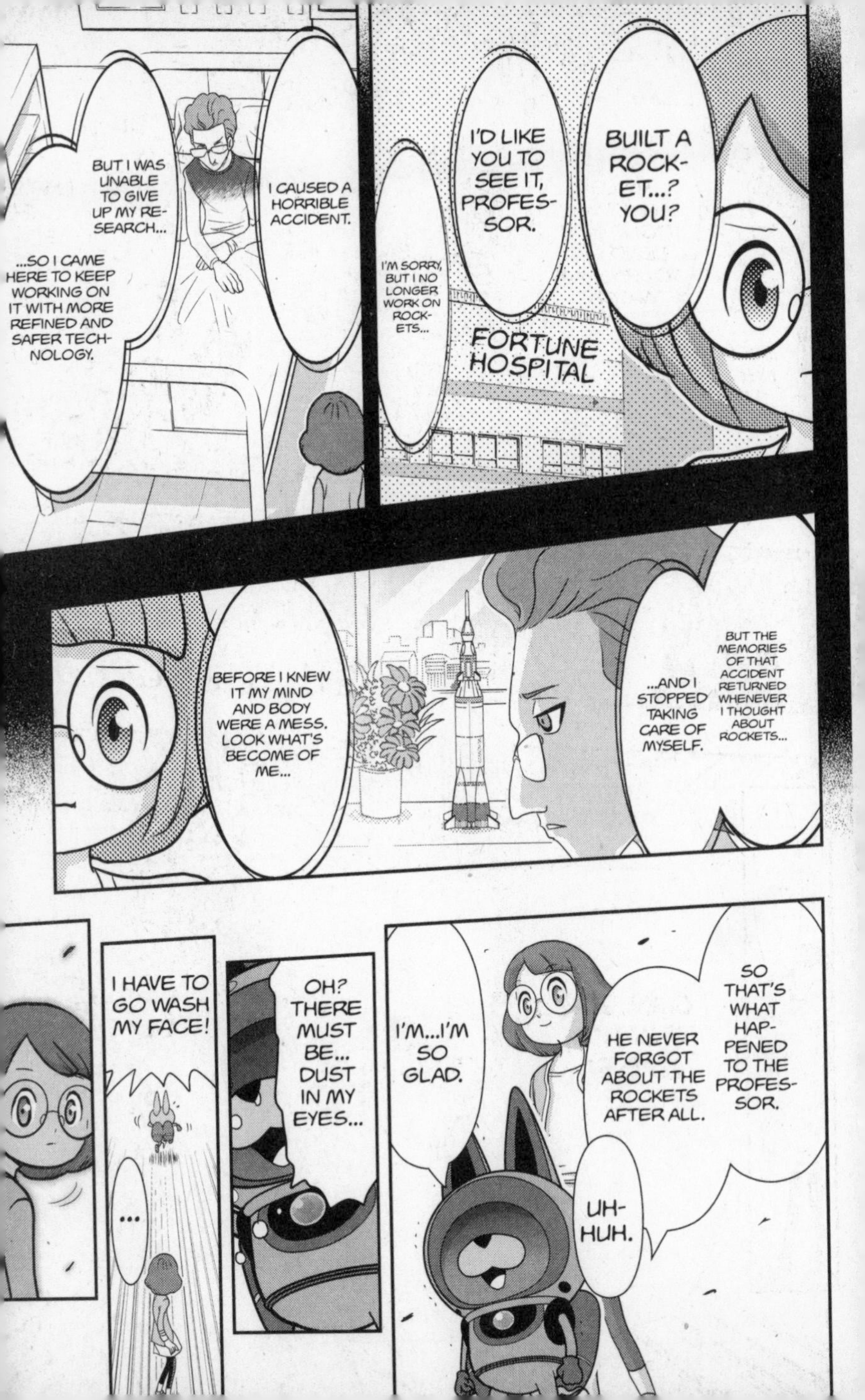
BUILT A ROCKET...? YOU?
I'D LIKE YOU TO SEE IT, PROFESSOR.
I'M SORRY, BUT I NO LONGER WORK ON ROCKETS...
FORTUNE HOSPITAL
I CAUSED A HORRIBLE ACCIDENT.
BUT I WAS UNABLE TO GIVE UP MY RESEARCH...
...SO I CAME HERE TO KEEP WORKING ON IT WITH MORE REFINED AND SAFER TECHNOLOGY.
BUT THE MEMORIES OF THAT ACCIDENT RETURNED WHENEVER I THOUGHT ABOUT ROCKETS...
...AND I STOPPED TAKING CARE OF MYSELF.
BEFORE I KNEW IT MY MIND AND BODY WERE A MESS. LOOK WHAT'S BECOME OF ME...
SO THAT'S WHAT HAPPENED TO THE PROFESSOR.
HE NEVER FORGOT ABOUT THE ROCKETS AFTER ALL.
UH-HUH.
I'M...I'M SO GLAD.
OH? THERE MUST BE... DUST IN MY EYES...
I HAVE TO GO WASH MY FACE!
...

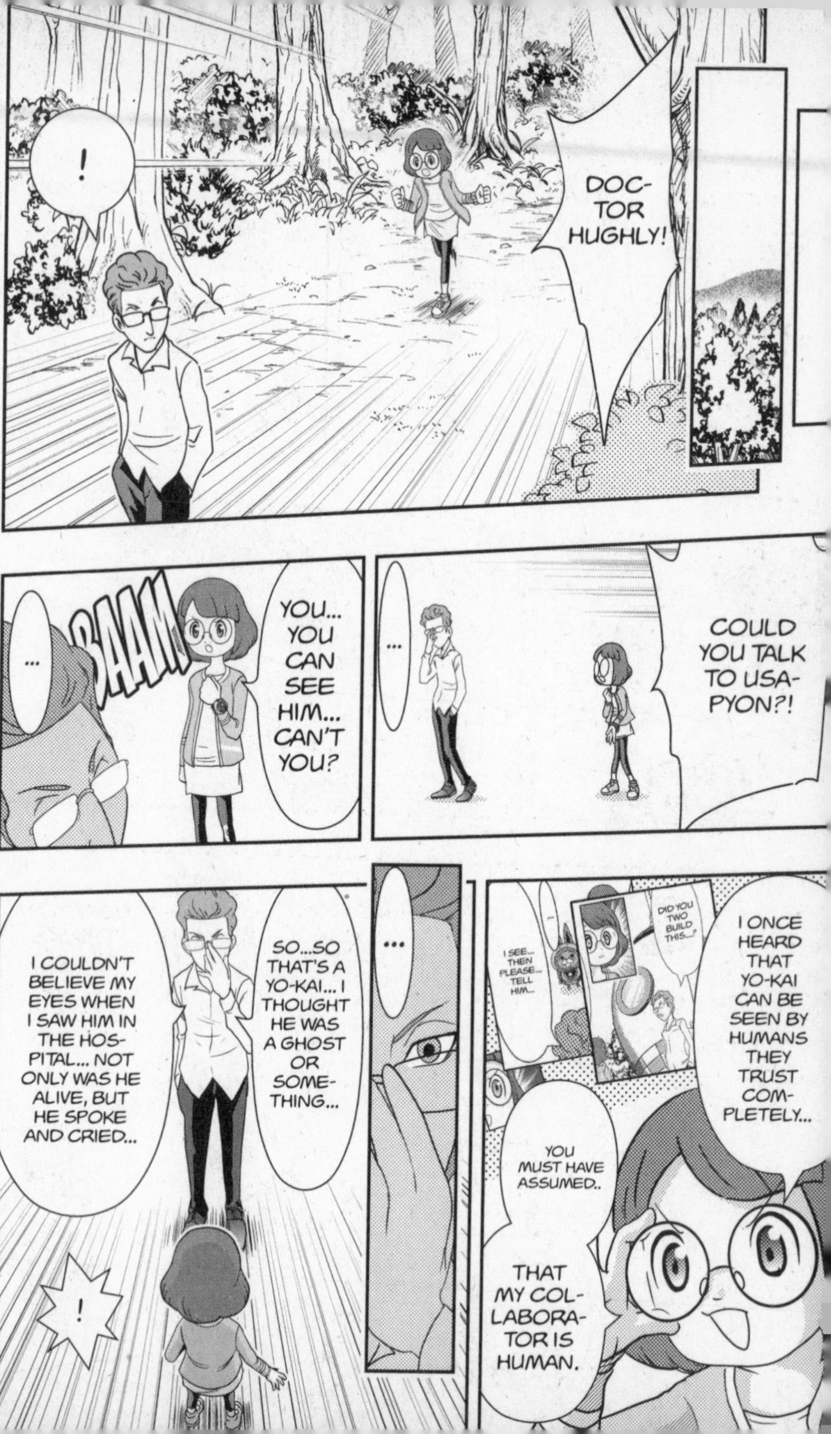
DOC-TOR HUGHLY!
!
COULD YOU TALK TO USA-PYON?!
...
YOU... YOU CAN SEE HIM... CAN'T YOU?
BAAM
...
I ONCE HEARD THAT YO-KAI CAN BE SEEN BY HUMANS THEY TRUST COM-PLETELY...
DID YOU TWO BUILD THIS...?
I SEE... THEN PLEASE... TELL HIM...
...
YOU MUST HAVE ASSUMED..
THAT MY COL-LABORA-TOR IS HUMAN.
...
SO...SO THAT'S A YO-KAI... I THOUGHT HE WAS A GHOST OR SOME-THING...
I COULDN'T BELIEVE MY EYES WHEN I SAW HIM IN THE HOS-PITAL... NOT ONLY WAS HE ALIVE, BUT HE SPOKE AND CRIED...
!

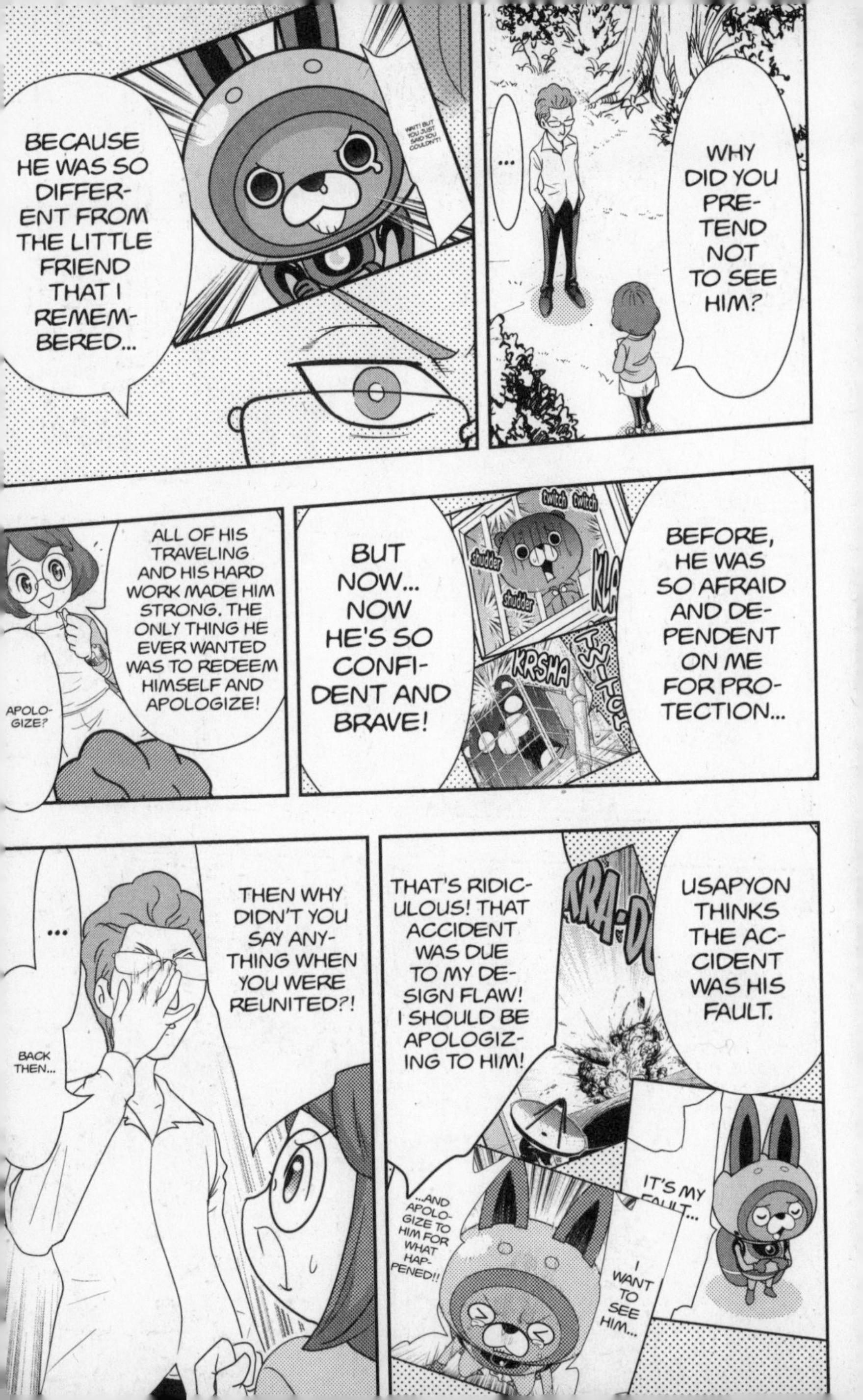
WHY DID YOU PRETEND NOT TO SEE HIM?
...
BECAUSE HE WAS SO DIFFERENT FROM THE LITTLE FRIEND THAT I REMEMBERED...
WAIT! BUT YOU JUST SAID YOU COULDN'T!
BEFORE, HE WAS SO AFRAID AND DEPENDENT ON ME FOR PROTECTION...
twitch twitch
shudder
shudder
KRSHA
BUT NOW... NOW HE'S SO CONFIDENT AND BRAVE!
ALL OF HIS TRAVELING AND HIS HARD WORK MADE HIM STRONG. THE ONLY THING HE EVER WANTED WAS TO REDEEM HIMSELF AND APOLOGIZE!
APOLOGIZE?
USAPYON THINKS THE ACCIDENT WAS HIS FAULT.
IT'S MY FAULT...
I WANT TO SEE HIM...
...AND APOLOGIZE TO HIM FOR WHAT HAPPENED!!
THAT'S RIDICULOUS! THAT ACCIDENT WAS DUE TO MY DESIGN FLAW! I SHOULD BE APOLOGIZING TO HIM!
THEN WHY DIDN'T YOU SAY ANYTHING WHEN YOU WERE REUNITED?!
...
BACK THEN...

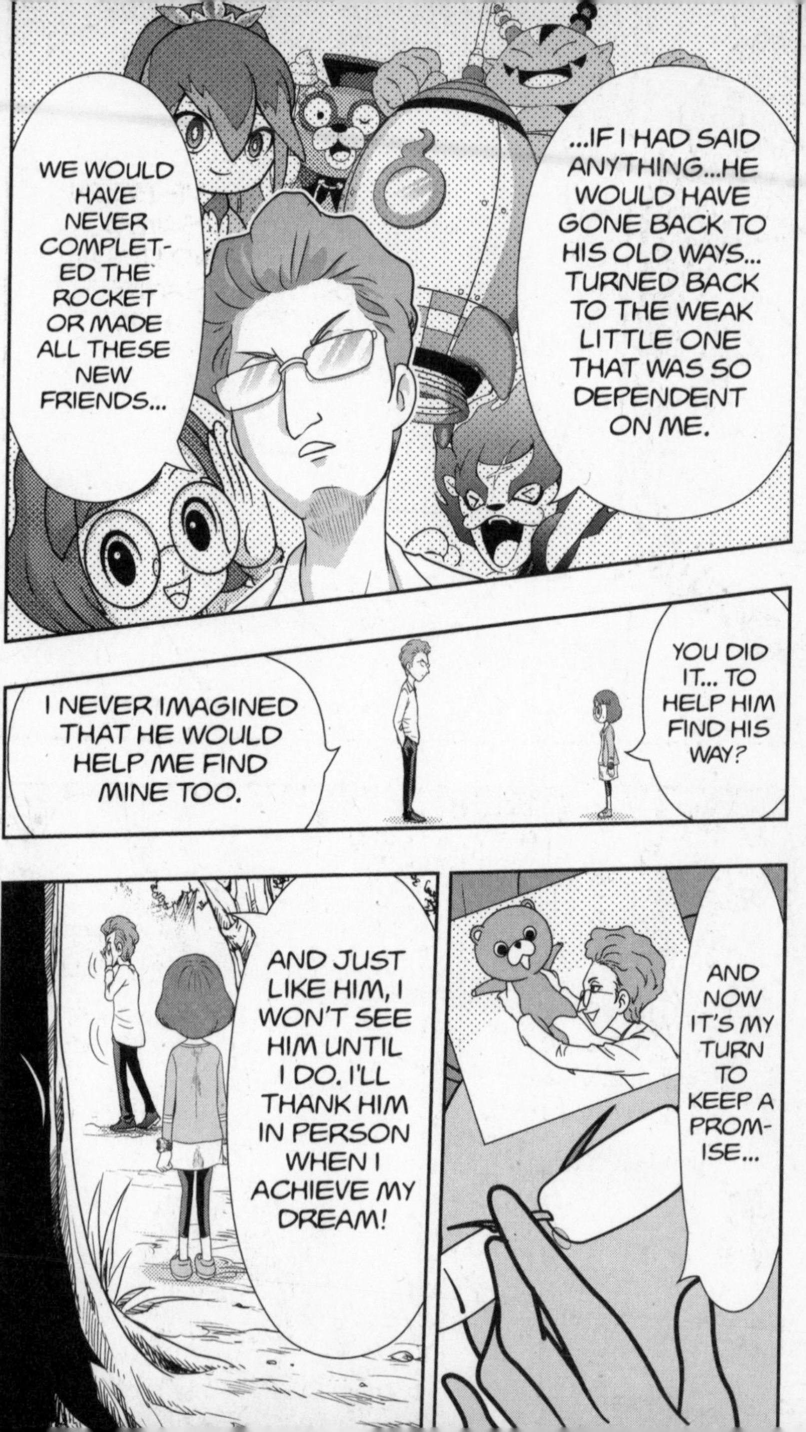
...IF I HAD SAID ANYTHING...HE WOULD HAVE GONE BACK TO HIS OLD WAYS... TURNED BACK TO THE WEAK LITTLE ONE THAT WAS SO DEPENDENT ON ME.
WE WOULD HAVE NEVER COMPLETED THE ROCKET OR MADE ALL THESE NEW FRIENDS...
YOU DID IT... TO HELP HIM FIND HIS WAY?
I NEVER IMAGINED THAT HE WOULD HELP ME FIND MINE TOO.
AND NOW IT'S MY TURN TO KEEP A PROMISE...
AND JUST LIKE HIM, I WON'T SEE HIM UNTIL I DO. I'LL THANK HIM IN PERSON WHEN I ACHIEVE MY DREAM!

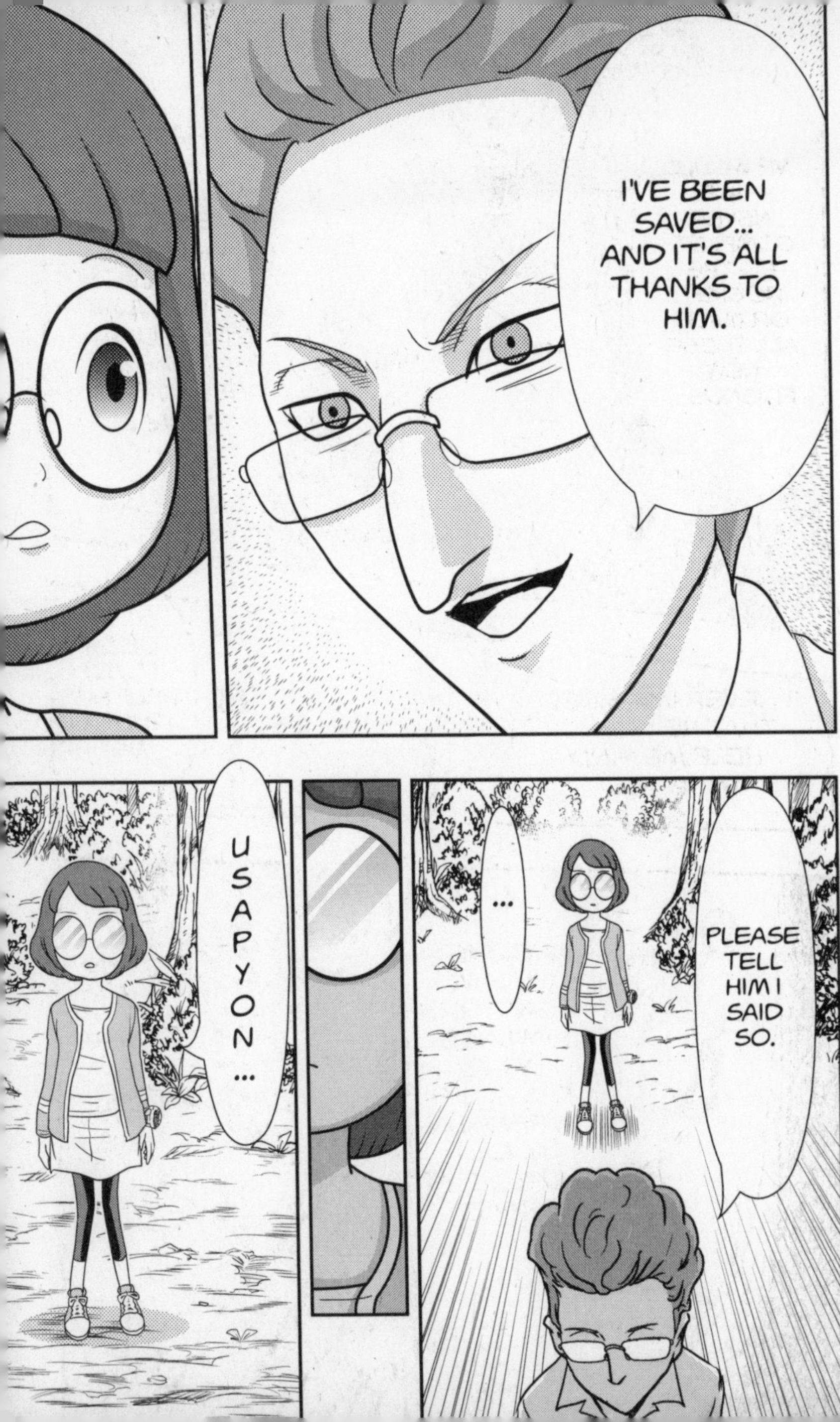
I'VE BEEN SAVED... AND IT'S ALL THANKS TO HIM.
PLEASE TELL HIM I SAID SO.
...
USAPYON...

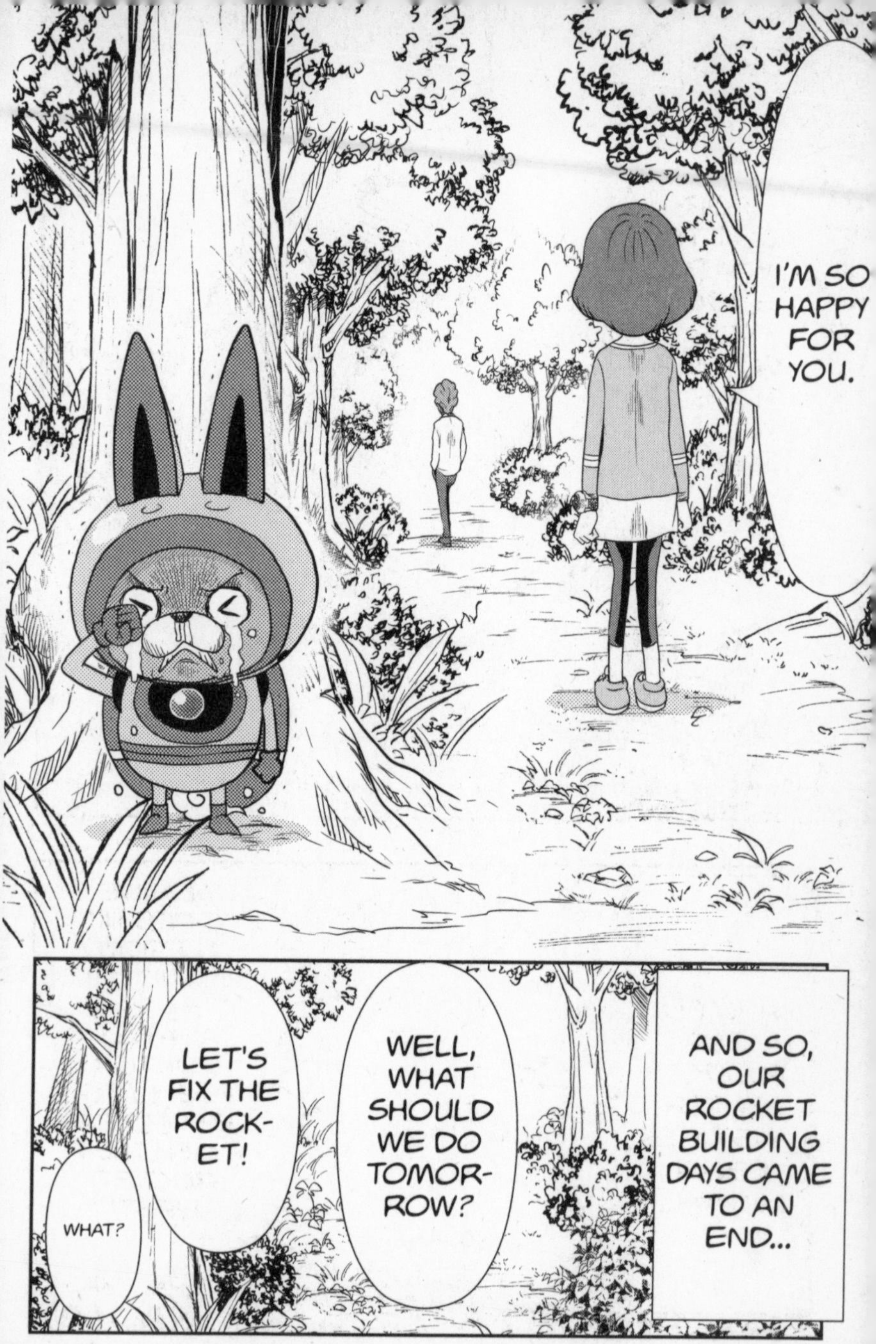
I'M SO HAPPY FOR YOU.
AND SO, OUR ROCKET BUILDING DAYS CAME TO AN END...
WELL, WHAT SHOULD WE DO TOMOR-ROW?
LET'S FIX THE ROCK-ET!
WHAT?

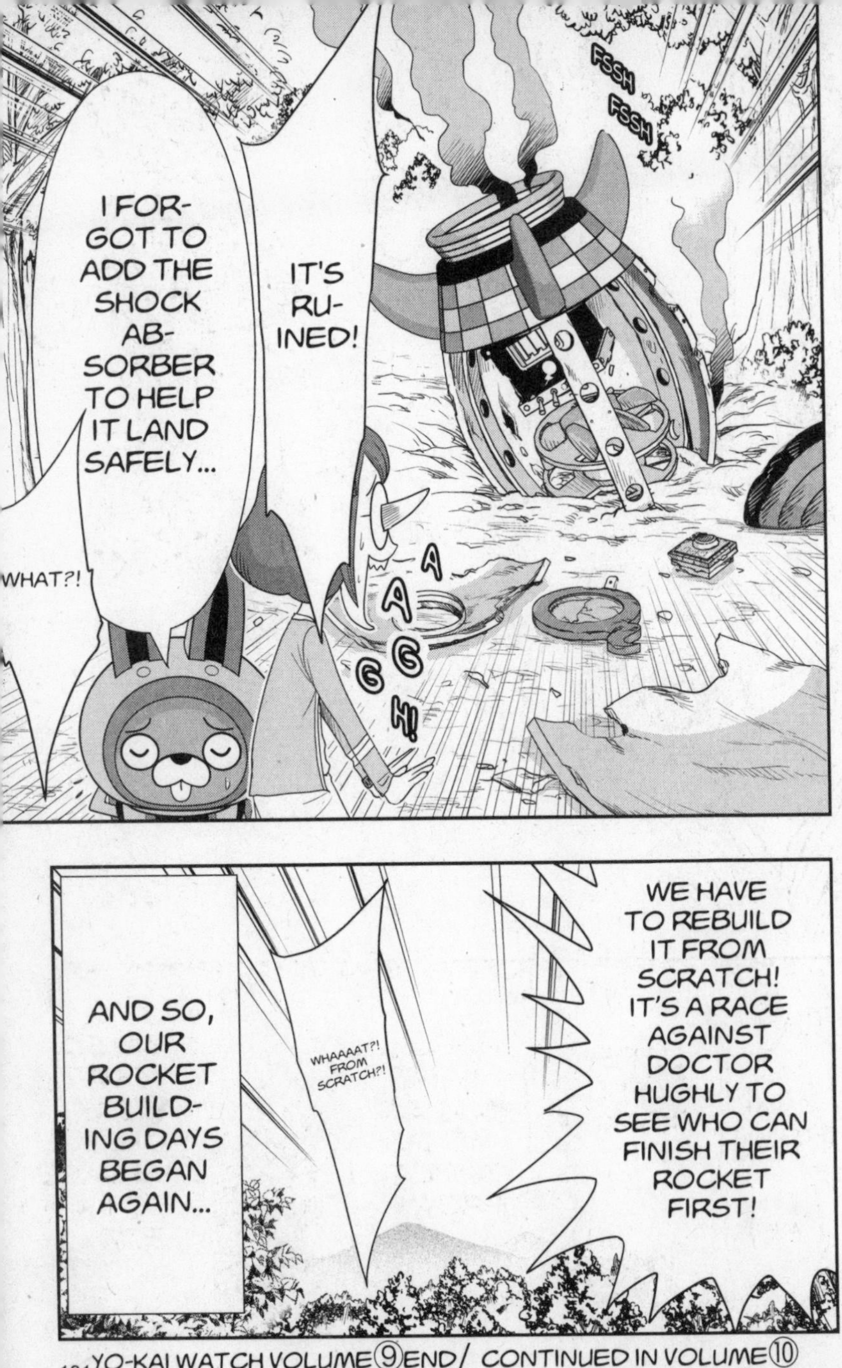
FSSH
FSSH
IT'S RU-INED!
I FOR-GOT TO ADD THE SHOCK AB-SORBER TO HELP IT LAND SAFELY...
AAGGH!
WHAT?!
WE HAVE TO REBUILD IT FROM SCRATCH! IT'S A RACE AGAINST DOCTOR HUGHLY TO SEE WHO CAN FINISH THEIR ROCKET FIRST!
WHAAAAT?! FROM SCRATCH?!
AND SO, OUR ROCKET BUILD-ING DAYS BEGAN AGAIN...

YO-KAI WATCH VOLUME ⑨ END/ CONTINUED IN VOLUME ⑩

AUTHOR BIO

Thanks to all of your support, YO-KAI WATCH is published in various countries around the world. There is an English version too, so I'm thinking about using it like a textbook to study.
—Noriyuki Konishi

Noriyuki Konishi hails from Shimabara City in Nagasaki Prefecture, Japan. He debuted with the one-shot *E-CUFF* in *Monthly Shonen Jump Original* in 1997. He is known for writing manga adaptations of *AM Driver* and *Mushiking: King of the Beetles*, along with *Saiyuki Hiro Go-Kū Den!*, *Chōhenshin Gag Gaiden!! Card Warrior Kamen Riders*, *Go-Go-Go Saiyuki: Shin Gokūden* and more. Konishi was the recipient of the 38th Kodansha manga award in 2014 and the 60th Shogakukan manga award in 2015.

ABSOLUTE SPINOFF "NEW YO-KAI WATCH?!"

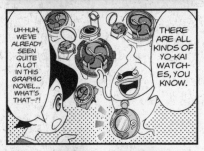

THERE ARE ALL KINDS OF YO-KAI WATCHES, YOU KNOW.
UH-HUH, WE'VE ALREADY SEEN QUITE A LOT IN THIS GRAPHIC NOVEL... WHAT'S THAT—?!
BAAM
THIS IS A POCKET WATCH-TYPE YO-KAI WATCH!!
IT'S HUGE... CAN YOU SUMMON A YO-KAI WITH THAT TOO?!
FWIP...
OF COURSE!
OKAY, JIBANYAN! COME OUT!!
OOH!!
SQUEEEE
G-GET ME OUT.
YOU STUFFED HIM INSIDE!! HE'S NOT A DOVE IN A MAGIC TRICK, YOU KNOW!!

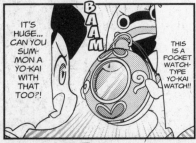

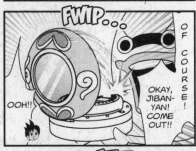

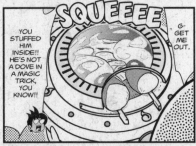

THIS IS THE END OF THIS GRAPHIC NOVEL!

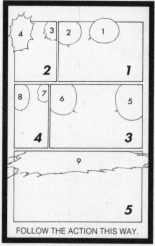

FOLLOW THE ACTION THIS WAY.

To properly enjoy this Perfect Square graphic novel, please turn it around and begin reading from right to left.